Watching The Principalities

Watching The Principalities

What you Don't See Can Kill You

William Songy

WestBow Press books may be ordered through booksellers or by contacting:

WestBow Press
A Division of Thomas Nelson
1663 Liberty Drive
Bloomington, IN 47403
www.westbowpress.com
1-(866) 928-1240

ISBN: 978-1-4497-9117-9 (sc)
ISBN: 978-1-4497-9116-2 (hc)
ISBN: 978-1-4497-9118-6 (e)

Library of Congress Control Number: 2013906387

Printed in the United States of America.

WestBow Press rev. date: 04/15/2013

The way of the wicked is like darkness;
They do not know what makes them stumble.
Proverbs 4:19, NKJ

Thank you God for loving us and forgiving us! Thank You for the opportunity to write this novel and serve in this capacity.

I want to thank my wife Darnell for her support and help. Without you this would not be possible. Thank you Heather, Kyra, Joshua and little Audrey for enduring the time I have spent writing.

I dedicate this to my parents Guy and Audrey Songy-I miss you mom.

CHAPTER 1

Screams echoed from beyond the haunting oaks, cutting through Marcus's soul at the instant realization of the source. It was *her.* Never had he heard such distressed sounds from a person. She was in trouble and in desperate need of his help.

The fear of losing someone he loved, yet again, surged to the forefront of thought. Could he endure it? He loved her, although he kept that emotion barred behind a door that he vowed never to open. Despite this, he would do whatever necessary to protect her.

The terror within summoned a surge of energy that poured through every fiber of his being. Incessant screams urged him to action. Yet, he paused in fear of the unknown. Anxiety intensified as he pondered the need to quick action versus effective action. Either way there was no leaving or escaping this one. This was real and it was time for him to respond. Whatever she was enduring was intensely brutal and she wouldn't be able to sustain it much longer. Time was precious, and possibly running out.

Marcus took a step into the direction of the house. Entering the darkness with reckless abandon could prove to be fruitless had he taken the wrong approach and was met with a trap set by whatever it was that tormented her. The house was somewhere behind an impenetrable black canopy of the late night. He groped his body in search of a cellphone and found nothing. Even if he had a phone, there was no time to wait for help. He had to move.

Marcus's heart was beating strong enough to bruise his ribs. His lungs pumped in and out large amounts of the cold moist air to the point of near hyperventilation. Growing tired of inaction, he lunged toward several majestic masses that danced tauntingly in the black night. The oaks slapped the ground, trying to trip him as he entered the hallowed area they protected. They became increasingly defensive and aggressively fought to block his passage. A cracking sound came from above. Marcus looked up. From out of nowhere appeared a glowing figure. It grabbed him and effortlessly tossed him forward as if he were a small child. He rolled and landed on his back returning a glance to see the tree sized branch crash to the ground digging into the earth's surface, dead center of his path. He certainly would have been crushed.

"Go!" An anxious voice screamed into his mind. "Go!"

Marcus rolled over and leapt back to his feet. A second branch crashed to the ground and he dared not stop and look back this time. He knew its purpose and where it had landed. He pushed forward like a soldier in combat. He was no longer scared, but fueled by the adrenaline that pushed him like nitrous oxide in a car.

The screams had yet to subside and strangely enough he considered that to be a good thing . . . she was still alive and breathing. There was still time.

A soft light guided him toward the front door. The three hundred feet he had traveled since entering the enchanted oaks seemed more like three miles. Blood surged through his body with such strength that he could feel the expansion and contraction of his circulatory system. The arteries in his neck pumped with such vigor that his head moved slightly from side to side with each heartbeat.

Marcus reached the door and listened intently as he heard a crash and the splintering of breaking wood. He pushed the door open and rushed into the structure in a defensive formation expecting to be instantaneously attacked by the perpetrator.

It *was* her after all. Despite the lack of adequate lighting in the house, Marcus could clearly see. Dawn was being held up in the air by something supernatural. She looked at him. She was no longer able to breathe and clawed at something that was around her neck. Fear blanketed her face.

Marcus ran toward the desperate woman and wrapped his arms around her thin waist. With all his strength he tried to pull her free. Something grabbed him from behind and tossed him across the room, and the coffee table dug into his mid-section as it crushed on impact.

Something jumped on his back and began viciously biting him. In a reactive measure, Marcus made a fist and swung while rolling over hoping to strike his attacker. He could see nothing as his fist passed through the air without resistance. Marcus swatted in the direction of an attack on his left calf, but his fist passed effortlessly through the air. Marcus rolled over a third time, trying to shake the undetectable assailant, but the attack continued. Painful puncturing bites were leaving trails of blood in random places on his legs and all he could do was endure and ineffectively try to fight back.

Dawn screamed again as whatever had cut off her breathing relented. Marcus looked up and watched a hulking mass in the darkness as it grabbed a fist of long blond hair and flung her in the manner of a catapult across the room in his direction. She landed with her upper-body on the couch and her knees on the floor. If he hadn't known better, it looked as if she were praying. She sat motionless and moaned lightly, exhausted and lacking the will to fight back.

Suddenly, an overwhelming force slammed against Marcus's midsection, ripping back his shirt. Several large punctures appeared in his chest. He tried to scream, but was unable to draw air from the pressure of the inward force. After several seconds compression subsided and blood instantly spilled out of the wounds.

Marcus could feel the invisible creature get off of him and grab his throat. He was lifted to his feet and supported. From the darkness he saw something emerge. He couldn't believe what it was that stood before him. Certainly such things existed, but never did he give any consideration to the possibility that he would ever encounter one. Even for a man of faith who believed in God and the spiritual realm, this was hard to absorb. Was this real, or was he losing his mind?

Marcus knew without a doubt what it was that now stood within a couple of feet and was leaning into his face. It did not speak, but observed, looking deep into his eyes and taking careful observation of his soul.

Dawn stirred and it turned to look at her. Marcus fought to speak and mumbled, "You can't have her."

The beast angrily looked back at Marcus and said, "You can't stop me! I have the right to torture her. She is mine! You cannot change that and you will die if you try."

The immortal creature grabbed Marcus and lifted him from the ground. Pressure from his neck subsided but the pain and pressure from the punctures was almost more than he could bear. Marcus found himself flying through the air again tossed like an unwanted toy. Twin windows exploded, sending glass and splintered wood across the front lawn from the impact with his body. He hit the ground and rolled over several times before settling face up.

His body felt torn and he was afraid to examine the damage. With the little strength he had left, Marcus pulled up his head, attempting to see what was happening to her, but could only hear the helpless screams. He had failed to help Dawn and was now too weak and injured to do anything.

Blood covered his body and he could feel it continuing to ooze out of his chest, down his sides and onto the ground. He realized that life would soon be over. He called out for mercy with what he perceived to be his last breath.

To his right, something approached. It was abnormally tall and well portioned and resembled a man. But, this was clearly no man. An implausible radiance illuminated the darkness in a way that the moon had failed to do resulting from the stingy and active cloud cover. The figure was so bright that it was difficult to look upon. Marcus was drawn to what looked like an outline of four large wings.

"An angel?" he asked aloud to himself.

The angelic being knelt beside Marcus as peace descended over him. Perhaps this wonderful angel had come to be his escort to God's presence. For a second he managed to put the pain aside and was ready and willing to go home.

He began to plead for the angel to leave him to help Dawn. But he maintained his focus on Marcus observing his injuries.

Marcus made another attempt to return to his feet and help her. The angel lifted his hand and stopped him from moving. He looked into Marcus's eyes and said, "Blessings and a gift of wisdom." The angel reached out with his index finger and touched his temple.

He gasped for air and opened his eyes. To his left, a large white blurry object quickly moved several feet away and stopped. Marcus anxiously raised both hands and examined his chest. There was no pain, punctures or oozing blood. However, a cold, wet substance saturated the abdominal area of his shirt. Marcus quickly moved into a sitting position and realized that it was his bedroom and it was morning. He was not on Dawn's front lawn bleeding to death, and for this he was instantly and eternally grateful.

He realized that the cellphone was ringing and was possibly what had pulled him from the horrific dream. He reached over and retrieved it from an oak night stand that held a lamp and alarm clock. The caller ID indicated that *she* was calling. How ironic, he thought, that just seconds ago he was watching her in torment and now she was calling to deal the punishment out to him.

Although he was uncertain of the reasons for the call, one thing was guaranteed: she had to be angry at him for something to call so early in the morning. He considered ignoring the call and just listening to the blistering voice mail. But after the dream he had just experienced, the sick side of him that was attracted to her wouldn't let him.

"Hello! Honey is that you? It's been so long since you've called. I thought you had forgotten about me. But now all is well. So, what can I do for you?" he said unable to resist the opportunity to mess with her.

"Uhhh . . . honey? I swear you're on drugs? Listen—"

"Do you wanna grab some breakfast this morning, or are you already on your way over?" He fought the urge to laugh.

"Do you want to know what I want? What I want is for you to get off the stupid radio. You know what I had to wake up to this morning? Your stupid song was on the radio. I turned to three different stations and they all were playing your stupid songs. I tried satellite and still . . . there you were. I check my email this morning and it's mostly about our little exchange the other day. It's bad enough that I have to see you in the park or put up with your stupid calls and your lame arguments, but now you're even haunting my mornings. How much do you pay them to play your junk?" she said.

"So, is this your way of asking for an autographed copy of the new album? Or, are you just having a difficult time with 'I love you?'" Marcus covered his mouth to mute his laughter. He could picture her angry, beat red face.

"I'll tell you just where you can stick your new album!" she said in a nasty tone before hanging up.

"Woof!" a freaked out Great Pyrenees named Zara barked assertively. She wagged her tail for a second then gave a turn of the head as if assessing her master attempting to discern whether or not he was able to understand what it was that she wanted.

Marcus felt the wet spot on his stomach, which had been caused by copious amounts of drool that often seeped from the huge animal's mouth. She had apparently been using him as a pillow.

"Woof . . . woof," Zara barked as she placed her paws on the side of the bed giving Marcus a look that suggested she was about to pee all over the floor if he didn't get a move on. The expression of desperation was followed by a series of short whines indicating that time was quickly fleeting.

"OK, girl," he said jumping out of bed and grabbing his robe. Then it hit him. "Love? Me . . . her . . . love? Where did that come from?"

He never doubted his attraction to her. She was beautiful and it was hard to imagine that every man didn't find her extremely attractive. But, love? He tried to shake his mind clear of the thought that had just taken his mind hostage, but a part of him wanted to explore the possibilities. What if her hatred for him really wasn't what it seemed? What if she was just afraid or was putting on a false front? What if she really did like him and was simply playing hard to get?

He let out a loud laugh and realized how funny even the thought of a relationship with her sounded. Marcus surrendered to the notion. "No, she really hates me!"

Thoughts of the dream resurfaced and he realized that it was a vision and noted the possible prophetic implications. He didn't consider himself a prophet, but realized that God could convey a message in any vessel or manner of His choosing.

Could this be the foreshadowing of future events? Was there some sort of imminent danger? He was uncertain of how to proceed or if there was a proper course of action to take in trying to protect her from a potential threat. He had no solid proof that anything threatening had loomed in the near future for her. Marcus realized that he couldn't follow her out of fear of being accused of stalking, despite having her well-being in mind. Future events had to play out and he would deal with whatever was to happen. He would be there for her despite her hatred for him.

CHAPTER 2

"Ed . . . thanks for calling the show," Dawn said, welcoming the caller before giving a stern warning, "now, give me your best shot and don't bore our listeners."

"Thanks. But there is no evidence anywhere to support your argument. If the Founders wanted there to be a separation between the church and the state they would have clearly defined it in the Constitution. I think they were smart or creative enough, without contradiction and with clarity, to do so. It was clearly not their intentions—" the frustrated caller said before being cut off.

"They *did* . . . . hello! The First Amendment clearly calls for there to be a separation!" Dawn yelled into the microphone in the manner of a prosecuting attorney seeking to build a case that would drown out any chance of "reasonable doubt."

"Show me! As I read it, there is no mention of any of the words separation, church or state. It is amazing that you quote a letter by Thomas Jefferson written in 1802 . . . which was years after the Bill of Rights—"

"Who was an *atheist*! Thomas Jefferson was an atheist and the . . . THE . . . source to cite when trying to understand the Constitution at that time. Want to know what they were trying to do . . . go to the source." Dawn interrupted again. It was her favorite tactic in getting over her opponent during a debate.

"You people—"

"What people? We people . . . the sensible ones? Like the Supreme Court Justices who saw the First Amendment our way and not your way?" Dawn asked bitterly.

"You are so blinded by your hate and your need to destroy the church that you can't see the truth. You know that these were liberal justices who had an agenda and legislated from the bench. This wasn't a simple interpretation of law, but a perversion of it.

"You fabricate these lies and feed them to the public. You're a lawyer, so it only makes sense that you don't understand the law. You worked for what I consider to be anti-liberty . . . or, at least, anti-Christian liberty groups who are left wing radicals. Your view is skewed to suit your need and is not in line with what the majority of the Founders had envisioned as per their own writings," the caller said nearly yelling into the phone.

"If Jefferson was such the hater or disbeliever in God, as you suggest, then why do his own writings not support this? Or, I guess his own words aren't enough evidence to support God . . . only to damage the Christian faith? It is par for the course for you to say that he just didn't know what he meant when he wrote, 'Almighty God hath created the mind free. All attempts to influence it by temporal punishments or burdens . . . are a departure from the plan of the Holy Author of OUR religion.' Yeah! That sounds like an atheist. He really segregated himself from all the religious 'nuts' with that one.

"Or, when he said, 'The doctrines of Jesus are simple and tend to the happiness of man.' Oh, I bet it burns your ears to hear that," the caller said angrily, as he had fallen into her trap. His arguments lost effectiveness with each increase in sarcasm. Conviction fell upon him, "I apologize if I seem a little sarcastic, but it is so frustrating to listen to you people lie, distort and get away with it especially when it is all documented," The caller said.

"Such anger! I rather liked it. You show yourself to be phony. I thought God was love?" Dawn said sarcastically while raising her hands into the air.

"God is love," the caller insisted.

"Sonny," Dawn said drawing the attention of her co-host, "did you feel loved just now? Because . . . I didn't feel love just now."

"Not at all," he replied and followed with a chuckle.

"He loved you enough to send His Son to the cross to die for—" the caller attempted to continue.

"Bla . . . bla . . . bla . . . all of us. We have heard all of this before. What a bunch of . . . bologna!" Dawn said withholding an obscene remark as it nearly slid off of her tongue.

"Have you ever wondered why is it that you are so verbally abusive and hate-filled toward Godly people? You are so profane and harsh with your comments toward people of faith. The reason is that you are being influenced," the caller passionately declared.

"Wait . . . what was that Satan? Tell him to jump off of the building and if his God is real then He will send angels down to save him? Ok. Hey, this voice in my head just told me . . ." Dawn said mockingly.

"Funny. He already tried that with Jesus and you know that. But the voices in your head are real and you are undoubtedly influenced by powers and principalities."

"By what and what? What are you an idiot?" Sonny yelled into the microphone.

"Powers and principalities?"

"Oh, really? What is that? Is that the reason why you are so stupid?" Sonny asked.

"Again there are the insults. It isn't a new doctrinal teaching. The oldest book of the Bible is a great example of—"

"That would be Job," Dawn chimed in.

"Right! Anyway, there are different levels of leadership in the spiritual world. Most people don't realize how organized the heavenly realm is," the caller said.

"That is why they are so good at controlling you and me," Sonny sarcastically said in a whisper while motioning with an index finger between himself and Dawn.

"You laugh and make fun of something that you cannot understand, but it is as real as you and me. In the book of Daniel, he prays for twenty-one days and when the angel shows up he tells Daniel about how the Prince of Persia held him up and the Arch Angel Michael had to come and help him."

"How do you know that this is one of those times when you literally interpret the Bible? Boy . . . you are really loopy," Sonny said.

"The Apostle Paul," the caller continued, unfazed by the remark, "wrote a lot about this spiritual realm and warns against the power they can wield on a person."

"But not you, right? Because you have been washed in the blood and all of that stuff . . . right?" Dawn asked. "The first time I heard that I thought of a horror movie. Like Carrie or something . . . you know when they dumped that pig blood all over her and she went crazy and killed everyone? Can't help it . . . that's what I think about."

"Blood baths don't sound good. Are they even legal?" Sonny asked.

"Freaked her out! She killed people with her mind. The whole eyeball thing with stuff flying around and locking doors and killing everyone. Kind of crazy." Dawn said jokingly.

"It isn't a physical bath in blood, but by the blood that Jesus has already shed on the cross. He ushered in a new covenant between man and God. When I believed in Him and accepted the punishment He endured for my sin, I am . . . what we refer to as washed in the blood. Meaning . . . that I am forgiven for my sins." The caller said.

"There goes that 's' word again," Sonny said.

"What, sin? We are all sinners. We are born to sin." The caller said.

"That would be us, right? . . . the non-Christians?" Dawn laughed at herself.

"Satan has you and millions of Americans believing his crap," the caller argued.

"Did he really just stay that? On our radio show where children could be listening? That may be a lower case cussword, but a cussword nevertheless young man and you should be ashamed of yourself. Did your mother ever wash out your mouth with soap?" Sonny asked.

"America has turned from God and it worries me. I pray that one day you will see the truth," the caller said.

"Look! No need to pray for me. Just stay in your confused little world of make-believe and leave me alone in the real world. Who's to say that what you are praying to isn't some universe jumping, disk flying little green man with buggy eyes that put all of us here? We're like this huge herd of alien cattle. I don't believe in your God or Jesus or Heaven or any of that non-sense. As I have said before. God is for weak minded people who fear death and need something to believe in. Otherwise they just couldn't cope."

"The Bible says that, 'every knee will bow and every tongue will confess that Jesus is Lord—"

"Goodbye! Enough of that!" Dawn said, cutting him off with the push of a button.

A commercial jingle came on and Dawn removed her headset and took down her hair. Long straight blond hair fell across her shoulders and two-thirds of the way down her back. She pulled it all back together at the base of her head and wrapped a ponytail holder around it. She animatedly exhaled out of frustration and looked at Sonny, unsure of what she wanted to say. The daily grind of talking about God was starting to wear on her. At first it was funny and good entertainment for those who listened but the novelty had long sense worn off. Her audience consisted primarily of non-believers claiming to refuse to bow to the religious establishment and wanted every vestige of such matters pushed exclusively behind church doors.

Dawn believed in science and evolutionary theories and refused to entertain the notion of a divine being. Creation, in her opinion, was nonsense and only those lacking in intelligence and education would hold on to something so seemingly silly. Many gods had been worshiped during man's reign on the earth and who was to say which one was real or the most powerful? Who was this Jesus guy? How arrogant was He to suggest and brainwash people into believing He was the Son of some phony God and that He was the only way to a salvation that didn't exist?

What was salvation anyway and what was so good about living for an eternity floating in the clouds with a harp. What fun was that? Life was about the here and now, not something unimaginably boring.

It was inevitable that she would get callers that would throw scriptures at her, to which she always countered by discrediting the Bible as flawed and written by man, and would finish by insulting their intellectual abilities. Insults were her weapon of choice and seemed to fuel the ratings.

Dawn didn't perceive herself as the product of a divine artist or the end result of a fantastic act of supernatural design. In her mind she was unexplainably the perfect byproduct of chance, Mother Nature's trophy millions of years in the making. She was physically perfect by even the strictest of standards. At nearly six feet in height with high cheekbones, strong blue eyes, long blond flowing hair that seemed to never be plagued by split ends or deficiencies and a supermodel figure, Dawn effortlessly treaded on top of the gene pool.

She was used to being the most beautiful and achieved person in a room wherever she went. All attention was usually instantly diverted her way upon entry. Men fawned over her and she treated them as if they were a cheap drink not worthy of her consumption. The more men that tried simply meant the more they did so in vain, and she loved every second of it. The attention was wonderful, but the power and control afforded by both her attractive nature and powerful position were more satisfying than the entertainer's salary that came with being nationally syndicated.

A former lawyer turned radio talk-show host, Dawn enjoyed her life. Along with all of her physical attributes were the intellectual and professional accomplishments of victories stemming from her time practicing law.

Dawn loved cases involving a question of civil liberty infractions, or as she saw it, the forcing of Christianity on those who were not believers. In her mind the law mandated a freedom from religion and she sought to use her talents in the legal war against the church. It was her goal to take the Thomas Jefferson 'wall of separation' and expand upon it and push the church underground and out of existence.

As with most atheists, she blamed the ills of the world on religion, believing that it was the primary reason why countless wars had taken place throughout the history of man's time on Earth. The Crusades and testimonies of fallen clergy who had perpetrated heinous crimes against nature were prime examples she loved to cite in justifying her zealous attitude and relentless efforts.

Dawn's world view perceived all religions as problematic and a threat to the national security of any nation that was dumb enough to tolerate them. Church leaders, such as pastors and priests, who had been caught engaging in immoral sexual activity or who had been found in violation of federal tax law in regard to how they conducted the business of the church or had simply fallen in any way, added fuel to her rage. The religious community was just as screwed up and flawed as the rest of struggling humanity and she was not about to give them a pass. Any member of the clergy or outspoken person who claimed to be of God that made a mistake was attacked during the monologue at the opening of the next show.

With no commitments to a husband or children, she married herself to her career and was enjoying the fruits of her efforts. Two hundred stations had picked up the show over a period of five years and more expansion was in the works. Her style infuriated and intoxicated listeners at the same time. Before Dawn, only conservative political talk-shows had achieved any sort of longevity. Most liberal radio shows had been boring and unappealing to the American audience.

"In Your Face" with Dawn McIntyre drew a faithful following from the young college and twenty-something crowd, who related to her rude and antagonistic approach. It was the way of Generation X and beyond. All sense of manners and politeness had accompanied the Bible as it was kicked out of the public school system and replaced with the federally-funded religion of evolutionary theory which taught no standards and provided no direction for leading a quality life. The selfish generation of "me" was coming of age and they had been taught to share in the godless beliefs of Dawn McIntyre.

Sonny passed a look from across the table and asked, "Powers and principalities? Where do these nut jobs come from? Where is the science in all of this? One of these days some scientist is going to find some gene that is responsible for making these people so stupid and actually legitimizes their mental condition. The Spirit that they worship is just in their heads and nothing more. At times I really believe that these people actually hear and see things much in the way a schizophrenic does. Only, THAT is a legitimate condition." He wiped his face in frustration and began sucking the last of the root beer through a straw that was sticking out of a lidless beverage container. He began to organize the papers from the notes he had prepared before the show.

"Powers and principalities? I think we can have fun with this one. What do you say we make it the topic for tomorrow's show?" Dawn asked as she considered the possibilities.

For Dawn, prepping for the next show was hands on. As a lawyer, the last thing she wanted was to go into a courtroom unprepared and subject to surprise and embarrassment. She carried this discipline with her regardless of the venture. Getting her facts straight, as she saw them, was unequivocally vital when debunking all who called to disagree with her. It was foolish to go into battle without the proper weapons or ammunition, especially when the topic involved Christianity. When talking with Christians or religious minded people, it was all about completely discrediting the opponent and not just winning the argument.

"You want to cancel the non-profit?" Sonny asked.

The show for the following day was to be on the tax exemption status of churches and the national movement to revoke all federal tax exemptions. David Drew, the founder of a watchdog group Secular Rights was to be the guest.

"I don't know. I just have this strong urge to do the powers and principalities thing tomorrow. It's just too good not to go after. I can't even imagine the calls we'll get over this one." She looked up as if a light had gone off and said, "Let's do it. Well, I have a lot of research before tomorrow, so let's get this last call over with."

Chapter 3

"Mike, I need to talk with you for a minute," Dawn said, entering the office of Mike Ferguson, the station manager at WZEO radio in New Orleans.

To Dawn, Mike's office was a great example of what was wrong with all men. Despite the new renovation that the studio had gone through, his office was overrun by a lack of willingness to maintain any semblance of order. Papers covered the desk and surrounding chairs. Coffee cups spilled over onto the floor as a green dented trash can was full to capacity and running over. Evidence of a diet rich in fast foods was predominantly displayed by the burger and burrito wrappers and empty soft drink containers that adorned the shelving, window stool and file cabinets.

"I have something you need to see," he said as he spun in his chair and moved toward a black metal stand.

A TV and DVD player was mounted to the top deck by a pair of orange nylon Velcro straps. He spoke inaudibly as he fought to push the small two inch rollers that supported the stand through the debris on the office floor. Frustration quickly got the better of him and he began to forcefully kick a stack of phone books that were up against the wall blocking passage from behind the desk. Several boxes of old promotional items that had once been stored in a hall closet and had been moved into his office during the initial phases of the station's remodel created a second obstruction despite being pushed into the corner.

Dawn refrained from laughing at Mike as he briefly lost control of his temper and viciously kicked the books and boxes with all of his might. His face turned red with the intensity of the assault and frustration at the refusal of the inanimate objects to comply. The chameleon-like transformation of his skin tone worried Dawn. If Mike was to have a heart attack, she hoped that it happened while she wasn't around so that it wouldn't interfere with the rest of the day. If the end result of Mike's poor dietary habits and years of lack in the care of his body was to result in a sudden shutdown of the heart, it wasn't of any concern and deserved no sympathy from her.

"Well, what is this about? Do you really need to do all of that?" she asked

Mike attempted to regain control of his breath. The phone books and boxes were now as damaged as the garbage can and the DVD was still behind the desk and had only moved several inches. Mike had accomplished nothing. He found an extension cord and decided it was more practical to bring the power to the electronic device instead of the other way around as had been his initial intention.

"This office is disgusting!" she replied while staring at the vacuum patterns on the carpet as they clearly cut around the clutter. "Perhaps the maid is afraid to touch anything in here. Maybe she's worried about releasing some . . . deadly micro-organisms into the air and causing some type of national pandemic. There is no way of telling what is in this office. Do you really meet with people in here?"

"No. That's why we have a meeting room."

Mike moved over to the center drawer of the antique mahogany desk and retrieved a fat cigar with the Dominican

Republic flag stamped on the wrapper. "I can smoke this. It will make the room smell better." Mike said, poking fun at Dawn's intense dislike of smoke.

"No thanks! I can live without cancer," she replied. "What is all of this about? I just wanted to tell you that I am going to change the topic for tomorrow."

"Well, this is short notice . . . whatever," he said with the wave of his left hand giving in to her desire. Arguing with her would be counterproductive and of no benefit to him. She would talk about what she wanted regardless of his opinion.

"So, what do you have for me?" she impatiently inquired.

"I am not really sure of what to make of this," he said, falling backwards into the leather chair rocking it backwards and lifting his feet off of the ground. Mike spun the chair toward Dawn and retrieved small black remote from the desk. "This is really interesting. Bob is a good lawyer, heck, you know plenty of good lawyers . . . if this turns out to be something."

"What are you talking about?" Dawn moved closer for a better angle at the television.

"There is a guy who calls the show, his name is Marcus Dillon," Mike said.

Dawn immediately rolled her eyes as she loathed the sound of the name. The hair on the back of her neck rose to attention and her hands rolled into tight fists. He wasn't just a religious nut, but a local celebrity who had found Jesus and made sure everyone knew about it. He had a significant fan base that extended across the United States and Europe.

The local media, with the exception of Dawn, portrayed the man as a saint. He always came off as nice, courteous and humble. He was loved and respected by the community and it made her sick. She longed for the day when the call would come in and Mr. Perfection would be found as a phony after an involvement in a major scandal. His arrest would be her justification. How she would celebrate on that day. Just the thought of it excited her.

Often, she had considered hiring a prostitute for the purpose of testing the man of God. Dawn would then have the woman come forth about the encounter and destroy his reputation. She was jealous of the attention he often received and only he was equal to her in regional popularity. But she managed to muster patience. He was a professing Christian and would fall on his own as most seemed to do.

She hated taking calls from Marcus and wanted to ban him from the show, but with his celebrity status the audience seemed to be addicted to their colorful exchanges. Often she convinced herself that she had gotten the better of him, but doubt usually resided somewhere in the back of her conscious mind. But, for reasons she could not understand, Dawn would grab onto their conversations and force a word by word review that often lasted for hours into the evening. At times the reenactment would make sleeping difficult. Neither music nor television could reclaim her thoughts and save her from reliving the conversation over and over. Some nights she wished she had his address so she could knock on his door and curse him out and not have to hold back out of fear of the Federal Communications Commission who, even in the modern flood tide of moral decay, would penalize her if she ever gave into the urges and temptations to cut loose on Marcus while on air.

"The last time he called you were talking about the separation of church and state several weeks ago, we were able to verify that he is the same Marcus Dillon . . . the musician." Mike said.

"I really appreciate all of the effort and detective work, but I knew that over a year ago. Christian musician . . . some self-proclaimed apologetic who calls in to defend God and argue with me . . . yeah. I asked him on-air," she said pacing back and forth while throwing her right hand in the air. She was growing increasingly impatient while waiting on his point.

"Have you ever talked to him in person?" Mike asked.

"I ran into him twice last weekend alone. I saw him at the Nevisian restaurant. He was there with some football player and they were raising money for some charity. Some people actually lined up to the get that idiot's autograph. So, I decided to play and got in line. He seemed a little surprised to see me and I had to make sure he kept his ego in check. I told him a few things that I had wanted to say. I kind of let him have it a little bit. After a few seconds I decided to get him to autograph my middle finger . . . if you know what I mean. I left him speechless.

"Then, I was in the park in front of my house and of all people, HE jogged by me. He likes to jog in the park. In fact, I noticed that he's there almost every day. He gave me one of those stupid 'Jesus loves you' comments and I couldn't get my mace out fast enough to reach him. I actually nailed the guy that was behind him."

Mike gave a concerned look, "You really tried to mace the guy?"

"Yeah, I did. You know he was just taunting me. The other guy was alright, it only went across his thighs. It wasn't as big a deal as he made out of it.

"Anyway, that was about a week ago and that is the last I have heard of him. Why? What's going on? Do you have some good news for me? Is he dead . . . killed by some stalker?" She asked.

"No . . . not hardly," Mike said.

"Too bad! If he really believes in Heaven, then maybe he should get there as soon as possible and leave the rest of us alone," she said coldly.

"I just found out yesterday who he was," Mike admitted.

"You could have just asked me. Anyway, why do you care about him?"

"It's not that I care about him, but you will be very interested in this," Mike pushed the button on the remote.

Dawn crossed her arms irritated at the thought of wasting more time.

"Ok. So, you know he is a local celebrity. I assume that you are not a big fan of his music?" Mike asked having fun with the conversation, but feeling a need to review his findings with her. "He had somewhere between three and ten hits in the nineties and kind of went off the scene for a while—"

"Probably to rehab like all of the other religious hypocrites. He came out and found Jesus," she said sarcastically.

". . . then began exclusively recording Christian music, which has done quite well for him. This last album has done quite well. His unique brand of music is selling very well." Mike said looking off of his list with reading glasses sitting on the end of his nose.

"Whatever. He is an idiot!" Dawn retorted.

Negativity and hate were a natural part of who she was and she embraced it as a strength. She was going to speak her mind and let people know where she stood. Those who opposed her deserved no sympathy or respect and often suffered brutal and relentless verbal assaults. If they were too psychologically unstable to take it, then that was their problem.

The image on the flat screen came to life. A man in his early thirties sat on a stool in the middle of a stage. Pleated khaki shorts, leather boat shoes and polo pull-over made up the bulk of his wardrobe. Years had passed since he had felt a burden to impress people with the quality of his attire and he preferred to be casual.

"We are on the stage of the Revelation Arena which is part of a new development on the Northshore called the Revelation Center just off of I-59. A lot of you have probably driven by here and have seen the development over the past two years. The only way to describe this place is state of the art. What a beautiful place this is. This is one of the few non-government funded arenas in the state. But what makes this development truly unique is that it is not just about the Revelation Arena. This is what is being referred to as 'a gumbo of mixed Christian based businesses' as described by the developer and owner, who is New Orleans' favorite son, Marcus Dillon," Ginger Sierra said, turning to her right to introduce Marcus.

"Well, thanks for being here. I am just one small part of this project," he said humbly.

"This place is beautiful. You guys truly have a state of the art facility here."

"Well, when you are representing the one and only true God, you need to be at the top of your game. We really want people to get the full theater experience when they attend an event here. So, we went all out to make it the best that it can be."

"Faith has played a big part of who you have become. I know that in the beginning of your career . . . I think you were . . . what about twenty-two when your first top ten hit came out. You kind of tapped into that rocky Caribbeanish kind of sound . . . you know . . . calypso, steel-pan drums mixed with guitar."

"We call it rock-a-lypso," he responded.

"That's what you called your first album!" she excitedly replied.

"I grew up on the beach and there was an artist who seemed to have a corner on that market. You know . . . the beach music. I loved his music, but hated the lyrics and all the stuff that it promoted. I wanted something that the entire family could listen to that actually promoted something worth promoting. Not the typical self-indulgent, do whatever you want foolishness that most artists today seem to live for."

"How much of this do I have to watch? What is the purpose?" Dawn asked impatiently.

"Well, I kind of lost the place. There is something that you really need to hear." Mike replied.

"So what happened in the three years you disappeared?" Ginger inquired, moving the conversation quickly in a new direction.

"Well . . . there was a great personal tragedy and I just had to deal with some things," Marcus said.

"Some things . . ." Ginger said in an attempt to lead him to further explanation.

"I experienced a personal tragedy and it took me a while to get to a place where I could deal with it. I suffered a great loss."

Ginger became more interested in the dirt than the actual reason for the interview and she began pushing for a confession.

"Please, if you don't mind . . . there was the loss of a loved one who was very special to me. If you don't mind I would prefer if we just left it at that," he said politely.

"OK. What about this new album you have released? Kind of different," Ginger said.

"Well, this is a kind of fun project that I had always wanted to do. We took old rock-n-roll songs and converted the lyrics to a positive message. I can always remember that when I would hear a song, I would kind of rewrite it in my mind. Usually it was funny. I wanted the songs to remain serious, but I want to have some fun as well."

"This brings me to one song in particular, the one the radio stations are playing. What about *Devil Dawn*?"

"I know where you are going with this," Marcus cut her off. "The song was not written about anyone local. It all kind of just worked out the way that it did," he said defensively.

> "*Devil Dawn . . .*
> *Everything you say is a great big lie*
> *And you don't know why.*

And did I hear you say
They're all stupid because they pray?
Are you are leading them all astray?"

She read from her scripted questions. "That sounds a lot like the relationship you have with Dawn McIntyre?"

"First of all, I have no relationship with Ms. McIntyre. She would rather shoot me then have any kind of relationship with me. Sometimes . . . I listen to her show and call it to point out some of her errant ways and misguided analogies. I respect her, but she is way off and way out of line most of the time.

"Ok? Now, I have answered this question before. It is not about that talk radio person," Marcus said defensively.

"He wrote a song about me? He called me . . . Devil Dawn?" She said furiously.

"You should hear all of the song," Mike said handing her a CD case with a burned copy in it. "The rest of the lyrics:

'The FM waves carry the lies that are crazy
Playing with the heads of those who are lazy
Her hands are waving around and the microphone is in the stand
Work' in overtime for that evil fallen man
Now in her broadcasting days there sat a pawn
The meanest woman to feast you ears upon
The Christians and the Jews should just run and hide
The fallen angel is taking her for a ride'

Then it just repeats the first verse again."

Dawn stood leaning against the desk tying to discern what she had just learned. A look of displeasure covered her face.

Mike placed a sheet of paper gently on the desk. He knew he had her when she was unable to speak. He liked stirring her up. It was good for ratings. She would certainly go after Marcus during the next broadcast and if he happened to call, it would certainly make for an interesting conversation.

"Now . . . now he said that he wasn't talking about you," he said, knowing it would only sharpen her anger.

Obscenities began to fly as she paced the room. Employees passing through the hall couldn't help but to peek in the office drawn by the rant. It was her face that was turning red now.

"If I were a man I would beat him up. That worthless piece of garbage! You read the lyrics. How can he be attacking anyone else but me? Who else but me? It is just too coincidental. He thinks I am a devil. Well, I will show him that the Devil has nothing on me. I will make his life tough. Then, I will sue him . . . I will!"

CHAPTER 4

Marcus exited the Range Rover and for the first time during the three year journey he allowed himself to take satisfaction in looking upon the nearly completed vision. It had been a huge and expensive task that involved the sacrifice of many, but it would pay huge dividends to the kingdom of God. He was not ready to compare it to the tremendous accomplishments of Noah or Solomon, especially given the unfair advantage with the increases in technology, but he was satisfied with the outcome.

He turned to look at the freshly paved parking lot and twenty randomly parked cars as there had yet to be any lines painted for division and order. Animation on a digital sign lit up the sky as he panned the frontage where a bustling Interstate 59 routed workers and travelers from Mississippi to the I-10 and into the New Orleans area. A loud and fast moving group of vehicles heading south sped down the interstate attempting to outdo each other as if in an urgent race to a final destination. A yellow Mustang moved aggressively from behind a slow moving bus that was traveling in the fast lane and into the outside lane cutting off a SUV and nearly causing the people to run off of the interstate and into a marshy area. Marcus said a silent prayer for the safety of the passengers of the SUV.

A rolling scripture caught his attention and he turned back from the traffic and toward the electronic billboard perched thirty feet above the interstate. "He that loveth not knoweth not God; for God is love. 1 John 4:8" and was followed by an announcement of an upcoming speaker and event.

He walked toward the forty-five hundred seat Revelation Arena and entered through one of six tinted glass doors on the main entrance. The main hall had been a primary focal point of the design of the arena as it was important to set the tone by helping visitors feel welcomed, comfortable and ready to experience the movement of God upon entry. Soft colors and greenery created a comfortable and soothing ambiance. Plasma televisions displayed various images of God's creation in coordination with soft music as it mildly penetrated the atmosphere. Marcus found it to be very soothing and comfortable. It was exactly what he had hoped the end result to be.

A newly installed electronic site map drew Marcus's attention and he walked over to make his initial inspection. He looked from left to right and slid his right index finger across the acrylic shield. On the left side of the acreage was an outline of the arena complete with a diagram of the bathrooms, ticket office, emergency exits, stage, seating areas and dressing rooms. In front of the arena was the Holy Grounds Coffee House with drive through service. On the right and behind the arena were two antique refurbished rail cars that were converted into an ice cream parlor and soda shop with décor from the fifties. Further to the right was a long rectangle outline of the two story world missions building and Christian book store as it sat behind a half-acre pond where a twenty foot cross stood in the mist of fountains. He was delighted when he noticed that the observation/service bridge that arched across the pond had been included. As he continued to his right, the L shaped school building and playground marked the end of the first phase of the development. He was well pleased and moved through the main hall and into the arena.

People moved purposefully about, attempting to fulfill their respective duties as rehearsals were taking place for a musical that was to serve as the opening event. Time was running short and a mild anxiety was clearly evident. Two women in a deep conversation passed within inches and Marcus stepped back to avoid a collision.

During his career in the music business, Marcus had always wanted to do a musical gospel in a theatrical setting. But, never had he been afforded an opportunity, until now. He worked with several local Christian screenwriters to craft a story line and coordinate it with a score of the songs from his forthcoming release.

The story followed a young man who was abused at the hands of an alcoholic father and an absent mother. The man's struggles as life takes him through various trials and challenges such as peer pressure, drug addiction and failed relationships. As an adult and on the brink of suicide, the love of Christ touches him when a stranger gives council and ministry. In the blink of an eye, the man of God disappears and the once lost soul calls out to Christ and is lifted from the bondage of his sins.

The storyline was nothing necessarily new in the Christian world of entertainment, but it was the focus on the spiritual presence that had worked behind the scenes to affect and direct the man and his decision making that gave it a new spin. Through life experiences Marcus had grown in his understanding of the spiritual world. He believed in beings such as angels and demons. Most Christians had a watered down understanding of such an existence.

As he approached the stage, Marcus couldn't help but to worship and move to the music as it stirred his soul. He gave a thumbs-up to Ronald Golstien, the lead actor/performer as he belted out the chorus of a ballad. Ronald fought the urge to laugh at Marcus while in the middle of carrying a note.

Marcus held his hand up in an apology for disturbing the flow of the rehearsal as he didn't realize how silly he had looked while dancing up to the stage. He was too stiff to dance and had never felt completely comfortable doing it. His moves were less like John Travolta in Saturday Night Fever and more like something out of Revenge of the Nerds.

Marcus panned the arena and watched the other performers walking through their parts. Three women began to powerfully give vocal support that caused goose bumps to coat his arms. His attention became instantly locked in on the stage. Marcus's eyes began to water as the sheer power of the performance further touched his soul. It wasn't until the end of the song that he regained focus on other matters.

Marcus looked around in awe at the realization of a dream. He meditated on the works of the mighty hand of God as He had been and would continue to be powerfully glorified. What was once a barren piece of unfruitful land had now been transformed into a life changing tool. Marcus paused and prayed for all who would enter the building and for all of the other Christian businesses that were a part of the development.

Marcus moved back from the stage and sat in one of the tan chairs on the floor of the area. He was glad to see the project near completion, but was also sad in an odd way. It had been a huge undertaking. He reflected on the attacks and obstacles of dealing with the corrupt local government officials, who attempted to siphon funds in exchange for their support of a necessary zoning change. Marcus stood firm against the bribes and the zoning was eventually changed.

Then the Permits Department repeatedly buried his requests and procrastinated in giving the necessary approval hindering the project. It had been a frustrating experience, but despite all the attempts to kill the project, here he was ten feet away from the stage. It had all come together. God's spirit began to flow and allowed him a moment to enjoy the fruit of his labor. It was a blessing as Marcus had taken the vision and was faithful to carry it out without wavering.

The task was to provide entertainment, shopping and eating alternatives that were Godly and family friendly. The goal was to develop a self-sustaining Christian Community that could witness, equip, educate people and confront the issues facing believers. It was a place of perpetual fellowship. The Revelation Center was not to be a typical or modern church project. It would, in a sense, be a reflection of a church age that had passed. Marcus had a passion to minister to the hearts and minds of a lost and hurting people and lead them to an understanding of who Christ really was and the spiritual battle taking place for the souls of each man, woman and child.

By creating a self-funding community, the ability to minister to people and work toward the preservation of a place for Christians in modern society would be possible. The Revelation Center would not function as a non-profit entity and would not suffer the limitations typically levied upon such organizations. Many churches had embraced their non-profit status and willingly allowed themselves to be bound and gagged for the sake of not paying taxes on revenues generated. Because of money, the Church had rendered itself voiceless and ineffective in regard to governmental leadership and public policy.

The Revelation Theater would be a place where church services would take place, concerts would be held on Friday and Saturday nights in order to get kids off of the streets and minster to them. Important political and/or social events would take place without fear of speaking of both God and politics.

"Hello, Mr. Dillon," someone called out.

He turned to see Sarah Marshal nearly ten feet away. "Sarah, how many times do I have to tell you? Please don't call me that. Just Marcus is fine."

"Well, Mr. Marcus . . ."

"A compromise then?" he asked with a smile.

At the beginning of construction, Marcus prayed that God would send him the right person to help with the Revelation Theater. Less than a week later while on the construction site he, was approached by Sarah. She was fresh out of Michigan State University with a Major in Theatre Arts Management and no real experience running a theater. She was energetic, positive, eager and in desperate need of a job. After deliberation, Marcus felt the peace of God upon him and looked past her lack of experience and persuaded the Board of Directors to offer her the job. Sarah was diligent, quick to learn and had been a tremendous blessing to him.

Marcus was astonished by her knowledge of the scripture and strength of her faith. In the modern age, it had been the norm for church going kids to leave their faith after going off to college. Peer pressure, secular teachings or influence by professors who were anti-God and liberal had helped many to stray from Christ. Her faith was tireless and firm.

"OK. The costume that we have for the devil, do you think it's too dark? It just seems too unrealistic to me and unlike who the devil really is. Can we make him more like the fallen angel of the Bible? He is supposed to be beautiful. Isn't that why he is so deceptive?" Sara said.

"Hey, we can go for the whole red-bodied, bull-horned pitchfork guy." Marcus jokingly said. Sara simply raised an eyebrow attempting to discern the nature of the comment. "Just kidding, I agree with you."

She chuckled realizing that he had indeed been joking. Enthusiasm welled up inside of her as she flipped open a tablet displaying a sketch for Marcus. The image was impressive in its detail. The tall perfectly portioned man looked like a model off of a magazine cover. Marcus's soul stirred and the evil nature of the fallen angel made him uneasy. He sensed a connection with the Devil, as if he were staring at an exact portrait of the beast from the past night's dreams. It was the creature that tormented Dawn, but in human form. The eyes gave it away. He remembered it being inches from his face. The detail was uncanny. The Deceiver had the same look of confidence expressed in the facial features and hint of delight for what he was doing to Dawn.

"I was praying last night and I felt that God wanted me to draw this. Once I saw it and realized what He was telling me . . . well, He is right." Then Sarah looked up and noticed the change in demeanor.

Marcus was amazed at how Sarah was able to catch the cunning deception of the deceiver in a drawing. "You are very talented. Well, I'm not going to say that he looks 'beautiful' like I imagined, but that looks pretty good. How do we get this suit in such a short notice?" he asked, trying to move on without sharing the vision with Sarah.

A disturbance caused them to turn toward the entrance of the theatre. Dawn McIntyre was standing in front of a closing door yelling at the first person she had encountered. The young man stood dismayed by the rude and angry woman.

"Where is he? Is Marcus here?" She made eye contact with him and stormed through a small crowd of volunteers walking, in the straightest possible line to get to Marcus while pushing over chairs and shoving people out of her path.

"Well, hello. It is great to see you. Are you here for an audition? What role are you interested in?" he asked jokingly, thinking of the conversation he had just with Sarah.

He knew that she was always angry, but her body language suggested that she had reached a whole new level of rage. It was no secret why she was there and he realized that the potential for such an encounter had existed. She was enraged and yet still so beautiful.

"What is this?" she asked, tossing the square case into his chest from five feet away?

"Uhmmmm . . . A CD. But, I may have to take it to the lab for confirmation," he laughed. "What do you want me to say?"

"You wrote a song about me—"

"I did? Apparently you didn't like it." Marcus said acting surprised while analyzing the CD. "Do you realize how beautiful your face is with that red tone . . . you know . . . when you're mad? You're absolutely breathtaking. I can see why you stay mad . . . you wear it well."

"Devil Dawn! Devil Dawn . . . don't play games with me," Dawn said. She had rehearsed the conversation over and over in her mind and he had already thrown her off with the beauty remark. It had been nowhere in her pre-confrontation run-through.

"Look, can you calm down? I didn't write a song about you. I disagree with just about everything you say, but I don't spend time doing things to try and hurt you." Marcus said and paused as the thought had occurred to him, "I'm in the Revelation Theater and I just had a revelation. How cool is that. But I did just realize something. Why are you so upset?"

"Isn't it obvious? You wrote a song about me and said that I am the Devil! You assaulted my character, accused me of misleading people and of being evil and I am not supposed to be upset?"

"But you even said that NONE of that stuff was real. Remember?"

"So?" she snapped.

"Well, I wrote a song. No, it's not about you. You don't believe in God or the Devil or anything spiritual so what is the problem?"

"Don't start that crap with me!" Dawn said.

"You say you don't. So, how can you be upset about some meaningless title given to something that doesn't exist? Unless you know that it, or he, is not so meaningless? Deep in your mind you know it is all true, don't you. Your being here is more of an admonition of guilt if anything. Perhaps your sub-conscious is telling you something." Marcus noted.

"Guilt for what? Helping people to see through your lies! All of you stupid church people who believe in your supernatural nonsense! Look, I don't believe in your fairy tales. One thing I do believe in . . . my lawyer. He is going to take you for all that you have."

"Then why get upset? Soon you will be richer and I guess . . . angrier," he said.

"Because you are trying to create a situation where some of your wacked-out fans will listen to this song and do something crazy to me because they believe that you called me the devil and they don't like the devil. I could be stalked and killed by some whacked out nut job Christian who is hearing little voices in his head telling him to do something to me," she said, making up the excuse as other rational reasons had yet to surface.

"I will always pray that never happens to you. I never want to see anything bad happen to you."

"Please, I am going to get sick. Sympathy from you . . . I'd rather have rabies."

"After the way you barged in here, you may need to be checked. I thought that I saw a little foam by your mouth. You knocked three people nearly to the ground and kicked several chairs over. How does it feel to be so angry all the time? Have you . . . for even a second in your life ever had a peace about anything? Do you always feel the need to attack someone? If I have a problem with a person, I go and speak with them in love and peace. I will have a one on one conversation with them and resolve the issue whatever it may be. I exclude the exhibition of a foul temper."

"Thanks . . . Dad. Don't lecture me! I don't need you—"

"I think God is talking to you," Marcus said, looking into her eyes.

"Look, I'm not weak minded and your Jedi mind-trick won't work on me. You weirdoes talk to, or believe that you talk to . . . Jesus. Let me guess . . . you saw a burning bush or Lake Pontchartrain parted for you . . . no . . . it was a bright blinding light that caught you as you were driving to Damascus? What makes you so holy? I think you were abducted by aliens and they fried your brain," she said animatedly.

"You don't have to believe in cancer, but it can kill you. I can't see the wind, but I can see the results of the wind. I can't see electricity as it flows through the walls of my house and when I tap into it, things happen. The bottom line is that you don't have to see or believe in God, but that doesn't mean He is not there. You can't just wish Him away like He is one of your callers.

"All of us with our thoughts and actions worship and follow one side or the other. You just can't see it because you believe that you can justify your thoughts. All of us talk to God, we just say different things. I say, 'Hello, I love you and thanks for saving me.' You say, 'Get out of my life, don't bother me, I don't need you, I can do it on my own.' You fail to see the true warfare that is going on within your own mind. You are being duped and it is truly sad."

"What is sad is that I have wasted so much of MY time standing here listening to this nonsense. There is no God and stop trying to throw that at me!" she yelled. "I wanted to stop and let you know that I am on to you and my lawyers, who are the best, will be getting in touch. I will sue you for all that you are worth!"

"What is the source of your perpetual anger? Where does it come from?"

Dawn looked in disgust and shook her head.

"Jesus loves you," he said as she turned to walk away.

"Save it preacher. You can bow down to your false . . . whatever. But, I live in the real world. If God is real, let Him stand before me and show Himself. Let Him tell me not to sue you. If He created me, then let Him deal with me!" she demanded.

"Listen, you need to watch what you wish for. You can't challenge God. That's just not smart," he said.

"Oooooooooh . . . what's He going to do? Take me to Hell?" she asked before finally turning away.

Dawn turned and began to walk around several of the chairs she had knocked over on the way in. Sarah was waiting and stepped in front of her. Without expression, she looked boldly into Dawn's eyes. She spoke in a calm clear voice, "Forty-eight hours shall pass and you will be touched by the living God and you will never be the same!"

The boldness of the young woman startled Dawn, and she froze for a second, attempting to discern how to respond. Instead of attacking the young woman, she turned to Marcus and said, "See! What did I tell you?" before stomping out of the auditorium.

CHAPTER 5

Marcus walked around to the right of the massive stage where the visit from Dawn had been a mild distraction. Actors and singers continued without interruption and the scene had hardly been a blurb to anyone who hadn't been pushed on or yelled at by the mad woman during her dramatic entry.

He walked into the office and sat behind his desk in a swiveling chair second guessing the song and feeling a need to pray for Dawn. His attention turned toward Sarah. It wasn't like her to act so boldly and almost confrontationally with someone or to give prophecy. At least not during the time he had spent with her. God must have moved powerfully upon her and this worried Marcus. First the vision from the night before and now a prophecy of something taking place within forty-eight hours? Marcus felt an overwhelming need to pray for God to have mercy—that He would allow someone the opportunity to get through to her.

He felt an unexplainable spiritual connection to Dawn, as if she had always been his mission. As strange as it seemed, he felt that God had intended for him to be her witness. That was why he felt so compelled to call the radio station and challenge her with frequency. He wanted her to see the truth and exposing the flaws in the things she promoted was a tactic that had proven to be fruitless.

Music was always in the plan for Marcus as it was his passion. However, it seemed more realistic to focus on the business side, as he had no desire to perform or tour and doubted the quality of his musical talent.

During his freshman year at Beck University, instead of spending his free time partying and wasting money like most of his fellow students, Marcus found LeJune Studio several blocks away from his apartment and began pestering the owner for a job. He eventually convinced John LeJune, the sole proprietor, to let him work for free in exchange for sitting in on scheduled recording sessions and getting some hands-on experience. John gave him employment in maintenance that included the studio and all four levels of the building.

Years of neglect had offered Marcus job security. What wasn't broken was covered in dust, mold or was in need of painting. For weeks Marcus scraped, caulked and painted the block wall exterior and then the redwood soffit and fascia on the main entrance.

Magazine St. served as the primary service and had been in a desperate need of beautification. Marcus re-landscaped the front with Chinese fan-palms, Dukes yellow, perilla, gold edger and added yellow and blue flowers according to season.

Although the finished budget was more than he had conceived, John was impressed with the work ethic that Marcus had displayed. It didn't take long to see that there was something special about him. He had possessed qualities necessary for success and John became anxious to help him grow and prepare to move forward in the business. There was no information that he withheld from his tireless employee. The relationship had proven profitable to both men, whose appreciation of and respect for one another grew.

One afternoon after sweeping the studio and de-cluttering the mess from a session, Marcus sat on the top of a bar stool and plugged in a green Fender Stratocaster that was in a stand next to a microphone. He began playing a song that the current client, Jackal's Edge, had been working on. The song simply didn't sound right. Marcus began strumming the strings and the song seemed to flow through him as if God Himself was guiding his hands. John silently walked into the mixing room and made a digital recording of Marcus while he was unaware that anyone had been in the studio with him. John played the recording back and was impressed by the changes Marcus had made to the bridge and chorus.

Marcus was startled as the PA called out and he turned to see John behind the sheet of glass waving him over. John played the tape back several times, complimenting Marcus's revisions.

It was nearly seven-thirty when the band arrived. Lance Ortiz, the vocalist, had written the lyrics and they were trying to fit the music accordingly. But clashing opinions and personalities had brought them to an impasse. Lance and guitarist Richard Lavene entered the studio fighting over the previous session's conclusion. Lance wanted to take the edgy riffs down a notch in order to allow the song's balladic appeal to flow and give the listeners a chance to focus on the story behind the song rather than the overwhelming guitar and drawn out solo. Richard demanded that the song remain as it was and was offended and accused Lance of letting his ego determine the direction of the music. Richard threw a punch with his right hand while lunging in anticipation of catching Lance unaware.

The influence of alcohol impaired Richard's ability to calculate the exact landing point of the punch, which missed its mark and made contact with the block wall that had made up the building's exterior structure. Screams and profanities rang out as the pain from broken bones pulsated throughout his hand.

He was escorted out of the building and to a hospital, but it left the band under contract and without a guitarist. John convinced the remaining members to listen to the changes Marcus had made.

The bluesy rhythm fit the lyrics perfectly and he was asked to sit in replacement of Richard for the night, which ultimately led to the rest of the recording secessions.

With a new found confidence and direction, Marcus assembled a few musicians from his church and began to cut some tracks. With no money, he had to continue on the barter system and negotiate for the services of the studio. In the time span of four months, ten songs, including one power ballad, had been completed.

After months of watching the boys as they prayed before every session and how they interacted with one another began to touch John. They didn't just talk their faith, they lived it. It was evident in their interaction. He had always been a rock-n-roller and in his youth had lived the life of "sex, drugs and rock-n-roll." He had never spent any significant time with anyone who was openly Christian before and the conviction of the men stirred his conscious mind. From afar, he had perceived Christians as kooky and weak minded at best, but his close interaction with the young men stirred his soul. Sub-consciously, he waited for one of them to slip up or come in inebriated or do something that would justify his past perceptions. But none came. During periods of frustration there was never a single obscenity or argument.

Thoughts of why Marcus had ended up in his studio began to creep up into his mind. Was there a God and was He attempting to reach him? He found himself considering the possibility of God more frequently. One night while Marcus was cleaning up after a session, John could no longer fight the urge to know more. After two years John had truly grown to like, respect and see a quality in Marcus that he had not seen in many people his age. Pushing his pride aside, he sat on a chair and asked Marcus if he could talk to him about God as the burden to know had to be satisfied.

They spent a couple of hours talking into the early morning hours about God and all of his creation, John still couldn't understand why accepting and acknowledging Jesus' death for his sins was vital to salvation.

Marcus explained by using a story. "You have a son who served in the Gulf War. Imagine . . . this is a horrible thing to do, but imagine that Robert was killed in combat. You bring his body home for a proper burial.

"During the funeral a man walks up to you and spits on his grave and tells you how stupid it was for him to sacrifice his life and what a waste his sacrifice was. 'Who was he to think that he could make a difference? Who the heck did he think he was?' He asks and continues to cuss the name and memory of your son. He turns to cuss you and verbally slaps you in the face as if you were responsible for the ridiculous mindset of this fool who died fighting for what this man views as nothing. How do you feel about that guy?"

"I would want nothing to do with him," John answered honestly.

"Another man walks over to you and humbly thanks you for your son and the sacrifice he made. He thanks you repeatedly . . . tears are in his eyes . . . he asks if there is anything he can do for the family and offers himself to you. He understands and accepts the gift of your son's selfless service. He is persistent in wanting to show his gratitude.

"How do you feel about this man?"

"I have a great appreciation for him."

"Now, one day there is a knock on your door and you go to answer it. Both of these men are standing there, which one are you going to let in?"

"I get it now. I think that's obvious," John said.

"Whenever we have an entire lifetime to acknowledge Jesus and what He did for us, and we choose not to . . . to acknowledge and accept the sacrifice . . . the Gift . . . how can God let us into Heaven if we reject the selfless act of His only Son? That is what we do every day that goes by and we ignore what He did for us.

The price has been paid. All we have to do is believe and accept the Gift in our hearts and give ourselves to Him and we are saved. God is awesome and waiting for us," Marcus said.

After several seconds of staring down in his lap in meditation, he looked up and simply nodded in agreement. The two joined together in a prayer and John became a brother in Christ. For Marcus the conversation had been inspirational and the most incredible witnessing experience. What would it be like to finally see Dawn come to Christ? What would he say if given the opportunity? How should he approach her? Nothing had worked till this point and how many opportunities were left?

Marcus picked up the CD and held it between his thumb and index finger and felt little need to listen. He had written every word and note. He knew the true intent behind the music. The song really had not been about Dawn, but that would be difficult to get her to believe.

Life was a funny thing, a never ending series of twists and turns. Twenty minutes prior Marcus was in total joy and in complete satisfaction and had now come full circle. The burden for Dawn McIntyre was not something he could explain. She was consistent in her hate for him, never leading on or giving any inclination that the possibility of a civil relationship existed. She was brutal and mean. Was it her beauty? The thought annoyed him, as he didn't judge who he witnessed to according to looks. Everyone was beautiful in God's opinion. The thought challenged him again, *'Is it because she is so beautiful that I keep putting up with this abuse? Or, am I genuinely concerned about her?'*

He spun in his chair to find that Dawn returned and had somehow found him in the office and was standing on the other side of the desk watching him. Her face remained like a stone statue chiseled to reflect anger. She held a document that described the future performance and looked as if she wanted to rip him some more. She reached out and snatched the CD from his fingers and stormed out of the office.

"Oh crap," Amy said, waking up and noticing tiny ray of sunlight slipping in from behind the thick motel curtains illuminating a spot on the wall. It wasn't part of the agreement to stay the entire night and until now she had a decent track record of leaving before dawn. She cautiously slid out of the bed and retrieved her garments.

Despite years in her profession, it was a reoccurring event to chastise herself as she dressed. As with each client, she felt cheap, dirty and violated. Amy wanted out, but knew that leaving was out of the question and any attempt to run away would result in her death. At times, it wasn't death she feared but the embarrassment that any publicity of her identity could cause, especially within the media who would certainly cling to the story and deluge the market with continuous reports. Death seemed to be a peaceful end to a wretched and miserable life that possessed no hope of ever getting better or truly free. She hated herself and despite having company nearly every night, Amy was so alone.

It was past time for her fix. Amy began getting dry mouth and a slight shaking in her hands. She needed to get out of the hotel room soon. She looked around and searched for what few belongings she possessed. Amy realized that she had not yet been paid for services rendered. Certainly, the John had provided plenty of party favorites and perhaps this was the reason he had fallen asleep before paying her. But he had to pay. If she returned empty-handed they would not be happy.

Amy recalled the last time she had shown up without the proper amount of money. Sam beat her until she fell unconscious. She woke up several hours later with both eyes swollen, knots in the back of her head and a major pain coming from her left ear lobe. She was unable to work for days and since she wasn't bringing in any money, her supply was cut down. The withdrawals were more painful and difficult to deal with than the beatings and regrets combined. In order to keep her hooked and cooperative after a day of suffering they would give her small doses.

She needed to get paid and didn't want to the wake the John up. If he woke up, he might expect more from her and she was ready to leave. With the exception of the dime sized circle of light on the wall, the room dark. Amy moved toward the bathroom and felt for the switch that turned on the light where the toilet and shower were. She eased the door shut enough to leave only a slither of light to aid in her search for the money. She looked on the table and night stand and found nothing.

She slid open the top drawer on the night stand and paused. A blue book with big gold letters that were supernaturally glowing in the dark strangely seemed to be calling out to her. She didn't really understand why. The Bible, after all, had never had any significance in her life before. Why did she stand here now staring at it? Why the desire to pick it up?

Amy reached in and placed her hands around the Bible and pulled it from the drawer. A noise to the left pulled her attention away as the John stirred. *What am I doing? This is stupid. I don't have time for this* she thought and put the Bible back in and shut the drawer. *I just need to get paid and get out of here.* She continued to look and noticed the man's wallet on the floor next to his shoes. Amy had two options: get the money from the wallet as she had done many times before, or wake the man and have to deal with him. Without hesitation Amy moved to the wallet and picked it up. She was relieved to find a large wad of cash, mostly hundred dollar bills. She took out the agreed amount and couldn't help but to give herself a little tip.

She bent to place the wallet back where she had found it, when the man grabbed her wrist. His grip was strong and she tried to pull away. He was unclothed and if she could get away and make it to the door the man would likely not pursue her. But, he proved too strong and pulled her to his face.

"What are you doing, thief?" He asked.

The stench from his rotten breath made her nauseous. She pushed away but the man now had two hands on her. In one quick move, she was pinned beneath him. The weight of the John painfully pressed against her bladder and stomach.

"What are you doing with my wallet?" he demanded.

"You didn't pay me and I need to go," Amy said through the pain.

"Why, so you can get another fix? Was I not good enough for you?" He took the money from her hands and counted it. "Looks like a couple of extra Franklins just accidentally ended up in your hands? You thief!" He yelled. The man raised his fist and brought it down across her face. The forced felt as if it had broken her neck and jaw. The taste of blood filled her mouth. He swung again with the other hand and she remembered no more.

CHAPTER 6

Marcus moved quickly through the aluminum door and into the lobby of the LeJune Studios. His hands were occupied by two hardcover books, an overstuffed black notebook binder, a can of root beer, a leather case used in transporting a laptop and tucked beneath his arm hung a stack of unopened mail. In passing, he looked over into the eyes of a very startled assistant and flashed a boyish smile.

"Well, good morning. Looks like you have your hands full," she said light-heartedly.

He entered the office and tossed the books onto a beige cushion on a chair, dropped the mail into a pile in the center of the desk and then waited briefly for Maryellen to comment about his new mess.

"I just cleaned that up," she said.

"Cleaned what up?" he asked, feigning ignorance.

"That desk! It was clean and now it . . . it has stuff all over it."

Marcus looked at the aging woman and affectionately said, "Job security. Just want to make sure you have something to do." He passed a small chuckle and pulled the computer from the leather bag.

After retiring from teaching in the public school system in her thirties, Maryellen Shea procured a job at LeJune Studios through a friend who knew John and his struggles to push the paperwork required to effectively manage his office. He hated the 'paper aspects' of the studio, as he liked to refer to it, and would rather put everything in a pile and turn it into ash. Music was his passion, but the bills and filings were not.

After purchasing the business and building from John, Marcus continued her employment. She was tenacious when it came to keeping the studio and office in perfect order and often gave him a cross look when he made a mess.

Maryellen raised the yellow legal pad she had been carrying while sliding a pair of reading glasses up the bridge of her nose, "No Surprise will be coming in next week to work on the final cut, apparently Review Board finally reviewed their finances and decided to send us a check, and I got cursed out by that angry woman who keeps calling here looking for you. So, I told her where she could find you."

"And she did." Marcus said.

"She is such a lovely woman. I have no idea why no one likes her. She must be single . . . probably like a black widow, if she had a mate she might kill him and eat him." Maryellen said with a serious expression.

"Wow! That is harsh. I think deep down inside there is a really good person who just needs the right opportunity to shine," Marcus said.

"Maybe black-hole deep! And there is no light in a black-hole. It just sucks up and kills everything it gets close to."

"Wow! You are a Christian woman . . . and a good one I might add. You need to give her a break."

"Break? I want to reach through the phone and pull her tongue out and stick it into an electrical outlet. It is soooooo annoying. She is so mean! The words from that woman's mouth would send a devout atheist into repentance."

"Did I tell you that we are getting married and she's going to leave radio and be my partner here?"

"Then . . . goodbye! I shall be on my way," she said with a smile and a slight wave of her left hand.

The phone in the office rang and Maryellen turned to look into the direction of the door. "Well I sure hope that isn't her. I'd rather the IRS call than to hear her voice again." She moved out of the room.

Marcus sat in the leather chair and began sorting through the mail like he was panning for gold. He pushed the envelopes around looking to determine if there was anything of interest to him or if he should just pass the entire pile off to Maryellen and let her go through it. A post card at the bottom of the pile became visible and Marcus picked it up.

He reclined back in the old leather chair and looked at the beautiful water and palm trees on post card. Marcus thought of John and his new life of adventure. He recalled learning of John's intentions to sell the tired old building and reaching him mere minutes before signing an agreement to sell to an interested party who was going to demolish the old structure and put up an apartment building. A deal for $2.4 million dollars was reached and within ten days the building belonged to Marcus. Sometimes he questioned the decision, wondering if it had been made in haste. But most of the time he was grateful. The price had been high, but the sentimental attachment he had, coupled with the possibilities of helping young men and women live out a dream, just like John had done for him, justified the expense.

After selling the building to Marcus, John left for what was supposed to be a seven-day vacation on a catamaran in the Virgin Islands. The outing turned into a permanent vacation as the wonders of paradise grabbed John and Denise and they simply couldn't leave. Once a month post cards bearing pictures of private coves and tropical beaches came in the mail full of stories and encouragements to visit the places the rejuvenated couple had been. Forty years of producing and dealing with egocentric musicians had negatively affected John's health and desire to work, but Marcus noticed an obvious refreshed zeal for life. Perhaps they had forgotten to send him pictures of the fountain of youth that they apparently had found.

Marcus looked on the peg board and read the back of one card mailed from Virgin Gorda. *"Marcus, What a blessing it is to be here. If I never would have met you or heard your music, I may have never come here. Is Heaven really going to be more beautiful than this? Wow! God Bless!"*

What a blessing John had been to Marcus. God had guided them together and created a bond, despite the age gap, that was insoluble. He could never repay God or John enough for the blessings of the relationship. How awesome it was to have a God who had provided and looked out for him so powerfully.

"Marcus," Maryellen called.

"Yes?" he said re-emerging into the conscious world. A bit of a panic came over him as if he were forgetting something. He thought for a second and began to look around.

"I just received a call from Matthew . . . you know . . . your agent Matthew, can you please call him back? He needs to talk to you." Maryellen called out from the front office.

"What time is it?" Marcus asked.

"Time to return you agent's call," Maryellen persisted.

Marcus put up his right hand in acknowledgment and spun his chair into the direction of the old radio as is sat perched on the new oak shelving.

As the new owner, Marcus decided to give the old building a much needed renovation and modern interior make-over. Everything from the mixing boards to the toilets had been replaced. Only the name and an antique radio remained.

Marcus turned to the radio and worked on the signal clarity only to be disturbed by a delivery truck that had stopped outside the window and was blocking the frequency as the driver talked on a CB. Once the truck pulled on he was surprised to hear *Devil Dawn* playing as Dawn's show came on air.

"Hello, and we are glad that you can be with us," co-host Sonny Brown said in a deep phony radio voice. "I want to start off the show today by reminding all of our fans out there that Dawn and I will be riding with the Crew of Dogmaticus tonight in the French Quarter. Remember, do not bring your kids to this parade unless you want to increase their education way beyond their years . . . what am I saying? Kids know more about that stuff than I do now. OK . . . well, it is kind of an adult's only parade . . . but suit yourself. To you religious yahoos out there don't say that you haven't been warned. Don't call here whining about what you saw. Thus let thy record sayeth that they have been warndeth," he said, mocking the King James Version of the Bible.

Historically, Mardi Gras in New Orleans had been an event suitable for the entire family. Over the years, the moral fabric that once strengthened local communities had been continuously ripped by the embracing of decadence and sexually deviant behaviors. Nowhere was this more evident than during Mardi Gras as women exposed themselves for worthless beads and trinkets. Binge drinking and open sex had become the norm in the French Quarter.

The Crew of Dogmaticus annually celebrated this new era of sin with an anti-God, vulgar and sexually promiscuous parade. Tasteless images of Jesus and Mary were shamelessly displayed throughout the rout in what was a ritualistic attempt at taunting God. New Orleans at Mardi Gras could sometimes seem like the second coming of Sodom and Gomorrah and some often looked to the sky for fire and brimstone.

"This show originally was going to be about tax exemption and 501(c)(3) and four organizations, but I decided to go a different route. After a little experience I had yesterday with one of our more disturbed and sick listener slash participants. He has a disease that I have appropriately diagnosed as En-simple-alitis. It is a new disease. It affects a lot of people these days although the numbers are falling as morc of you are getting cured. Some of the symptoms include talking to someone you can't see and asking for healing and stuff and really expecting an answer. Or, you know how Christians read the Bible and they say that it is a living word?"

"Uhh . . . I think so. You mean like closed caption?" Sonny asked, urging her on.

"No. Sadly these words are not electronic but printed. They don't really go anywhere. They are kind of stuck to the page like in any book.

"If you read living words and imagine angels . . . you may have En-simple-alitis. Or, quite simply . . . you may be simple and need special attention. But, this particular case of En-simple-alitis has this infected person seeing demons or believing in demons and the whole devil thing."

"Well . . . ," Sonny asked with a laugh, "can it be treated, doctor?"

"So far the only known cure is to transplant the brain of a chicken . . . or any fowl will do. Either way they're getting an IQ boost. But, this particular patient . . . I have in my hands a copy of this here document. He has spent the last couple of years or so developing that property off of 59 and that first exit. Well, it turns out that this place is made up of a theater and other business that are all Christian-based. Guess that makes them better than all the rest of us."

"I never really thought of Christians as having a lot of money. Aren't they all poor and buck-toothed?" Sonny asked.

"You would be surprised . . . some inherit. Well, this theater is going to host all kinds of events that will entertain these people," Dawn said.

"What . . . like Big Bird and Elmo?"

"No. How about the devil himself?"

"Well, YEAH! I would pay to see him. Of course, he and I are like brothers. I could probably get free tickets and back stage passes if you want."

"According to this flyer I got last night, running for the first week is this production about a boy who grows into man and his lifelong battle with drugs and depression nearly kills him. How these unseen things . . . you know demons . . . affected him and drove him away from God until a stranger changed his life. It says here that this musical is a dramatic representation of 'powers and principalities.'"

"Wow! Just like the caller yesterday. How long is the show? Man I would really get tired of hearing that pipe organ after sitting through that," Sonny said.

"You know, I have to admit that I did see a guitar. Someone was acting like he was playing it, but I still saw one," Dawn said.

"Do you believe in guardian angels protecting people or demons creeping around making people do bad things?" Sonny asked.

"Stories like this really are in the Bible. There was a scripture written on this flyer . . . I guess I wasn't supposed to have it, so I looked it up. In this particular story we are supposed to believe . . . well, several things happen, again this is according to THE BIBLE, so, take it for what it is, anyway, Jesus and his disciples were sailing across the Sea of Galilee. Then this mysterious storm pops up and blows them across to the far southern side of the Sea. I don't know if Jesus supernaturally knew that there was demon possessed men there or not. Perhaps he just got in the boat without knowing and the Judeo-Christian God blew him to where He wanted him to go. But anyway, there are these two men with . . . like . . . several thousands of these spirits in them. He actually talks to them . . ." Dawn said before being interrupted.

"Like in the Exorcist? Did they turn their heads and spit green-pea soup?" Sonny asked.

"Yeah! Something like that. I just don't remember any description of spraying vomit. But, hey it's a story add whatever you want. Anyway, he says that his name is Legion because there's a lot of them. Jesus supposedly tells the spirits to jump into these poor pigs and then they just run and jump into the Sea of Galilee and drown. My question to you out there if anyone who reads or believes the Bible and knows how to work a phone, why don't you call me and explain this whole powers of darkness or principalities and powers fairy tale, or . . . can we coin a new phrase? How about Christian mythology? Explain this thing to me. Anyone? We will also be doing interviews to determine if you have the dreaded En-simple-alitis disease." Dawn said, projecting the sarcastic overtones of her comments as if she were playing the lead in a Broadway play.

"Powers and Principalities sounds mythological. Maybe it was some ancient alien contact," Sonny said, hinting to Dawn that she needed to take her comments farther.

"Whatever. This is nothing more than bad fiction written by a bunch of men who spent a little too much time alone. If you know what I mean! They didn't have music or television or anything to keep them busy. So, what else were they to do with all of their time? Apparently they weren't very good fishermen. If I'm not mistaken, it was a miracle when they actually caught fish. While they sat there doing nothing their minds were working overtime. They created some really scary and colorful stories in order to scare people into following their beliefs.

"I mean, come on, there is this elaborate and organized structure. Demons have different ranks and importance to the 'order' of things in the spiritually dark world of the, let's say, umm . . . the evil one." Dawn laughed into the microphone. She was having fun.

Throughout her youth, Dawn had been nurtured in the atheist beliefs established by her mother, Keri McIntyre. As a scientist, her life ambition was to find the 'missing link' and prove that evolution was the ultimate answer to the origin of all species in an attempt to end the controversy forever. Often she engaged intelligent design groups, during which she always became hostile and abrasive, serving as a role model for her child.

Dawn was programmed to believe that all who followed God were clueless, wacko right-wingers that didn't stand a chance against Forest Gump in an IQ test. They were the lowest form of life on earth and the very targets of the atheistic beliefs of natural selection and in reality, shouldn't even exist. The only question being was why there were still so many of them.

By the time Dawn was eighteen, she had become her mother's equal, bold and confident. She withheld nothing that was on her mind. Dawn's height gave her an intimidating feature as she was able to get into the faces of most men and woman who attempted to disagree or debate with her. After passing the Bar, she donated a lot of time to various 'civil liberty groups' in matters of the First Amendment and the squelching of Christianity.

Dawn, nick-named by a segment of the Christian audience as Devil Dawn, was gaining popularity daily. Even those who hated her wanted to tune in every day in anticipation of what she may say, taking the label of "shock jock" to a previously unimaginable level.

Every Sunday all across the nation, many church bulletins included her name at the top of their prayer lists. Perhaps, since the pre-conversion days of Saul's life, there had never been a more determined zealot against the Christian faith and way of life.

Since her days as a young adult, she had used any means possible to hurt Christians, labeling them as mind-numb robots who just needed something to believe in to offset their fear of death or misery from failure.

She took great pleasure in answering the letters and e-mail from people who admitted being followers of Christ. For Dawn her payment was throwing a legal victory via court decision that injured Christianity into the faces of each person of faith who had written her. Every injury to Judeo-Christian liberties was one more step toward the total annihilation of religion.

"It's soooo dumb it wouldn't even make a good enough script for one of those really bad 'b' movies. These spirits are just running around and tormenting people and causing them to do evil things? Well . . . that certainly took a lot of imagination. It really does sound like a really lame horror/fantasy fiction novel. Their sole, sorry, no pun intended," she said, laughing, "reason that these spirits exist is to prevent people from going to Heaven or to make people who are saved miserable?

"So, every crime that has been committed was not really the criminal, but the criminal or demonic influence within. Well, we should just let all the convicts out-maybe everyone in prison is telling the truth. They really didn't do it. What kind of back woods, drunk on moonshine, hillbilly non-sense is that? Are you people for real? This isn't Ancient Greece and all of those mythological creatures and stories. We have real science and history and a lot of evidence that proves beyond a doubt that we are not living in some fantasy, Never Never Land utopia. What you see is what you get. Have you ever wondered why the Bible tells you to live by faith and not by sight? Are you smart enough to figure that out? Apparently not!" Dawn said.

"Now Dawn, you know that the only reason you said that is because some demon put that in your head," Sonny added. "Dawn, I know that I say this a lot, but as lawyers you and I have dealt with a lot of Christians while helping in certain important matters of civil liberties, and they always seem to be so narrow minded and simple. And we love you all the way you are . . . simple, confused and funny. We are always going to know what to expect when you are asked a tough question 'the Bible says it and I believe it.' That's it . . . done! What else is there to say?

"A great example of this is your belief that there is only one way to Heaven. I get so sick of hearing these evangelicals preaching that the only way to Heaven is through Christ. They call this guy's death a victory. Now, I am applying common sense here. It makes no sense to me because in war death is counted as a loss. A family member dies it's considered a loss. If your child dies, that is certainly not counted as some victorious gain. Am I missing something here? If this guy couldn't save himself, then how can he do anything for anyone? Besides, he's dead now. Who are they to say that they are the elite and the only ones worthy of going to Heaven? What makes them so sure that they have it right? How do we know that Heaven really exists and is worth going to anyway?"

"Let's take another caller," Dawn said.

"Sid from Viagra Falls, just kidding, I mean Niagara Falls, New York," Sonny said, amazed by his own wit. "Sid, welcome to the show."

"I love the show. Thanks for taking my call. So, the Christians believe that we are under the influence of little worker spirits that steer us to do bad things like cheat on our spouses and break all of the Ten Commandments and rob banks and stuff like that?" the caller said in a heavy New York accent. "It reminds me of the cartoons we used to watch as kids where this little red devil would come to them and stand on their shoulder trying to get them to do something mean or bad. Is it kind of like that?" the caller asked.

"In a NUTshell . . . yes," Dawn said, opting to never pass on an opportunity to launch an insult.

"That's freaky!" the caller said in astonishment. "So, I am supposed to believe that these worker spirits can influence me to do things that are bad?"

"So, what we need to do is petition Washington to invest billions of dollars toward an evil spirit harnessing system. I can see it now. There will be this task force, kind of like that *Ghost*—whatever movie. Then we can put all of those ghost whisperers or Demon Squad members on payroll. Won't that be the business to be in? They will go around catching and storing all of these demons and all crime and evil in the world will go away. All the money we save on the prisons can pay for this program. I guess they can be a branch of the Homeland Security or National Guard or something," Sonny said with an angry, sarcastic tone.

"Humm . . . so, get rid of the spirits and get rid of crime. Well, I guess *possession* really is nine-tenths of the law after all," Dawn said.

"Do these little worker spirits also make us sick? How do Christians get sick if they are protected from the worker spirits?" continued the caller.

"Well, what about children? What about the dog or pet that you love so much?" Dawn asked for the sake of giving her audience more to ponder.

"Thanks for the call. It's time for us to take a break. You're listening to 'In Your Face' and I'm your host, Dawn McIntyre. We'll be right back," she said, as music faded in.

"Will these people ever get it?" Marcus asked into the receiver while the program faded and a commercial jingle began.

He turned in his chair toward the mahogany desk and removed a daily planner encased in black leather. Marcus popped off the strap, flipped it open to the calendar and began to review the scheduled events that remained for the day. He thought back to when he heard his song coming off of the last commercial break.

The realization of Dawn playing his music generated a bizarre sensation.

Quickly he forgot the schedule and began contemplating a call to the show. While in deep thought about how to approach this topic in an effective representation of the Christian perspective, the radio began to squeal and hiss. Another big truck had stopped at a red light in front of his office and the driver was yelling into his CB. The radio crackled while Marcus turned the dial attempting to fine tune the frequency.

"Why don't you just get a new radio? That thing is so old I believe that it was passed down from Mosses!" Maryellen said re-entering the room and dropping a stack of papers on his desk. "I . . . ," she said before being interrupted.

"Shhhhhh!" he said while waving his right hand in the air, trying to focus on the radio.

She frowned and continued despite his focus on the old radio, "I noticed that she is using your song. That's weird."

"Hold on Maryellen," Marcus requested in a polite tone while dialing in the correct frequency. "It's coming back on."

Once again, *Devil Dawn* led in.

"So, you're going to call her? Again?" she asked.

The light changed and the delivery truck moved on. The static dissipated leaving a clear reception.

"Yes, but the Bible says that, 'We deal not with flesh, but Powers and Principalities,'" the caller argued.

"Here we go again. The Bible says . . . so I believe it. Look! How many times do I have to ask you and all of you who read this book and put all of your faith and belief in it. Where you there when it was written? Did you really see who wrote it? The guy that wrote Daniel probably smoked more dope than ninety percent of the people in the music industry. How do you know what is true and what isn't?" she asked.

"Because God says that . . . ,"

"Yeah, yeah! We have heard all of that before. Can I ask you a question?"

"I guess," the caller answered cautiously.

"Why can't you people just give a straight answer to a question? How about this one, have you ever experimented with drugs? Have you ever done . . . acid? Have you ever seen anyone on acid? Let me tell you, it is certainly a trip to watch those people. Who knows what kind of drugs they had back then or what they were on, or what caused these dreams they had. If any of these people lived today do you know what they probably would do for a living? They would be screenwriters in Hollywood and they would be extremely successful with the imaginations they had. Now . . . goodbye!"

CHAPTER 7

"Can you believe that we get paid for this? Is this a radio show or a shrink's office? I have a hard time telling the difference sometimes. You people are too funny. And I'm saying funny to be nice.

"I was watching this Christian television station last night, I think it was on satellite, and this auditorium was full of people and they were falling down . . . like on the ground and crying and stuff. This is really bizarre. Some people were screaming about being healed. I am sometimes tempted to sneak into one of these things and just sit in the back and watch. But, I don't think I would be able to contain myself. It's just too funny . . . and really, really sad at the same time," Dawn said.

"Why don't we do it one day? We'll sneak in some cameras," Sonny asked.

"Well, like I said. It wouldn't be pretty."

"OK. Mel from Mobile. Can we call you Double M?" Sonny asked the new caller.

"Well, if you want." Mel said in a nervous, cracking voice.

Something about the caller stirred Marcus. The man's nerves came through and he feared that the caller was about to be humiliated by taking on the tag team.

"I see them. I've been there and it is real," Mel said.

"Seen who? Been where? Wal-Mart, Disney . . . where?" Sonny asked.

"I've been to Hell. I've seen demons."

"So have I. It's called the DMV or the Department of Motor Vehicles. Ever try to get through there? It is Hell," Sonny joked.

"No, you are not listening . . . I have been there. I see things. Weird things that no one else, or, at least no one that I know, can see."

It was clear to Marcus that the man was extremely frightened of something he either truly saw or believed he had seen. "What do you think of this?" he asked, turning to look at Maryellen.

"Well, the man certainly sounds afraid or convinced of something. It doesn't sound like some joke . . . at least not to him. Anyway, you really shouldn't ask me about things like this."

Marcus was surprised by her response and was suddenly disinterested in the radio. "Why? Does it offend you or something?"

"No, not offend. I just really believe that people, even today, can see angels and demons. I believe, for whatever reason, that some people have open windows into Heaven or the spiritual realm. I believe in the presence of God. I believe in angels . . . they are right here in this room as we speak. Plus, I cannot look at the world without coming to the conclusion about the existence of unclean spiritual things.

"I believe these people who die, come back and say that they have gone to heaven or hell. Sure, some are liars or confused, but some are certainly honest. I believe so strongly in those places and those beings that I believe that people really see all of that." Maryellen said passionately.

"Well, I absolutely believe. We produced a musical about it. But I always thought it would be really neat to see an angel. Often I have even prayed to see one, but it just hasn't happened. Maybe

God doesn't want me to see one. However, I also believe the testimonies," Marcus responded, turning back to the old radio.

"Look, tell me what happened and let's see if we can get you fixed up. Doctor Sonny is in the house. See, I have a real passion for these people," he said, looking toward Dawn.

"Yeah . . . this ought to be good," she replied.

"I know that you think that I am crazy, but I think that God wants me to share this with you. He is reaching out to you. He loves you. Can't really say why or understand why it happened, but I was just sleeping one night and it was like I left my body. Before I knew it I was in this black . . . I mean, this darkness was so thick I could *feel* it. My body was so heavy that I could hardly stand up. I could hear all these sounds around me . . . falling things and screams. The screams were filled with panic and pain. It was awful. Something hit me, kind of like it ran into me with its body. I flew into a wall or something. It was hard to get up.

"Before I knew it I stopped in front of the burning lake of sulfur. Hell! I could see the faces of the tormented souls in the pits. The horrified and desperate looks . . . the screams were chilling and unrelenting.

"Then I looked up and noticed the worst thing of all . . . you can see Heaven from the lake of fire. I could see and know that it was Heaven and that I was never going to go there. It's strange. You see them celebrating and welcoming in new souls. They were rejoicing and I was in torment beyond belief. I screamed, but no one heard or even looked in my direction. They cannot see Hell from Heaven.

"Then, all of a sudden, I was back in my bed full of sweat." The man paused when he realized that Sonny was laughing. "You're laughing," he said somberly.

"Look dude! You called here. What did you think was going to happen?" Sonny asked.

He ignored Sonny and continued. "The next day I began to see things. Weird things. Strange creatures . . . some huge and some small. Some white and some all kinds of colors. Some are heavenly and some are evil."

"OK! That was great. Look, we wish you the best with your little . . . whatever it is that you have going on. Your little band of spirit brothers or whatever," Dawn said, irritated.

"I had to call. I had this prophetic thought about you Ms. McIntyre. I'm so sorry to have to tell you this, but God is going to deal with you. Last night I was told that before this weekend is over that something huge was going to happen to you."

She remembered the crazy girl who had cut her off and had told her basically the same thing in the arena. Perhaps the two knew each other and they were playing a game with her. Either way, she became a little unsettled and a chill ran up her spine. But despite her fear, she refused to relent. "Listen you kook, I don't appreciate your calling here with this story and phony warning. If God wants me, then here I am. Let Him come. I am not worried. You want to know why I am not worried, because He doesn't exist!"

"Sure, God wants you. God is reaching for you . . . reaching for you like He did with the Prodigal Son. But, you have weighed Him in the balance and have decided to worship the creature rather than the Creator. The deceiver is coming for you. You are without excuse."

"Man! We have heard all of this before. We have been through this a million times. Last year a man called in . . . heck, it may even be you . . . with a threat like this to me. I am still alive, kicking and laughing at you right now," Dawn yelled into the microphone.

"They follow you . . . the both of you, all the time. You do their work when you are on the air. You never fail and they use you . . . both of you," Mel said in a monotone voice.

"Speaking of used, you have used up enough of our time. Got to go Double M. Be sure to be a stranger to the show. Will ya please?" Sonny said, inviting Mel to never call again.

"Wow! That was interesting," Marcus said. "As you know, Dawn came to the center last night and after she had thrown her tantrum the strangest thing happened. Sarah—"

"Oh . . . I do love that girl. She is so sweet," Maryellen interrupted.

"Well, yeah. But, she did the strangest thing. When Dawn turned to leave, she got right up in her face and said that 'forty-eight hours will pass and you will see the living God and you will never be the same!' Dawn seemed kind of freaked out. Then she looked over and blamed me . . . what's new about that? But that guy on the radio just said that last night he was told something about forty-eight hours for Dawn. That is so strange. Do you think that God is really trying to send her a warning . . . a prophetic word? Prophets did that with the kings and men of the Old Testament, but how often does that happen today?"

"Either, like she said, they conspired the whole forty-eight hour thing, or she better watch her butt. I must confess that I am really concerned for her," Maryellen said.

"I . . . had this really graphic dream. You know when your dream is so real that you can smell and feel and remember everything? I dreamt that Dawn was being attacked by two demons or evil entities. She was tortured and was screaming. I wasn't able to help her. I didn't even come close to doing anything remotely beneficial. Kind of funny timing to have such a strange dream. I wasn't sure if it was prophetic, but now I'm certain."

"I have seen some incredible things. These were not dreams. When I was little my older sister went through a serious time of rebellion. She was really bad. Doing really bad things every night my mom and dad would lay hands on me and pray that God would protect me . . . that His hedge of protection would surround me.

"One night I saw this huge angel come into my room from the window and sit on the floor next to my bed. He was so big. Even though he was sitting on the floor, I had to look up at him. I could see him as I see you right now. I asked him why he was there and he said 'to protect you.' I asked all kinds of questions and he answered a lot of them, but some he would just say 'ask God.'

"About an hour after he came in, I saw these . . . what I guess were demons, coming into the room. When they saw him they would turn and leave. The demons were only there when she would come home and they followed her when she left. Then one day, my angel stopped appearing to me. I guess the demons stopped following my sister in the house and her attitude was a lot better. I don't know what happened, but she really straightened up.

"Now, do you think I am a quack?" Maryellen asked.

"No. I do have some experience with them. Although I have never seen anything physically manifest in its spiritual form. We have prayed for and have seen people delivered from unclean spirits. Plus, the Bible is full of accounts of demonic possession and oppression. I absolutely believe you," Marcus said.

"The angels were easy. It was the dirty spirits that were hard to look at. That was a real challenge for a little girl. Be careful what you wish for," Maryellen warned.

"Well, I've seen a lot of incredible things during my time as a Christian. We cannot explain everything. But, we have to be able to give an account for what it is that we believe and take the fight to the enemy. That is hard to do if Christians just write off spiritual warfare as some pre-modern Christianity occurrence that doesn't affect us today. That is a lie from the Deceiver himself," Marcus said.

He pressed the speed dial and waited for Sarah to answer. Without wanting to take too much of her time Marcus asked her about the word of knowledge and the possible co-conspirator Mel from the radio show. Sara promised to have had no contact with anyone named Mel for any reason and was very interested when Marcus had shared the events of the call with her. He concluded that the guy was genuine and his warning was to be heeded.

Marcus grew increasingly weary and felt the anxiety about Dawn's eternal condition move up a notch. *Two, perhaps even three warnings,* and he looked at his watch to do the math. *Last night was about eight o'clock when Sarah talked to her. It's after eleven now that is about fifteen hours. But, they both said that within forty-eight hours something was going to happen* he thought. He knew he had to try so he pressed the button with the preset number and waited.

Toby, the producer, looked at Dawn through the glass and gave the thumbs up that Marcus was on the line. She became excited and followed the monitor and pressed line two.

"Oh, Marcus. Is this my Marcus?" she asked with a hint of sarcasm. She rolled her eyes and loathed the notion of talking with him again.

The question threw Marcus off a bit and he paused for a second to consider a witty response, "Well, I guess it is. I always knew that you liked me. So, now the truth is out for everyone to know. The tabloids will be lit up tomorrow."

"Ha, ha. Now you are writing songs about me. Is that right?" Dawn asked.

"Like I told you before . . . no," he replied. "Look, to make a long story short, two years ago I was doing some mission work in North Kurdufan and there was this story the local Christians told me about this person named Fatimah Obkik. She was a ruthless soul and had infiltrated the underground church. She led many Christians to the slaughter and most were apprehended while worshiping one Sunday morning. She was called the Devil at Dawn or Devil Dawn. The song is truly about international Christian persecution, but inspired by her."

As much as Dawn didn't want to admit it, the story was somewhat original, if not convincing. She had never heard the story and couldn't prove that it was a fable. "What about the comment about the microphone and radio waves?" she asked.

"She was allowed to broadcast from an underground FM radio station. It helped her reach the multitudes of Christian believers with false meeting places and times. The military went to these meetings and arrested everyone. At this very moment these people are being tortured and starved to death on the southern border," Marcus answered. "Look, I called for a different reason. Sure, I think you have the wrong idea about Powers and Principalities and I can give you a million reasons why you are wrong."

"Sure you can. I expected nothing less from you . . . our own personal little spiritual authority," Dawn replied snidely.

"I say this and I don't mean to seem like I am attacking you or Sonny, but this show is a great example of how prevalent . . . strong and effective the spiritual war is. You slam the Church and Christians all the time. Your show thrives because of how rude, ruthless, vile and offensive you can be. Shock talk, or however you want to categorize it, is how this show gains in popularity.

"I'm thankful that my father was a church-going Christian, but I was not. I wanted to make sure of who God was and if He was even real before I could make the same commitment my dad had made. So, I explored the evidences of God. I analyzed historical and scientific evidence—" he said before being cut off.

"Scientific?" Dawn said laughing. "Hasn't science proven evolution and the Big Bang? You got nothing if you want to start talking science."

"Absolutely not! The Big Bang sounds like something a five-year old made up. What an original name. I have five words for you about the 'big bang'—and write this down . . . the conservation of angular momentum. Now, test your science!

"Anyway, science hasn't proven evolution; just the opposite and I can provide countless sources. This entire conversation is exactly what I am talking about. You get on the air and make all of these assumptions and accusations and it doesn't seem to me that you have thoroughly examined the truth. You wouldn't know the truth if it was a brick and it landed on your foot. You read what other atheists and secular sources have said and regurgitate their talking points. That is irresponsible. You can criticize me all you want, but at least I reached my conclusion by looking at the entire issue and making and educated determination according to the evidence.

"I realized that God is real and that He has an adversary in the devil. There is a war for the heart and soul of men. Heaven and Hell are real. You guys are guided or misguided . . . and the reason is spiritual. You are just too blind to see it. You're puppets." Marcus said challenging them.

"Hey Kermit, you feel like a puppet?" Dawn asked Sonny.

"Alright! You think you have it all figured out? Well, I come from a Christian home and I was forced into a private Christian school. There were more hypocrites in there than anywhere I had been. The only difference I saw was just a façade. Behind the scenes they were no better than anyone else. I didn't see or experience anything that proved to me that God was real, just the opposite. I prayed and read the Bible and experienced nothing. I didn't see any healings or radical changes. Just a bunch of foul-mouthed, sexually active, drunken drug users just like every public school I had been in. If you were an athlete you could get away with murder. If you were a slightly below average student you got no mercy and was asked to leave the school because you didn't measure up. Where is the love in that? Is that Christ-like? Throw them out if they don't measure up!

"God is just some marketing tool. Look at all of these 'ministries' making boat-loads of tax-free money off of mind-numb Bible-thumpers like you. I have seen NO evidence of God, the supernatural, miraculous healings or anything that supports your non-sense. The bottom line is there is no evidence of God or any other gods. You weak minded people just need a crutch to blame all of your failures on. That is why this spiritual warfare thing is so important to you. It is your excuse for everything," Sonny said.

"Well, I am not going to be able to convince you of anything until God shows you how wrong the both of you are. Dawn—"

"See how your little song has turned people against me?" she interrupted. "That crazy girl last night and that caller just a few minutes ago are crazy. Since spirits don't exist I guess you put them up to it. Is this some scam? Trying to scare me to your side?"

"I honestly can say that I wish you were right about that. But, the truth is that I am worried about you. I talked to my assistant and she knew nothing of this other caller a little while ago. God is warning you! I beg you to consider what they are saying. I am not sure what is going to happen. But, I will tell you that God loves and cares for you. I am willing to bet that you are thinking about it and you know something supernatural is about to happen. You know!"

The truth of his statement caused goose bumps to race across Dawn's arms. But she had to maintain her tough unaltered persona and replied, "What I know is what I have said many times . . . you are a fruit loop. Forty-eight hours from now I will be fine and waiting for you to call this show. Only you won't because you and those two others will look like the fools you truly are."

Everything was a blur as Amy strained to open her eyes. The darkness of the room conjured panic as she was unable to initially discern where she had awakened. She wanted to sit up in order to observe the surroundings but was met with opposition from her aching limbs. The pain in her arm was only superseded by that of the face and head.

Amy's thoughts were groggy. She remembered the hotel room and the man's repeated punches to her face and body. She fought through the pain and pushed herself up against the headboard and moved a pillow behind her back for support.

Amy rested her throbbing head against the top of the headboard and began to cry. How many times had she been beaten over the years? Would she ever escape from this life, and if so, what could the future possibly hold for her? Amy had long since given up on the notion of the perfect husband, 2.5 kids, a house with a fence and a dog named Chewy. This was *her* American dream—physically and mentally abusive men controlling every aspect of her life. What was the point? Life was ruthless and tough. She refused to lie to herself about the dismal prospects of the future and just wanted it all to end. These people would never leave her alone, she knew too much. If she ran away they would find her and kill her.

Why did I ever leave home? Why was I so stubborn and ran way? Why didn't I ever go back and ask Mom to forgive me? Why not try? Would it really have been that bad? she thought. But now it was too late. She was a prostitute, a drug addict and an embarrassment to both her high-profile sister and mother. No one could ever love her even if they were family. She had ruined any chances of a descent life and would either die of a drug overdose, at the hand of a crazy John or Stan would just do it for the sake of not having to deal with her anymore.

Often she wished to enter into eternity and be done with all of the hurt and pain of her disappointing life. *Do it! Why not kill yourself? No one will ever notice. You don't matter.*

I can cut my wrist. I can steal a gun and shoot myself. I could hang myself . . . it's not like I have never been choked before. She sat and considered the possibilities of success and failure with each. She scanned the room and looked into the closet and realized that there was no way she was hanging herself in there. As soon as she ruled it out, her thoughts seemed to take life, *what is wrong with cutting your wrist. Can it be all that bad? Susie had the courage to do it and it worked for her. Why not work for you? There is a glass by the sink. Just drop it into the sink and get a piece and do it.* Amy looked over at the large mirror and scanned the countertop. She could barely see a drinking glass that had been placed next to the faucet. She rolled over to her side and heard a clanking sound on the floor. She continued to roll over and looked down. The small glass container lay motionless on its side. She moved out of the bed and picked it up and noticed that it had been emptied. Amy's hands started to shake at the realization that her daily ration had been taken. Her mouth became dry and she started to panic. Amy knew that her dependence on heroin was one way they controlled her and another reason to be ashamed. She hated having a dependency, but couldn't live without it and wanted it badly. Before leaving with the last John, Stan had given her a dose and now it was gone. The man must have taken it after knocking her unconscious. That would explain why the container was out of her purse.

Amy wondered how she would get more. She longed for it and needed it. If she approached Stan now and asked for more, it would open the door for more humiliation. They would mock her and make her do 'favors,' as they called it. They enjoyed having power and control.

Amy began to cry and looked at the ceiling. *Come on, let's end this. What is there to live for? Things will never change.* Her thoughts began to betray her again.

A slight movement in the curtain caught her attention. She looked and saw nothing out of the ordinary, but was convinced that something had been there. A beam of golden sunlight found a way around the thick window treatments of the hotel room and cut through the darkness. The beam landed on something that Amy couldn't see clearly enough to identify. The blinding light was painful and caused her to blink. She looked around in search of whoever was responsible for moving the curtain and allowing the light to enter the room.

She found nothing and considered her sanity while concluding that she had been seeing things. Amy pushed her legs off of the bed and made her way toward the sink. She looked on the floor as the purse and its contents were scattered over a three foot area and maneuvered through them without stepping on anything despite her weak and shaking legs and poor balance. She reached the counter and braced herself by leaning on both hands despite the burning forearms and triceps. She looked in amazement and gingerly rotated her head back toward the window. As it was before, the curtain and air conditioner were the only visible objects next to the door.

On the counter was the grey Bible from the drawer. She hadn't taken it out and doubted the abusive John had either, unless he was the type who, while the world was watching, pretended to be a Christian but secretly lived the life of a devil. Perhaps he would read some scripture to settle his mind in light of the things he had done while in the hotel. A cleansing before leaving the stench-filled room.

Something in her heart rejected that thought and convinced Amy that the occurrence was all about her. The words were in red and she knew enough about the Bible to understand that these were the words of Jesus. The ray of light coming from the window lit up a single scripture. She leaned over and read it aloud, "As the Father has loved me, **so have I loved you.** Now remain in my love . . . John 15:9." A thought crossed her mind that Jesus was talking to her and she wept and fell to the floor. She didn't know much about Jesus and could not understand why the scripture had penetrated her so deeply. It had been a long time since anyone had acknowledged any type of love for her. She felt so unworthy of love.

Chapter 8

Dawn crossed the threshold and slammed the entrance door from the garage behind her. She paused and kicked her shoes off to the side of the brown fleur-de-leis floor mat before walking by the open counter area that separated the kitchen and dining room. Out of frustration, she blindly tossed her keys. The sound of nickel and aluminum sliding across the granite rang through the room and crashed loudly as it slammed into the plastic casing of the phone. The impact startled Dawn, causing a momentary distraction from her consuming, angry thoughts.

She looked over at the phone and the blinking light of the answering machine and briefly considered hitting the play button. She paused, bearing in mind the possibilities, and refused to give in to the daily habitual practice of checking the messages. The day had been long and irritating enough without giving life another chance to slap her in the face. The last thing she needed was to find out that some false prophet had illegally gotten a copy of her phone number and was calling to let her know how life would be radically affected sometime within the next day or so.

Although she had not outwardly expressed any concern with taking the prophesies seriously, Dawn knew that getting out of the building without anyone seeing through her amateur acting abilities was a miracle in itself. The truth was that something within her had been disturbed. Despite not believing in the supernatural, she feared the unknown. *What if by some strange stroke of luck they are right? What if someone is planning to hurt me? Something will happen very soon,* she sorted through a gumbo of thoughts and her concern grew. In order to stave off the fear, she fed her anger by blaming the Christians with wishing or cursing her to some ill fate.

A burst of confidence seemed to take hold and she considered how she would humiliate Marcus and his stupid little assistant and the moronic caller on Monday when she arrived at the radio station in perfect health. She would taunt them and take great pleasure in doing so.

But just as quickly as the thought of victory came, doubt and fear unexplainably crept back in. Dawn walked across the living room and jerked open the blinds covering the twin six foot windows that gave her a view of Audubon Park, nearly ripping the two inch wooden curtain rod from the wall. She crossed her arms and looked at the crowd of people going about their day. Their lives were probably unfulfilling and simple, she pondered. But no dark promise hung over their heads. Then again, they were just ordinary people with mostly useless lives and nothing to show for it. She was accomplished and this was often the price to pay for being at the top. People often wanted you, and in some cases, wanted to hurt you.

Her thoughts were random and uncontrollable. One second she was fuming over Marcus or the stupid blond who worked for him. Then she would unexplainably find herself focusing on the forty-eight hour prophecy against her. The lack of control was as irritating as all of the thoughts combined.

A thought came across her mind to curse God. Dawn raised a finger and opened her mouth to speak and pulled back. She was baffled at her own action, or rather the lack of it. God was not real and she should have nothing to fear from an ancient fable, but found that something stirred her to silence.

Dawn became unsure of what was happening and realized that she needed a distraction to move her mind onto other more profitable things. She turned on the television and adjusted the lime green leather sofa while pressing the buttons on the remote in anticipation of finding something of interest. It was out of character for Dawn as she passed over the news stations without stopping and getting the breaking news or items of the hour. She strangely longed for something entertaining that lacked serious subject matter. Oddly enough, she wanted something that would make her laugh.

The green pillows on the couch were stitched with a picture of a conquering matador. His cape was thrown back while proudly and victoriously stabbing a bull. The massive animal, as determined by the scale, hunched over in defeat as blood ran down its sides and pooled beneath its torso spewing from the sword's penetration points. After attending a bullfight in Spain, Dawn was enthralled by the event and couldn't resist purchasing multiple items to remind her of the experience.

She, too, was a matador, only in a different fight and with a different type of sword. Here weapons were words and a modern interpretation of the Constitution. Dawn had been able to levy heavy blows against the church and took great pleasure in doing so. She longed for the day when she would drive that victorious last dagger into the beast of Christianity and it would fall to the ground in ruin. The fall of the once strong and impressive bull represented the future of the body of believers. Each day small victories were won and the day of celebration drew nearer. The pillows were a reminder of the goal.

Thoughts of Spain reminded her of the need for a vacation. Perhaps she would return there, or perhaps Rome. The Colosseum would be a nice visit since Christians had actually been killed there. An off-the-wall thought came to mind about the kinds of souvenirs that could have been sold during the various events.

"God! Who needs a god?" she said angrily.

Dawn leaned back attempting to settle in for a moment in order to rest hoping the mind would follow the body. She fell into the waiting leather and cushions of the sofa without concern as she had done numerous times before, but was surprised at the sensation of continued momentum. Initially, Dawn thought that perhaps, despite being pushed up against the wall, the sofa had rolled over backwards. This was quickly dispelled when she realized that it was no longer beneath her and nowhere in view. The walls, the floor and house were all gone. She was freefalling as if thrown from the top of a mountain by an unseen source. Fear of the unknown and uncertainty of the situation summoned a great sense of panic and instinct for survival. She kicked and reached for anything that would stop the fall. She desperately sought a place of refuge and found none.

Layer after layer of the earth's strata passed before her eyes, disappearing into the distance that passed between her and the surface. Dawn fruitlessly continued to fight for anything to break the fall and could not grasp the reality of how her hands passed through what should have been solid substances as if they were a gas. She looked at her hands while moving her fingers. She could see, feel and control the extremities and concluded that the physical makeup of the earth had made a sudden and impossible ghostlike transformation. Out of a growing confusion and disbelief, Dawn waved and watched her hands as they continued to effortlessly pass through. She screamed with all the breath she could muster, but there was no one who could help.

Darkness began to dominate her surroundings. The strata continued to pass and she sank deeper into the expanding abyss. Within seconds it covered her like a constricting shroud, intensifying the fear. Dawn was freefalling completely blind. Despite the loss of vision and lack of awareness for her surroundings, Dawn continued making frantic attempts to grab onto something.

After several minutes and near the point of exhaustion, Dawn stopped fighting the fall and conceded to the notion that either death was imminent, or that she was going to fall forever. If it was time to die, she hoped that it would be quick and painless. Before the thought had completely exited her mind and without warning she came to a sudden and violent stop crashing into something that had remained solid. Every inch of her body felt the impact and she wondered if every single bone had been shattered. Yet, she was unexplainably alive and conscious. The entire world seemed to have been turned to gas, but the solid bed of rock that caught her had somehow maintained its original physical property.

Dawn stirred to look and was met with limited mobility. She made an exhausting attempt to push herself up to get a better view in hope of finding a source of light or life. The same oppressive blackness that had accompanied her on the way down coated everything within the reach of her vision. She looked anxiously around like a child and was frightened of the darkness, desperately yearning for the relief and immeasurable comfort offered by light. Even the tiniest spark or smallest of flames would have seemed mighty and powerful here. It wasn't simply the absence of light that created an overwhelming hopelessness and gave an overpowering authority to the dark, but it unexplainably appeared to have the ability to steal life. It was like nothing she had ever known and it possessed a strange tangible quality. She couldn't understand it, but the darkness seemed to live and take pleasure in exploiting the fears of anyone foolish enough to wind up here. She could sense it mocking her.

The darkness was having its way and she panicked as if waking from a deep rest only to find that she was fighting the suffocation and claustrophobia of being buried alive in a coffin. Dawn could feel the darkness wrapping around and touching every inch of her body. She felt exploited, weak and completely subjected to the will of whatever it was that had engulfed her.

Dawn was lying on her side in an awkward and painful position. The need to get upright and escape ascended to the forefront of the multitude of competing thoughts and emotions as a searing heat scorched every inch of her body, in direct contact with the solid ground. She pulled her hands into her body near the chest area and was surprised that they responded instead of lying limp and unwilling to cooperate. Her bones should have been broken into micro fragments, but amazingly had remained intact and functional.

Dawn put her hand on the scorching ground and pushed. There was no traction and her hand slid through a thick greasy substance that coated the ground and smelled like rotten garbage. Her sides burned. She pulled the hands back and used better positioning that allowed for a more vertical effort and less of an angular one. Through the pain, she forced herself to roll over. To Dawn's astonishment, despite the fall's impact, her arms and legs hadn't sustained any noticeable punctures or lacerations.

Once again combating the claustrophobic feeling of the darkness around her, Dawn wrestled desperately to get to her feet refusing to cede to what was either sheer exhaustion on the part of her muscles or a massive increase in gravitational pull. She rubbed her side attempting to subdue a none-existent fire. Her back no longer hurt from the fall, but had lingering effects from the intense heat of the ground. Dawn pulled her knees upward into the chest, positioned her weight over her feet and pushed upward.

She stood on burning feet, fighting for breath and trying to contemplate her circumstance. The density of the air made it a struggle to breath and she sucked the oxygen-depleted air like a fish on land, opening and closing its mouth in desperation for the passage of water over its gills.

Dawn realized for the first time that she was naked, which was soon forgotten as the piercing screams demanded her attention. The black void held many ghastly mysteries and hid the source of the screams that surrounded her. Still blind in the living darkness, she considered a rather desperate act of randomly selecting a direction and attempting to feel her way around. The risk of falling into another chasm or a potentially worse situation outweighed the thought of remaining stationary.

Dawn wondered if there had been some massive earthquake, which was nearly unheard of in Louisiana, and she had been swallowed up by a crack in the surface. Perhaps there were others that had unexplainably survived as she had. If there were others, they could possibly help each other and collectively figure out what happened and a way to get out.

A sound interrupted her thoughts and summoned a new fear. Grunting noises like that of a huge boar were close and moving around her. She planted her left foot and turned in a circle following the sound in order to keep whatever it was in front, which provided the best possibility for defense should the need arise. Several times she turned in complete circles, following the movement of the sound in anticipation of an attack. It was only natural to fear the unknown and she had to assume that the unidentified presence was stalking her with intentions to do harm. She began to weep and considered taking a chance and running into the opposite direction of the circling grunts. Maybe there was a rock or something that could offer refuge, a weapon or something for protection.

Before she could turn, a pair of glowing, red-orange eyes appeared inches from her face. Despite not being able to see the full facial expression of the thing before her, Dawn looked deep into the eyes and sensed a hate so profound that it sent chills down her spine. She became paralyzed in fear. There was no chance for an escape now. Giving into fear and indecision had cost her. Whatever the small window of opportunity had been, it was now closed.

The creature stood for a second and bent back down letting out a bone-chilling scream inches from Dawn's nose. Her forearm could fit horizontally between the creature's eyes. A word typically not included in her vocabulary came to mind . . . evil. The thing was pure evil.

Its breath was like an intense wave of heat from a furnace and smelled of burning flesh. Dawn recoiled pulling her hands to her face expecting to find melted skin and burning hair. Once again there was no evidence of damage. The eyes narrowed slightly as the creature moved back within inches from her. A sudden burst of tremendous pain shot through her back as the beast dug its claws into her shoulders. The huge demon picked her up and seemed to play like a child that had caught a tiny and helpless insect. The beast stood erect and moved Dawn up to its face which she estimated to be at least fifteen feet off of the ground. The overwhelming pain once again beckoned unrelenting screams. She kicked in a desperate but useless attempt at self-defense. Both arms were locked at her side in the grip of the evil creature. Every muscle in the upper body ached and screamed for relief.

The pressure from the claws increased digging in farther as she moved briskly to the right and was thrown. Her head met with a rock, which caused her body to swing and spin sideways like a wheel rolling horizontally through space. Several seconds passed and she crashed down to the ground and rolled to a stop.

Dawn forced her hands to move and inspect the bodily damage once again and found nothing. This was as perplexing as the entire ordeal. *How is this possible? I should have been decapitated. I should be dead. I should have died from the first fall*, she thought. *This is just crazy!*

It was at this point she realized the full and eternal extent of her situation. "Is this . . . Hell?" she asked. She looked around with a new sense of loss and terror. Dawn pulled her hands to her breast and pushed upward to stand for a second time. The newness of her reality overrode immediate fears of the beast. Was Hell a real place after all? Had Marcus and all of those callers over the years been right? Was she now destined to an eternity here? *I never really hurt anyone. I was a good person. Sure, I was just open and honest about what I believed with people who I didn't agree with. I have done nothing to deserve being here,* Dawn thought.

A voice pierced the wall of darkness and was followed by another and then dozens. The echoing voices were all familiar. Despite the seemingly random broadcast of countless conversations at one time, Dawn could discern each and remember precisely the details and account for every word calling out like testimony during a trial. Countless conversations of hatred and rejection toward God and His Son were piercing her heart.

One brutal, profane filled attack after another called out and slashed her soul like a double-edged sword. Each word penetrated deeper. Conviction now consumed her and she covered her ears desperate to deflect the condemning testimonies. The chorus of verbal accounts against her grew louder and louder, concluding with her own words, *"Save it preacher. You can bow down to your false, whatever . . . but . . . I live in the real world. If God is real, let Him stand before me and show Himself. Let Him tell me not to sue you. If He created me, then let Him deal with me!"* Dawn fell to her knees and screamed out to God for mercy.

Her soul ached as it gave in to the reality of the righteous judgment she now faced. She, more so than many others, had numerous opportunities to acknowledge the truth. In her mind she realized the countless times God had reached out to her only to be slapped and spit on. Rejected like some loser in a bar making a pass. She was blinded by the lie she had so zealously coveted and now it was time to pay the price.

It was easy to write God off and deny Jesus. Then there was no commitment and everyone accepted you. It was an era where the world had out grown the need for a god. Those deemed 'religious' were ridiculed and mocked by everyone, not just her. They were the outcasts who had really not given any convincing account of God. Simply declaring that, "The Bible said it and I believe it," was hardly scientific, not good enough in a world ruled by tangible and visible evidence. It was an educated and intelligent society that needed physical and substantial proof before believing in anything outside of a Hollywood rumor.

A lot of people went to church, but away from the pastor and church family, where it was assumed that no one was watching, they lived no differently than the rest of the world. There had been no clearly defined line of delineation, border or impasse. Some had seemed to be just like the rest of the Godless world. She couldn't tell the difference. They were all hypocrites and justified her way of life.

A new thought pierced Dawn's soul as she tried to absorb the reality of her situation. *How many have I led to this place? How many were misled? Souls may end up in my situation for an eternity as the result of my actions.* It seemed impossible to sink deeper into a pit of desperation, hopelessness and ultimate failure. Perhaps she was deserving of this place after all. She felt wicked and vile.

Suddenly, a huge explosion rocked the underground cavern with the force of a powerful earthquake. Reaching into the supernatural atmosphere, a glowing blue plume rolled upward like a giant mushroom and lit up the area around her. She could see her nakedness and confirmed there was no visible damage, even from the huge claws that had torn at her flesh. She scanned the area and saw huge underground rock formations that trailed off into eternity. She pushed herself back onto her feet and looked into the direction she had been thrown and saw the huge beast moving quickly toward her.

A second explosion erupted and Dawn turned in time to see an incoming wall of burning sulfur as it knocked her back to the ground and coated her body. She screamed, violently jerking to get free. Relentlessly, she swatted the burning elements off of her. Thoughts of cursing God came to mind as she was suffering. She jerked and rolled moving in any direction or manner that would free her from the blanket of fire. No longer did she have tears to cry. No part of her body had escaped the fire.

In the short time in this place, whether it was Hell or just some chasm in the earth, she had experienced unfathomable fear, pain and hopelessness. Dawn screamed out God's name and begged for mercy and forgiveness going against the indwelt desire to curse the creator of Heaven and Hell for her suffering. An image of Marcus came to mind. *He was right,* she thought.

Dawn stood once again and surveyed what she could as the fading explosion had seemed to defy the extraordinary gravitational pull and lit up the area for several minutes. But it began to fade and darkness was once again approaching. Dawn quickly turned in a circle and was horrified to see that the huge beast was being followed by at least twenty other deformed and wretched creatures that were headed toward her from the original direction from where she had been thrown.

The demon stood fifteen feet high, with a pair of singed and mangled wings that seemed to offer no assistance in flying, but served only as a reminder of its fallen state. The former wings lacked the membranous webbing required to give propulsion. A set of broken and disfigured frames flopped in place where a once mighty set of angelic wings had been. A tattered and dirty garment covered a portion of its body. Its round head was crowned with awkwardly formed horns, similar to those of a ram. The nose seemed to dangle on the left side of its face, bouncing from cheek to cheek, and was possibly the reason for the grunting noises.

She turned to run but felt magnetically secured to the ground, barely able to resist the force and pick her feet up and move. Running was nearly impossible. The gravitational pull was too great. Pain ran through her back as the first beast overran her position slapping her in the center of the back with an open fist. The blow knocked her down. The creature grabbed her left leg around the thigh and jerked her mercilessly into the air. It began to swing her around. Its claws dug deep into the thigh and once again she was airborne. Dawn hit a series of boulders skimming across them before free falling off a rocky cliff and landing flat on her back on a series of smaller pieces of rock.

Exhaustion now completely consumed her. She no longer wanted to move, but the heat from the rocks was more than she could bear. Dawn once again rolled over to get back on her feet and paused. She wondered why she should bother if she was only going to be grabbed or knocked down by one of the beasts again. But the reality was that the chances of escape were zero if she were to just lie there. Thoughts of a conversation with Marcus came to mind about Hell as an eternal destination where there was no chance of egress. He had told her the story of the rich man and Lazarus. She remembered it with clarity as if she had just read it.

She rolled over to her right and began to hear the screams. Dawn sat up and looked in the near distance at a glowing and endless sea of blue flames. She knew what it was and wondered if that was her fate. Was she going to be helplessly tossed into it? She turned to find a way back up the rock wall that made up the cliff she had just fallen from. Dawn crawled to a rock and desperately attempted to pull herself upward. The exhaustion combined with the magnified weight proved to be too much. She made attempt after attempt.

On her fourth try she looked up to find that one of the beasts had jumped from the cliff and landed behind her. The giant demon stood angrily looking as if it wanted to rip her into pieces. It reached out and wrapped Dawn's hair in its fist and picked her up by the head. She screamed and clawed in terror.

The demon turned and began to walk slowly across the smaller rocks toward the blue abyss. It stomped through the rocks and kicked the large boulders out of the way. She screamed and called out to God and begged for mercy. With every pain-filled and fearful step she called out for God to listen to her petition and grant her mercy. She now believed in Him, the spiritual world and the existence of beings that had not been seen by many living souls.

She could see the shore of the burning lake as they drew nearer. The stench of sulfur filled her sinuses. Dawn screamed intensely. Slapping, scratching and kicking seemed to be useless against the beast. Out of a sense of urgency and desperation, she frantically jerked and tried to pull out her hair, but it held firm. Dawn became increasingly desperate, screaming out for God to intercede with mercy.

The beast stopped on the shore as blue flames of different heights danced on the rocks that outlined the pit of suffering. The tormented souls screamed in agony and desperation. Some cursed God and others fruitlessly begged for mercy for themselves and their families. The demon seemed to take delight in the suffering and in tormenting Dawn. Like a puppeteer, it moved her down to the edge to a boulder just big enough for her feet to touch and let her dangle and observe the lake for a few seconds.

Two feet away from Dawn was an empty pit. Next to it stood a woman who looked ghostly and horrid as she screamed and moaned in torment. She turned and looked at Dawn with an empty, lost expression. She reached to the top of the pit and was able to extend her hand nearly a foot out.

Dawn felt the beast pull forward, dragging her off of the rock and over the blue flames. She fought to stay over the shore, but found her feet swinging toward the empty pit and the hand of the condemned soul. She continued to beg for mercy while looking into the open pit of burning sulfur. The hopeless soul of the woman wrapped her hands around Dawn's ankle. The heat from the soul's hand was intense and would have melted normal flesh. She jerked her foot free and kicked at the woman.

Slowly, the demon began to lower Dawn into the pit. The flames leapt up to meet her as if hungry for the new addition. She pulled her feet up, bringing her shaking knees into her chest. There was no escape from the growing intensity of the burning sulfur. With soul-crushing finality, Dawn realized that this was a place of no escape, that she was destined to an eternity of suffering. She screamed and continued to fight to get out.

Chapter 9

Time was running short and the worst part was the uncertainty of what to do. Helping Dawn would certainly be a challenge even if the matter wasn't spiritual. Discussing the will of God with her would be equal to swimming with a bull shark or having dinner with a tiger.

He reached down, touched his toes, and held for a count of ten seconds, stretching out his leg muscles to avoid injuries as did most runners. Audubon Park was one of his favorite places to take an evening run. On this day, there was no coincidence that the preferred route crossed directly in front of Dawn's house, where he had prayed to witness a miracle. Marcus was gravely concerned and getting desperate. He found himself in continuous prayer over her. Perhaps she would see him in the park, stop him and unleash another tongue lashing. Either way he didn't care. It was about helping her out of the darkness into the light.

He thought of Jesus and how He had been brutally nailed to the cross and yet had asked His Father to forgive the very people who had crucified Him 'for they knew not (understood) what they had done.' Marcus would gladly take her verbal abuse if it opened a door even if only for one more time to give the gospel. *Abuse me, oh Lord, just let her be alright. I'm not sure what your plan is. Just give me one more chance. Give me the words she needs and the wisdom to deliver the message.*

It was unusually warm for early February. Marcus hated running in sub-freezing weather and was grateful for the passing of a recent Arctic blast that had, only days prior, held temperatures in the twenties. There was very little chill in the air.

He stood and took a long slow breath and began a slow pace from Magazine Street to East Drive and then Dawn's house. It was difficult jogging at the pace of an out of shape beginner, as he usually maintained a consistency of consecutive six-minute miles. However, Marcus lacked confidence in the situation and was buying time in order to sort out or receive a revelation of what to do. He couldn't just stop by, knock on the door and say, "Did I ever tell you that Jesus loves you? Can I tell you more about Him?" Certainly she wouldn't just invite him in for a spot of tea.

He had already tried that approach and recalled her 'mace attack.' The poor unsuspecting fellow that had been standing behind him got a leg full of the pepper spray that had seemed to be quite painful. *Man she is mean!* Marcus thought. *There has to be a situation where her guard would be down.* He moved slowly because he felt that he was missing God's instruction or that He just needed more time.

The distance to her house was shorter than he had desired. He made his way past the line of live oaks and the familiar Chinese fan palm in the front yard became visible. He slowly moved down the trail and slowed to a stop a hundred yards from the fork in the asphalt that led to Exposition Boulevard. *Nothing, not a word*, he thought. *Lord, what do I do?*

Marcus became somewhat discouraged and really didn't want to act in haste. If it was God that wanted him to speak to Dawn, then He would make a way for it to happen. Perhaps it was he that needed a lesson in patience and it was not yet God's timing. Or, maybe God wasn't going to use him in this situation and would resolve it another way.

The only logical thing to do was to make another lap and continue to do so until God moved. It would be a disaster if he went across the street on his own authority and knocked on her door. Marcus turned from Dawn's house and took up a brisk pace, content to make the lap around the park and golf course. He would do so until either God moved or he was exhausted and no longer able to move.

Just as he got to full speed, something moved quickly from the left and into his running lane, leaving no opportunity to maneuver out of the way. He felt like a quarterback getting nailed by a linebacker on a full-out blitz, and Marcus couldn't avoid running into the man who was now face to face with him.

The man was tall and wore a black leather jacket with gold stitching. As the two collided, the stranger reached out and grabbed fists full of Marcus's shirt at the shoulders and pulled him to the ground. Marcus instantly realized that the man had gotten in his way on purpose; this was not a by-chance incident. The man stared intently into Marcus's eyes and rapidly spoke in a language he did not understand. After a few seconds, the unknown man reached up and placed his hands over Marcus's eyes. For a reason unknown to Marcus, he did not feel threatened or the need to move.

The man pulled his hand away and said, "God will be with you and will give you the wisdom to help her. Now go! They come for her!" Then he pushed Marcus aside and leapt to his feet.

The force caused Marcus to roll a few times and he sat up looking at the man in confusion wondering what the whole hand over the eyes thing was. *How bizarre*, he thought. There was no need to clarify who the 'she' was, only how he was going to help her. But it was confirmation that there was imminent danger.

The man stood, pulled off the leather jacket, and tossed it in the air where it vaporized and was no more. Two pairs of gloriously white wings unfolded and the man now stood to nearly twelve feet tall. The angel looked down the asphalt trail in the direction that Marcus had just approached from. Three beings nearly as large as the angel moved confidently down the jogging trail and pulled out what looked to Marcus like swords that were an inch thick at the base and nearly seven feet long. The three creatures were different in their appearances despite being covered in hooded garments.

They yelled in a language that reminded Marcus of Aramaic. He had no idea what was going on and could only assume that the one was of God and the others had to be demons, possibly sent to do Dawn harm.

The angel held out his right hand and a sword materialized. It was of equal size, but alive with blue flames. He said nothing and stepped forward eager for the opportunity to challenge the oncoming demonic warriors. The giant angel brought his sword down onto the first demon as if trying to divide it into two equal parts. It raised its sword in time to block angel's attack. The strength of the angel knocked the demon several feet backward. It reached down and dug its claws into the ground like a brake but slammed into an overhanging limb of a live oak. The beast swiftly regained its footing and came back for more.

The other two moved in, simultaneously sensing an opening. The opportunistic demons allowed several feet of separation between themselves and attempted to come at different angels from his back side. Not wishing to waste valuable time raising the sword high into the air, one of the demons simply lunged with the sword pointed at the angel, going for a wounding shot.

With speed that surprised the opportunistic demon, the angel spun around and drove the sword into the ground while kicking the second demon in the head sending it end over end. The third demon swung wildly and was aggressive in its attack. But skill and experience was on the side of the angel as he deflected every shot, then kicked the legs out from under the beast. The first demon quickly recovered and was back on the offensive.

Marcus, still on the ground, gazed in awe at what he was seeing. A man walked by Marcus and asked him if everything was alright. He blinked, looked at the man with a dumbfounded expression, and asked, "Don't you see that?"

"See what?" the elderly man asked as he followed Marcus's gaze.

"That!" he said pointing at the four huge beings that were fighting.

"Do you need me to call a doctor? You were jogging and just fell down. Perhaps you are having a stroke," he said.

He didn't even see the man before he knocked me down turned into a twelve foot tall angel, Marcus thought. "I'm not having a stroke, I'm fine. You didn't see the man that knocked me down?"

"Son . . . I don't want to argue with you, but you fell on your own. I was sitting right there." The man pointed to a bench opposite of where he sat on the ground.

Marcus observed the other people in the park as they passed by, oblivious to the warring angel and demons. Each carried on as if they were alone, lost in conversation or thought, completely unaware of anything out of the ordinary.

The confused expression on Marcus's face as he stared out over the field near the pond caused the man concern. He pulled a cell phone from the pocket of his slacks. "I'm going to call for an ambulance."

"No! No . . . that won't be necessary," Marcus said, getting to his feet. "I'm alright . . . thanks for checking on me. Have a good walk, or sit or whatever it is that you are doing. Thanks again."

The man walked away, complaining to himself, "All these people are on drugs today."

Marcus moved to an unoccupied bench and sat wondering why he was able to see the beings while no one else seemed to be able to. The angel grabbed a demon by the throat and threw it across the pond and into the golf course.

An open window into the spiritual world! How awesome is that? Marcus thought. He remembered the angel touching his eyes.

Two of the demons were now circling the angel as the third tried to recover at the base of an oak tree. It stood and seemed to gather itself while calling out directions. A fourth and larger cloaked demon walked from behind a live oak and moved in to join the fight.

In an aggressive move, the angel rushed one of the demons and overpowered it, driving his sword through the chest cavity and pinning it to the ground. The creature screamed and convulsed before descending into the earth.

The angel turned and lunged for the last of the original assailants.

"What are you waiting for? Get going now!" a second angel demanded as it appeared from thin air, standing in front of Marcus. His voice was deep and had a mild echo. The angel was clad in golden armor and had an unsheathed flaming sword. "Go!" he said looking up at Dawn's house.

Marcus looked up and was alarmed to see a man walking down the driveway toward the house. Perhaps this man was going to try to hurt or even kill Dawn.

"What do I do?" he asked.

The angel looked at him with wise, reassuring eyes. "Just go. You will know."

"There she is again," Reed said pointing down the block to where Amy sat.

"Look at her, she is shaking. Daphne said her name is Amy," Paris said sympathetically.

Reed held a square to-go box from a local restaurant, filled with a fresh hamburger, fries and apple slices. Paris carried a tall Styrofoam cup of Coke with a little ice. They prayerfully approached the shaking woman and would try to open a line of communication with an expression of compassion, as they did with all of the women.

Amy sat on the top of an overturned metal garbage can and seemed to be oblivious to everything and everyone around her. She shook violently as the withdrawals assaulted her body. She pulled a cigarette to her lips but struggled to find her mouth and take a puff.

As they drew closer to Amy, the more pronounced the shaking appeared, and concern for her well-being grew. Reed wondered how in the world she was going to eat the food they had brought for her if smoking a cigarette had proven to be such a challenge. To Reed, it looked like it had been days since her last meal. She would need to eat soon or run the risk of serious long-term injury, if not death. Malnutrition was evident, and grave.

God's mission for Reed and Paris was twofold. For Paris it was reaching prostitutes and rescuing them from their destructive lifestyles by showing them the redemptive love of Christ. As with most mission work, there was a price to pay. Rejection and verbal assaults were a way of life and Paris had to develop thick, near-bulletproof, skin. Their five years in the Crescent City had mostly been spent witnessing in the French Quarter, which had proven to be fertile ground for such ministry. Desperate woman appeared at nearly every turn. Drugs were abundant and the money continuously moved as the prostitution and drug business flourished.

Paris always sought the trust of the lost women of the streets. She would begin to minister to them by first living as an example of Christ and His love, displaying His abundant mercy through her actions. This had proven to be effective and often led to open doors. Then she would powerfully deliver a testimony of God's love and His desire for their lives. The end result would often be rejection, as the strong hold of the spiritual forces had reign on the hearts and minds of the oppressed woman. Some hearts would turn from stone to flesh, bringing to life a repentant spirit and a conversion of thought.

After convincing a woman that she could trust them to help her, they were taken out of the city to the Rehab's Place, a non-profit shelter for abused woman, where they would be provided food and shelter while detoxifying, rehabilitating and learning career skills.

One of the great pleasures Paris took in her work was watching the women come to an understanding of why they had led such lives and why Christ was the answer. The knowledge of freedom offered by accepting the gift of the Lord granted indescribable liberty that was often passionately embraced. The second great pleasure was reuniting the rehabilitated girls with their families. The reunion was usually emotional and brought Paris to tears each time regardless of how often she had been blessed by the experience.

Reed had proved to be a tremendous asset, in the matters of a spiritual understanding of why their lives had been such messes. His mentoring on the scriptural accounts of the unseen perpetual battle was powerful in giving the women confidence and tools for victory.

For Reed, his calling wasn't limited to the teachings of spiritual matters to the women Paris helped; he also engaged in the infiltration of satanic cults. For him, this made Amy, alias Freedom Girl, a more intriguing challenge as she was both a prostitute and practicing Satanist. Reed found it ironic that anyone in her situation would use the alias Freedom Girl. She was a slave to her circumstance and would die without intervention.

They approached, and Paris led off, "Hello, I thought you might needed something to drink."

"Thanks," she said, taking the cup and dropping the cigarette on the ground.

Reed moved his foot over and stepped on the burning filter. He raised the takeout box of food and offered it to her. "It's still warm," he assured her.

The charity displayed by the strangers was a foreign experience to her. From rumors and overhearing conversations about the two, she knew that they had helped some of the other girls and believed that they were preachers or something to do with religion. However, most of the Christians who routinely patrolled the Quarter were angrily shouting out scriptures and carrying on about Hell and suffering the eternal judgment. Often they would get in her face, complaining of the upside down cross necklace and pentagram tattoo on the inside of her forearm. They walked around with tall crosses and big mouths, spitting out angry and condemning scriptures. She hated them.

These two seemed different. They had always seemed kind and pleasant. Several of the girls who encountered them were no longer on the streets and the word was that they had helped them to a new life. She really wasn't sure what had happened to the girls, but knew that she was desperate for a change, even if it meant death.

Amy remembered what had happened after Daphne had disappeared. Stan made threats and swore that he would kill those two if they were to ever show up in the French Quarter again. An order was given to his men that they were to be taken out if they were seen. The expense of losing and replacing the girls was costing him dearly and he wanted Paris and Reed to endure for the pain they had caused him.

Amy became slightly fearful of what might happen to her if she was seen talking with them. She was tired of being beaten.

She started to ask them to leave, but thoughts of the morning's Bible experience had been on her mind all day. She considered talking to them about it, but remained reserved.

She lost her balance and nearly dropped the food, but Reed was able to steady it for her. "Thanks," she said, looking at him.

Looking past the malnourished, tired and drug-worn effects on her body, Reed saw a beautiful woman with a lot in front of her. Somehow she had managed to keep her teeth healthy for the most part and her long brown hair was combed and pulled back.

Reed wondered how long she had been hooked on whatever substance it was that made her shake and suffer through withdrawals. His heart longed to help her.

"Well, look what we have here!" the man said, approaching from Royal Street.

Reed and Paris turned to see the two men who had worked for the thug that had controlled Daphne and now treated Amy like a worthless animal.

"Doing, what you won't. We are giving the girl some food . . . not drugs like you!" Reed said, standing his ground.

"Ain't that real special? We take care of our girls."

"She looks well cared for!" Reed said turning to look at Amy.

"You got a problem. You want some?" one of the men said.

"Stan said we should really put a hurt'n on them if they ever came around again," the short stocky man said, reaching behind his back and pulling out a knife.

Amy sat and looked at the two men that she had known all too well. Interfering would only guarantee that she would receive a beating as well. She slid off of the garbage can with the disposable container and Coke in her hands and turned to face Reed and Paris.

Reed had been through the scenario many times before and knew what was going to happen. They were in just the perfect spot to be shoved down a twenty foot wide alley where few people would have an opportunity to witness the assault. Reed decided not to wait for that to happen and to take matters into his own hands. This would give Paris a chance to avoid injury and escape. He kicked the heavy man's wrist, breaking it and sending the knife into the alley. The second man seized a tiny window of opportunity and drove his fist into the back of Reeds head, managing to get him into the alley. He stumbled forward into the stocky man who was furious over his limp right hand and began swinging with the left fist. Reed swung upward with all of his might, driving his fist into to stocky man's private area. Instantly he fell to the ground, fighting for breath and cursing violently.

Paris ran from the alley and called for help. No one seemed interested in offering assistance and just passed by, willing to mind their own business. Several men peeked down the alley and suggested that she call the police and simply went about their way.

The second man was on Reed's back. Reed reached down, grabbed the lower portion of the left leg, and pulled up. Both men went down to the ground. The wall was closer than Reed had hoped and his right elbow forcefully met with the red brick and a portion of skin was peeled back as they slid down the wall and onto the ground. Numbness ran through Reed's lower arm.

Fortunately for Reed, the back of the man's head slammed into the wall as well and was cut open and began to bleed, but he maintained his bull dog grip and refused to let go. He re-positioned himself into a chokehold on Reed determined to send him into the unconscious world then beat him till disfigurement. Reed tried to grab the man and get free but was unable.

The stocky man got back on his feet and winced and yelled angrily. He picked up a two-foot long piece of pipe that looked like it had once been part of an exterior emergency escape. He limped over to Reed and began hitting him about the legs and arms. But in his anger the man made a second and more costly mistake, and Reed once again kicked him in the privates, leaving the man incapacitated.

The pipe fell and Reed used his feet to pull it to his left hand and began driving it into the shins of the man on his back. After a few powerful shots, the thug let go and began punching Reed in the head again and attempting to push him off so that he could get back to his feet. Reed spun around and perfectly caught the man's fist across the knuckles in mid-punch. The sound of cracking bones was unmistakable. The man was now helplessly on the ground, grabbing at his injured hand.

Reed stood and looked at the two men who had assaulted him and wanted to violently hurt both him and Paris. They moaned and groaned and were now defenseless. He thought about all of the women the men had abused and hurt at the will of this person they called Stan. A flesh fed anger welled up in him and he knew in just a few seconds, and with a few strategic strikes, he could take the men out indefinitely; his military training had taught him that.

Reed walked over to the first man who looked up while grabbing his fist. He brought the rod across the right ear of the thug's head sending him to ground. The will and desire to destroy the two men was hard to push aside. A part of Reed wanted to hurt these men worse than they had ever hurt anyone before. For Sharon, Nichole, Diane, Daphne and Amy and the abuse they had suffered.

Adrenaline was flowing through his veins as he focused on the thugs. He raised the pipe and moved close intending to finish the job. He wanted to levy a heavy penalty on the men for the evil they had been responsible for.

"Reed! They just did what they were instructed to do. You have defended yourself. That is enough," he heard the voice say over his anger.

"Just turn and leave. I will finish this," he said.

"NO! That's not how we do things!" Paris insisted.

He paused and lowed the pipe fighting his rage, anger and hate for the men. There was no remorse, only the need to finish what they had started. Both men were scum and should be taken out. Both deserved his judgment.

"Reed! No!" the voice of God said.

Reed did not want to listen to God. His state of mind was not on spiritual matters, but on the flesh, and he struggled to let go.

"NO!" the Lord shouted into his head.

Reed suddenly looked up as if waking from a dream. He had been transformed back into a soldier trained to fight. He turned and tossed the pipe down the alley and stumbled back into the street. His body ached and the sensation was returning to the right hand. Blood streaked down his right forearm from the elbow.

Several policemen made their way to the scene. Reed sat on the curb watching the two men and ignored the police who brushed past him and into the alley. He thought about how close he had been to killing the two and remembered the faces of those he had killed during active duty. That was war and he was justified in doing his job. But this was different. In his anger, he felt a sense of duty to take the two thugs out and God had stopped him. For this, Reed was grateful, but yet worried about the ability to control himself. He had enough blood on his hands. Those days had been over. He was supposed to show the love of Christ to people, not the sting of a steel pipe. He questioned himself.

CHAPTER 10

Dawn swung wildly with her arms, searching for a weak spot or any opportunity that would offer her an escape. Punching and clawing violently at the demon, she refused to give up and accept the eternal sentence. Desperation usually brought forth action that wasn't supported with the proper thought or a well-structured plan. Dawn in her irrational mindset hadn't realized, as she hung over the lake of fire, that getting free would only expedite her punishment. The beast was the only reason she was not encased in the burning sulfur.

Suddenly the pressure subsided and her hair was free once again. The beast had released her. Eternity was here. She screamed and feared looking down into the pit. Her knees were up in the chest reducing the length of her body delaying the inevitable even if only for a fraction of a second. With nothing to lose, she continued to fight for an escape and heard the crash of the lamp as it met the wall.

She paused and noticed that the intense heat was no longer present. The pain in her neck and scalp still lingered, but was far less intense. Dawn's entire body was sore and sensitive to the touch. She opened her eyes and gasped in relief of the familiar surroundings. She was back in her house lying on the floor and looking up at the ceiling. Only now she was turned around with one foot on the couch and one on the end table with her head and back on the carpet covered floor of the living room.

There didn't seem to be an inch of her body that was not affected by the experience. Dawn felt as if she had been seared like a piece of meat on a grill. While continuing to lie on the floor, Dawn tried to inspect her condition, but gave into the sensitivity of her skin. Her clothes were dry and her body was just beginning to profusely perspire. She was radiating heat and her eyes were dry and burned as if she had been roasting in an oven.

She placed her head back on the floor and continued her cry, only now for a different reason. The relief of being back at home was as emotionally powerful as the entire experience. It was all too much to bear. Dawn believed that she had somehow escaped an eternity in Hell and would deny its existence no more. Despite the pain, she curled up in a fetal position and wept.

Dawn was unexplainably more lost than ever before. She didn't know why God had sent her back. Why was she able to return? What was the purpose of her return? What was expected of her? She was willing to do anything if it meant that she would never be sent back again.

Her body was now coated in sweat, which was being absorbed by the living room carpet. Dehydration was coming on quickly and she longed for a drink of water like never before. The roof of her mouth was dry and sticky and the back of the throat began to hurt. Dawn rolled over and pushed upward and stood once again. Her hands and legs shook, still affected by unparalleled fear.

Dawn stumbled into the kitchen like a drunkard, pushed the sink lever to the right for cold water and pulled the faucet head out of the temporary housing. With little concern for the floor, counters or proper etiquette, she pulled it to her mouth and drank. The water was satisfying like it had never been before. She drank and couldn't seem to quench her thirst.

The cold water on her lips felt good and satisfying. She began to spray the area of the face, neck and back of the head as it brought great relief. She couldn't resist putting her arms over the sink and washing them off. Like a hot frying pan dipped in a tub of cold water, Dawn's skin cooled off and was restored to normal, despite being pink and discolored.

The rest of her body demanded attention, so she turned off the kitchen sink and moved quickly down the hall, leaving a trail of water behind her. She pushed open the door to the hall bath and jumped into the shower without undressing. The relief the water brought was like nothing she had ever experienced before. Usually when showering the heat would be at steam level filling the bathroom with a thick cloud of moisture. Dawn doubted that she would ever need a hot shower again. The cool water was intoxicating and helped to calm her nerves a bit. She turned and spread the water as quickly and evenly across her body as possible.

She pulled her soaked garments off, dropped them into the bath tub, and wrapped in a towel before going to the bedroom to get a fresh set of clothes. She looked back at the fifteen hundred dollar outfit lying in the bottom of the tub and turned toward the door.

Dawn entered the bedroom and moved past an eight foot free standing mirror and opened the closet door. She was still very much on edge and swimming in her thoughts of the entire experience. *How long would it take to get back to some semblance of a normal life? Never! If normal landed you back there again, then normal is not what I want. Please let me abnormal.*

Dawn thought about Marcus and a part of her felt strongly about confiding in him. After the way she had threatened and mocked him, certainly he wouldn't give her the time of day. He would be justified in his rejection. *Should I go and ask him to forgive me? Beg? I don't deserve his help. Why should he care? Three hours ago*

I wouldn't have had a care in the world if some tragedy had swept over him. It would have been a great thing that I would have used to hurt him as much as possible. Now, I want his help? She chastised herself.

After pulling a pair of jeans and a black and gold sweatshirt off of hangers, she walked over and sat on the edge of the bed and thought. Marcus had been the only person who had seemed genuinely interested in helping her. He suffered humiliation and embarrassment to tell her the truth. Despite all of the harsh treatment, he continued to call the show and dealt openly with her. He was always transparent. His manner was always polite and sincere and never the hint of anger. He could be sarcastic, but never angry. Rejection after brutal rejection seemed to do little to stop him. He was relentless in his quest to open her eyes to the truth. She now saw Marcus in a new light. He was not crazy after all. It brought her to tears to think that he had endured so much to deliver the truth and give her a chance to avoid an eternity in Hell. He, if anyone, would understand and be able to explain what it was that she was dealing with. Despite the potential embarrassment, she would take her medicine and ask him to forgive her. He would either turn and walk away, or help her. She hoped it would be the latter, but knew she deserved to be treated equal to what had been dished out.

Dawn stared at the floor at the base of the mirror while she considered the immediate future. In the reflection of the mirror, something large moved toward the back of the room. Dawn blinked. She tried to focus her irritated puffy eyes and could see nothing in the mirror. She stood and turned into the direction where the intruder should have been. There was nothing but open space. She looked back at the mirror and then turned again to the corner of the room. Dawn was certain of what she saw and looked a third time.

Am I going mad? I did see something. It was big. How can it just disappear? I must be losing my mind, she thought.

With a new sense that perhaps the experience wasn't completely over, Dawn fearfully left the room and dressed in the hall. She tossed her towel into the hall bath nearly running back into the kitchen.

The water puddle was larger than she remembered. She pushed the faucet back into the housing and retrieved five beach towels and spread them out over the wet area.

What just happened in the room? she thought, standing and looking at the floor. Her hair hung down and she noticed that it was desperate need of a brushing, but she was not willing to go back into the bedroom or bathroom for a brush.

It was imperative to know why and what she was to do next. Had that simply been a warning and a last shot at redemption? Was a larger more significant and eternal event close, like a deadly tsunami after the warning of a rapidly falling tide? Was this part of the prophecy against her? How could she prevent or stop what was already set in motion?

Instinctively she turned to go into the living room, but caught a glimpse of the lime green pillows, quickly decided against any immediate return and resolved to take a position in the breakfast area instead. Just looking back at the room caused her to want to cry all over again. Despite the experience, she was still a strong woman and had to get some control over her emotions if she had any chance at figuring out what to do.

She looked at the blinking phone and hoped against hope that Marcus would somehow get the number and call to check up. But such hope was silly and almost childlike. She would need to call him. After all, she had done so before, even if the sole reason was motivated by hate and the need to scorn. She felt filthy and wretched.

Dawn reached over and pulled out an emerald green pen with LeJune Studios and the phone number written in gold on the side. She wanted to call and seek his council, but felt bad about putting her new problems on him. She was Dawn McIntyre and could call anyone in the city to talk to—except for Marcus Dillon. Something in the sub-conscious said, "No, he is the only one you can talk to. Put away your pride." She conceded and dialed the phone.

She felt like a school girl calling a boy for the first time. Each ring increased her nervousness. How would he react? What if he didn't help? After several rings no one answered and she assumed that they had gone for the evening. The sound of a disappointed sigh filled the air.

Was God real? she found herself asking for the first time, as if the possibility existed that He had indeed been a real being. "If Heaven is real, then Hell has to be real. If God is real, then Satan has to be real," she recalled Marcus telling her.

"If He isn't, then who the heck was I calling out to? Who was I expecting to come and help me?" She asked

> *That was Hell. I won't deny that. That was no natural place. You just don't fall through a couch, floor and layers of earth and simply pass through like you don't exist despite the fact that gravity is still pulling on you. Then crash land on some rock that seems to be solid when all the other layers are like vapor. I hit so hard it was like a bug on a Mac truck going a hundred miles an hour and I wasn't even unconscious, or, much worse . . . crushed.*

The pitiful, horrible look on the condemned woman's face was something she would not soon forget. The image would haunt Dawn for the rest of her natural life. Next to the thought of Hell itself, the suffering soul put another burden on her heart. She felt a sense of guilt having been given a second chance. Dawn would do everything within her power to avoid ever seeing that place again. The tormented woman would have no opportunity to escape and would be as she was, forever tormented. Dawn thought she could hear the screams and began to weep in agony over the lost soul that had no hope and understood Marcus's angst.

Dawn couldn't let the sun set without understanding. She had to have the security that came with knowing she was marked for salvation. How did she make it all right and find favor with God before the opportunity was lost and she ended up in the blue prison cell that had apparently been set aside for her? While the experience was horrible, if she could correct her relationship with God and enter into Heaven for an eternity, then it would have been an immense blessing. She certainly deserved no less than what the tormented soul of the unknown woman had received, but Dawn was unwilling to side with apathy and chance.

She remembered the Bible she had received as a joke from Sonny on her twenty-ninth birthday. She often used it in preparation for the show to provide counter arguments. The margins were coated with thoughts and notes that were blasphemous and filled with hate. The intent was to destroy the scripture and anyone who dared to defend it. The trick was finding contradictions, or at least crafting an argument as if you had. To do so often meant that scripture had to be distorted. In some cases the Christian callers were not speaking from knowledge, but what they had been told about the scripture, and convincing them of error was easy.

She slid from the bar stool and moved past the living room into the study, walking cautiously and looking around uncertain of what she might see. The room was cold and had been unused for several days. The mahogany desk was neat and orderly, with only the wine colored Bible out of place. Dawn walked hurriedly across the room, wanting to get out as quickly as possible. She reached for the Bible and turned to leave, but something moved from behind the desk, causing her to freeze and turn back. Like in the bedroom, there was nothing. She took a step back and crouched to floor level and looked beneath the desk for something that may have been hiding. There was nothing but the two-inch black plastic wheels that were giving support to the leather chair.

Once again calling her sanity into question, Dawn moved behind the desk and rolled the chair back. Nothing. She rounded the corner and briskly walked out of the room, then shut the door.

On the counter, Dawn picked up the phone and pushed the speed dial button labeled "Mom." She knew that Keri McIntyre was the last person to talk to about such matters, but this was a desperate time. Just hearing a familiar voice would provide a level of security. The phone rang four times and was sent to the answering machine. Without knowing exactly what to say, Dawn hung up. It was for the better, she thought as Keri may have her committed to the mental ward if she talked about seeing things and a trip to Hell.

She scanned the handwritten list looking for someone who may have slipped her mind, but none of the names jumped out at her. Then she placed the phone back on the charger, feeling alone and discouraged. She needed someone to talk to and the loneliness became a tremendous burden. The anxiety grew as thoughts crept in with an unrelenting authority and new power despite her attempts to push them back.

Dawn sat back on the bar stool and through fresh tears, opened the Bible looking for scriptures that would help. It seemed odd to use the Bible from the perspective of assistance and truth and she couldn't settle on what to do or how to proceed. Dawn wiped the tears away for what seemed to be the hundredth time since the return and tried to focus on the small print.

The silence of the house gave way to random noises and was growing annoying. Dawn thought she may go mad if she didn't turn on something to soothe the nerves or get focused on other things, which was what she was attempting to do when the whole ordeal began. She reluctantly walked over to the couch and looked for the remote. On the wall was a large dent and scratch in the paint from where she had obviously jammed the remote during the backwards fall.

Dawn stepped back and looked at the four green leather pillows with the matador stitch in disgust of what the image represented. She no longer could stand to have them in her presence and snatched each up one by one tossing them by the back door to be turned into refuse.

Buried behind one of the pillows that had given support to her left shoulder was the remote. Dawn cautiously leaned down to the couch afraid of falling through the same portal that had taken her to Hell. She grabbed the remote and moved back quickly. Sheetrock was embedded in the seam between the two pieces of plastic that encased the electronic components. Dawn picked it up and walked over to the breakfast area using her left thumbnail to scrape out the white substance before selecting a local station.

The forty-two inch plasma television was easy to see from the open area of the kitchen, despite the angle. The five o'clock news was plugging the upcoming forecast to follow the commercial break. Dawn and Kat Conners, the weather girl, had a long standing friendship that stretched back to grade school. She watched every evening and was thankful for something familiar.

Despite focusing intently and reading the words aloud, the scriptures seemed to be in some language that she just couldn't consume. It could just as well have been written in the original Greek or Hebrew. Her mind was hopelessly unsettled. She tried again and continued to struggle for discernment and meaning.

For years she debated Christians who had tried to be a witness, but in her time of need, Dawn couldn't recall a single passage. Certainly the people who had made the most compelling arguments had believed the Bible in its entirety. Marcus was one who seemed to know just what to say every time. Strangely that was the reason why she hated him and it was now the reason she desperately sought his council. She longed for his knowledge and would gladly sit and listen to him without debate.

Certainly she would have to do something. It wasn't as easy as looking toward the sky and saying, "God, can you save me?" There had to be more than that. That was just too easy. If what she understood about Jesus was true, that was an awfully steep and brutal price to pay for it to be so easy for dirty and vile people such as herself to enter by mere words.

John 3:16 entered her thoughts. She had heard it many times and hoped that there was something to the scripture.

She turned to the gospel and read aloud, "For God so loved the world that He gave His only begotten Son that whoever shall believeth in Him shall not perish, but have everlasting life."

"Belief . . . is that the key?" she asked out loud.

The flat screen exploded to life with the blue and green colors of a weather map of the United States. Quickly locating New Orleans on the side bar, Dawn noted the spring-like high of 65° for Saturday and briefly began to consider whether or not she was going to be around long enough to experience the awesome forecast. The thought was brief as a bright eyed and chipper young red head who had been lecturing to the unseen audience from off camera bounced back into frame.

Kat smiled and moved with purpose and was flawless at finding the targets on the monitor while pointing to the blank screen behind her. She sold the weather forecast and could have done so with a poster board and a box of crayons. Kat was polished, confident and effective. But despite her perfect appearance and love affair with the camera, something was wrong. Dawn couldn't quite make out the problem, but something was out of order in what she was seeing. She wondered if perhaps the expensive television had been in need of adjusting or just wasn't working properly.

Dawn walked back across the living room for a closer look and to make an attempt to adjust the T.V. if there should be a need. Behind Kat, there appeared to be an odd sort of shadow. Every time she moved it seemed as if her shadow lingered for a split second and was lazily following and catching up, but always slightly behind. Even more perplexing, her arms and legs had no matching shadow, only a renegade dark spot.

Dawn reached for the remote control and froze the DVR hoping to get a better understanding of what was happening to the television. Nothing stood out and the image seemed to be clear. She pressed the button and commanded the machine to rewind until reaching the beginning of the broadcast. Dawn pushed the play button. Still, there was nothing.

"Humph. I must have something wrong with my vision," she said, returning the DVR to real time. Once again the lingering shadow appeared and moved out of sync with Kat, only now it hardly seemed to follow her at all. The shadow had a mind of its own and moved completely independent of Kat. Once again, Dawn rewound a few seconds of the live coverage and pressed play. The shadow was not visible it just seemed to disappear. Kat was all alone in front of the screen and camera.

Dawn stood in bewilderment. The thing she saw clearly existed and stood out. It wasn't a question of some trick of light or bleed over on the part of the television. There, as with the rest of the events of the evening, was something amiss. She returned the DVR to real time.

"What in the world is that?" Dawn blurted out.

The camera zoomed in on Kat's face as she was making a humorous comment about the co-host's tie. The camera locked in and Dawn moved in closer looking at a series of distortions in color and texture in Kat's face. Her skin appeared to morph and change shape and color. Green and black splotches were surfacing and disappearing repeatedly.

Dawn dropped the remote and recoiled when a second face that was behind Kat's natural one pushed to the surface and dominated her features. It wasn't simply a shadow, but the face of something evil. She clearly saw it push out for a second and was reabsorbed by Kat's body.

Its eyes were black and separated farther than that of its host. It looked to have discoloration on the epidermis in areas where lacerations seemed to never have healed. The thing had a mouth full of tiny blunt-tipped teeth and a wicked smile.

The camera pulled back to capture the images of Kat, Jason and Megan once again. Dawn blinked and continued to look on in astonishment as creatures or unknown animated beings, which appeared to be some three or four feet tall, flew around and through Jason like bees protecting a hive. The things were much faster than any insect or bird, leaving only a blurry trailer in their wake. Their speed didn't allow Dawn much time to get a mental image by which she could scientifically analyze for positive identification.

The heavy activity around Jason created a fog-like appearance, making him hard to see. One of the creatures seemed to get a little curious or daring and begun straying from the others by flying in large circular patterns that took it steadily closer to Megan. With each pass the distance narrowed methodically. Its intentions were without dispute.

Dawn lost her breath for a second when a pair of huge white semi-translucent wings coated with a magnificent iridescent multi-hued sheen came into view standing just within the camera's range.

"Is that an angel?" Dawn couldn't help asking out loud. She began waving her hands excitedly like a child at Christmas. Just seeing the angelic being gave her a sense of comfort she hadn't had in hours. "An honest to goodness angel?"

The darting, arching black thing continued on course and was about to reach Megan on the next pass. Like an orbiting satellite, the strange being looped around Jason and seemed to thrust itself toward Megan. Within the twinkling of an eye, the huge hulking figure with the wings moved to the side of Megan and snatched it from the air by the neck. The thing jerked and fought angrily trying to loosen the grip of the angel. It spat and tried to bit the huge hand that now gripped it. Like a small shark, rows upon rows of teeth were visible throughout its mouth. Its appearance was an evil version of the artistic misrepresentations of the cherubs who were painted as powerless babies. The camera pulled away and into a commercial.

Quickly, she pressed the rewind command on the remote control. She rewound as far back as the computerized digital memory would permit. Once again Jason and Megan sat behind a crescent shaped desk repeating the familiar dialog from the previous minutes. But there was nothing. No large, swarming, toothy, black things. She patiently watched and nothing out of the ordinary appeared. She searched for the winged man, but he never appeared.

"God, what is going on?" she pleaded. "Can you please help me figure this out? Can you help me . . . please? How come I can see these things live, but not when I play it back?"

Dawn waited, expecting the audible voice of God to answer. After a few minutes, she walked back over to the granite overhang where the Bible sat open. Nothing was coming together. The clock displayed the time at near five thirty. Two and a half hours had expired since the visitation. Her nerves were on edge. Every little noise effortlessly garnered her attention.

The unquenchable thirst for knowledge was only overridden by the physical need to replenish her bodily fluids. Green citrus tea came to mind and she moved around the counter to get a bottle out of the refrigerator.

A movement down the hall caught her attention. The closed doors of the bedrooms limited the light at the end of the hall despite the penetration of the afternoon sun. Dawn was certain that something had moved. She stopped in mid step and froze in observation of the hall. This had been the third time such a thing had happened in the time since her return. It was all too coincidental and she had to know what was going on.

She reached for the switch to the hall light and flicked it upward. Doing her best to push aside fear, she walked down the hall anticipating something supernatural. In her mind were visions of the beasts in Hell that had tortured her.

The bathroom door was partially opened and needed only a light shove. She was relieved to see the towel balled up on the floor as she had left it.

She stepped in, looked into the bath tub and gasped. The clothing had been moved as if purposefully laid out for someone. The empty arms of the blouse were bent at the location where the elbow should be and angled to the midsection. The tub looked like a coffin and her clothes had been spread out in waiting.

The hair on Dawn's arms stood to attention. She backed out of the bathroom. She hoped that someone was in the house playing tricks on her. She moved down the hall, longing to see a living person and not more spirits. Moving slowly was certainly of no advantage to her if the intruder was supernatural. Moving with more authority helped Dawn with her nerves.

Dawn pulled her shoulders back in a posture of what was really a false confidence and marched down the hall. She pushed the door with her foot and turned on the light.

The fan was turning from the center of the step ceiling. The palm shaped blades cut quietly through the air. A wallpaper border patterned with lush pink, magenta, purple and pink bougainvillea woven together by thorny vines lined the inside of the foot high step ceiling and matched the Caribbean theme of the house. Lemon Tart paint covering an orange peel texture backed the border and matched the walls of the room. Her eyes followed the wall down to a large painting of a traveler's palm set in an antique frame Dawn had found in her mother's attic. It was centered on the wall between the closet and bedroom entrance doors. Everything seemed normal.

Since the bathroom a few seconds ago a voice of warning continued to reverberate through her conscious mind. She couldn't believe that she hadn't run out of the house already. But, what weird circumstance waited for her out there? Her thoughts competed with the thumping heart. Her hands began to shake more vigorously.

The sound of a click came from the hall. Dawn turned to look. The hall light had been turned off.

Unsure of what was potentially waiting in the hall or what to do, Dawn just knew that she desperately wanted out of the house. She had to leave. Her nerves just couldn't take anymore.

Another movement and she quickly searched the room near the windows. The thick multilayered drapery that had been designed to insure that the early morning sun, as it rose out of the east, would not disturb her all-important sleep, had been pulled away from the window on the right corner.

The intense bronze reflection of the afternoon sun reflected off of the glossy finish of the bamboo floor and temporarily blinded Dawn as she unexpectedly looked directly into an area of heavy concentration. Normally a flash of bright light directly in the eyes would spark a migraine, which was the last thing she needed.

Several seconds passed and Dawn could see again. An odd shadow stood out in the right corner of the bedroom on the other side of the open bi-folding closet doors. She considered for a second that the light was causing some kind of shadow casting effect on objects within the room. Instinctively she looked back toward the floor and returned to the corner.

The ability to fully focus had returned and she was able to make out a figure of something standing and hiding in the shadow cast by the drapery. She looked closer and clearly discerned the feet of something or someone that was standing and watching her. The huge feet were covered in with thick extremely coarse hair and toes crowned with deformed black claws that were cracked and pointed in different directions. A long black cloak covered the body. The costumed man or hooded beast stood over six-feet tall and was just short of matching the height of the closet door jam. A hood rested on the rim of a large round nose. Black lips were flat-lined.

Dawn felt like she was in one of those horror movies where some sick pervert or cult member would break into a house dressed up in a ridiculous costume and torment and brutally murder young women.

Quickly, she tried to qualify her best options. She wanted to turn and simply leave the room and try to pretend that she hadn't seen the thing. But she was far too anxious for that and considered running out of the room and possibly fighting her way out of the house. Whatever it took and whoever was waiting outside would just have to be dealt with. This was enough; too much, in fact. She couldn't spend another second alone in this house. Dawn couldn't help but turning to the intruder one more time to make sure it wasn't moving in on her.

The hooded thing began to defy gravity and slide up the wall. Dawn looked in astonishment as it continued to move from right to left in front of the curtains pausing long enough for Dawn to see the transparent nature of the strange being. She had no option but to step out of her intellectual comfort zone and consider the supernatural. Ghost or spirit, she was not sure of the difference or if she had even cared. The experience was unnerving.

As if not satisfied with the current position, the thing reversed position and hovered back to the corner and did not settle on the floor. It just hung in the air. Its thin black lips started to move and a red snake like sliver of a tongue moved slowly back and forth as if testing the air like a serpent.

How do you defend yourself against something that can defy gravity? What defense was there against the supernatural? Dawn pondered.

In a move that was completely visceral and devoid of rational thought, she stepped forward and threw the remote at the hovering intruder. The remote passed through the trespassing thing and smashed into the wall.

It expressed astonishment at the realization that it had been seen. The thing produced a pair of scaly hands and aggressively threw the dingy hood back. It looked down toward the chest cavity where the remote had passed through and then back to Dawn who turned to run out of the room.

Hate-filled eyes sank into deep eye sockets and were canopied by an exaggerated brow. Lesions and random growths peppered the facial surface while two triangular pieces of skin appeared tightly stretched over deformed bone where a nose should have been. The eyes had no pupils but ice-blue flames that illuminated the concave area of the face. A carpet of wild, black, coarse hair covered the head and ran down the neck into the cloak.

Dawn ran for the bedroom door fueled by an unbridled fear desperate to escape. She no longer cared about the possibly of what could have been waiting for her there. She slid across the tile floor in the hall and smashed into an eight by ten picture. It crashed to the floor, sending shards of glass in all directions. She wasted no time morning the damage and continued to move as fast as her injured body would go.

There was no longer a need for planning or thinking. That time was long gone. The options were few as she would have to pass by the kitchen and through the foyer in order to get to the front door. It seemed to Dawn that her chances of getting out of the house were slim considering the supernatural nature of her pursuer.

She had no idea what limitations the thing had. She thought about God, and perhaps this creature was sent to punish and torment her as a result of her years of blasphemies. Maybe the entire evening had been about some sort of pre-judgment and she would be back in Hell before the chase was over. Best case scenario, if she survived the night, there would a major need for therapy. The entire evening had already changed her world forever.

The creature seemed to recover from the reality of its discovery and was now enjoying the sport of the chase. It met her at the edge of the kitchen tile with outreached hands beckoning her. Blue flames leapt up from the open palms and cast shadows of demonic beings on the sheetrock. The creature laughed and licked the air, taunting Dawn.

"OK to die, it is. Come to me love. Take away all your pain, I can. Me and you it has always been. Became who you are all by yourself . . . you did not?" the creature said, talking directly into her mind.

She shook off its words. "I don't know you!" she yelled.

"But you do. A team we are. Sent many people to my master you have. Confused you have become."

With nothing to lose, she lowered her head and trudged forward determined to run through it. She was surprised to see that she passed with no resistance and her momentum carried her to the foyer where she slammed into the decorative table sending a crystal vase of freshly cut lilies crashing to the tile floor.

Dawn reached for the foyer table and yanked with all of her might to get back up and pulling over and onto the floor. Dawn pushed up and yanked open the oak door and ran out. Powerful hands grabbed her shoulders and she screamed at the realization of being caught.

Chapter 11

Dawn bolted through the door and slammed into something that was neither ghost nor spirit. The intruder had transformed into a physical being in order to carry out its plan against her. Momentum was on her side and she decided to use it. With all of her strength and ability she pushed the creature over the sidewalk and onto the front lawn. It grabbed her and Dawn started swinging. Though her eyes were closed, she could feel the punches landing. Dawn was in a fight for freedom and life and she was going to give the beast a fight.

"Ouch . . . stop!" the voice said, startled.

Dawn opened her eyes, pulling back in mid-swing before landing a punch on the left side of the jaw. She had attacked Marcus and not the strange creature from the house. He was on the ground just looking at her and grabbing his nose. Never had she been so happy to see him. She grabbed him and wept in his chest.

Marcus was not sure how to react. Dawn had tackled him? She flew out of the house and tackled him, then threw punches and now was hugging him so hard that only a little air was able to get into his lungs. It wasn't the physically aggressive side of Dawn that had him unsettled. He always suspected that she would hit him one day. It was the manner in which it had all transpired. She didn't seem to know who it was that was at the door. She was scared. Of that he was certain. The angels had warned him that something was after her leaving Marcus to his imagination. What could have broken such a strong woman?

Marcus struggled to push Dawn up and knelt in front of her. He pulled up the front of his white shirt and tended to the bleeding nose. "Is he still in the house?" Marcus asked assuming that a man had forced entry with the intention of doing her harm.

Dawn wasn't sure how to answer and remained silent. If she answered truthfully he may think she was crazy or on hallucinogenic drugs. Certainly he was open about his faith in God and spiritual matters, but this was different. This was pushing the envelope. It seemed more suited for Hollywood than scripture.

When Dawn remained silent, Marcus looked up and noticed as something seemed to move inside of her. Instantly he understood her problem. Marcus watched as a demon walked out of Dawn's body and stand behind her. Its lips were moving and speaking to Dawn. Marcus couldn't hear what it was saying, but Dawn undoubtedly reacted to the thoughts it was placing in her head.

Marcus realized that the vision was not limited to the event in the park. His facial expression gave her further reasons for concern and she asked, "What is it?"

"OK. I guess you really *are* upset to see me," Marcus said thinking quickly and trying to divert her attention and allow some time for God to instruct him on how to deal with the demon. This was new: angels and demons fighting in the park, and now he was kneeling in the grass, in the front of the person who hated him more than anyone on planet earth, watching a demon mess with her mind. He forgot about the trickle of blood as it continued to run over his lip and drip onto the ground between his knees

"No!" she replied.

Marcus was taken aback by the certainty of her answer. He had no idea to the extent of what she had been through and expected to be rejected regardless of what was in the house.

"I am glad you are here. I . . . even tried to call you. I'm not really sure why, but you are the only one I think I can talk to."

Infuriated by the comment, the demon went into a rage, opening its wings and flying in the air and slamming itself into the trunk of a large live oak at full speed, then back into the air and to the ground. It punched and bit viciously at the earth's crust, growling and screaming as it did so.

Marcus was not sure how to react to what he was seeing. The entire experience wasn't just odd, but freaky. The demon plucked itself off of the ground and stomped back over to where Dawn was.

Looking directly at Dawn was difficult with the demonic spirit moving in and out of her. He wanted to stand and rebuke the stupid thing, but had no experience at casting out demons and he didn't want to alarm Dawn. He needed to buy some time. He needed to get some Godly guidance.

"What," he asked. "What is wrong? Did someone try to hurt you? Is he in there now," he asked despite knowing the answer to the question. Marcus could no longer look at her while the spirit treated her like a voodoo doll poking and manipulating her.

Anger at the demon was beginning to become an issue with Marcus. He had no fear of the creature as he was a child of God and could stand against the demonic host. It was the potential physical and mental injuries that could be inflicted on Dawn as she was unsaved and unprotected.

He needed a moment for himself and used the house as an excuse. Marcus stood and walked into the foyer looking to see if other spirits were present. He recalled the demons that possessed the men at Gadara and the 'legion' that was in them. Was he fortunate enough to only have to deal with one or was there more? Perhaps hundreds more similar to some of the accounts he had read about.

Marcus became unusually nervous and had to control his breathing. To the right an antique table with clawed legs and a walnut finish was on its side as if thrown over during the fight for the front door. On the floor beside it were large pieces of a crystal vase. A puddle of water covered nine square tiles and in the center was a pile of fresh Lilies and two broken crystal candle holders.

Dawn began to stir and Marcus suggested that she remain by the front door until a search of the house had been completed. He called out to God and prayed for strength and protection for what he was about to encounter. It wasn't by any power of his that this or any demon would be cast out of Dawn. It was Jesus who had the power and authority.

The problem would be Dawn. There was obviously a long line of generational curses and being reared in a home that not only ignored God, but actively preached against Him, Dawn wasn't simply a confused person or devout atheist. She was a hard-core activist against God and hated the notion of His existence. That had to be a powerful manifestation of the demonic possession and oppression that had been with her every step of her life.

She was an earthly warrior for Satan and he was not going to just let her go. Marcus needed God's strength and presence. He had longed for the opportunity, but had never really understood the challenge and potential disaster in its entirety until now. The reality was that these demons would try to kill her before they would let her escape and run to God. This was going to be brutal, painful and could even send Dawn into further shock. She had no covering, no protection and he was inexperienced at casting out spirits. She needed a prayer covering, but how much time was there for that now? Perhaps the previous week's prayers of the churches would be sufficient and God would pour out His mercy.

He stepped through the foyer, walking around the water and stood on the threshold of the living room. As he continued to pan back and forth, the broken glass and wood from the frame directed his path toward the rear hall way. Eagerly he moved down the hall expecting to find that another demon was in the house. Shards of glass shifted and broke against the tile floor as he walked toward the open door of the bedroom. He leaned and looked in. With the exception of the clothes in the tub, there was nothing out of the ordinary there.

"I will be with you. You are protected. Satan will certainly try to take her life, but he will do so regardless of what you do or say," God said to him.

"I think the house is clean. I looked in every room and the garage and there is nothing. Let me help you in," Marcus said.

"No! I don't want to come in," she replied.

Marcus looked at the gathering crowd from the park, "Do you want me to take you somewhere else?"

Leaving her home didn't guarantee that the experiences or visitations would stop. There was the potential for something to happen to which there would be other witnesses and would result in major embarrassment and permanent damage to her reputation as a stable person. Dawn had always valued her privacy and it was enough to have Marcus see her at this low point in life. The only thing worse than being chased by a demon would be having others watch and be entertained by her torment. They would certainly think she was nuts. She changed her mind and decided to once again enter the house. As long as Marcus was there, she would work to find out what it was that God wanted and stop the occurrences.

Nervously she asked, "Will you stay with me a while?"

"Sure, if you really want me to."

"Then I want to stay here," Dawn said.

Standing in the foyer door, Dawn was wincing in pain from the experience a few hours earlier. Marcus walked over to help her into the house and stopped to move the debris out of the foyer. Marcus decided against an immediate search for a mop or towel to clean up the water. It was best to direct Dawn around the wet tiles and to get her into the house before the entire neighborhood was abuzz with rumors and false stories of the misunderstanding in the front yard. The newspapers would be overrun with exaggerated tales of her tackling and punching him in the nose. That was the price for their celebrity.

"You look like you are in pain. Should I call the police or an ambulance?"

"No," she quickly replied, knowing that an explanation would land her in the psycho ward at the local hospital. She reached out in acceptance of Marcus's hand and felt no ill effects of pride and was glad for his help.

Marcus recoiled slightly and looked away from Dawn. The demon had once again possessed her and was sticking its head out of the top of hers in stern observance of him. It stared coldly with ice blue flames for pupils. Marcus didn't want it to know that he could see into the spiritual world until the time was right.

By his actions, Dawn sensed that Marcus saw something. Rather selfishly, she hoped that he saw something at least similar to what she had earlier. If he saw the demon then she wouldn't be alone and explaining her experience to him would be easier.

"What?" Dawn inquired, hoping that Marcus would freely divulge information and that she would not have to be the first to admit to witnessing the strange being.

"Nothing," he replied quickly, putting on a normal demeanor. He knew what she wanted to know, but realized that the element of surprise would be taken away if the impure spirit knew.

He looked away while reaching out and grabbing her hand for a second attempt. In the manner of assisting an elderly person, he guided Dawn to the breakfast area where the Bible had previously been open to the Gospel of John. He let go of her hand and moved away. After reaching a safe distance, he looked upon her again. There was nothing.

Dawn searched the counter. The Bible was gone. She looked left and right and saw no sign of it.

"What happened?" he asked. It was strange. He had always believed that she was his mission. A challenge God had set before him. The idea of physically seeing the back side of the front door was a victory in itself, but to be in her house and potentially able to help her in matters that involved God was an opportunity he was not going to take lightly. Why he always believed her to be his mission, Marcus had never understood. He did realize that the ways and reasons of man were not comparable to God's. But trust and faith in God to have a plan was enough. His approach was one prayer, word, sentence and conversation at a time as God opened doors. If this soul could be snatched away from the Deceiver and won for the Kingdom, what a powerful and life changing testimony she would possess. The entirety of Satan's governing authority in the New Orleans area would be sent into turmoil as untold thousands could be reached for Christ. A mighty and injurious blow would be delivered to the Deceiver.

"I am not sure . . . or even if I can talk about it," she said nervously. She stared at the floor and then moved her eyes to meet his. For the first time she saw the golden radiance like the female news anchor had. In seeing this she felt peace. She fought briefly with her desire to share the experience, but continued to wrestle with her thoughts.

"I thought I saw an . . . intruder and I just panicked and ran out of the house," she said, lying as a protective measure.

Not wanting to press, Marcus sat patiently in a continuous state of prayer and waited for a few minutes while dabbing a cloth on his injured nose. He wanted her to lead in the conversation. "Are you sure that you don't need any medical help?"

With the pain in her side subsiding, Dawn stood in an attempt to show Marcus that she was alright and capable of self-reliance. "I'm fine," she said, walking over and surveying the foyer mess up close.

The hate she felt for him had disappeared. The Godly radiance about him was extremely comforting. However, embracing this new found sense of trust, in this situation, was difficult beyond measure. Dawn desperately wanted to come clean, but the two had yet to have a civil conversation and confessing a trip to Hell and a gravity defying, snake tongued intruder was difficult.

The demon was no longer visible and Marcus watched her hands and face as she struggled to hide the fear that was clearly present. This normally strong woman was visibly shaken and hiding something. She stood and moved robotically from the breakfast area to the foyer and then the living room.

A teak coffee table with carved legs gave support to several travel magazines and photo books on New Orleans graveyards and Mardi Gras. The leather sofa made a ninety degree angle and took up a large portion of the living room. A television broadcasted a national news program and was mounted on the wall opposite of the couch.

Dawn walked toward the living room window that overlooked the park and pushed back the olive colored curtain with her right hand. A small burst of a scream filled the room. Dawn was back-pedaling, once again desperate to escape something that was by or at the window. The coffee table met with the back of her calves obstructing her momentum. Long blond hair trailed in the air as she fell onto her butt breaking the carved legs at their narrowest and weakest point. The splintering teak ripped through her jeans and raked against the back of her right leg peeling off small trails of skin. The injury to the calf went unnoticed and she was unable to break her focus on the window.

Marcus was up before she landed on the table. Instinctively he reached down to help her while continuing to search the window. Her face was frozen in horror.

The head of a huge demon was in the window, screaming and growling. This creature was different from the ones in the park. Marcus started to recoil, but gained his composure and starred at the thing in the window unwilling to take his attention off of it. Dawn reached up and grabbed his hand. Her grip cut off the circulation to his fingers.

The thing laughed and snapped at them both. Long stringy grey hair was flailing back and forth with the rapid gyrations of the demon's head. Its greasy hair wrapped around large pointed ears. Veins popped out of the putrid blue grey epidermis on the forehead and body much like a professional body builder in the midst of a strenuous set. Its mouth housed canines four and five inches in length. It looked enraged, wanting to tear them both apart.

Marcus realized that for some reason the demon was not able to get into the house. He was glad, but wondered how or why this was possible. The blue eyed demon possessing Dawn re-appeared and was standing behind her. The lesion riddled face was looking to the window and began yelling or speaking to the thing. They were communicating. Marcus discreetly looked back and forth between the fiery blue eyed demon in the hood and the huge hulking monster outside the window.

"They are demons," he quietly said to Dawn.

The hulking creature stopped suddenly and looked back and forth between Marcus and Dawn and wrinkled its brow in agitation as if intelligent enough to understand that they were watching him. The smaller demon now looked upon Marcus with interest and back to the window for instructions.

"Pray!" The command rang out as if spoken directly into Marcus's mind.

"I bind you in the name of Jesus Christ. Now be gone!" He demanded.

Eyes filled with red pupils looked up and rolled back and forth. The demon lord reached up with a scale covered hand and pointed a bloody claw at him. It became agitated and reformed the fist. The beast was yelling and making threats toward Marcus. Suddenly several new demons joined the scene at the window. They were smaller and possessed no permanent features and continuously morphed and changed shape and colors as commands were given.

Dawn recognized them as having the same general appearance as the things on the news that had been caught by the angel. One second the creatures could look like a small human, the next second a random ball of mass.

Marcus was inexperienced when it came to casting out demons. "I said that you have no authority here. I am a child of the Most High God and I command you to leave this place at once!" Marcus said, yelling at the hosts of Hell.

The group of smaller demons now turned to him and darted through the wall. One of the demons stopped several inches from his face hovering and looking him over. Dozens flew through the walls and filled the house. They laughed, spit and fought amongst themselves.

The hovering demon darted at Marcus and passed through his chest and stopped several feet past him and looked back anxious and unsettled. Suddenly Marcus bent over and grabbed his abdomen. Breathing became very difficult as the pain covered the entire chest cavity. Marcus didn't know what the demon had done to him or how to counter it. Dawn screamed as she looked at him and the demonic spirits tearing up her house.

"God! God help him!" she screamed.

A large angel entered from the back wall putting aside other business in order to help Marcus. With his huge fist, he grabbed the portly demon by the arm and hurled it into the chest of his Lord who had been watching from the window. The two went tumbling end over end stopping nearly two hundred feet from the point of impact. The larger demon quickly regained its footing and drew a huge sword and began to strike the ground in anger like a kid during a tantrum. The smaller demons darted through the walls and disappeared behind their lord for whatever protection he could offer.

The angel reached out to Marcus and prayed. A brilliant radiance came from his hands at the point of contact with Marcus's body. The light was intense and nearly blinding. Healing quickly came and Marcus was relieved of the pain. He stood and looked to Dawn and found her distressed by the continued demonic presence in her house. The angel swiftly exited where he had entered, resuming his responsibility to other matters.

Marcus quickly moved to the window and pulled back the drapery blocking any view of the outside world. It took several seconds to regain his breath. He was surprised that the demon was able to attack him. Had it not been for the angel, it may have killed him. Strangely, the experience gave Marcus a new confidence instead of increasing his fears.

The blue-eyed demon ascended from the floor and looked at Marcus. It tauntingly smiled at him and spoke telepathically, "You know I will kill her before He can have her."

There was no doubt that this was the demon that had been given a special commission to guide, or more aptly, misguide Dawn. The creature's power and ability were evident in the success it had achieved in her life. It was this evil creature, when certain that Dawn was going to walk in light and turn from the darkness that would certainly try to kill her.

By the look of the activity, Marcus assumed that God's plan to reach Dawn must have sent the entire region of Satan's kingdom into a panic. An even stronger sense of purpose, determination and opportunity came over him. He prayed to God that her heart was ready. Any uncertainty on the part of Dawn would insure a long and drawn out battle. The demons would have the right to possess her if they had an invitation or an open door.

Even if receiving salvation, they certainly would continue to manipulate circumstance and try to attack her health or anything to try to destroy her relationship with God. It was always good for them if members of the body of Christ were to backslide and lose their testimony. If the primary goal of taking souls to Hell with him for an eternity was to fail, then the loss of the ability to witness and win others away from Him was a minor victory.

He thought of a scripture that had always bothered him because he was never really able to fully understand it. Many people had many different interpretations and explanations, but his understanding was not set. "When an unclean spirit goes out of a man, it goes through dry places seeking rest; and finding none, he says, 'I will return to my house from which I came.' And when he comes, he finds it swept and put in order. Then he goes and takes with him seven other spirits more wicked than himself, and they enter and dwell there; and the last state of that man is worse than the first."

"Can I help you?" Marcus asked breaking the silence

"No. I can get up on my own," she said. "I know you saw what I saw."

"Let's cut to the chase. It's obvious that we both saw the same thing. I was attacked by one of them. Those are demons who want to kill you. Jesus is the only way to have victory over Satan. You need to receive him in your heart. After all you have seen can you deny that Jesus is real? That He can and will save you? Will you make Him your Lord and Savior?"

"Yes" she said.

The demon jumped on her back and began to choke her. Only it had made a critical error, it had waited too long. Despite the absence of an audible declaration of faith, her heart was already set on the Lord. In her heart, she had already given herself to Him but had yet to make the verbal profession.

The living room was suddenly robbed of light as a wave of demons re-entered the house like a flock of wild birds. A tornado of activity ripped through the house, tearing curtains down, cabinet doors flew open and dishes crashed to the tile floor. Food flew from the refrigerator smashing against the walls. Plastic containers of mayonnaise and fruit juices punched holes and were embedded in the sheetrock.

A piece of the broken crystal vase from the foyer struck Marcus in the neck and was quickly followed by a second. Marcus looked up as a demon was picking up a third piece. Ignoring the minor threat, he turned back to help Dawn.

"I rebuke you!" Marcus yelled.

The demon ignored him and continued to hold the grip. It snickered and laughed at Marcus as Dawn was fighting for air. She looked at Marcus, pleading with her eyes for help.

A brilliant golden light entered the house from the ceiling. A four winged angel descended and drove a huge fist down on the demon knocking it off of Dawn. The angel grabbed the creature and flew out through the blinds of the living room window. The blinds flew backwards at the passing of the angelic being. Finally, the demon was gone. Dawn tried to control her desperate gasps for air.

Two angels chased the smaller spirits, cutting them down with flaming swords. A third and fourth sharp piece of crystal struck him in the head. Marcus leaped to his feet and ran over to the demon and fought with it over the remaining large pieces. The creature pulled his hair and bit him on the arm. One of the angels grabbed the pestering spirit and slammed it toward the ground where it disappeared. Marcus nodded in thanks. Within seconds the room was clear.

Marcus looked at Dawn who was in tears on her knees face down on the floor. He ran to her side and placed his arm over her. She looked up cautiously and slowly looked around fearing that she may see another spirit or be subjected to another attack.

The mess was huge and would take weeks to completely repair. There wasn't a single picture or glass decoration that wasn't broken. The kitchen cabinets looked to be empty and piles of debris were on the floor. Somehow the only thing within view that remained intact was the television. It apparently had no value to the vandals.

"They weren't happy you switched sides." Marcus said, searching his scalp for blood.

She wept and he knelt beside her. She cried on his shoulder again.

A few quiet minutes passed and it seemed that it was finally over. The blue eyed demon didn't return and the pestering little unformed demons were all gone. Marcus moved to the window and quickly threw back the blinds the returned to the bathroom where he had remembered seeing a box of tissue. It was no longer on the shelf, but had been tossed into the bath tub on top of the now ripped up clothes. He reached down and peeled several strips of cloth off of the box and picked it up. He decided not to tell Dawn about the shredded outfit and handed the box to her.

"Thanks . . . I went to Hell," she blurted out.

"Hell?"

"Yes. I was sitting over there, mad at you. I was cussing you and that girl and planning Monday's show. All of you were going to get it. I was going to let you have everything I had even if they kicked me off the air . . . I didn't care.

"I was so angry that I had to turn on the TV to try and calm down. I grabbed the remote and sat back and the next thing I knew, I was falling." She told him about the entire experience including the physical pain she still felt when she returned.

"Well, I guess that explains the sunburn. I've heard of people having a near death experience. But it's not too often that someone is just taken to Hell. That's certainly a life changing experience," Marcus said.

"I was so alone down there and when I got back I seemed to be just as alone . . . confused and not sure what to do. I needed someone to talk to, and you seemed to be the one person. That's the reason I hated you so bad, isn't it?"

"Afraid so. This was apparently in the works for some time and they knew it was going to happen. They knew that getting you to hate me was critical. And man did they do a good job of it. At least until God was ready."

"Well, not anymore," she said through tears.

"Today's broadcast . . . you talked about Powers and Principalities and you were pretty harsh in your criticism of the Biblical teachings. Maybe God wanted you to have a first-hand experience. He took you there and gave you the ability to see them here so that you couldn't deny that they existed.

"The whole unseen spiritual world, as you now know, is very real and well structured. Now you need to understand several things from the beginning. First, this is no cake walk. When you are open about your faith and stand firm . . . you will be rejected. The majority of your friends and family will drop you from Facebook and stop calling the second you try to tell them about Jesus. You are about to find out who your true friends are. Sure, some may really like you and *tolerate* your spirituality, but a lot of them will not stand to have you talking openly about your faith and will just ask you not to talk about it. However, we know what is at stake. You went to Hell. Do you want to see anyone end up there for an eternity?"

"No!" she replied shaking her head.

"Having a strong passion to help people understand what is at stake isn't always enough. They are too in love with their lives to want to change for any reason. The one lie that we have very little ability of overcome is that they are all convinced that there will always be time to get right with God before they die. And that's the hurdle for the ones who believe. The ones who are like you used to be have to get hit in the head with a frying pan just to get them to listen. Their hearts are hard like stone.

"But you, in contrast, are a woman with a lot of strength and authority. You can have a major influence on the countless number of people who have listened to your show. Your conversion . . . your testimony will stir the hearts and souls of people everywhere. The media is going to be all over you for a while and it will be a good thing. But Satan will continue to come after you. He comes after me all the time even before today. You are strong enough to deal with it."

"Was . . . I . . . ."

"Were you . . . what?" Marcus asked.

"Possessed?" Dawn asked fearing the answer. "You were looking right at me when you rebuked that spirit. Right at me."

"Well, certainly *oppressed*. Thanks to that angel the demon wasn't able to linger long, or I'm not sure what would have happened. But then again, I truly believe that your heart was ready. Sometime after the Hell trip something happened and I think your heart changed and you accepted who Jesus is. You needed to make an open confession. But, it's about your heart, not your mind." Marcus said.

Dawn nodded in agreement then asked, "But, how can you see them? Have you always been able to see them?"

"Well, I was running through the park trying to come up with an excuse to talk to you . . . to try and witness one more time. A man in a black leather jacket tackled me and I guess he prayed over me. Before he let me go, he touched my eyes. Then I saw these demons coming after us. He said that I needed to help you that . . . they were coming to kill you. I guess that God has given us both an open window."

"Open window?"

"Yes, open window. In the Bible in Second Kings, there is a story where the Syrian army surrounded the city of Dothan. Elisha's servant was worried and didn't know what they were going to do. So, Elisha prayed and his eyes were opened. He saw horses and chariots of fire . . . this vast army of God was protecting Israel from the Syrians. That's one story. I guess that is the kind of experience that we are having. I'm not sure if it only lasted as long as it took for you to get saved or if this is something we will carry with us for a while."

Marcus was tempted to go to the window and look but wanted to keep all of his concentration on ministering to Dawn. He knew there was going to be a lot to explain.

"I . . . can't . . . stop . . . crying," she said. "Is it supposed to be like this?"

"Sometimes, but it is different for everyone."

CHAPTER 12

Dawn was physically exhausted, but the house was a mess. To suggest that it looked like the middle of a war zone would be conservative. It was still hard to fathom all that had happened. But the tangible proof of its reality was scattered throughout the house. There was a lot she didn't understand. Marcus was doing his best at ministering to her needs. The Bible that had once been placed on the top of the granite overhang had yet to be found. Marcus decided to go back to his house and get a Bible and materials that would help Dawn.

While he was gone, Dawn decided to begin the restoration of her home. The task seemed overwhelming. There were about thirty holes in the walls, all of the pictures were in piles of broken glass, indoor plants had been uprooted and the dirt tossed everywhere, expensive drapery was ripped up and on the floor and from her vantage point, it didn't seem as if a dish was left in the kitchen. The destructive demons had made a mess.

As she surveyed the back side of the kitchen by the dining room, the green pillows remained as she had left them. She stared at the matador and the dying bull and thought of the irony of now being a Christian after seeking so vigilantly to discredit and destroy the faith, to kill God, as if it was possible. She no longer saw herself as a matador stabbing the life out of the Christian faith. She envisioned herself fighting the matador and inflicting injury on the deceiver. She would have to undo a lot of the damage that had been the result of her lack of knowledge. She would never know how many people she had pushed away from God.

She saw the woman reaching for her again. The hollow eyes and horrified expression was haunting. Dawn wondered if she had any hand in the woman's eternity. Was that why she was able to see her? She had to do everything in her power to change the destinies of all who had ever listened to her.

She called out to God, "Father, it was my mistake . . . my words . . . my actions that have lead many people away from You."

"It was their hearts. You just told them what they wanted to hear. You gave them what they were already looking for. They hated Me in their hearts before ever knowing you. You must forgive yourself," a voice spoke into her mind.

Dawn felt a peace. But she still resolved to walk and talk with boldness and make a difference. She would have a platform to use, and she planned to make the most out of it.

She walked over food and broken dishes to get to the pillows then pushed open the door and stuffed them in a large blue garbage can, now seeing herself on the other side of the fight.

What are Sonny and Mike going to think? What do I do about the radio show? Before the two questions were complete thoughts, Dawn realized that she really cared about neither. Her life was going in a new direction even if she wasn't certain of exactly what to do.

The events of the day had undeniably altered the rest of her natural and eternal existence. It was no coincidence that Marcus was there at that particular time in order to catch her at the door. The timing was too perfect. She knew that when God was involved, nothing happened by mere chance. Marcus was now a positive and welcome part of her life.

How odd, she thought, to have possessed such total disregard for a person and for that person to return her harsh treatments with kindness. Certainly he had encouraged her on occasion with witty remarks, but she owed him an apology. "I asked him to sign my middle finger," she said aloud, remembering the night at Nevesian Restaurant.

She shut the door and stumbled over a mound of matching plates, saucers, salad bowls and coffee cups. She paused at the recognition of the china. It looked like the entire set was ruined. It had been in the family since the early eighteen hundreds and in her care for less than three months. Every piece now destroyed with nothing left to salvage. She knelt down and picked up a piece, looked it over, then tossed it back into the pile. Dawn stood and vowed not to get upset over it and decided to try and find a matching set online.

Where do I start? She considered attempting to formulate some type of strategy. The only thing in the front of the house that was untouched was the TV and she decided to lighten the mood. She had enough of the fear and tears and felt a sense of peace about it all. Hell was no longer going to be a part of her future and that alone was worth celebrating. They could get a dozer and knock the entire house down for all she cared.

She walked over to the couch, picked up the remote and searched the digital radio stations on the satellite and selected Contemporary Christian. It was different than what she was accustomed to, but it seemed soothing.

An odd beam of light pierced the ceiling and shined on the floor. It was golden at first glance, but a closer look revealed hundreds of brilliant colors mixing and moving continuously throughout. Slowly the radiance grew both in coverage and intensity first shining down on the broken teak coffee table and expanding to cover Dawn's feet. She backed up and watched in amazement. It looked like a piece of the sun had fallen to earth and landed in the middle of her living room. Golden rays bounced off of glass shards, metals and crystal producing a light show. Lasers shot into all directions while the source of the brilliant light continued to descend.

Dawn moved as far back as possible. She was enamored by the beauty and became anxious for Marcus to return. This was something he would be disappointed in missing. The light was beyond description. She remembered the lost and hopeless feeling of being in the dark and was now experiencing the absolute antithesis. This light gave her a peace and joy. She was happy to see it and wanted to meet the source.

A pair of large leather sandals emerged from the concentrated center of illumination. A large perfectly portioned frame floated down and settled on the floor in front of her. An angel stood in the center of the ridge facing Dawn. He was nine feet tall with two sets of enormously large outstretched wings that were barley contained within the walls of the living room and cut off the rest of the house from view. The transparent nature of the layered feathers fixed upon his wings sparkled with breathtaking iridescence. A multi-hued sheen produced rich colors that moved like electricity with every angular change set off by even the slightest of movements. The brilliance was enthralling to Dawn.

Long white hair draped down and over the shoulders and shared the sheen and characteristics of the feathers enhancing the strong blue eyes. His facial expression exuded both sincerity and purpose. Certainly this magnificent creation had not exposed himself to her without proper cause or reason, she considered. This was without doubt an angel of superior stature and ability.

In an act of self-control, Dawn forced her attention from the light show on the wings and in the hair. She recognized the visitor as the same angel who had chased off the demon that was choking her at the time of her attempted profession of belief. Only now, instead of armor, he wore a linen garment bordered in purple and gold that hung down to the buckles of his sandals. A large sword was fixed by his right hand if the need arose to fight.

"Yes, it is as you are thinking. The Father has sent me to you. My Father calls me Asher. I am here to give you council," he said in a deep but soothing voice.

Without hesitation Dawn asked, "Why did God show me such mercy? Why did He spare me and not the woman in the pit next to where I was supposed to be? Why did I receive this kind of mercy?"

"The Father's ways are not your ways. Your thoughts are not the Father's thoughts. He who sits at the right hand of the Almighty, is righteous and just. The Lamb of God slain for your transgression and that of all man, He will judge all. It is not for us to discuss or judge." He knelt down to get face level with Dawn.

"Can you tell me what is going on? Why can I see these things? What is happening?"

"You have been given a gift. As you now know, there is a world all around you that has contributed a great deal to your life. You opted to believe it all to be a lie therefore choosing to believe *the* lie. Man is bound by his need to see and yet the attributes of God are everywhere and still he sides with ignorance over truth.

"God has granted many people an open window into the Heavenly realm. But has never given anyone the ability to share what they see with the world as you are able to do."

Dawn's brow rose in interest. "Show?"

"You and Marcus have been given a special opportunity. Anyone you touch will be able to see everything you see. They will see the open window as you two can. If employed properly, it will open ministerial doors and multitudes will understand," Asher replied.

"Really?"

"Time is short so pay attention. Dagon, the spirit that haunted you, has been able to control just about every aspect of your life since you were thirteen. He has grown to be a powerful spirit who will try to hinder you in any way possible. But don't worry, you won't be alone," he said, putting his hand up.

"Do you remember that day in eighth grade when you used profane language against your teacher over a B she gave you on a test? That was his first success with you. Once your temper was had, you were a willing accomplice. Over the years he was able to manipulate you.

His greatest injustice against you . . . ," Asher paused as if he didn't want to go any further. "Dagon's greatest victory was that night in the dorm . . ." he said, not wishing to draw painful memories and push Dawn away, but to help to get an understanding of the seriousness and effectiveness of the Deceiver's army to destroy man without limitations or boundaries.

Dawn looked at Asher with a face no longer wrought with fear, but a since of understanding. His last comment had the desired effect. She straightened her back regaining composure, "So, that happened because this Dagon created a situation that set all of that up? My rape was because this demon wanted to mess up my mind and get me to hate Christ. My rape, by the son of a preacher, was carefully orchestrated?"

"I remember how you reacted when you found out that the boy was a preacher's son. You blamed all Christians for your rape. You harbored that hate and used it as fuel as you, in a sense of speaking, declared war and took out your revenge on the church . . . on Christ. Why were you never satisfied? Where did your uninhibited hate come from? It came from the influence of Dagon. He kept your heart hardened against the body of Christ.

"Jesus understands and has forgiven you since you asked." He became animated as her countenance revealed a pressing guilt. "The purpose of this conversation is education and is not meant for condemnation. Don't you, for a second, hold on to the past. Jesus has forgiven you. You are now a child of the living God. Anything you said or did is now gone . . . forever! The deceiver used you and now you have a chance to stop him from lying, hurting and using other people."

"Why didn't you protect me?" she asked in a somber voice.

"I tried. While you did not ask to be raped and God certainly did not want that to happen to you. You chose to go to that party, a place of drunkenness and sin . . . a place where a person like that may be lurking. That was your decision as a person given free will by the Father. Your rape was not a punishment from God.

"Remember that thin red headed kid with the really bad complexion that you always picked on?" she thought for a moment and nodded. "He asked you that night to go to church with him to see the Christian band, Seven Days Straight. He was really persistent and trying to convince you how great an experience it would be. You were really aggravated by his refusal to take no for an answer. When all else failed, he bared all embarrassment and abuse and tried to witness to you . . . because God had put you on his heart. You wouldn't listen. I tried to get you to go, but you listened to Dagon and not me. I tried, but I cannot, even now, impede your free will.

"Would you mind walking with me in the park? It is time you saw the big picture," he said.

"I have been given charge over you since the day of your conception. Where you have walked, I was there. There was no tear nor laughter nor thought not recorded by my hands as I would have been forced to be a witness against you, but now seek to help you. For seasons I have longed to welcome, protect and embrace you, but you would not have me as your denial of the

Father and the gift of the Son had isolated you from the rights of His elect. You were on a course for eternal damnation and separation from your Creator, but you have repented and have seen the error of your ways.

"You have been given a special privilege, but it does not come without a cost. Men are to have faith without sight, but because of your previous arrogance, the Father has marked you for such experiences. Many lie in your future. What you have seen already has proven difficult, but we will help you. God has called you and Marcus for a purpose such as no man has been before. However, you have the right to deny your calling as He will never interfere with the free will of His creation. His commitment to this has been painful as many have chosen eternal separation from Him and sided with your former lord, the father of lies.

"There are a great number of matters of which you need instruction and knowledge. I will help you with your lack of understanding. If you please, can we venture into the park. There is much I want to teach and show you." He gestured toward the front door.

Dawn wasn't sure what to think of this request. The special privilege granted to her by God himself conjured conflicting emotions of excitement and apprehension. She considered why someone of her low stature as a new Christian with very little understanding and severely shrouded in lack could be worthy of such concession by the Father.

Fighting through severe nervousness, Dawn stood. Her legs were shaking and she fought to stay upright. The presence of the angelic being and the revelation of what her immediate future was going to look like caused her to be unsettled.

Asher's wings began to shrink and disappeared while the tall frame reduced to that of a normal man. The robe changed into a pair of casual slacks and a tightly woven cotton shirt. The angel was now less intimidating and easier for Dawn to converse with.

Out of impulse she reached out and poked him and said, "Well you are definitely a solid form."

"He said you would do that." He smiled at her.

She looked upon the seemingly normal man and wondered how many times in life she had encountered one of these servants of God and not known it? How would any mortal man have known?

Without moving, the door swung open at a normal pace guided by an invisible force. Dawn passed over the threshold and walked cautiously toward the park. Instinctively, she scanned the area and was relieved to see no sign of the huge beast or any of the other demons. The park had never looked more beautiful than it was at this point in time. It was normal again as she once knew it. The wind rustled the leaves of the live oaks that lined the asphalted walkway and encircled the park. Tiny ripples formed and expanded while dancing patterns of unseen air revealed itself by pressing into the surface of the pond and moved crazily across to the opposing shore. A squirrel zoomed down a tree leaving a trail of disturbed air-born leaves and ran up another scaring several blue jays into flight. Turtles sunned on top of logs and bees flew aimlessly into all directions in search of their bounty. Two joggers were passed by a little girl on roller blades as a yellow lab pulled her from a red leash hooked to a harness.

Dawn savored the fresh air and felt, for the first time, alive and free. The exhilaration made her want to cry tears of joy. The day had become quite warm and perfectly invigorating. A beautiful little girl, she estimated to be near four years old plopped down onto the ground next to her mom and fell backward allowing a thick carpet of grass and purple wild flowers embrace her tiny body. Long, tightly curled red hair bunched up like a pillow beneath her head. Several minutes later, giggles filled the air as she lay in peaceful bliss pointing into the sky calling by name and talking to mom about God's master pieces. A rhino, an elephant, a manatee and a dolphin paraded through the atmosphere giving a private performance to a very special spectator.

How nice it would be to just lie in the grass like an innocent child and stare into the clouds searching for resemblances of creation? What it must be like to have no fears, worries, tears, pains or concerns? she thought.

"That is Heaven. There is no fear, worry, pain or concern in Heaven. For you and all of the saints, that is what waits. It is a perfect place void of all those things," came from an audible voice in her mind. She knew it had to be from Asher, who was patiently enjoying her delight of this performance of nature.

Dawn was not one to desire children and had never taken the time to reflect and study a child before. Her eyes filled with tears as she watched the innocent child and studied her. The little girl lipped something to the sky as if talking to one of the performers. Dawn wished she knew what was said and to which character she spoke.

"She named the manatee 'Abby' and told her 'hello.'" Asher said as the little girl began to feverishly wave her hand upward.

Several feet to the right of the little girl a husky dark haired angel appeared. Two sets of wings were folded and compact behind the large frame. His upper body was covered in polished gold and brass metals that had scriptures in Aramaic engraved around the borders of each plate. Separate guards were strapped to the forearms and shins, each with large embossed crosses in the center. Lying on the ground next to him was a large sword. The blade lived as blue, orange and red flames danced back and forth in waves from edge to edge and tip to handle.

He sat cross-legged in the grass reclining back onto his right hand. With his left he pointed into the sky and orchestrated the show. The clouds swirled and moved according to his direction. He quickly opened his hands spreading his fingers and stopped in a curled position. A lone cloud began to swirl by itself and caught the attention of the little girl and Dawn. The cloud stopped in a near perfect circle and two acorn shaped holes appeared as a new animal was about to join the parade. A snout and then a mane finished off the lion's head. As it crossed the blue sky, the cloud's movements gave animation to the roaring lion giving commands to his pride.

Upon recognition, the little girl gasped and clapped in excitement. The angel took great delight in her amusement and nearly fell onto his back in laughter. As Dawn watched, the love of the angel for this little child was overwhelmingly sincere. She noticed that she too shared in that love despite not knowing anything about her. Again, she wept.

Asher motioned for Dawn to take a seat on a bench which had been abused by years of public service as fingernail polish, markers, knives and gum had all been used in various forms of vandalism. She sat fixed on the girl and the angel while attempting to take in the supernatural new world.

"Faith," he said looking at the little red-headed girl. "She is a beautiful healthy child and God loves her so dearly . . . as He loves you." He briefly turned his gaze to Dawn. "Zenon is the one who watches over her. None of Satan's warriors can take him by themselves and believe me, they have tried. Many a battle has already taken place over and around that sweet child. She doesn't know it, but the fights have been intense, some lasting for weeks at a time. God has marked her for greatness as He has you. As tough and brutal as these battles have been, matters will only multiply in the future and Zenon will face the greatest challenges of his existence trying to protect her. Lucifer wants her."

Dawn realized that it wasn't by chance that Faith was in the park at that time. She felt a connection with her.

"For now, she is innocent and protected by the Father. But, when she grows up and makes her own decisions, Zenon, despite his strength, will not be able to defend her unless she willingly calls upon the Lord. The hardest thing to do is watch while your charge falls for the lies and deception," his face traced off as if reliving a great failure of his own.

"I'm sorry," Dawn said sincerely.

"The battle is being set and the deceiver plots to destroy this child while she is young and impressionable. Unsaved parents are easier targets as the father is without salvation and are slaves to the flesh and ways of the world. They will try to keep him this way. The father has a special duty to pray over his child, but Faith is without. As he has attempted to do in the past, Satan will seek to destroy the covenant of marriage and separate the parents. This will weaken their focus on Faith and all but ensure that she will never have the proper prayer covering. She will be exposed. If he is successful, then influencing Faith will become much easier and will increase the challenges Zenon will face when she grows and enters the 'free-will' portion of existence.

"As with Faith, God has gifted many with the abilities to be great advocates and powerful witness for the Kingdom. He gives them wisdom and knowledge and abilities to do many things. He will place people, events and situations in their lives to help them grow and mature. But He does not force them; they must do so willingly, and the Prince of Deception is there at every turn. God will carve the path, but they must choose to walk down it to become all that He has created them to be. Sometimes the prince of this world wins by deception . . . I know that you are familiar with Charles Darwin, whose teachings have been a tremendous problem as evolution is the new religion of the secular world and has been one of his most effective weapons injuring man. Like a piece of rotten bait dangled in front of the human race, despite its revolting flavor, the world feeds. The cunning angler reels man into the abyss. A great and cunning lie indeed! Other times he seeks to destroy life before it can have an effect and bring others into the kingdom."

"Before they are born?" Dawn asked.

"Yes," he motioned toward the couple, "Rachel and Paul started courting in High School. Both grew up in church, but moved away from God during college and Paul has followed the ways of the world ever since.

"They have certainly never seen the things you have experienced and have no idea why they struggle and why things seem to work against them. They don't believe that Satan wants to devour both of them." A large purple and gold scroll appeared and hovered in front of Dawn. Two large wooden spools housed the sections of the huge document. The sections rolled several feet into opposite directions exposing a single scripture for Dawn's view. '*Proverbs 4:19 The way of the wicked is like darkness; for they do not know what makes them stumble.*' Like you before today, Rachel and Paul do not understand what it is that works against them. Billions of unsaved souls do not understand and are lost, but worse than that is the millions of Christians who don't believe the scriptures."

Dawn watched Rachel as she reached over and tugged on Faith's flower coated sun dress in an attempt to get her attention. Paul seemed distant, not fully a part of whatever discussion that was supposedly taking place.

"At the time when they learned of Rachel's pregnancy, financial hardships had fallen on them causing some fairly serious marital problems. You see, Satan knew that God had marked this child for many great things. Satan's solution was to kill Faith while she was still in the womb. Pigos, Ipos and Labal, three of the deceiver's most cunning demons, created an environment of financial hardship and marital strife then planted thoughts of abortion and lust for another man in Rachel's mind. Zenon, who worked to protect Faith, was limited in his options as man's law gave Rachel the right to take the unborn life. This was a very difficult undertaking, but under no circumstances does the Father impede free-will. But, He hates the shedding of innocent blood . . . the burden will be heavy on the Day of Judgment.

"The three wretched creatures worked and planted traps that would promote fierce confrontations where hateful and destructive words were weapons of great injury. The finances continued to falter further complicating the situation. Pigos intensely pushed Rachel for the procedure using friends to convince her that the marriage was over and she would need to devote one-hundred percent of her time and energy to a career. Being a single mom would have been too difficult, and a broken home was no place for a child. Rachel was mere wax in the hands of Pigos as she was broken. Orifiel, an angel of God was sent to care for her, but had no real means of protecting her since she chose to be separated from the Father. It is a painful thing to watch as man's flesh destroys its soul and spirit."

Several feet away from Rachel, a new angel appeared standing in attention and appearing to be alarmed by a threat. His head was stationary and focused on something by Paul that Dawn could not see. Armor covered his body as a battle seemed imminent. "That is Orifiel. He cannot match the size of mighty Zenon, but he is quite powerful and most skilled in battle. I can assure you."

Asher paused for several seconds in deep thought, then continued. "On her way into the clinic a dear saint, Emily is the name of this precious soul, approached Rachel in the parking lot. Rachel's mom had her church praying for the broken couple. God heard these prayers and commanded Orifiel to reach out to dear Emily. He pressed it upon her heart to be there that day and to seek out Rachel. It was a divine appointment . . . you see." He paused again, allowing Dawn to absorb all that he was teaching her. "Emily was able to convince Rachel to walk across the street for a few minutes with her to a little diner and have a cup of coffee before she entered the clinic. The Holy Spirit led Emily in the conversation with her and they talked about the Father. God touched her heart through that conversation. One of the weaknesses of Satan is that he can push too hard and can lack patience. This often pushes people into the wonderful, open arms of our loving Father. It is in everyone's heart to want a relationship with Him, but it can be hidden for a while until tough times or a crisis brings Him to the surface to be realized and embraced. Rachel, for the first time, understood that God was there for her and the child and He had a plan for them both. God softened her heart, and guilt poured over Rachel at the realization of what she had almost done. She called out and poured her heart out. Just like what you did today. After an impressive performance, God commissioned Orifiel with Rachel's permanent care."

If you could have seen the battle that took place during and after that prayer in the diner that day, it was one for the ages. Satan was delivered a mighty blow. This child Faith is someone very important and special. She will be great among you. Rachel appropriately named her . . . Faith. I do love that name."

"I thought you said he couldn't do anything until she had accepted the Father," Dawn interrupted.

"She did; her heart had changed. That is the key. It was a heart conversion. Not some misleading and useless head conversion thinking you know God and thinking you called on God and thinking you have a relationship with God when nothing had ever changed or was ever from the heart. Millions of people call themselves Christians though they have no relationship with the Father. The scriptures warn of this. The mind, while necessary, can be an awfully damaging obstruction. Calling out to God is completely fruitless if the heart has not changed. Have you ever noticed how little the mind effects the heart, but how profoundly the heart can affect the mind. When the heart changes the mind effortlessly accommodates the change.

"Let's just say that you are in a relationship with a man. He shows a great deal of love and respect for you, which you like, but you have no love for him. Can you convince your mind that you love him? No, it's impossible. I've seen it too many times. On the opposite side of this, you are in a relationship with a man and you genuinely love him. You would be willing to do just about anything for that person. It is amazing what people will do when they have a heart filled with love for someone. Countless books, songs, movies and poems have been celebrating this emotion . . . of true love. Jesus is instantly aware of those whose heart is full of love for Him."

Dawn nodded in agreement with Asher.

Asher continued with the story, "Orifiel and Zenon were unleashed onto Pigos, Ipos and Labal. Great pleasure and time was taken in running them through like wild pigs! What a sight it was.

"As you can see, Faith is a healthy, happy little girl." He moved into Dawn's view staring deep into her eyes, "You and Faith have a more in common than you know."

Without acknowledging Asher's last comment, Dawn said, "When I prayed and was attacked . . . when I couldn't breathe, it was you who knocked the thing from me and took it out of the house?" She asked seeking conformation.

"That thing is one of the most skilled and deceptive in all of the Dark Kingdom. He has had the charge of driving some of the most influential people down a path in service of Abaddon. Dagon is a nasty and relentless spirit. He comes from the order of Principalities. You are sure to recognize his most famous body of work. It is largely responsible for the movement that led to the legalization of the procedures that almost prevented you and Faith from leaving the womb alive."

Dawn blinked and thought for a second, "Both of our lives . . . do you mean—"

"Today wasn't the first time I had to fight over you. There were many battles at the beginning of your existence that were much like the life story I just shared with you. I picked this family, not without reason."

"Well, I understand that I was under attack. Like you said, I didn't realize all of this was really going on," she said.

"You were also marked from the beginning of time and yet you were very near to having no time at all," he said.

The reality of his point was like a dagger into her heart. "Mom tried to abort me."

"She came very close. Dagon used the same convincing argument as he did with Rachel. This is an effective tactic.

"Thankfully God didn't give animals the freewill He gave to people. It was a confused and scared French poodle that saved your life. It was quite an opportunistic situation that worked out perfectly. Your mother was driving down Veterans Boulevard. There was this lost dog aimlessly walking around looking for food. The animal found its way in front of your mother's car and instinctively she swerved to miss it and hit a bench and light pole.

"It was the day before she was to have the procedure. We tried to change her mind. This was the only way. Thankfully her leg was injured and needed surgery."

Dawn sat in stunned silence.

"Using one of our many methods of persuasion, we arranged for a nurse to come in and do an ultrasound on you. It was your tiny beating heart that changed her mind.

"Don't be mad at your mom, Satan had deceived her like he does even to this day. Your mom believed that you were just 'reproductive material' as the demon in the clinic had told her. She didn't see you as a person, but the ultrasound debunked the lie.

"Dawn McIntyre," he started, "as a very special person and of great interest to our Father. Since the beginning of time God has marked men for their purpose and you and Marcus have a calling like no other in the history of this creation. If you both take this charge, you will see and experience things in a way that no other has ever experienced and greatly change the world.

"We are in the seventh day. The end of man is near. All who have lived believed this, but *this* generation will certainly not pass from this earth before the Lord's return. Time is short and it is not the will of the Father that any should parish."

The idea concerned Dawn, but she sat and listened without comment. She turned her eyes from the joyous and innocent display in the grass and toward Asher.

"Satan has manipulated and deceived man for thousands of years. His goal is to take as many of God's creation into the abyss with him because he knows that it pains the Father that anyone should parish."

"Then why does He do it . . . send people to Hell?" She asked.

"God cannot allow sin into Heaven. It is a pure and clean place. What if when you were in the hospital and had to go into the operating room for the procedures necessary to save your life and the room was filthy and unsanitary? What if the scalpel and other surgical implements were not sanitized? You would get infections and have major complications and quite possibly . . . die, or lose your earthly body. Under no circumstances can the purity of Heaven ever be allowed to be compromised again.

"Every kingdom on earth has had an inner circle. Where there is power, there is a covetous desire by another man for that power. The dealer of inequity hardens the hearts of all who will listen, manipulates them into following him and the King suffers persecution from his own subjects through a militarily led rebellion. Let me say that many of these rebellions have been justified, and many have not.

"The King of Kings picked His twelve and then Judas became the betrayer. Despite all he had seen, he opened a door and allowed Satan to enter him. He betrayed the one true King.

"Satan coveted all that God is and wanted that authority. Jealously consumed Lucifer and he wanted to take the kingdom of

God for himself. He built an army and brought war into Heaven. He was cast out and made to be prince of this land. He now takes his revenge on God's creation. He will devour man and destroy this world until his destiny with eternal judgment has come. Make no mistake he will destroy every man that follows him.

"God came himself in the flesh and as a part of this world. Satan attacked Him and tried everything to destroy the foundation that the Lord was installing for man. One of hope and a promise that would lead people to Him if they would only open up their eyes long enough to see and trust in Him.

"Satan has used man to build on this foundation a house of ill repute. The prostitution of the flesh for evil pleasures and pursuits outside of the will of God is a spiritual cancer that has only one cure . . . one resolution, The Christ."

Asher turned his eyes off of Dawn and toward the little girl. Dawn followed his gaze. "During man's time on earth, he has always been subjected to rule . . . to authority." The scroll spun quickly and settled on a new scripture, "'When the righteous rule, the people rejoice. But, when the wicked rule, the people groan.' The deceiver's war on man has become increasingly easier as your governments have fallen into corruption. The God of Self is in the hearts of the people and your leaders. Corruption and wickedness abounds. The end of time has come. The battle for man will greatly intensify in this last day."

With the wave of his hand a new world appeared before Dawn: the world of the supernatural was exposed to her. Columns were as numerous as the trees and disappeared into the sky. Flaming chariots pulled by enormous winged cat-like creatures filled the air and one landed on the ground several feet in front of Dawn. The angelic traveler seemed to be on a mission of great importance and quickly moved out of sight.

Dawn turned to the family. Paul was covered in the smaller demons like the ones that had destroyed her house and choked

Marcus. A new, larger demon stood over Paul and possessed a physical quality. It looked as if it were stuffed with black, grey and red veins to the point of bursting. These innards were in constant movement, circulating through the body as if pulled by a current. The clear epidermis had a smooth silky texture. Its mouth was open like a panting dog revealing no continuous rows of teeth, but snakelike fangs that moved between the top of its mouth down toward a forked tongue with each exaggerated breath. Large black bulging eyes devoid of lids were fixed in an open position.

Its wings flapped in excitement when taking a position behind Paul. The demon viciously jammed its claws into his head causing Dawn to recoil in horror of what she was watching. It jumped, stomped its feet and snapped at the air in a frenzy of excitement as Paul lashed out at Rachel no longer willing to hold back his comments. Rachel put up a defensive response. Several demons were flying overhead in search of mischief and sensed an opportunity. They fell from the sky and hit the ground running, snapping and spitting as they moved toward Rachel despite the presence of Orifiel. Swiftly he stepped around Rachel and punched his sword into the ground freeing his hands. He lunged and grabbed two of the demons by the throats and smashed them together. A petroleum-like substance splattered and vaporized. Orifiel jumped several feet into the air and slammed both demons fist first into the ground hurling them through the earth. He spun and grabbed his sword and raked the fiery blade across the back of a third demon. It turned and fruitlessly charged. Within a fraction of a second, the creature was aimlessly traveling through the earth like its two companions. Orifiel surprised the demon on Paul's back as he unexpectedly spun and removed its head, the tip of the blade barely passing through on the opposing side. The creature fell and was absorbed by the earth.

Paul regained composure and showed regret for what he had said. He apologized, and Rachel hesitantly accepted.

"This is what it is like all around us? This is what you see all the time? How can you stand it?" Dawn asked.

"Since the fall of man," Asher replied.

"Why didn't . . . ," she struggled to recall the angel's name.

"Why didn't Zenon help? He didn't need to. As I said, Orifiel is quite capable."

"Those demons were flying through the air and just fell to the ground and ran for Rachel. What was that about?"

"Sharks can smell a drop of blood in an endless sea and know that there is prey. Demons can sense the smallest of open windows. When a human gives into anger, lust, hate or any destructive behavior the demons can sense it. They will take advantage and will move in and do all they can to influence and push the situation. They will stay until they are forced out.

"When Botis, the one who no longer has a head, sensed an opportunity in Paul, he took it and convinced him to lash out at Rachel. Paul didn't want to be in the park today and only did so because Rachel had demanded that he spend some family time. Paul was increasingly aggravated as he wanted to go and drink with his buddies. Botis set him off. With the unsaved, the demonic hosts don't need much to work with."

"Orifiel is supposed to protect Rachel, then why did he attack . . . ," Dawn lost the new creature's name.

"Botis? God, for His reason, must have given him the authority to take Botis out. Zenon was reaching for his sword and would have done it himself.

"Marcus is coming," Asher announced.

Dawn turned and saw Marcus as he passed the threshold of the front door. He headed into the direction of the park in search for Dawn. From all directions, out of the air and from underground, demons charged Marcus. Dawn wanted to yell out a warning to him as a demonic militia of nearly sixty charged him.

From an unseen location, a large demon who resembled the one in the window of her house earlier that day, had been pre-occupied with the torment of another, ran and jumped into the air flying toward Marcus. With each flap of its wings, electricity shot into the air. The smaller demons fought with each other jockeying for position to get at Marcus. The larger demon bowled over them sending the smaller ones air-born in all directions. Above Marcus, a large and majestic angel patiently followed watching the activity. He didn't seem alarmed by the surge of demons or the large wicked spirit.

"I left the door open after we exited. Marcus returned and began to fear and worry over you as he searched the house. As soon as he was out the door, he realized that you were here on this bench. That very temporary stress was sensed by the servants of darkness. The door was closed when he saw you, but the scent has excited them into a frenzy. Now they desperately seek an opportunity to get at Marcus. He is a prize that they covet and would love to take back to the master.

"Marcus is well protected. The Lord is with him . . . and you. Argos from the order of Powers is watching over Marcus," Asher said.

"The large beast is Palatos. He is the second in command, so to speak, in this region."

Dawn watched the new evil entity as it moved in front of Marcus, backpedaling while he continued walking toward the park, spiting and snorting as if trying to intimidate him despite being invisible. Palatos' eight-foot frame made Marcus look like a child. Huge muscular arms flailed in the air in a fit a rage, as if taunting Marcus. The beast had the forehead of a great bull on which rested a pair of twisted horns nearly four feet in length that the creature raked back forth in the air above Marcus's head.

Enraged, it stepped back and lunged forward, attempting to drive its horns into Marcus's chest. The large demon failed to penetrate and slid off of Marcus's torso, its momentum nearly taking it to the ground. Palatos quickly recovered and jammed its huge canine's inches from Marcus's head screaming in anger as it bent down to inspected the alien human. No mortal had ever busted Palatos in such a manner before, and it wanted to rip him apart.

Palatos stepped back and raised its claws to the sky. From the base of its back where there should have been a spine, a new appendage became free and rolled upward. The giant tail of a scorpion arched over the head of the massive creature and hung several feet in front of its snout.

Dawn began to panic and call out to Marcus. Asher touched her hand and calmed her. "Disease. That is the weapon used by that beast. Palatos gets into the body with that stinger and plants infectious diseases. He is quite vile."

Argos landed and walked next to Marcus with a smile on his face. He was near twelve feet tall and was larger than the demon. He was unfazed by the display of rage.

The smaller demons began to bypass the larger demon in an attempt to get at Marcus despite the performance being put on by Palatos. One by one they crashed into him and bounced off as if met by an unconquerable force field. Each burst into flames at the point of contact. Smoke trails filled the air as each foolish demon squealed in pain and flew aimlessly into all directions in search for relief. Seconds later the screams and trailers had faded into the distance.

Argos decided that he had had enough of Palatos. Simultaneously he drew the fiery sword and thrust the palm of his left hand into Palatos' chest sending it backwards. The membranous wings kept the best upright as Argos' power forced the demon out of balance. The large tail and stinger were now in front of it jabbing in the direction of Argos. It waved back and forth, not willing to give Argos an easy shot at removing the deadly stinger.

In a move that startled Dawn, Argos stood and sheathed his sword. The beast wasted no time and charged the mighty angel. Argos grabbed the appendage and flew into the air, swinging the demon above his head and then driving it into the ground. The recovery was nearly instantaneous, but Argos was far too agile and quick and was in Palatos' face with the sword. He removed the stinging tail at the base. The creature screamed and wanted no more of Argos. The standoff had lasted only a couple of minutes as Marcus, unaware of the fight taking place, moved from the house toward the bench where Dawn was.

"Why can't he see what's going on?" Dawn asked.

"He hasn't received a full release yet."

Desperate to share the event with Marcus, Dawn quickly grabbed his hand and turned him around in time to see the conclusion of the standoff. Palatos conceded and dove headfirst into the earth, disappearing from view. Argos sheathed his weapon and walked toward the bench.

"That thing was attacking you . . . or trying to attack you," Dawn said.

Marcus looked at Argos as he walked up. The angel looked at him and gave a smile and a nod. It was a nearly overwhelming sight for Marcus as he looked from the scene of the fight toward the couple and the little child and scanned the park. Demons, beasts and Angelic beings surrounded them.

His gazed followed a column upward and he looked toward Heaven seeing no end to the massive structure. Instinctively, Marcus reached for it, but his hands passed through unobstructed. Chariots and angels were numerous as they patrolled by air and ground. Creatures of various likenesses fought each other, attacking humans and fighting with angels. After several incredible minutes, Dawn released his hand and the world returned to its normal state.

Marcus turned for the bench, needing to sit down and take in what he had just witnessed. The vision from earlier in the day paled in comparison to this one. The experience, while brief, was full of unimaginable beauty and unspeakable horror. Dawn saw Argos place his left hand on Marcus's shoulder and talk into his ear. A peace came and he recovered his spirit and once again looked up. For the first time, he noticed the man sharing the seat.

Marcus recovered his breath and said, "Oh, hello Asher." He was not sure why Asher was there and what part he had in all of this, but if he wasn't aware of the supernatural world Marcus had just seen, than Asher would consider him and Dawn to be slightly on the loony side. Marcus really hoped that he had not been a coincidental bystander watching him attempt to grab an invisible column or look upon an unseen world.

"So, you two know each other?" Dawn inquired, surprised.

"Yes. Mr. Asher has been a real saint. He has volunteered and really helped me get the Revelation Center off and running. Whenever there was a problem with the Parish Council, building code issues or the fire marshal, he was there. He is a real godsend."

Dawn realized that Marcus had no idea that Asher was an angel and not a human. She was left searching for options about how to handle the situation. Could she just introduce him as her guardian angel?

Asher stood and moved in front of the two. He quickly grew in stature returning to his full height. Four large white wings reemerged and stretched out spanning eighteen feet from tip to tip. Instead of the linen garment he originally wore, armor covered his body. The chest and abdominal armor were comprised of hundreds of one and a half inch strips of metal fastened together horizontally. Each piece moved independently offering support and comfort. Bronze plates covered his shins and forearms embossed with Hebrew text bordered by moving electrical currents.

Three new angels appeared at his side in matching armament. Each was slightly smaller than Asher, but looked prepared to fulfill their duties. "This is Tios," Asher said, motioning toward a red-haired angel. "This is Idio." A blond haired angel nodded. "And this is Goad."

An angel with long brown hair made a fist with his left hand, covering it with the right. Goad pushed them into the air in front of his chest, stepped forward and nodded in an agreement of service and stepped back into line. Asher looked at Marcus and Dawn. "You both have a challenging mission before you." He looked at Marcus and opened the widow into the heavenly realm, "You have been a faithful servant of God, stay faithful and He will give you peace. Dawn will explain all that we have discussed . . . ," he looked back at Dawn, ". . . and this will be a difficult, but critically important task. The time of man will soon pass. Reach them . . . the lost. So many are in darkness . . . you must reach them.

"Because this is a most unusual commission, special provisions will be granted to you both. Dawn, for you Tios, Idio and Goad will watch you. For you Marcus, Argos will be with you as he has since the day you entered the body of Christ. You will not always see them, but they will be with you." He sensed Dawn's random thought. "No, not in the bathroom, dear one. You will bathe in peace. You will have privacy in your home.

"Now I must go. This war will take a new turn and there is much to be done," he said, then launched straight into the air like a missile, disappearing in a flash.

Chapter 13

Rustling dishes prematurely summoned Dawn back to the conscious world disrupting what was a peaceful rest. The long and event filled day had physically taken its toll. Her body was stiff and achy from head to toe. Dawn groaned lightly as she rolled over to her right side, contemplating whether or not she wanted to risk leaving the comfort and security offered by the bed, for whatever might be waiting for her beyond the bedroom door.

A thud made from the placement of a drinking glass on the dining room table reminded her that Marcus was still there. There was a second noise of something sliding. *What's he doing?*, she wondered.

She considered where she would be if Marcus had not shown up, or caught her at the door? Would the snaked tongued thing, she paused to recall its name, Dagon, have chased her through the park? How would it have appeared to all of the park visitors to watch her run franticly screaming about something no one else would have been able to see? What about the other demons? How would she have handled that? What a blessing—she thought for a second, yes—*blessing* it was that he was there. It was without a doubt, orchestrated by God. His mercy was unfathomable.

On top of a white bamboo trimmed night stand the green display on a digital clock read 9:35. She couldn't recall falling asleep. They returned from the park and were talking while sitting on the couch and she assumed that she had fallen asleep and Marcus put her in the bed. She panicked briefly and pulled up the cover to inspect her body. *Same clothes*, she thought and gave a sigh of relief. *Surly he wouldn't have changed my clothes*, she realized.

She tried to recall their conversation as they had attempted to make sense of and fully understand all that had happened. Dawn assumed that she had fallen asleep as a result of exhaustion. She struggled to recall the final minutes before she had fallen asleep.

In the back of his mind, Marcus wondered if Dawn would come out of the bedroom the same person she used to be. Would she be offended or uncomfortable with his being there? She was nearly out of it when he had put her in the bed and she asked him to stay for a while. *What if she doesn't remember asking me to stay and wakes up as her old self again and becomes angry? What if she thinks that I did more than just put her in the bed and cover her up? What if?* he thought.

He pondered the possibilities of what would transpire had her mom or Sonny came over while he was there and Dawn was sleeping. They would undoubtedly be rude and vulgar despite the appropriate manner in which he had always conducted himself. They would certainly continue their accusatory ways and ruthlessly seek an opportunity to cause some sort of injury to him.

He realized how silly he was being and decided to ignore his concerns and do what was right. Helping her was his priority. On the way out of the room broken glass from the picture and random debris crunched under his feet. He decided that a necessary labor had to be performed on the house as disarray lurked in nearly every corner. If she were to exit the room half awake, there was the possibility she could suffer a significant injury.

Marcus braved the world outside and drove home to gather several large garbage cans, boxes, a broom, a large shovel and digital camera. For insurance purposes he thought it proper to take detailed photos of the entire house. What kind of story would she give to the insurance company, he was uncertain. She would certainly be met with raised eyebrows and an excuse that it didn't necessarily fall under the 'Act of God' clause in her policy. He decided that if need be, he would pay for the repairs and would clean up the mess after the photos were taken.

The most obvious place in need of attention was the hall near the master bedroom. He quietly picked up the frames and large shards before sweeping the smaller pieces and other trash toward the kitchen into a pile at the end of the hall. He used the snow shovel to pick up piles of the china, crystal glasses, dishes, and regular serving glasses which were separated and placed in boxes for sorting and identification. A smaller box was filled with the damaged silver and stacked to the side with the other boxes. After an hour and a half, the hall, kitchen and walls of the living room were free of debris.

Unlike most homes with garages, Dawn had not converted hers into to mini storage and junked up all areas that surrounded the parking space. He moved the boxes and teak coffee table against the far wall on what appeared to be the least used side.

During her state of panic, Dawn had pulled the foyer table over and damaged the wall, leaving an arching white and walnut colored gouge. Marcus stood the table up cleaned up the sheetrock dust and removed the damaged crystal and pottery. Without a secondary vase or any idea of what to do with the lilies, he filled up one side of the kitchen sink as temporary housing until a replacement could be found or purchased. The broken holders and vase fragments were put into a small white plastic grocery bag and placed in a box in the garage.

After the first step of ridding the house of disorder, Marcus thought that it would be a nice gesture of friendship and took the liberty of ordering Dawn some takeout food. A quick scan of the phone book revealed a list of orders that had been written by what he surmised were her favorite takeout restaurants. Wonton Soup, egg rolls and fried rice had been ordered from Lao Tien Chinese Restaurant. Chicken alfredo from a place Down Town called Nickie's, and a shrimp Caesar salad from Bucky's Steak House.

Then he entered a new quandary: which would she be in the mood for? How can he possibly be certain to get the right one? The only possible solution was to order each. Marcus was eternally thankful for delivery. Since all of the plates and glasses were in thousands of unusable pieces, he purchased two sets from the souvenir shop at Bucky's.

He prepared a place for one at the table as he did not want to invite himself or make anything seem improper. He washed and placed the second setting in the empty cabinets for Dawn to use later. This was all about helping her as any good Christian should feel blessed to do. Marcus arranged the food by restaurant giving slight attention to presentation. He left the containers unopened hoping they retain the heat until the time she woke, which for all he knew could possibly take place the following morning.

He wanted to help her with all that was ahead, but feared the hate she once harbored for him would rear itself once again and prove to be more than she could overcome. The reality of her salvation had stirred him at times, but he understood the conundrum and the persuasiveness of the deceptive forces who were experienced, motivated and in numbers that couldn't be counted. Every man who had walked the earth with the exception of Jesus, who was the only one to not give in, had been manipulated in some measure. The unseen dark kingdom was powerful and mightily effective and had been throughout man's existence.

The possibility that she would enter the dining area, snub the food and order him to leave was a reality. What condition would she be in mentally after she had a nap and time to reflect?

What if she had opened some door and allowed herself to be, not possessed, but once again oppressed? He prayed against that possibility.

While the food sat and Dawn had yet to emerge from her room, Marcus set up a laptop and portable printer at the end of the table. He placed a binder with documents that would help her adjust as a new Christian and deal with spiritual warfare. He put a ream of paper and a hole-puncher to the side for Dawn to use if she found something she needed to copy for referencing.

Spiritual warfare was real and Marcus had always understood that to be the case. Different denominational beliefs either embraced or ignored the truth, but it was undeniable. God was a spirit, Lucifer was a spirit and the angels were spirits. It seemed pretty simple to understand that an unseen world was out there.

What an opportunity for a ministry, he thought. The potential gave him chills. Visions of what he had seen in the park played out in his mind . . . the spirits interacting with people who just had no clue. If he was to show someone a demonic attacker, what would the reaction be? Certainly some may run the risk of having a heart attack, so there was a need to exercise caution. But what would be the average response? It couldn't be denial. Many would still reject Christ, but would not be able to deny the existence of the heavenly realm. Millions would be reached and converted as the truth would certainly set them free. Testimonies would receive international attention and there could be a situation where he and Dawn will be overwhelmed by the attention.

How anyone could look upon the world and not see the manifestation of evil and clearly identify it was beyond his comprehension. Certainly man's perception and definitions in regard to what evil was had certainly evolved over the course of man's existence. Behaviors that were mere decades removed from being illegal and immoral were now common practice and protected by federally appointed judges. Violent crime and drug use overwhelmed police departments, suicides destroyed teenagers like at no other point in history, broken homes increased as divorce was now as common as marriage, corporate corruption worked to destroy the financial structures of nations and ever-expanding governments tax businesses and citizens to financial ruin.

Marcus stood with a broom in his hand and the large shovel on the floor ready to pick up another pile of Dawn's broken property. He was lost in his thoughts and was excited about making a difference. Although he had missed most of the conversation with Asher, Marcus had a Holy Spirit-led understanding of what had to be done.

A noise in the hall broke his train of thought and he turned his blank gaze from the empty shovel and broom to the disturbance. For Marcus, it was a moment of truth as Dawn emerged. She had put on jeans and a long sleeved shirt and pulled her hair back into the familiar long, straight, blond ponytail. To his relief, she gave him a quick smile and began to notice and praise all of the work he had done while she slept.

"Wow! You have done a lot of work. I feel bad that you did all of this by yourself. It isn't even your house. Why . . . why did you do this? Thanks so much." She walked over and gave him a kiss on the cheek.

Marcus smiled and nodded and asked, "So, are you feeling better? Did you have a peaceful rest?"

"Yes. I feel much better. I really needed some sleep. The only problem is that I probably won't be able to sleep tonight," she said.

"Are you hungry? Your phone book gave me some ideas about what you like to eat." Marcus said as pointed to the dining room table.

She was speechless. He had gone through a significant amount of trouble and some expense to insure a good meal for her and the sentiment touched her deeply.

On the table was a single yellow octagon plate with a white napkin in the center, matching saucer, fork, knife and wine glass that awaited her arrival. Two large and small containers had been placed in a line with a small white paper bag in the center. "Am I to dine alone? Have you already eaten?" she asked.

"No. This is your house. You have been through a lot and I am sure that you need a good meal. I just hope that you can eat something."

Dawn was touched by his humility. She rose and entered the dining room while he continued to fill the garbage can with the remnants of the refrigerated projectiles.

She peeled back the plastic lids and removed the foil seals from the temporary containers. Dawn held out hope that at least one setting of some kind had remained in the cabinet. She pulled open the doors and found the extra set that he had purchased.

It was the horse logo on the plate that gave him away. "Did you buy these from Bucky's?"

"I had to. There really wasn't much time for shopping and it was convenient."

"Expensive," she said and looked back at the plate on the table and the napkin. "I guess you don't like the horse logo. I see you've covered it up."

"Kind of silly I know. But, I just couldn't stand to look at it."

She placed the matching set for him next to hers. She asked him to wash his hands and then demanded that he sit and make a selection. Dawn moved the chicken alfredo from the container to his plate and then served herself the caser salad and an egg roll.

She moved to the chair next to him and cupped his hand and looked into his eyes, "In the very short time . . . well, today actually, I realized how wrong I have been about a lot of things God and Christ and the entire spiritual world and eternal life . . . all of it. But, I was equally wrong about you. You were treated unfairly and despite all of the nasty things I have said and the threats and public insults, you never got angry. You never stopped trying to help me. From my heart . . ." she noticed the swelling in his nose from the wild and desperate punch and asked, "Does it hurt?"

"No, it is going to be alright," he said jokingly. "I think I know where you are going and—,"

She cut him off, "No, I need to say this. I am truly sorry for the way I treated you. You deserve better than that. I was so stupid and blind to so many things. The way you were treated, I can't even fathom why you are still here, spent this money and did all of this. You should hate me. I don't deserve your friendship."

He interrupted, "Dawn, first of all, I couldn't give up on you no matter what. God wouldn't let me. I am not a perfect person and am no better than you at any point."

"Nothing changes the fact that I was wrong," she said.

"It is fine. I wouldn't have any part of anything that has happened any other way. Can we forget all of that and move forward?" he asked, sliding a new Bible over to her. "I hope you don't mind, but I couldn't find the other one and picked this up."

"You really are a saint. You cleaned up my house and bought me dinner and a Bible. Are you hiding anything else?"

"No, but you don't have to thank me." Marcus said.

"Obviously I have a lot to learn. I want to apologize in advance for any mistakes I may make," she said.

"Well, the first thing you are going to have to learn is that we all make mistakes and none of us are perfect, or even meant to be perfect. We will never be perfect until the day we are in Heaven. We should strive to be like Him. Please don't feel any extra burden to think that you need to be without flaw and spotless every second of every day. We need to watch or tongue and control ourselves, certainly. But we will never, at any point, live mistake-free. Just accept that now."

Marcus prayed over dinner and they began to eat when his portable printer clicked and searched the barren tray for new blank sheets. Marcus left the table, refilled the tray and returned with several papers in his hand, setting them on the table.

Dawn looked at Marcus and asked, "What is your real story? How did God reach you?"

"Well, which version do you want, the long or short?"

"I will listen to whatever you feel like you want to share. You know all about my conversion," she said with a smile.

"Well, I grew up in a Christian home and we went to church almost every Sunday. But, like most teenagers, I kind of wanted to experience life for myself and it really didn't include God for a while. I am ashamed of that. If I would have died, I would have deserved to have been denied entry in to Heaven.

"I spent all of my time either playing music or beach volleyball—"

"You liked beach volleyball. I figured you more for a basketball player," she said, poking fun at his six-foot three-inch frame.

"Height is good for volleyball too. I loved it. We would play for eight to ten hours a day sometimes. Anyway, we were playing a charity tournament in Biloxi and lost in the quarter finals. These were just amateur tournaments that we would play for fun. Since we had an early exit, I went to the beach just to hang out and relax and I kind of met someone."

"Someone special?" she asked.

"Very. Her name was Allison LeBlanc and she was with a church group who decided that the beach would be a very interesting ministry field. They were walking up and down passing out tracks and witnessing to people. I really don't know how they did it in the heat with regular clothes on.

"She said my name and I didn't know who she was. It kind of fed my ego, I thought she saw me in the tournament and was impressed or something stupid like that. After talking with her, I realized that she knew nothing about the tournament and I was really confused as to how she knew my name. She witnessed to me and we sat and talked about God for a while. When the sun set and I decided that I wasn't quite ready to repent. I was just interested in her. Her ability to communicate and to witness was really powerful. But my pride was a major obstacle that had to be dealt with.

"The following Sunday, I saw her at my church. I lived with my parents and they made me go. I had no choice. Apparently she attended the same church, which, at that time, had about four thousand members. I had never seen her, but apparently my mom had been asking the youth group to pray for me. God had burdened her heart for my salvation. Funny thing is that she ended up on the same stretch of beach in Biloxi that I was on. God brought her right to me an hour or so away from the church. Go figure that one out."

"Kind of like He burdened your heart for my salvation?" she asked.

"I guess it was the same. She tried again after church service, but I figured that if I had accepted, this beautiful young woman may not be interested in talking to me anymore, so I declined again. I think this infuriated her. I saw her the next weekend and she tried again, only she looked a little different than the week before and again I declined. Later I learned that she had fasted all week. That is why she looked so tired. She had sacrificed all week for me. I ran out to her car in the parking lot and she was praying and tears ran down her cheeks. She was praying for me . . . for me!" He intently focused on the round plastic bottle of green tea from which had had been drinking. "I felt horrible. I confessed to her what I had been up to and realized by her sacrifice that God really wanted me. Anyway, I accepted and the rest is history," he said, wanting to end the conversation about Allison.

Dawn didn't pick up Marcus's emotion and pressed, "Well, what happened to her? She sounds like a great girl."

Marcus paused and continued, "Well, I went to Beck and she went to LSU, but we remained committed to each other. Four years later, I was twenty-two, *An Island Love Song* went up the charts and my music career took off. Now that I had a significant income and what I thought was a road map of the future, I proposed to her. We were walking the beach while the sun was setting when I finally got up the nerve and fell to one knee. At first she thought I was just goofing off . . . then I pulled out the ring."

Dawn couldn't explain her emotion, but a sense of jealousy came over her as he passionately talked about Allison. She fought to repress the renegade thoughts as she couldn't possibly have these feelings for him. They had only just become friends and she realized that she was coveting the love he expressed for Allison through the passion in the tone of his words.

"We purchased this house that we were gonna live in after our wedding and had a lot of fun decorating it and all that stuff. We had actually moved a lot of our stuff into it. We were at her parent's house and it was about ten on a Friday night. The wedding was about a week away and we all had this spontaneous agreement to go for a nighttime walk on the beach. We drove over to the house to get some light jackets and whatever else. I ran to the bathroom while Alison ran to a closet in one of the bedrooms to get the jackets. I remember this horrible scream. I ran to find out what had happened to her and the guy was still over her. It was dark and I didn't know exactly what had happened, but I knew that he had hurt her. I dove at the guy. I beat him furiously until he stopped moving.

"I was exhausted and ran over to Allison and there was blood everywhere. This guy was a drug addict who had been watching our house and knew that we usually didn't go there at night, so he jimmied the back lock decided to spend the night there. Allison walked in on him and she was stabbed."

"I am so sorry," Dawn said, cupping his hands and looking sorrowfully into his eyes.

"She died. In my arms . . . a week from our wedding . . . she died," Marcus's eyes were tearing up. "I bulldozed the house and made a park out of it . . . was about five acres. The city takes care of it now. It will always be a memorial to her." He picked up his fork and continued to eat.

"Is that why you disappeared for a while?"

"Yeah. I was angry at God, at myself, at life. I began to hate everything. I was angry. There were a lot of times when I just sat in a room and beat myself up. I can't explain it, but that night I had a really bad feeling about going back to that house. We could have just borrowed a couple of jackets, but it was the adventure of going to OUR home . . . kind of silly. Something was warning me and I just ignored it. Stupidly, I shrugged it off. I should have known better than to go there at night.

"There was no way that I could write music or tour or anything. Everything . . . food or life, it all lost its flavor. After a while I just couldn't take it anymore and bought a one way ticket to the island of St. John and stayed there for a while. Some people get drunk or do other things to deal with their misery. I thought that getting away would help."

"That was about nine years ago? This may be a stupid question, how did you get right with God?" she asked.

"I thought I was on a secluded beach on the island and I began yelling at God. I was really venting my anger, my hurt. I wasn't holding anything back. I let God have it. I saw this catamaran coast into the little cove where I was at. Apparently this guy had been anchored on the point beyond my line of vision and was listening to my rant. His wife guided the craft to my exact position and nosed up onto the beach. I refused to leave my spot.

I felt violated by the intruders and was going to stand my ground and keep them from the beach. I was mad. The vessel continued to nose directly towards me with this tattoo-covered man in sunglasses standing on the bow with a rope in his hand, just watching me watching him. He threw the rope at me and told me, not asked, but told me, to pull them in. I almost pushed the boat away from the shore. I wasn't going to let them dock. I just backed up and let the rope fall into the water. There was no way that I was going to help them."

"Boy, a feisty side of you," she said in surprise.

"Well, you know . . . I am in this private cove. There hasn't been a boat for days, at least none that sailed into the cove. Then this ugly tattooed biker rides up on a catamaran and invades my territory. Yes, I was mad. I almost threw a coconut at him.

This big guy in his late fifties jumps off of the boat with this small aluminum beach chair and plops himself down in the surf and just sits and looks to the horizon. For ten minutes he just sits there and I am wondering what is this guy doing and why he has invaded my beach?

"Without taking his eyes off of the horizon, he says in a voice that reminded me of the actor Sam Elliot, 'The thoughts of the wicked are an abomination to the Lord, but, the words of the pure are pleasant. What have you created lately?' I said that I had created nothing. He replies, 'Exactly right! God is the creator of all things. He gives and He takes away. None of us can understand why, but we must trust. Son, when are you going to stop blaming God? He loves you and doesn't want you to hurt anymore. Your real problem is that you need to forgive this man who took Allison's life if you are to ever have peace. You need to forgive yourself and face your hate for him and stop turning it toward God.'

"I asked him what business it was of his and asked if God had sent him here to tell me this. He admitted that he had been listening to my yelling for about a half an hour and God stirred his heart. He said, 'The world is an evil place. If you can't take it then perhaps you should get out of it. If that is what you decide, I have a gun in the boat . . . you're welcome to it. If not, stop your whining and move on with life.'

"I became so mad that I wanted to punch him. Instead, I asked him how he knew what I was going through.

"'Julian, my beautiful wife and I lost a daughter at the tender age of six. We lived in Colorado and it was winter. The roads had ice on them, but I had driven in ice and didn't really concern myself with it. I was a big, tough, bad man. Ready to fight for any reason and often went out looking for trouble. I didn't need to listen to Julian's demands for caution. What was a little ice going to do to me?

"'I was doing about sixty when I attempted to make a sharp turn when it happened. We slid into the guardrail and into the side of the mountain. Neither of us noticed that Mandy had not put on her seat belt. She was ejected from the car and didn't make it. A little ice did more than hurt me . . . .

"'The guilt I felt was unbearable. I tried to run by joining the military and volunteering for the most dangerous jobs, hoping someone would kill me. Four times I thought the job was done, but I always recovered. When that didn't work, I tried suicide seven times and never died. Finally God reached me and helped me to forgive myself. Julian forgave me for not listening and did her best to grieve while trying to protect me from myself.'

"He turned and looked at me for the first time and took off his glasses, then continued, 'Things happen that we cannot understand. He gives and He takes away according to His will. Allison is not hurting anymore and is where she had longed to be . . . in the arms of her Savior. She, despite what most people foolishly believe, is not in Heaven watching you drown in your self-pity. YOU are the only one enjoying the show. Son . . . who in this world will ever get out without dying? Are you Elijah? Did Jesus die? Sure, He was resurrected. We will all die at some point and only He knows why Allison was brought home. The question is, what are you going to do?'

"He said, 'Satan's got you right where he wants you. Right now you're weak and he can control your mind. But, when you win . . . and you will . . . you will be much stronger and closer to God. It is an *amazing* experience. However, you will continue to lose this battle if you insist on blaming God. Call upon Him, let go of your anger. Stop blaming yourself and forgive the man who did this to her.

"'Would Allison have been better off to have never lived? Would you have been better off never to have known or loved her? Be grateful for the six years you loved each other. Be grateful for the twenty-two years she lived and did God's work in this wretched place. She led many to Christ . . . including you. But, be most grateful for the fact that she is in Heaven right now. She can never suffer again.' Those things . . . I didn't tell him. I never talked about her age and how long we were together or even that she had witnessed to me. He just knew.

"His wife . . . Julian, jumped off of the boat and served us fried redfish sandwiches and we talked a great while longer. That experience really set me on the course for forgiveness. I realized what I needed to do. I flew home and went to see Henry Boone—"

"Henry Boone?" she asked.

"The man who murdered Alison. I began to visit him about once a month and eventually was able to forgive and witness to him. He is involved in a prison ministry now."

Dawn wiped the tears from her face and said, "I am glad that she was able to witness to you . . . obviously. And I am glad that you were here for me. I am truly sorry for what you've been through," she said, her voice breaking. She wanted badly to confess something to Marcus but pulled away.

"Mr. Boone and I have had many conversations and it was through the bizarre things he told me that opened my eyes to spiritual warfare. Not as something metaphoric, but real. I was able to get a real picture of how the deceiver had manipulated and controlled his life. He never made the claim that 'the Devil made me do it.' But he realized afterward how he had lost the spiritual battle. Heck, just about the entire world, including this country, is losing that battle. Unfortunately, Satan is not stupid. Maybe reckless and out of control, but not stupid. He is very cunning, extremely intelligent and sometimes successful even with people who believe that he is real and know that he wants to deceive them. He absolutely controlled me during that time of my life."

Dawn reached over, put her arms around him and kissed his cheek, "She was very blessed to have known you. I am truly sorry."

Marcus touched her hand and thanked her then turned to the documents on the table. There was no title on the page, but, after a brief scan, Dawn realized the contents pertained to the organization and structure of the spiritual world.

"I remember Asher, when talking about a couple of the demons or angels and said something about being from the 'order of.' Is this what he meant?" she asked, looking at the paper.

Without looking, he nodded in agreement and said, "It seems like the traditional belief is that the order of angles is: the Seraphim, Cherubim, Thrones, Dominions, Virtues, Powers, Principalities, Archangels and Angels. Each order has a specific purpose or role in the Kingdom. Now, Billy Graham has a different order, which I agree with and I am no expert. It just makes more sense to me." He picked up a sheet that had been placed on top of the quickly filling binder, "He believes that the order goes: Archangels,

Angels, Seraphim, Cherubim, Principalities, Authorities, Powers, Thrones, Might and Dominion.

"Now, Archangels . . . some believed that Lucifer came from this order and others believe that he came from the Cherubim order. For several reasons I can't see him as a Cherubim. It may be simple or silly, but I can't help but think of the Ark of the Covenant. It was the most sacred item ever made by man, on which God himself rode and guided the Hebrews. We know this is a holy chest . . . the most holy. Why would God insist upon having two Cherubim on the cover with their wings touching and watching—protecting the Ark when it was a Cherubim who had betrayed him and wreaked havoc on the world of man? It just doesn't make sense to me. Plus we are told that he was second in the kingdom, the first behind God and not the second order in line, depending on which order you believe. Most believe that he was an Archangel along with Michael and Gabriel who seem to me to have direct access to God and take orders directly from Him."

Dawn grabbed a second paper from the large half circle of printed items on the table that arched around Dawn and her chair. "Well, it says here that there are seven of them: Michael, Gabriel, Chamuel, Jophiel, Raphael, Uriel, and Zadkiel. That would have made eight with Lucifer. This goes on to talk about the numbers and how important they are to God. Seven is perfection and eight means a new beginning. Do you think, if this paper is right, that if he did fall that there were originally eight of them or that another angel took his spot?"

"I am not sure how anyone can really be certain of anything that is outside of what we know from the Bible. So, I am not sure what to think.

"Speaking of numbers, think about this . . . the Bible says that when Lucifer was cast out of Heaven that one third of the angels, represented by the stars in the sky, were cast out with him. Some astrologers believe that there are eleven trillion stars for each person on earth . . . eleven trillion. That is an amazing number and is hard to fathom," Marcus said.

"Where is the greatest need? In other words, where are they most successful, do you think? It is obvious that we need to fight him. How? In what area and in what way do we fight him?" Dawn asked.

"First, that is something you—"

"Why just me? Aren't we in this together?" she asked fearfully.

"For as long as you want me, I am with you one-hundred percent. There is no shortage of people who can benefit from this ministry. If I must confess, there are two specific burdens that I have. But, God is going to call the shots. I think He will let us know what to do."

"Well, I know that I am new at this, but I see an entire city in need of help. It is hard not to see evil at work here. It is a great place with some great qualities and all of that, but there is a lot really bad stuff going on. Corruption, perversion, lust and greed are at the heart of all of these problems."

"As far as ministering goes, besides the message of salvation, my heart . . ." Marcus touched his right hand to his chest, "and I can't speak for where God will lead you . . . is for the children. They are easy targets and he seems to be having tremendous success and doing irreversible damage in the lives of children. Look at the adults and how they are acting and you can see the evidence of a misled, misguided upbringing.

"Abortion, hunger, poverty, malnutrition, abuse, deformities, educational needs and orphaned children . . . there are so many areas of need. I don't want to use a cliché, but they are the future. Whatever future is left before the Lord comes back. I see such a battlefield when it comes to the children. I know that none of us can save the world, but they are defenseless and that is why he can have his way with them," Marcus said.

"But, I thought they were innocent and protected," Dawn replied and remembered Asher and his explanation.

"They are, to an extent. Children are two for one with Satan. Get to the parent and you automatically injure and influence the child." Marcus said.

"Asher taught me about that today before you showed up."

Dawn flashed back to her childhood and Amy came to mind. What fun they had until the day everything changed.

CHAPTER 14

"Were you really going to throw a coconut at that guy?" Dawn asked laughingly.

Marcus looked at her for a moment without saying anything. Then he replied, "That is the first time I have had the chance to see you smile. It looks really good on you."

"No sarcasm?" she asked.

Marcus looked like a speechless little boy and nodded his head.

She smiled again. "That is the nicest thing you have said to me."

"I'm not really sure. I looked around, but couldn't find one." He continued to answer her, trying to get out of the increasingly awkward moment.

"What?" she asked.

"The coconut. I couldn't find one. Yes, I would have nailed him with it."

"Oh. OK," she said recovering from the distraction. "Sounds like you can have a fiery temper yourself."

Her smile faded and she became serous again, "I have to confess something. You have come clean about Allison and I have a burden I need to share."

Marcus looked up and focused on her. "OK."

"I keep thinking back to what Asher said about my mom that she almost aborted me and how little Faith was almost aborted. That is just hard to deal with. Before today I was pro-abortion. I really was. Since Asher told me those things and how these demons are manipulating the parents to hurt . . . kill the unborn, I am really sad for them. Abortion seemed fine until I saw the other side of it. I mean . . . my mom was going to kill me. Kill *me*! Maybe she loves me now, but I can't help but think of all those kids who will never get a chance to be loved by anyone."

"Look, you have the right to feel this way. You can be angry," he said.

"How is it OK to be angry?"

"There is such a thing as righteous anger. Jesus got angry and cleared the temple, was he not justified? He chastised them, turned tables over and chased them out."

"Well—"

The garage door opener jumped into motion and the sound of the lifting door startled them both. Dawn moved quickly from the dining room table, through several areas of trash and into the kitchen. She looked through the window over the kitchen sink and gasped.

Marcus followed her to the window and looked at the sky-blue Mercedes pulling into the driveway.

"Your mom?" he asked.

"How did you guess?"

"Five second ago you were talking about how angry you were at her and now, here she is. That's how it works. Never fails." He paused and said, "Well, let's go out and greet her."

Dawn nearly laughed at his suggestion, "OK, well . . . she hates you. Like *really* hates you."

"What did I do? Why?"

"The same reason I did. That's who I learned from. She will shoot you if she gets a gun. Really . . . she wants you dead." Dawn said.

"I didn't realize I was such a controversial person. What did I do to her?" Marcus asked.

They both watched as Keri McIntyre was sitting behind the wheel and staring beyond the now open door. A dumbfounded expression consumed her face while staring into the garage at something Dawn couldn't see.

"What is she looking at?" Dawn asked.

"I put the broken table and boxes of the broken china and glasses against the far wall to keep them separated and get them out of the house. I guess she can't get in." Marcus said.

"What is she going to say when she sees you?"

"Hates me?" he asked, unable to get over what Dawn had just told him.

"Sorry. Most of that is my fault. She listens to the show and rants every time you call in," Dawn said.

Two demons hovered over the car and fell back remaining in the street as the car entered the property. One resembled Dagon, the snaked tongued demon that had chased Dawn out of the house. A missing ear distinguished the beast from its near twin. The other demon was larger. Its face was highlighted by a large wolf like snout and solid black eyes. Dark, black, coarse hair covered its body.

In unison the two yelled into the direction of the house and Dawn assumed that they were receiving the notice that their rights of passage no longer existed to which there was protest. They moved forward with unsheathed swords, taunting and daring Tios, Idio and Goad to advance on their position. Hissing and high pitched shrieking filled the air and rang through their ears.

Like a bolt of lightning, Goad was on the ground at the property line, pushing the two stubborn demons back. They swatted the ground and made a fuss, but didn't push Goad.

This was an unexpected visit and Dawn didn't have sufficient time to contemplate the introduction of Mother McIntyre to her now Christian daughter. To explain this would be difficult and would initially be met with denial and rejection. She would demand separation from Marcus and some sort of unorthodox spiritual rehab to chase God out of Dawn.

There would certainly be an attack against Marcus and it would be brutal. All of the blame, like two teenage kids that had been caught doing something forbidden like drugs or fornication, would fall on Marcus.

Dawn wondered if she was ready to have such a conversation with anyone, especially her. Her confidence quickly began to wane. How could she explain the supernatural world she had been introduced to? Certainly she could grab her and let her see the demons, but they would not be accompanying her into the house. Keri could look at Dawn and Marcus in their golden glow and cheesy grins. That lacked power and authority. They could look out of the window and into the park, but it was quickly getting dark.

Agitation and profanities were certain to abound. Any explanation Dawn offered would be instantaneously rejected regardless of any help offered by Marcus. Keri McIntyre hated him worse than Dawn had and would often call after the two had butted heads over theology during the show. She vented her hatred and brutally attacked his character as a human.

She climbed out of the driver's side and continued to look into the garage. She moved out of the way and shut the door while moving to the house. She stomped over to the boxes that were obstructing her parking spot to observe the contents.

A scream rang out. "THE CHINA! What happened to the china? The crystal is broken too!" she panicked and ran toward the door, then paused and ran back to the car. She reached into the seat and pulled out her purse and dug for the cell phone.

"She must have brought me dinner," Dawn said, and looked toward the dining room where two settings remained. "She is going to freak out."

"Yes, we covered that," he replied.

"Just making sure you are ready."

Dawn closed her eyes and prayed from her heart. She asked for guidance and the best possible result and that at minimum, seeds would be planted. She opened her eyes and wondered where the seed portion of the prayer had come from as she had not been familiar with the terminology. She decided to ask Marcus about it later.

Keri pushed the rear door of the Mercedes closed with her foot and the two demons attentively moved into position at her side as if they were two members of Satan's secret service and were protecting an ambassador negotiating the terms of war. Tios flew down and landed in front of the wolf-faced demon while Goad took position in front of the one eared deception dealer. Idio positioned himself in the middle and raised his hand ordering the demons to cease and challenged them to make any advance on the house. The three angels towered over the demons, but they were undaunted, determined to have their way.

Keri moved toward the garage for the second time. Tios was the first to move and traded a few blows of his swords before doing a spin move and grabbing a fist full of its garment and overpowering it to the ground where the two disappeared below the concrete driveway. Goad was only a split second behind Tios and flew into the chest of the second demon, sending it flying into the park. Several other demons saw Goad pounding their comrade and came to its defense. Within seconds, nine demons jumped on Goad. Idio darted in and gave assistance. The angelic warriors fought nine demons and seemed to have their hands full. Goad popped out of the ground and tossed fists full of the demon's black hair onto the ground. He quickly joined in the fight and evened out the odds. It was now of ratio of one to three and the angels refused to back down. Argos left Marcus and joined swords with his brothers.

Tios sliced the arm of one the demons and its sword hit the ground. The unclean spirit screamed and Tios kicked it in the face and sent it flying end over end. With a jumping thrust kick, he knocked the second demon off of his feet allowing Argos to make quick work of him.

The diminishing favor in regard to the odds began to worry the demons. One by one they fled into the protection of the darkness. The angels decided against giving chase and returned to the property.

The door from the garage swung violently open as if kicked in by a federal agent. Dawn and Marcus turned to greet Keri in dreaded anticipation of her reaction. Idio ascended from the foundation and stood in the room with them. Dawn moved away from Marcus to greet Keri.

"Dawn . . . Dawn," the voice called out while entering the house. "Why is the china broken? Why are all of your glasses broken? Your dishes? Why is the coffee table broken and in the garage? What happened?" She turned from Dawn and noticed the rest of the house. She gasped in horror and was speechless.

She looked at Marcus and asked Dawn while animatedly pointing, "Is this . . . is that who I think it is?"

"Yes ma'am, Marcus Dillon," he said, smiling and nodding at her.

She stared coldly at him. Anger resonated on her face as she assessed the situation, quick to assume some felony had been perpetrated against Dawn by Marcus. "You! You are responsible for all of this. What are you doing to my daughter?" She looked at Dawn, "Has he hurt you? Is he keeping you against your will?" She reached for her cell phone and considered punching in 911 and confronting Marcus as they waited for the authorities to arrive.

The lilies in the sink caught her attention since it was not a typical place to house flowers. Instinctively Keri turned and looked into the direction of the foyer where she recalled filling a vase the day before with an arrangement of fresh flowers and realized the vase and candle holders were no longer a part of the foyer décor. The large arching scar in the sheetrock further added to the mystery of the recent sequence of suspicious activities. Marcus had to be at fault, she thought. Perhaps he broke in and was holding Dawn against her will and she was just in time to save her from this deranged religious fanatic. Perhaps he was some serial killer or rapist. Keri pulled a small container of mace from her purse and pointed it at Marcus while dialing her cell phone.

Two seemingly innocent and used dinner settings were on the table in the formal dining room further advancing Keri's confusion. She canceled the call and turned to face the two. "What is going on here?" Keri vociferously demanded. "Dawn, what on earth happened in here? The broken table the messed up sheetrock and the vase is gone and the lilies I put here yesterday are in the sink! There is trash all over the floor. All of your dishes have been broken." She turned her attention to Marcus, "What is he doing here? Has he hurt you? Do you want me to call the police?"

Without looking, Dawn set the papers on the counter, and walked over to Keri in order to assure her that things were alright. "Mom, everything is fine. I know it looks bad, but it's not what it looks like. Yes, we had some vandals today, but everything is alright."

"Church-goers right. Members of *his* church no doubt. They got mad at you over the show today and tore up your house. Now he came down here to inspect the job. She stepped forward to get a better look at the house and kept the mace pointed at Marcus. She turned to see the sheetrock full of giant holes from the jars and canned goods. "That wall looks like Swiss cheese. The house is damaged, furniture is broken. What is it supposed to look like?"

"Mom, everything is alright. It is OK. Marcus is here at my request and is helping me with something."

"What in the world can he help you with? Oh, I get it. He decided to write another song about you, only this time he decided to get your approval," she said in sarcasm.

Marcus thought about the song and the media attention it had received and was amazed. Certainly free press was always good for record sales, but this song was potentially painful to Dawn. He was glad that he had addressed the situation a week earlier despite the present fallout.

She walked Keri from the kitchen to a stool in front of the bar. "Can you give us a minute?" She asked.

Keri was dumbfounded by the comment. Sarcasms eluded her and confusion was near paralyzing in its control of her thoughts. She wanted to jump from the bar stool and launch a no-holds-barred verbal assault directly into Marcus's face, but was unable to as Dawn grabbed his hand and quickly pulled him down the hall and into the bedroom.

Stunned by the actions of her daughter, Keri was compelled to follow.

"What am I going to tell her?" Dawn asked not realizing that Keri had followed them and was listening through the door.

"Tell who, what?" She demanded.

Dawn partially opened the door and asked Keri for a few seconds of privacy adding to the irritation of Momma McIntyre.

"This is really weird!" Keri continued as she paced the hall and noticed the hooks where the pictures used to be. "The pictures too? Do you have any pictures left? Something really weird is going on here. Unless I have stepped into the Twilight Zone, or maybe there is some hidden camera. You hate this man. I mean really hate him. He is everything you hate, everything you abhor . . . . stands against everything and stand for as an intellectual member of society and now he is, by your invitation, in your bedroom . . . IN YOUR BEDROOM! Has the world gone mad?" She paced back and forth unsettled by the festering anger to the point of physical agitation. "I'm coming in," she said as she tried the locked door knob.

Dawn ignored the intrusion of privacy. "We didn't even talk about how to address this situation. We are still trying to figure things out. I don't know how to do this—"

"Figure what out? Do what? Dawn, are you in trouble? Do I need to call an attorney . . . or a shrink?" Keri interrupted.

"I don't see any on her . . ."

"See what on me. What am I supposed to have on me? What are you two loons up to?" Keri demanded.

"How can I show her, if there aren't any on her?" Dawn asked.

"Well, just tell her," Marcus replied.

"Oh . . . yes. Please do! Tell me. I would just love to hear it. Did he hypnotize you or brainwash you or something?" Keri said as she continued to eves drop.

"No, mom," Dawn replied with slight irritation. "Do you think if we pray, that Asher would . . . you know . . . let her see him?" she whispered into his ear so there was no way that Keri could hear.

The intimacy of the move struck them both and despite everything at stake, Dawn realized that she was attracted to Marcus. Not only had she displaced her hatred, but her feelings had somehow morphed in a more than positive emotion.

"It will be a little hard for her to understand. We can pray and see what God will do. Or, you can take her to the window and show her. Maybe Tios, Goad or Idio would do something," Marcus said.

She pulled her mind back to the situation for the moment. "I am afraid that seeing," Dawn paused in reflection of all she had seen. It wasn't exactly the Haunted Mansion ride at Disney World, a Hollywood production or makeshift haunted house during Halloween. This was real and brutal in appearance and disturbing in reality. The mere sight and knowledge of the unseen world could, since she wasn't under the protective covering of the Lord, cause her to have a heart attack or perhaps a nervous breakdown. It would have to be done in a manner that would maximize any opportunity for Satan to take Keri out before she could be witnessed to.

"I can't take her to the window. I know that she is only sixty, but what if she can't handle it. I'm not sure why we haven't gone crazy. That in itself has to be supernatural. There is one thing I understand completely, is why God hid that world from us to begin with."

"Then how are you going to use . . . this ability you have to witness to people. You have to show the world. God knows the numbers of hairs on everyone's heads. Let Him deal with that. Let's just do what He guides us to."

Dawn took a deep breath, slid down to her knees and prayed for God to give her direction, strength and mercy for Keri. They exited the room and Keri was quickly on them giving Marcus a stern look.

"Look, mom. I was a little startled by something and I didn't notice the table and fell on top of it. Marcus helped me up and kind of took care of me. He cleaned up the table and put it in the garage."

"Well, I'm moving in," Keri said, abruptly fearing a loss of control over her daughter.

"No . . . no, you don't have to do that."

"You two aren't . . . no. You can't be!" Keri said, as if the realization of some bizarre hidden truth had sudden fallen upon her. "All this time, you have been secretly seeing each other? This whole hate thing has been a lie? You are secretly involved in a relationship," she said giving no attention to the denial offered by both. "How . . . in this world FULL of losers, did you end up with this one? So, this is the big secret? Well, I can certainly understand why you didn't want anyone to know. I'm embarrassed for you!"

"Mom! Will you just stop for a minute? That is not what is going on!"

Keri looked at Marcus and noticed the redness and swelling on the bridge of his nose. Suspicion continued to evolve imaginative false situations and circumstances. "What about his nose? I guess he got that cleaning out his sinuses? Or were you two having a lover's spat? How was I not able to see it? All of that on air stuff was a hoax. You lied to me and your audience with all of those phony arguments," she said angrily.

"That is not what is going on. But, I am grateful he is here. He has been a tremendous help to me," Dawn said.

"Oh, I bet he has. In ways I don't even want to think about," Keri continued.

"It is not like that! Now, stop ranting and listen!" Dawn demanded.

Marcus became increasingly uncomfortable with the dialog. He wanted to go to her in kindness, but felt compelled to remain silent. Asher had told them the house would be a refuge and that the spirits would not be allowed in. Was Keri's confusion and battle with reality a matter of the flesh or was it spiritual?

A disturbance caught his eye over where Keri was standing. He turned in time to see part of the snout of the larger demon as it pierced the wall before being grabbed by an unseen angel and drug away. The battle for entry was still raging on and the three angles were having success.

"OK. I do like Marcus. As I said before, he has been tremendous in helping me. Like you, I was wrong about him and have asked for his forgiveness. He is helping me with something," Dawn paused and just let it go. "I got saved today."

"Saved? Someone did attack you?" She quickly replied.

"I think we are talking about two different interpretations of the word here. Marcus is ministering to me."

Suddenly it all dawned on her. "Saved? Certainly you don't mean that kind of Christian kooky kind of saved, do you?" She nearly had to sit down. Several seconds passed and she pulled out her cell phone and began to dial. "I'm calling Dr. Branton. We need to have you checked out."

"Why are you calling him? Besides, it is late." Dawn said.

"Something is not right with you. I wonder if—"

Dawn walked over to Keri. Without thinking, cupped her hands over her mom's and closed the phone. Keri looked up and saw the glow. Both of them had a radiance about them. She pulled away and stared for a second before walking over to the kitchen counter. She dropped the cell phone into the purse and quietly began walking toward the garage door exit.

"What? Why are you taking this so hard?" Dawn asked.

"'Hard.' You don't know what 'hard' is." Keri replied.

Without thinking, Dawn said, "Why were you going to have me aborted, Mom? You almost killed me as an unborn child. You mean to tell me that a dog was the only thing that stopped you. A car wreck and an ultrasound?"

Keri turned and stared at Dawn. "How do you know that? Who told you that?"

"God told me everything," Dawn said.

Keri turned her head away from Dawn and walked out of the house and to her car. Marcus and Dawn followed her into the garage and watched as the demons took their positions around Keri and followed above the car as she drove off.

Dawn turned to say something to Marcus and noticed his closed eyes. Slightly moving lips mouthed the prayer as it was released from his mind and sent to the Father in the name of His Son. The burden he felt for Keri and the bondage she was in caused his heart to grieve.

"She doesn't understand," he said and looked across to the park.

As it had been earlier in the day, there was a frenzy of spiritual activity. The saved and unsaved moved through the park completely oblivious to the world around them. Spiritual darkness was all he could see. He wanted to run into the park and call everyone together and witness to them. Perhaps God would work a wonder as He did on the day of Pentecost. Even if just one was to be saved it would be worth it.

Dawn gripped his hand tightly and demanded his attention. "I really am sorry for all of those things she said. I know that I already apologized, but you deserved better." She leaned in, kissed his cheek and wrapped her arms around him, and he returned the embrace.

CHAPTER 15

Chancellor Reed sat on the reclining lounge chair and observed the small lake. The moon was bright and the clouds were few. The temperature had dropped into the forties but Reed had prepared for it. How he enjoyed his time talking with God and meditating under the stars.

The deck was thirty feet by forty feet and was built just over the water's edge where the small waves could be heard lapping against the shore. The sound was most comforting and often put Reed to sleep. Some nights when a peaceful rest seemed impossible, he would make the two hundred foot trek from the bedroom to the deck with pillow and cover in hand.

It had become a place of prayer, reading, meditation and reflection. The deck was the place where he could vent his anger and get council from his heavenly Father. Reed sat trying to talk to God but succumbing to a reoccurring cycle of un-forgiveness and hate that he hadn't dealt with. The inner struggle had nearly cost two men their lives mere hours ago and if he didn't deal with his lack of control over the Haiti incident, it may cost him more than psychological torment. It may cost his life.

Somehow he had always managed to keep the full extent of his struggle from Paris. He had no need to burden her with it. Even after years of marriage she had no idea of the thoughts that would sometimes weigh on him and he preferred to keep it that way.

Reed reflected back on the incident in the quarter. His arms and legs were knotted up and sore, but he had suffered no significant injuries, at least none that were worse than the elbow.

He had wanted to kill the men. It was hard not to after the stories they had been told and the condition of the women they had rescued. They were treated worse than dogs and a part of Reed wanted to beat them until they couldn't hurt anyone ever again. If that meant death, then death it would have been.

His thoughts drifted back to Haiti and the events that had a stronghold on him, to the horror that Filipi had turned into. Often he thought about the dead and the surviving family members and put the blame on himself. At times it was unbearable. At first Reed would let the spirit of shame beat him up, then the spirit of sorrow, then revenge would play out dramatic accounts of how satisfying it would be to take the deranged man's life. Reed took brief pleasure in the mental images of standing over "The Ax of Filipi", as Reed called him, as he begged for his life. He would show no mercy, making him suffer for each life lost that day.

This cycle repeated itself hundreds of times over the first year until Reed was physically and mentally exhausted and at his wits end. Thoughts of taking his own life began to supersede the desire for vengeance. He was not willing to surrender all of the hurt and shame to God.

At times God would minister to him about the hate in his heart, to which Reed would pull back. It was an injured part of his soul that he didn't want fixed. Despite his love and belief in the Almighty Creator, Reed refused to let Him have that one piece of himself. It was going to be for him to deal with.

Reed was on a three-week mission trip in Haiti delivering Bibles, learning materials, food and drilling wells for the impoverished indigenous Navass people. The tribe was the last of the Tairo Amerindians who were the natives to Haiti pre-Columbus and the Spanish invasion.

One of the elder Navass tribesmen, knowing the missionaries were Christians, invited the group to travel to the nearby town of Filipi to witness a religious ceremony, as a white man was to conduct the service. It was the talk of the village.

It didn't take them long to recognize the symbols and style of worship to discern that it was a satanic ritual. A black and brown goat had already been offered by the time they had arrived and the high priest was covered in the blood of the goat that had been drained into a wooden bowl. He chanted to the demonic hosts while trails of red fluids ran from his mouth down and over his bulbous stomach. The presence of Satan was strong and he and fellow missionary Asa Brooks pushed aside fear and began to proclaim the word of the Living God, not willing to be mere observers. They boldly challenged the men and yelled rebukes to the devils that were present.

Several Navassians grabbed Reed, Asa and the other missionaries and pulled them out of the ceremony before a potentially murderous riot ensued, leaving the ceremony to chaos. The group of about eighty was worked up into a frenzy like a pack of wild hungry dogs, waving machetes and screaming something that was indiscernible.

Reed and Asa were pulled into the thicket and brush and off the trail where finding them in the dark would be difficult. Several members of the cult initially pursued them, screaming as they ineffectively pushed through the thick undergrowth in multiple directions with no real idea of where the men had disappeared. After an hour, the angry mob seemed to give up the chase.

Later, after arriving back at their shelter, Reed had an overwhelming burden to pray for the lost men from the ceremony. Reed asked Asa to follow him to a point on the side of the mountain that he had found and liked to pray. It was quiet and provided an uncompromised view of the region.

Asa was the first to notice the distant screams and disturbance in the village. Small fires began to pop up, two and three at a time, lighting up the Caribbean sky. The two men ran to the village to find the Navassians and the missionaries under a heavy assault as masked men with machetes were mercilessly chopping down every living person.

The shacks were ablaze without hope of putting the fires out. The villagers fought against the odds using buckets and various open containers to throw on the blaze desperately attempting to salvage their homes while being chopped down. Asa ran back up the trail to a spot where he recalled seeing a bucket and Reed ran into the center of the village.

Instinctively he charged the first person he saw with a weapon. The man laughed at Reed, who was empty-handed and stupid enough to stand and not run. With little need of playing games with the man, Reed bull-rushed the murderer. He jammed a fist into the Satanist's throat, caving in the esophagus and sending him to the ground before he could swing. The killer's eyes were wide and filled with fear as he struggled to breathe, knowing that death was upon him.

Reed grabbed the machete and brought it across the head of a second man who was torturing a young woman. The strike caught the man completely unprotected. Reed moved from man to man taking them down and inflicting injury. In a matter of minutes the group began to pull back, satisfied with the blood they had spilled.

Reed walked behind one of the huts searching for a screaming woman. There was the bald white man still shirtless and covered with blood. In his hand was a well-used hatchet. Flames of the burning huts reflected off the fresh liquid that dripped to the ground. He was standing over a man he had mercilessly sent into eternity. The villager's wife had been forced to watch the deadly assault. He took a step toward her. Reed ran at the man with his weapon raised. The killer looked at Reed, tossed the hatchet at the woman then disappeared into the woods. She screamed as the blade head dug into her leg. Reed reached the woman as was torn between helping the victim and allowing the murderer to get away, or pursuing the beast into the woods and delivering swift justice.

Reed, fighting his strong desire to hunt the killer down, picked the woman up and carried her from behind the hut and brought her to an area where the injured were being tended to. Many of the injuries were too great for the medical supplies of the missionaries. Disease would become an issue if they didn't get significant help. Survivors were tending to the wounded and trying to control the fires. To Reed, the scene was intensely brutal and dire. His heart mourned and felt instant responsibility for the deaths. Had he simply left peacefully and had not disrupted the satanic service, the attack may not have happened.

Reed ran into the location where the man had entered the woods and tried to pick up his trail. He searched throughout the night, but was unable find him.

Time had not healed the wounds and Reed harbored the hate and longed to kill the man he named The Ax. The images were burned into his conscious mind and only vengeance would help that horrific chapter to close. He longed look into the eyes of the white devil as his life drained out of him. Only then could he be healed.

After an investigation by the local government, Asa was able to identify him as a South African by the name of Clifford Ross a man of wealth and means. Further detective work found that Ross had a mission to propagate the lies of the deceiver. Ross was responsible for cult activity all over the world and had been rumored to practice human sacrifice. Reed wanted him dead with no chance for salvation. As a Christian, this presented a major internal conflict. He couldn't forgive the man and completely move on. He had to confront him. Reed had to kill him and refused to forgive.

Marcus reached over to his MP3 player, plugged in the external speakers and pressed play. Sixpence None the Richer provided a relaxing ambiance. Marcus adjusted the volume. He looked around the house and reflected on how quickly the portly demons had messed the house up and how tiresome it had been to clean.

He said, "I can deal with the fact that she hates me, but because I am a Christian? It just seems so weird and not to insult your mom, but just speaking about the world as a whole. There is a receding tolerance for Christianity, but an increasing tolerance for deviant behaviors. We help people. Feed the homeless, fix people's houses for free after disasters, help orphans get a place to live and provide food and medical attention. Why . . . how can anyone think so negatively about Christians unless there is something spiritually wrong?"

"When I was in Hell and I saw the woman, it was as if I was looking at everyone who was down there. They all suffer and will never . . . ever see the light of another day. The darkness of Hell represents the darkness they chose to embrace when they were alive. I just can't get that image out of my mind. I just want to go down there and pull that woman out of that hole and give her one more chance. Just like the one I had."

"Look, I agree with you. I understand your emotion, but we don't know what lengths God went through to reach her. We just don't know. To think that way would be like saying that God isn't just and that we can administer a more fair justice. God doesn't want . . . Hell wasn't created for man. Man was never supposed to be there. But we are eternal beings and there is only one of two places to go. He cannot let sin into heaven. Under no circumstance is He going to do that. Why should He, if a person can't even do something as simple as understand, appreciate and accept that we are all sinners and cannot enter Heaven in our current condition. The lost cannot understand, appreciate and accept what He did by coming down. Remember in the Old Testament they always had to offer up sacrifices to atone for sins? He came down and changed all of that and willingly became the sacrifice. Then it is as simple as accepting the sacrifice and calling out to Him in humility. Why should He waste His time on us? God doesn't need us, He wants us. Use that image in your mind for motivation, but don't think that God doesn't deliver justly."

"I think it was only fifteen minutes, but it felt like I was down there for hours. When I got back, I was lost and really alone. The worst part—and this may sound silly—is that I didn't know how to change it. I didn't know what to say or pray or anything. With the exception of you, I didn't even know who to talk too. I was shaken. It really scared me.

"It was so dark. The darkness seemed to be alive like one huge dark soul that covered me. It was thick and weird . . . I felt like I was being violated. There was no part of me that was immune to what was happening. It really scares me to think that anyone will go there. I may be a hypocrite for saying this, but if there is even a one percent chance that you could end up in there, why risk it? Why not make sure that you're not going there?" Dawn asked.

"There is darkness in the world. The funny thing about darkness is that it isn't created or maintained, light is. Darkness is simply the result of the lack of the presence of light. Darkness exists if light is not created and invades it. This is both earthy and spiritual in the sense that the sun and Son bring light and life into the world. Nothing lives or exists without either.

"The sun and the Son both break the darkness, help us to see, give life, hope, direction, growth and nourishment. Take away the sun, everything on the earth dies. Take away the Son, man dies to his natural sinful self. The world would be like in one of those Mel Gibson movies . . . *Mad Max*.

"Darkness is easy because unlike light, it requires no effort. The natural order of things, as I see it, is that people are willing to suffer and do without because it requires no effort. There are many who will suffer eternal torment because it was too difficult to deny their fleshy desires and do what is right. Too many just can't and won't say no to themselves no matter how selfish and stupid the desire.

"Christianity is not easy, especially these days. The secular humanist can do whatever they want. The jails and prisons are full of people who wouldn't say no to themselves. There is no discipline required. Everyone wants to live unbridled by any laws or standards. Well, to live the life Christ has for us, that is not an option. It requires discipline and effort. Billions aren't willing to do the work, and it will eventually cost them.

"Think about how everything is structured. It is easy to lie in bed and refuse to go to work, but it is difficult to get up every morning and make the commute and work all day. It is easy to eat fast food despite how unhealthy it is, but it is difficult to shop and prepare a proper meal. It is easy to deny God and live by man's standard and it is difficult to commit to God and live according to His standards. That is just the way it is now. The Deceiver has really been effective in appealing to the lazy side of man." Marcus said.

"So, are all these people in the world who deny God . . . are they demon possessed?" Dawn asked.

"I can't say that . . . . oppressed perhaps."

"I have something that I need to confess. I've done something really awful and a confession isn't going to make everything alright, but I need to tell someone," Dawn said.

"What can be that bad?" Marcus asked.

Dawn turned to him and answered, "I have a sister. Her name is Amy. When we were little girls we were so close. We hardly ever fought. It was nice having a little sister around. We had a close family.

"After dad died something happened to her. She just got out of control. Amy went crazy. She wanted to mess around with all of these boys. She snuck out more than she stayed home. She was unbelievable. It became impossible for mom to control her. The sneaking out and stubbornness and determination to do everything she was told not to do . . . there was just no way to do anything about it.

"By the time she was sixteen she had run away twice, had an abortion and was hooked on pills. Mom just couldn't control her. I was just embarrassed by her and wouldn't have anything to do with her. I was in college and moving forward with my life, I didn't have any time for her. Mom was near a breakdown and when she ran away the last time . . . she never came back and was never found. Well, I say never found.

"For years I was really mad at her for all of the pain she caused mom, but I was worried that she was dead. After college, you know about my career. A couple of years ago I hired an agency to see if they could find out what had happened to her since the police never could. I wanted to know if she was still alive and how she was doing . . . I never told mom about this. You are the only person I've ever had this conversation with. Please keep it here until I know what to do," she urged.

"I promise. But just be certain that this is something you want to tell me and not something you should confess to your mother. She is the other person involved," Marcus said.

"No. I can't tell her yet," she replied.

"I understand."

"It took a while as the trail seemed to go from New Orleans to Houston and then Atlanta and back to New Orleans. If I understand correctly, what they found was that she hooked up with this guy who was a pimp and she became one of his girls. It seems that this guy had an upper-class clientele, so she was traveling a lot within the states. Amy was beautiful and I am sure she made him a lot of money.

"Apparently she was hooked on pills and other drugs and would have done just about anything to support her habit. After a while, I guess she became less attractive or profitable and he cut her off and tossed her out on the street. Maybe her drug habit became so expensive he could no longer afford it. I'm not sure.

"She met this guy Donnie Dye, he calls himself Dyenomite. He drove a black seventies model Corvette with . . . I think it is DYNOMTE or some stupid play on his silly nick-name on the license plate. Anyway, he was her pimp and supplier at the time. I'm sure that has changed by now.

"Meanwhile, everything was going good for me. I had money, success and popularity. I was on top of the world, the big shot with the big ego. When he gave me the address to where she was living and told me all of this stuff, I had some really negative thoughts and question myself as to why I was doing this. I knew she was alive, but she was a total loser . . . a prostitute and a drug addict. What was I thinking was going to happen? That she was just going to go with me and everything was going to be perfect?

"After a couple of days, I decided to go ahead and drive to the address given to me. It was an old beat up trailer. I saw the black Corvette and license plate and I knew it was the right place. There was trash all around the front of this rotten porch like thing. I guess they tossed the trash out and animals got into it or something. It was gross.

"Insulation was hanging down all underneath the trailer. It looked like some really big pipe was leaking and making this large puddle. Mildew covered the whole thing, even the windows. There were holes in the side walls and the door was so bent and messed up, I'm not sure how it closed.

"I heard the noise and walked up to the porch and listened through the door. They were inside. She was begging for something he had. I assumed that it was drugs, her payment of services rendered . . . I suppose. She begged and he teased her and laughed and was having a grand old time. It was pitiful. This went on for the ten minutes or so that I stood by the door. All desire to help her disappeared and I began to blame her for the way she lived. She made her own decisions and she chose a life like the one she was living. No one made her run away or take drugs. I lost my dad too. Mom lost a husband. It was not expected, it was painful and we all lost someone we loved. Why had she been so weak? Her selfishness made things worse and even more difficult for us. I became . . . somewhat self-righteous then mad and turned away from the . . . if you want to call it a home . . . and never looked back. Her life was her problem. She made her bed and she would have to lie in it.

"I really justified not helping her. Hooray for me and literally to heck with her. I guess that was my attitude," Dawn said as guilt broke her down. "I have to help her. I can't let her go to that place. Now I know why that happened. I understand now. It wasn't all her fault. Sure . . . freewill, but now I know why. I am going to help her. I can't let her end up like that woman. I can't. I don't care what people think or what the media thinks. I can't let that piece of crap," she said in reference to the deceiver, "have her anymore. I will find her and she will know the truth."

CHAPTER 16

The ceiling fan was turning in the center of the step ceiling. The palm shaped blades cut through the air stirring a gentle breeze and made a monotonous clanking sound that strangely comforted Dawn and would soothe her into a peaceful rest.

She opened her eyes and looked around the room with a new appreciation for life. It was truly a new day and she could not deny the difference she felt within herself. It was odd, and she couldn't put her finger directly on it. She felt truly liberated and free. Dawn believed that she could sense the spirit of God in the room.

During the events of the past day in the midst of the chaos she had forgotten about the curtain and failed to push it back. A brilliant golden radiance filled the room and had to be partly to blame for her early rise. She threw back the covers, dipped her feet in the magnificent rays and thanked God for the light.

The burdens and cumbersome weights that had once been upon her were gone. She had confessed her sins and explored her weaknesses and the experience was beyond compare to the point of being intoxicating. Certainly, she had shed a lot of tears and felt as if there had been a purging of her soul. No longer did she have to live with the sins of the past. This was a new day, a new life with a bright future; one that would not be filled with regret, anger and hate. Her spirit leaped for joy.

The peace, contentment and rejuvenated spirit caused her to smile. How odd, she thought, for someone who was in no way a morning person to smile only seconds removed from a deep sleep. For the first time, a genuine sense of being happy and free of burden energized her soul. No longer would she have to fight the demons who were the keepers of her bondage. Dawn found that life was not hers and there was a God who really loved her and had poured out immeasurable quantities of mercy and grace. A once misunderstood and haunting concept was now a comforting reality. He was in control and the burdens of life no longer had any substantive quality.

She raised her hands toward the ceiling and thanked God for his mercy. She poured out praise and adoration up to Him and began speaking the things that were on her heart. She prayed for God to watch over Marcus and bless him as he had been a blessing to her.

For a while, she thought about the events of Friday and was still in awe of all that had happened. God's plan for her was evident and the more attention it received the more lucid the plan became. A slight and temporary frown came when she thought of the food stains and gaping holes in the sheetrock that had to be dealt with.

Remembering Marcus pulled her mind from the world of deep thought as she recalled that he was sleeping in the living room. She had all but begged him to stay, even offering him her bedroom while she slept on the freaky and apparently sometimes bottomless couch. He declined and decided to take the sofa and spend the night in the event that something should happen.

She quickly climbed out of bed and hoped that she could surprise him with breakfast since he had cleaned the house, bought dinner and honored her request to stay. She dressed and grabbed her purse and car keys since a trip to the store would be required thanks to the childish actions of the demons that had ruined all of the food in the house.

The scent of fresh coffee and chicory caught her attention as the door swung open and she realized that Marcus had not only been up, but also at work. Dawn rounded the corner and found a spread of covered serving trays and containers on the granite counter top. Three large coffees with full compliments of sugar and cream were placed by an array of foods. She uncovered the dishes. Blueberry pancakes, scrambled eggs, sausage, biscuits with assorted jellies, and a large glass bowl of sliced and prepared fruits ranging from strawberries, wine grapes and cantaloupe all placed in line like a buffet. A tray of fresh powdered beignets, sliced pineapples and blueberries filled the last dish. She jokingly wondered where this guy who was so thoughtfully taking care of her had been all of her life. The selection was impressive, but it was the presentation that touched her the most. The strawberries were stacked in a cross surrounded by loose wine grapes and cantaloupe.

The lilies were out of the sink and in a new clear vase that stood on the counter. On the bar was the morning paper and a note. "*For He shall give His angels charge over thee, to keep thee in all thy ways. They shall bear thee up in their hands, lest thou dash thy foot against a stone.' Psalm 91: 11-12*

"*Dawn, I pray that you had a great night of rest. Enjoy your breakfast it should help you get some energy back. I ran home to take a shower and let the dogs run in the park. I will come by later.—Marcus.*" She read the letter out loud.

A slight feeling of solitude came over her as she placed the note on the counter. For years, she had been self-relent and enjoyed the freedom of being independent. It was better that way. Relationships were messy and painful. She questioned herself, was it about Marcus or the need to have someone there who understood?

She removed the lid from one of the coffees added cream and sugar before picking up the newspaper. She unfolded it and scanned the headlines of each section for anything that may warrant her attention then flipped the pages habitually looking for headlines. "Local Musician Pulls His Own Work" caught her eye in the Saturday only printing of the Entertainment section. She pulled it out and began to read. "Local musician and studio owner Marcus Dillon has made a deal with his label Rea Records to have, of all things, his own CD recalled. It is unknown if the recall is tied to the controversial song *Devil Dawn*. It is alleged that Marcus Dillon wrote the song with slanderous intentions against WKZO radio personality Dawn McIntyre . . ." She put the paper down and wondered why he would have the album pulled. Was it an admittance of guilt? Had he in fact written the song about her and made up the Fatimah Obkik story? There was too much at stake financially for the CDs to simply be pulled just before its release.

Either way didn't matter to her. She didn't care if it had been written about the old Dawn McIntyre. That was behind her.

She looked beyond the food and noticed the Bible. He had found it somewhere in all of the mess. Embarrassment came over her at the realization that Marcus had noticed it and quite possibly had read some of the contents. The notes in the margins were certainly not meant for the ears of children. The comments were pithy and nasty. Dawn wished that she had put more effort into finding the book and giving it a proper disposal. She grabbed the leather casing and picked it up and thumbed through imagining the things Marcus had potentially read. Page after page was full of embarrassing obscenities and blasphemous side notes she had written. Multi colored messages filled nearly each page and the word contradiction written in all caps made the most frequent appearance.

Looking through the text from the perspective of a believer was her first true taste at being on the other side. "Wrong . . . wrong . . . wrong . . ." she said audibly. "I can prove this and this and this . . . ," as she continued her reexamination of the former Dawn McIntyre.

A big star drawn with a blue ink pen caught her eye. It was the fifth Proverb. A red pen had been used to underline several verses, '*Her feet go down to death, her steps lay hold of hell. Lest you ponder her path of life—her ways are unstable; you do not know them. Therefore hear me now, my children, and do not depart from the words of my mouth. Remove your way from her and do not go near the door of her house . . .*'

And yet He came to me, she thought.

The Holy Spirit tugged at her heart to forget the old desecrated Bible. Christ had died just as much for her as He had for all of mankind. She was as worthy of salvation as all of the apostles, prophets and keepers of God's words were. "I love you regardless of what you did. Forget it and move on as it can never be used against you again. Walk in righteousness," he said to her heart.

The immensity of the unconditional love set off an explosion of praise and thanksgiving. She left the room and wiped the tears from her face.

She ran to the front door and looked across the street into the park. A huge ball of white hair slowly moved across a small open area that was bordered by large live oaks. A massive white dog vainly chased after a smaller and much faster black Labrador as if it were a puppy. A long pink tongue hung out of its mouth and dangled down the right side of the jaw allowing the maximum amount of airflow possible. It was clear that the white bear of a dog was out of shape and in need of losing some considerable weight before it rolled over and died. The Lab ran circles around the larger animal and barked as if taunting the white mass as it moved in a speed difficult for the young dog to fathom. The dog stopped suddenly and fell to her belly and was motionless. Dawn thought the white animal had a heart attack from overexertion. The Lab wagged his tail and ran up for another taunt and was surprised when the big paws tackled him.

Dawn opened the door and stepped out. She looked cautiously around to see what was going on in the spiritual realm and was delighted at the lack of activity. She braved the elements and took a full breath of fresh air before sipping the hot coffee. She thought about walking down the street when everyone was up and active for the sake of discerning the spiritual condition of her neighbors. Perhaps she could shock the Christians with the news of her conversion. Watching the jaws hit the ground would be priceless. The idea occurred that some, as did Momma McIntyre, might think she was a fraud and only used religion to line her pocket book. She couldn't recall ever having a conversation with anyone or seeing anything blatantly pro-God in the neighborhood. Then again, who would confess that to her?

Dawn continued to consider the prospects of knowing her Christian neighbors. It would be truly nice to have other believers close. She considered walking around the neighborhood and testing this new vision of the heavenly realm.

It was early and cool despite the abundant sunshine, and a few joggers and early risers made their way around the park. A small woman in jogging pants and ear buds was being escorted by an angel. She was singing and raised her hands waist high and turned her palms up toward Heaven in praise. Marcus wished her a blessed day, which she happily reciprocated.

Marcus sat in the grass behind the dogs laughing. He gave commands and the dogs instantly obeyed. He yelled something, clapped his hand twice and the happy canines returned to him. He tossed small pieces of bacon treats into their mouths, which they excitedly received. He scratched the white dog's obese belly and both back legs began kicking the air. The lab picked up a stick on his way back, dropped it on the ground so he could receive the reward for listening and then returned his attention to the piece of oak. He began to gnaw on it while lying upright, then rolled over to his back. The pup suddenly forgot about the stick and jumped to attention. He sat panting and looking to Marcus's right, letting his master know about the close proximity of a visitor.

"Fat, but smart," Dawn said laughingly.

Marcus turned to see Dawn then jokingly looked down at his belly. "Me?"

"No silly, the dog. What a . . . large animal."

"Zara is a Great Pyreneese and she eats and sleeps very well."

Zara ungracefully rolled her large body onto her feet and trotted toward Dawn. She panted heavily while inspecting the new acquaintance.

"Be careful, she might stick her nose in your butt . . . Zara is bad about that. She's just checking your ID," he said. "How do you feel?"

"Actually, I feel better than I have in years. It is not like something I can understand . . . the physical side of it all. There is this peace that is so comforting, but then it is almost like a part of me isn't really sure that it is all real. It is so weird."

"This new gift of ours—" he started.

"Is it really a gift?" she asked.

"I think it is. I've prayed for years to have an open window into heaven. I will admit, however, the demons are more than I bargained for. I thought they would look different than the angels, but since they are fallen angels, I kind of expected a different but similar appearance. I'm a little taken aback by that. I hate to say it, but Hollywood was good for something. With the millions they spend on garbage, I am glad that I can say that now.

"I like the idea of knowing who is saved. Did you know that your neighbor in the third house was saved? Man, she has as many angels as you do."

"I wonder why. She never tried to convince me that I was wrong. Not once. I'm not judging her, I'm not mad or anything . . . just wondering."

"She would have been chased out of the neighborhood. You were pretty ruthless," Marcus said.

"Yeah, maybe," she replied.

"Maybe?" Marcus laughed.

"You found my old Bible," this was more of a statement than a question.

"It was actually out in the yard. I noticed it when I left this morning. I was going to copy a proverb out of it and it was kind of . . . well . . . after a page or two I kind of closed it and set it on the counter," he replied.

"I am sorry for that. I would look for reasons why not to believe. It's just that simple. It is so embarrassing."

"That is one of the true signs of a saved person. You feel guilty and remorseful. That's good. The Lord said to repent, which is probably the most misunderstood word in the history of man. Move from the old path of sin and seek a new path, one of righteousness that only a person who has Christ and the Holy Spirit as their guide can find. In your heart you knew it was wrong."

Dawn nodded in agreement and she rubbed Atlas who had sat at a distance until she called him over. She scratched him behind his left ear and he began to kick with the left leg scratching the air and getting extreme pleasure as a result.

Dawn noticed the slumping posture of a woman walking in their direction who, for some reason, looked familiar. She was petite and beautiful and looked to be in her early twenties, with brown wavy hair. Despite having the golden radiance about her, she looked tired and beaten down by grief and sorrow. Behind her walked an angel who was similar to the others and was large and well portioned. He walked with his mighty arm around her shoulder as if trying to console the sad woman.

Dawn tapped Marcus on the leg and pointed to the scene. "Look at that."

From an outreaching limb high in a live oak that crossed over the asphalt walkway a demon jumped out of the tree and on to the angel. In several one-hundreds of a second ten more came from various hiding positions behind the pond and from underground. They slashed at him with daggers and swords and viciously drug him to the ground. The demons attacked like a pack of ravenous wolves, devouring their prey. Without ceasing, they stabbed, punched and bit the angel. He retaliated, inflicting injuries on several of the demons, but was overpowered.

Two more flying overhead swooped down and stood next to the attack and watched looking for an opportunity to join in. One demon had a solid form and was hairless with a swollen head with mostly human features. His arms were covered with what looked to be either fresh blood or red paint. The creature laughed at the sight of the fallen angel and jumped up and down in celebration. It removed a six inch dagger from the sheath on its side and hunched over looking to jump in to the already crowded assault.

One demon was extremely odd and Dawn found it to be intriguing. The creature managed to pull its attention away from the fracas and walked over to the woman. It walked by her side and morphed into a creature that matched her perfectly. The deceptive spirit was walking behind her talking and summoning confusion and deflecting clarity causing increased frustration. She continued to pray and call out to God, but the demon refused to back off.

With the forearms of her blue shirt, the woman wiped the tears from the right side of her face and stopped walking. She looked up and closed her eyes and spread her hands out opening them to heaven. Dawn heard the faint echo of the prayer as she poured her heart out to God and called out for His help.

As if hearing the prayer, Tios flew over Dawn and made an arcing landing onto the asphalt. He stared into the direction of the struggling saint and became insulted and angry. He drew his sword and lunged forward taking two steps before becoming a bullet of angelic fury. He flew several feet off of the ground and went through the praying woman, driving his shoulder into the chest of the demon. The beast rolled down the asphalt fighting to regain control and launch a counter attack on the unknown adversary. In a rage of fury, Tios was on the demon before it could gain its bearings. He swung relentlessly slashing the demon and sending it to the abyss.

The second demon wasted no time and moved toward Tios. Goad had approached from the opposite direction and cut the demon down from behind. It never saw him coming. He moved quickly to the pile of agitated creatures and began swinging his sword. He looked like a man clearing a field with a swinging blade. Parts of demons were cut free and flew to his right and left, as one by one they fell, refusing to acknowledge his presence, but focused on the wounded angelic being they had taken down.

Tios helped from the other side, but a second wave of unclean spirits tried to join the fight. They were much larger in size than the first group, although smaller in number—in the range of nine to twelve feet and looked very human. The countenance on their faces gave them away, but Marcus was surprised. Had they not been in opposition to Tios he would not have been able to discern what side they were on. These demons bothered him far more than anything he had seen yet because of the resemblance to the angels of God.

Tios turned and met them over the water. It was a small group of five and he was pushed back. They were overpowering him with ease. Argos left Marcus and flew to the aid of his brothers in an attempt to help Tios push back the five. But they were far too quick and strong. A fourth unrecognized angel quickly descended from the sky and landed in the middle of the fight and initially helped to stop the advance. The three regained ground. One demon overcommitted when swinging his sword at Tios' abdomen. The mighty angel seized the opportunity and cut him to the ground. A second quickly fell and at the realization that they were now out manned, the remaining three pulled back and retreated to fight another day.

The three quickly ran back to Goad, who had cut the pile of demons down and now attended to the fallen angel. The attack had inflicted severe damage to the heavenly being. Goad reached down and picked the angel up and in a ray of light, disappeared into the heavens.

Peace fell upon the woman, who wiped the final tears from her face and nodded her head as if getting the answer she needed. A clear improvement in the lady's disposition had taken place. Dawn nodded and prayed for her and asked God to let them meet one day before realizing who she was.

"Megan?" she called out.

The woman looked into her direction and tried to quickly recover and hide her imperfect appearance. "Dawn McIntyre?"

"How have you been? I watched you just yesterday, you are as beautiful as ever," Dawn said.

"Thanks. Well aren't you sweet!" Megan replied with a smile. She was bemused by the positive, nice demeanor exhibited by Dawn. This was a side she had never seen before.

Dawn wanted to grab Megan and spin her around to see the angels as they held hands in prayer over their injured brother who had tried to defend her.

She motioned over to the man sitting with the dogs and asked Megan, "Do you know Marcus Dillon?"

Her face took on an odd expression and she smiled, "Yes, certainly I do!"

"Why don't you join us . . . if you have a minute," Dawn asked.

Megan walked over and greeted Marcus and stood looking back and forth at the two, "OK. I'm sorry, but I have to ask. What is going on here? You two hate each other and now you're . . . hanging out in the park together. Where you can be seen? This is a little hard to understand. What gives," she asked with great interest.

"Well, to be honest with you, I had a rather difficult situation and Marcus was there for me. He also witnessed to me," she said.

Megan pointed at Dawn and asked, "Witness . . . like God, Jesus and the Holy Spirit? That kind of witness?"

"Yes," Dawn answered.

"Man, this has been a crazy day. Excuse me, but I need to sit for a second," Megan sat on the ground and crossed her legs facing Marcus and Dawn.

Zara moaned and rolled over and forced herself up onto her legs. She took what looked from her perspective to be an open invitation and waddled over to Megan and plopped on the ground. Her head rested on Megan's calf. She looked up, anticipating a long and thorough scratching.

"So, let me get this right, you guys are friends, or are you more than friends?" The reporter side of Megan was starting to ask the difficult questions that the public was certainly going to want to know.

They both were quiet, and contemplated the 'more than friends' comment. "Both," they answered simultaneously.

"Wow, this is news," she answered. "You are a Christian. How does the world's . . . top atheist just become a Christian? Please don't be offended, but this whole thing is rather amazing . . . almost supernatural."

"No, it's supernatural alright. That is exactly how it happened," Dawn replied.

"Can I ask how?"

Dawn looked at Marcus who simply looked at the congregation of angles and nodded his head. Megan followed his gaze and then returned it back to Dawn.

"Can I show you?" Dawn asked.

Intrigued, Megan couldn't resist. "Absolutely."

Dawn walked on her knees several feet to where Megan was sitting. She looked a little uncomfortable with the unknown and seemed to wonder what she had gotten herself into.

"Can you look in that direction and tell me if you see anything . . . unusual?" Dawn asked.

Megan turned to the spot that she thought Marcus had looked just seconds ago, "No, I don't see any . . ."

Dawn touched her hand. Instantly Megan began to see. Dawn was extremely relieved that what Asher had told her about sharing the open window worked on Megan.

She sat entranced by what she saw. "Angels? There's two of them standing and praying. They don't look happy like you would imagine."

Dawn told her the story of what had happened when she was walking up. She looked down at Zara and scratched her behind the ears.

"Well, I really didn't believe in demons quite to this extent. But, I can't explain it. A couple of days ago I found out that I am pregnant."

"Congratulations," Marcus said. "I bet Rob is excited."

"Oh, yes. Very much so. But, I can't explain it. I woke up this morning worried and then I kind of got depressed. It was really strong and I couldn't shake it. I came to the park to clear my mind, but it just didn't work. I guess now I kind of know why."

Dawn realized that Megan and Marcus had known each other before this encounter. She became slightly curious as to the extent of their relationship.

They told her in brief about some of what they had learned since the angelic encounters had taken place. She was excited and appreciative of their willingness to share. Argos returned and stood about fifteen feet away from them watching and looking around. Megan asked if she could see him.

Dawn touched her foot and the angelic warrior came into view. Megan felt a little silly for looking, but needed conformation of what she thought she had seen.

Marcus noticed a gradual increase in activity in the park and realized that he needed to get Dawn back home. The longer they stayed the worse it would get. Dawn seemed to handle the earlier battle well, but he knew that they would be sought out by the demonic spirits. He asked Megan if she wanted to join them for breakfast and she declined. Megan hugged Marcus and was surprised that touching him also released the energy and visions.

They entered the house and the dogs were put in the back yard. Zara made for a blue grey bowl filled with water while Atlas stood on his hind legs and drank form a concrete bird bath. Dawn fixed Marcus a cup of coffee and placed several beignets, a handful of wine grapes and blueberries on a plate. Marcus grabbed several biscuits, jelly and strawberries.

Dawn led Marcus through a six-foot French door into the back yard. Chinese fan palm fronds brushed against his shoulders as he passed through the door and onto the concrete covered porch. To his left sat an impressive summer kitchen with stainless steel appliances, flat screen television and a small round wooden table with two bar stools positioned across from each other.

On the television, a minister was excitedly pacing back and forth on a stage and slapping his Bible with his left hand, determined to get the word of God to resonate in the hearts of the congregation. Exterior speakers exploded with life and Marcus nearly spilled the coffee Dawn had prepared for him.

"Hallelujah to the Lamb of God . . . . Hallelujah. Give him praise and glory . . . Amen," echoed throughout the backyard before Dawn found the volume control button on the remote.

Marcus looked into the yard and found Dawn on a square area of brick pavers surrounded by seeding queen palms. Atlas had left the bird bath and was chasing a squirrel as it gracefully moved across the six inch dog eared fence boards that enclosed the back yard. Zara took a break from the bowl, stared at the dog and seemed to wonder what the stupid pup was up to.

The landscaping and exterior décor gave him much to look at as nearly every inch appeared to be part of an incredibly detailed plan. Split leaf philodendrons and bamboo blocked the view of the back fence. Washingtonia and Chinese palms served as center pieces for several landscaped islands. The yard was lush and full of life in the early spring morning.

Dawn moved past the covered porch area and set her breakfast on a table in the open sun. Several black aluminum chairs surrounded a round table topped in mosaic tile. After empting her hands she pulled out a chair as a gesture for Marcus to sit.

"So . . ." she started cautiously, "why did you do it?"

Marcus looked befuddled and asked, "What . . . breakfast? Is that really a mystery?"

"Why did you pull the album? That was a lot of money," she asked nicely not wanting to accuse him of anything, but desiring to leave the floor open.

He nodded, acknowledging that they were on the same page. "How did you know about that?"

"It was in the paper this morning," she said.

"That song was released almost three weeks ago. Almost from the very second people heard it, Bill, my manager, started getting one call after another. The general consensus was the same as yours. So, a little over a week ago we decided to pull the album out of production and cut the track. A new song is going to take its place."

"Look, it doesn't matter to me now. I deserve to be called that for what I was. I am not and will not be mad if that song is about me."

"As a Christian my words are supposed to lift people up, encourage and help. That song didn't do any of those things. If it could in anyway hurt or upset you, for me, it wasn't worth having on the market. I wanted to fix it. So, we took care of it."

Dawn was moved by the gesture and wasn't sure how to respond. She felt a sense of guilt for being overly sensitive about the entire matter.

CHAPTER 17

"Are you sure that you are up to this?" Marcus asked out of concern for Dawn after all that she had been through.

"I'm going to have to be. I don't have a choice. We need to find her before something really bad happens. Before she overdoses or worse . . . I need to try and reach her," she replied. "When I had her tracked down, one of the detectives said that she worked in the quarter, which was obvious. I'm not even sure if she is still there."

Marcus navigated the SUV into the narrow gate, entered the parking lot next to Jax Brewery and placed the ticket on the dash. He took Dawn's hand and prayed for the Lord's supernatural protection and guidance as they searched for Amy. Having an open window into the spirit world would be extremely difficult to manage in the Quarter. Marcus was nervous about his own sanity and strength. It was an evil place after dark and what they had witnessed in the park would certainly amount to child's play compared to what was in the Quarter. He prayed for God's strength and mercy.

"It is right at seven o'clock and it's kind of dark. The later it is the crazier it probably gets," Marcus said, hoping for a miracle and swift results.

Dawn stepped out of the Range Rover and faced the river, attempting to hide her apprehension. She dreaded looking into the direction of the Quarter as it was certainly the hub of sin for the region. The demon Lord was certain to reside here. She sensed the demonic presence which was powerful enough to make her knees shake.

Ramped drunkenness, open and mixed sexuality, drug use and every other sin imaginable took place nearly on a nightly basis. When it came to the French Quarter, there was a severe lack of moral standards and hedonistic virtues were pushed without limitations, akin to the Biblical cities of Sodom and Gomorrah. Police and government officials turned their eyes for the sake of incoming tax revenues and paid little attention to the foul and heinous perversion that was now simply a part of the French Quarter experience.

She looked down at the picture in her hand and wondered how anyone would be able to recognize Amy in a photo taken nearly thirteen years ago. She and Amy had their faces pressed together in order to fit in the frame while shooting a close-up. The beach sunset served as the backdrop. Amy had pig-tails, a burnt nose and a huge smile on her face. It was the last time Dawn could recall her sister being happy or content. She treasured the memories of what was to be the last weekend that the McIntyre family enjoyed unity and happiness. Life was about to throw them a challenge. A surge of negative emotion began to surface, but Dawn pushed it aside. She had to be tough.

"I will be with you," the voice said as she prayed a third time and the peace of God came over her. She raised her right hand, looked upward and thanked Him.

Marcus reached for Dawn's left hand and led her up the weather stained concrete steps to the platform that provided an elevated view of Jackson Square. A homeless man slept on a black metal bench with bricked planters and flowering bushes on each end. In the planter by the man's head rested an empty bottle of cheap wine.

A tall lanky demon sat atop the planter with a huge pair of hairy feet resting on the chest of the sleeping drunkard. The demon looked down toward its hands, paying no attention to Marcus and Dawn as if disinterested. Its head was covered by a hood which did not allow them to see the facial features of the creature. The hands and feet of the demon were covered by the same black extra coarse hair they had noticed on other evil spirits.

Marcus wanted to walk over and wake the man and witness to him, but he was drunk. It would have been useless. If he had the opportunity, he would certainly attempt to help. But Amy was a priority and he was focused on the mission at hand.

He turned to look toward St. Peter Street and Jackson Square and nearly fell backward onto the sleeping drunkard. "This isn't quite what I had expected," he said.

Dawn stood motionless and looked upon the thousands of angelic beings who stood perched in elevated places surveying the actions of man in the midst of his sin. The radiance from the angelic presence arched upward illuminating the sky and was visible over the fading presence of the sun. Beams of multicolored light penetrated the atmosphere, creating a covering of iridescent pearl.

"That's God's Superdome!" Marcus said.

"That is the most beautiful thing I have ever seen. Way better than any sunset . . . ever! That is absolutely amazing," Dawn said after catching her breath. She wanted to sit and just look at it for a second and vowed to spend more time doing so after Amy was found. She pulled Marcus to the top of the rounded steps that led toward St. Peter Street and they were both helplessly frozen in awe.

"Not that I am an artist, but I have never seen colors like this," Marcus replied.

"Well, Asher and all of the angels . . . I have seen this same pearlescent color to their wings. There must be tens of thousands of them over there. It looks like millions and millions of soft lasers of different colors moving and mixing and—"

The loud, obnoxious and wicked laughter of a woman distracted Marcus. She sat at a table of a woman who was reading tarot cards and must have given joyous approval to whatever demonic revelation she had just received. The elderly woman reading the cards continued as a small demon stood next to her and whispered into her ear enough truth to give support to deception. An angel sat ten feet above on a live oak branch that had provided the woman with shade during the day. He gently shook his head in disapproval.

The demonic hosts did their work and seemed to have little concern for the numerous angelic beings that shrouded the area. Small groups of people ventured toward the heart of the French Quarter as demons joined in and followed them excitedly, plotting and waiting for opportunities to promote sinful activities.

Marcus watched as one demon directed a young man's attention toward a sign that advertised forty-ounce containers of beer for four dollars and excitedly pushed for the group to get the party started.

"I guess the job gets easier when they have alcohol in their systems. Kind of let your guard down. That thing is pushing awfully hard," he said, drawing Dawn's attention to the activity.

"You know, I have to admit that seeing all of them really makes this a lot easier. Knowing that God is with us and that the angels are everywhere . . . really is comforting. I really thought that this would be the last place to find such a presence of God. I had no idea that there would be so many here."

"Well, it is the sinner who needs salvation and we must provide the light," he replied.

Marcus and Dawn briskly walked down the arching steps and made their way across St. Peter Street and stood before the old tarot card reader. She wore a blue do-rag and silver cross earrings swung with the movements of her head. The old woman looked deep into Marcus's eyes as if seeking knowledge from some supernatural ability. He tried not to stare at a cataract in her right eye that was working its way across the brown iris and toward the pupil.

"Excuse me ma'am, have you seen this person? She's a little older now and—" Dawn placed the picture in front of the lady. The demon jumped up and down and screamed into the woman's ear in a fit of rage.

She calmly looked up and asked, "What are you . . . a couple of cops or got some kind of fantasy your lookin' to fill? Just take your pick. We got lots of hookers, runaways, drug attics here. Low-lifes, no-lifes." She chuckled at herself.

"Please, have you seen her?" Dawn pleaded.

"Show me a badge or get lost. Do you freaks have ears, or do they just not work?" she bitterly replied.

Marcus drew weary of the old woman's nasty attitude, but understood the demonic stronghold and asked, "Do you know that those cards are evil? And that you are being influenced by a demonic entity?"

She rolled her eyes and replied, "For years you holy rollin', mightier than thou morons have been harassing me with your non-sense. If you want a reading, then sit down. If not, then get out of here. You're hurtin' my business!" she replied.

The demon jumped up and down, spinning itself in tight circles in the manner of an excited monkey. Its red eyes left trailers in the air as it turned in rapid succession.

"What if I told you that you had a demon talking into your left ear? What if God showed it to you?" he asked.

The demon stopped and looked at Marcus. He leapt onto the table and attempted to stare into Marcus's face. "Would you like to see? He is right here." Marcus said nearly touching the nose of the demonic being.

It recoiled in confusion, falling to the ground and looking upward to the angel sitting on the oak branch as if seeking an explanation. It hopped back onto its clawed feet and looked toward Dawn who was digging into her purse. The demon quickly moved to the woman's ear and tried to convince her to discard the two fools.

"I am not in the mood for cheap magic tricks. Save it for the drunks in the Quarter. Now, get out of here!" She nervously looked at Dawn as she dug into her purse. "What, are you going to shoot me or sum thin? Look I ain't seen her. Now, just leave me alone!"

Dawn pulled out a five by seven mirror from her purse and set it in front of the woman and said, "This is no trick," and grabbed her hand. Dawn was too slow as the demon quickly entered her body and was no longer visible. It gained a stronger control over the woman who briefly laughed at the empty air to her left. The demon placed scales upon the woman's eyes and she couldn't see the spiritual world around them.

"Oooh . . . there is a tree behind me. Weirdoes! Now get out of here!" She demanded.

Dawn placed the mirror back into her purse and decided that, for now, they had wasted enough time with the demented woman. They would return later to finish God's work.

"It's all about the money, aye? Well, I'll give you ten dollars for your earrings."

The woman looked at him and nodded, "What cha want with these?" She pulled them out and held out her hand for the money. Marcus traded with the woman, then stuck the jewelry into his pocket.

Marcus placed a tract on top of the cards and tugged at Dawn's hand. They continued down St. Peter.

"Why did you buy her earrings?" Dawn asked.

"She's a tarot reader. It's just not good for people who don't understand to see a woman reading tarot cards and promoting symbols of Christ. There was no way she was going to say no to a few bucks. It was the best thing to do."

For several minutes they silently contemplated the tarot card reader and considered a solution to the new problem they were certain to encounter.

"That was strange. I guess that is something we need to prepare for," Marcus said.

"Should we have cast out that demon?" Dawn asked.

"I can't explain why, but I felt as if we needed to move on. We'll have another opportunity to talk to her. I've seen her there before."

Marcus looked up as a burst of movements caught his attention. Past the Royal Street intersection angels gathered and stood in the middle of the street behind a group of young adults. A small assemblage of large demons moved into the area swooping down in front of the angels attempting to irritate them before taking a position on top of a shallow pitched roof overhang that had provided them with an unobstructed view.

A tall thin blond man stood with a Bible in his right hand, waving it toward the line of people seeking entrance into the world famous Hurricane's night club for an evening of alcoholic indulgence. Michael Beason stood calling the irritated line of sinners to repentance.

Hurricane's opened nightly and gladly assisted revelers in the removal of all burdensome extra cash that would be quickly converted into expensive, but worthless urine. After a night of emptying their bank accounts, the indulgers would receive further rewards in the form of massive hangovers, sexually transmitted diseases, unwanted pregnancies and memories they would not be able to fully remember. To Michael and most other Christians, it all made perfect sense, while making no sense at all.

"Go away you losers," a voice came from within the line.

"You don't need alcohol. Repent from your sin and get drunk on Jesus! Get drunk in the Spirit of the Almighty God!"

A man wearing baby blue t-shirt and a brown multi striped knit cap strutted arrogantly over to the preaching man. A short obese man with a full head of black curly hair followed closely behind.

"What? You some kind of preacher or something? You think you are better than us?" Cool Man asked.

"No! Absolutely not!" he boldly proclaimed, "We are all born to sin and destined to an eternity in Hell if we don't accept the gift of forgiveness. We all need the shed blood of Jesus."

"I don't need your Jesus. Your Jesus is just in your head. There ain't nothing here but us. We rule and make the rules," he said and hoisted a green long-neck beer bottle into the air toward the crowd as if he were an actor engaging in street theater. "Oh god of alcohol, product of barley and malt and holy water, will thou come in to me . . . I needeth you." Cool Man took a long, drawn-out gulp of the contents as the crowd cheered and clapped in approval. He lowered his head back down to Michael and spit the beer on the Bible and into his chest. Beer soaked his shirt and coated his beige slacks, stopping just above the knees.

Michael leapt backwards and hurriedly wiped the burgundy colored leather cover of the Bible without consideration for his soaked slacks and shirt. The crowd's roar intensified and hecklers joined in from every direction.

"So tell me . . . was that a sin? Turn the other cheek, brother!" Cool Man said as he arrogantly walked back to the end of the line.

The over-weight man turned and expelled bodily gasses toward the center of the grouped Christians as he moved behind his friend. They shared a laugh and celebratory high-fives from the crowd. Before getting into line the spitting man turned, looked at Michael and dropped the bottle into a round black metal garbage can marked by the Hurricane logo.

Dawn complained to Marcus about his grip as he drew angry because of what he had just witnessed. "I'm sorry. That was just uncalled for! That guy needs to be taught a lesson."

"Certainly you're not going to beat the guy up!" Dawn reacted.

"Where does this 'beating up people' come from? I don't want to beat anyone up. But I believe that God has given me a better idea," he said before leading her toward the man.

Two young woman gathered napkins and any absorbable items they could find and helped Michael clean the Bible and himself. A second young man, who looked like he had endured a rough life on the streets before his relationship with Christ, stepped forward. A large scar arched over his left eye parting his brow and his nose looked like it had been broken several times as it crooked back and forth. He spoke with an elegance and style that surprised Marcus and Dawn.

"I have been where you guys are. You are all searching, yearning for something . . . seeking fulfillment in a place where you will never be satisfied."

Marcus and Dawn walked past the young ministry almost ignoring the group. Hordes of agitated demons now blocked their visibility of most of the crowd as they attempted to navigate toward the creep by memory. Tios motioned for them to follow as he kicked demons sending them flying and rolling in to other groups of demonic spirits causing them to turn on one another and fight. They found the man in the knit cap and approached. Marcus let go of Dawn's hand. Several demons appeared from behind the brick wall on which the drunkards leaned upon as they awaited entrance. Several blasphemed God in recognition of His Children. Idio remained with Dawn and Argos with Marcus. Goad and Tios stood several feet back.

They drew nearer to the knit capped man who was undressing Dawn with his eyes during the last half a block of their walk. He did little to contain his lust for her, giving no heed to Marcus.

"What's up," Cool Man asked arrogantly addressing Marcus without taking his eyes off of Dawn.

"That was really good over there," Marcus said, laying out his hand horizontally in order to exchange a hand slap for a job well done.

The man paused and looked back at Dawn again and considered what he may have to do to get between her and the loser she was with. He knew he was far cooler and of more physical worth and such a woman deserved the best the world had to offer. He decided to stud himself out to her for the night if she got rid of the loser.

After a short pause, Cool Man moved his hand from the blue jean pocket and lazily moved it toward Marcus's hand. Upon contact, Marcus grabbed him and held tightly. A surge of power moved through the sinner as he fell back to the wall. Cool Man's eyes darted from place to place, never settling in one location for more than a second.

Fear was now his master. Panic came over him and his eyes stretched open beyond what seemed to be humanly possible. He screamed, "Demons . . . Angels . . . they are everywhere!" He was cool no more.

Marcus put a confused look on his face and turned to the crowd, suggesting that perhaps Mr. Cool was really Mr. Crazy. "Drugs," he said and shrugged his shoulders as if confused by the sudden change in continence and acted as if he was trying to help him.

The short, gaseous man moved in to survey the condition of his friend and grabbed his shoulder to stabilize him. The electric impulse charged through him and the spiritual world opened up. He shook violently and began to cry. After a few seconds he wet his pants.

Tios and Goad moved back and let several demons pass. They got into the faces of the frightened men. Cool Man began to scream like a scared child as the sulfurous fiery eyes of a demon snapped at him. Large canines slapped together at the tip of his nose. A second demon with bulging red-orange eyes and a wolf like snout lapped at the short man with three tongues that moved and danced independently and dripped a thick green substance. On the tip of each tongue was a large stinger. He recoiled and fell to the ground away from his friend and covered his face. He fought to catch his breath and the fierce pounding of his chest cavity scared Dawn. A new two-winged angel appeared and touched his chest. He regained control and closed his eyes.

"Thank you Jesus! Thank you Jesus!" he cried.

The members of the ministry had gathered and stood behind Dawn, looking in awe. "What is going on? What is he doing to him?" a young woman asked.

Dawn ignored her and focused on Marcus. The heavy man seemed stable, but the man in the cap wasn't looking so good.

Cool Man continued his struggle as he was too weak to pull from Marcus's hand. Dawn was afraid that he might overdo it. She started to interfere, but Goad motioned for her to stop. Two more demons joined in, more hideous and threatening than the first two. They stood over eight feet tall and Cool Man's neck hurt looking up at them. They were dressed in armor covered with pentagrams and blasphemies. A voice spoke into his mind, "We are going to take you to Hell. You will be with us. You worthless piece of refuse. You will burn!"

The hulking figure on his left raised a large hammer above its horned head and started to swing down. Argos moved between the man and the beast and knocked the hammer away.

Marcus let go and leaned in. "Still think that we are all alone . . . Cool Man? Think about it next time before you mock God, or spit on one of His. You got me?"

He shook his head in understanding, "Man . . . what was that? I don't want to go to Hell," he said while sliding down the wall onto the filthy, urine-covered side walk. He began to weep as he shook uncontrollably.

Michael and Joseph heard the man mention his fear of Hell. They were unsure of what had happened and how Marcus had scared Cool Man to the point of an instant conversion and sudden concern of his eternal destiny. They looked cautiously at Marcus then moved widely around him to give assistance to the shaken men. Michael opened his beer-soaked Bible and ministered the Gospel. Marcus took a knee with the ministering men.

"Hi. I'm Mandy,"

Dawn turned and said hello and did not offer her hand in a formal greeting. "Nice to meet you Mandy. What a great thing you guys are doing out here. I admire your courage."

She stood and looked at Dawn in confusion.

"You know, for the ministering. For proclaiming the word of God to all of these people out here."

"Oh . . . right. Yeah . . . thanks." Mandy nervously asked, "OK, are you guys . . . like angels or have like this super power or something? I mean, what gives? He completely turned these guy's brains to mush. One minute they were all like . . . tough and demon possessed and now they're like a couple of scared babies that need to be put in diapers. What is that all about?"

Dawn instantly loved Mandy and wanted to reach out and grab her fidgeting hands. "Well," Dawn started, unsure of how to answer, "perhaps one day we can sit and talk about it. I can't explain everything right now. It is kind of complicated. No, we are not angels, but angels are all around us right now."

Her face lit up with excitement. "I knew it. I haven't . . . like, ever seen one before. But, I always knew in my heart that they were there. Hold on . . ." Mandy walked over and grabbed the arm of a third man who had been ministering. "This is Josh. He doesn't believe that angels and demons are really walking on the earth. He believes that the evil that man does is something that is in us. Like a part of our DNA or something. Can you straighten him out?"

"Well, I can only tell you that I have seen angels myself and that they are certainly real—"

"She, like, has an open window . . . dude! Said that they are right here, right now with us," she excitedly poked Josh in the arm as she spoke.

"Look, two drugged out psychopaths," he said, gesturing toward the men who were now standing up and leaning against the wall, "isn't evidence of anything spiritual. I told you, haven't you noticed the decline in dialog about demons and angles since modern science has been able to detect and understand the many forms or variations of mental disease and disorders. Like A.D.D.," he directed at Mandy, who did not respond. "That is not evidence. What kind of man walks up to a stranger and spits beer on them?"

"One who is demon possessed," she answered.

"OK, whatever! You have your belief and I have mine," he said.

"What if you could see one? Are you in love with your doctrinal belief or do you really want the truth?" Dawn asked.

"What?" they asked in unison.

"Can you handle seeing one? What if God was to open your eyes right now? Can you handle it, or would you fall on the ground like those guys?"

"First of all, you're saying that those guys really saw demons and angels and that you can make that happen? No offense, ma'am, but New Orleans is full of em." He turned to walk away.

"This guy is a Christian?" Dawn asked Mandy. "Wait, I didn't say that I was going to make it happen. I will ask one more time, can you handle it? If they were real, and you could see the heavenly realm, would you be able to handle an open window into the world of the supernatural?"

"Yeah, sure. Why not?" He replied.

Dawn watched as angels moved in and formed a protective barrier around them. "Mandy, do you want to see angels?"

"Oh, it would be so cool. What do I have to do?"

Dawn reached out and joined hands with the two. Mandy flinched at the surge of energy. Her hypertension ceased and she stood in awe looking at the huge angelic wall that surrounded them. In search of an end to the continuous angelic barrier, she turned as far as she could without breaking the bond with Dawn's hand. Like a coiled up spring, she quickly reversed position and continued in the opposite direction and looked upon the angelic hosts. Tears streamed down her cheeks.

Josh blinked and had a hard time initially adjusting to the majestic glare, "Whoa . . . whoa . . . whoa," was the extent of the dialog as he went down the line looking at each angel individually. One in particular caught his attention and was the only one who had refrained from looking back at him. He was among the shortest of the angels and stood proud and gripped a sword, ceremoniously displaying it in a vertical position in front of his torso.

He couldn't explain it, but he felt a connection. This particular angel had to be one that watched over him. Was this the warrior that had been commissioned to protect him? Josh wondered what battles this angelic being had endured at the cost of protecting him especially when it had resulted from his own foolish decisions. He maintained the posture of a stone-faced body guard as his eyes continuously paned the outer regions of the angelic wall which were not visible to Josh who was far too short in his flesh.

Dawn was thankful that no demons had been allowed to penetrate and enter the spiritual circle. Such hideous creatures could have left haunting visions in the minds of the two youths and would have taken the attention from God and for the moment it was all about bringing Him glory.

She released their hands and stepped back. Josh's face was beaming in excitement, while Mandy wiped her face and was lost in emotion. The two shared a smile.

Mandy punched him in the arm. "Now, Mr. Fuddyduddy! What about that? That was AWESOME!" Mandy exclaimed no longer able to retain the fountain of excited energy within her. "That was sooooooooooooo cool! How did that happen? How can we see . . . what is . . . ? Are you sure that you're not an angel?"

Dawn watched Mandy and rapidly grew to appreciate her personality. She was as transparent as they came and she loved that quality about her. "No, I am not. That's completely a God thing," she said.

Several moans caught Dawn's attention and she turned to their direction. The spirit of God had fallen heavily upon the immediate area and backslidden Christians were moved by the Spirit and were sitting, calling out to God and shaking. Three were against the wall ten feet away from where Marcus ministered to the two men. They shook and looked around in wonder. Neither had ever experienced a powerful movement of God and was at a loss for an explanation.

Behind Dawn, a lady in her forties sat on the curb next to a man who was calling 911, fearing that his wife had just suffered a stroke. She calmly reached out and closed his phone and told him of the powerful spiritual experience that had affected her. He began to dial the phone again believing she had lost her mind as a result of a stroke. It was only after she sternly told him to stop that he relented. With outreached hands, she openly praised and thanked God for deliverance from her backslidden state.

Dawn saw angels everywhere ministering to people. They prayed and praised along with the people.

Several more called out prayers of repentance from behind a portable hotdog vending machine as it sat on the curb under a street light. Only their feet were visible to Dawn, but the sound of their voices carried. *What an amazing thing*, Dawn thought.

Amy came to mind and Dawn decided to show Mandy and Josh her picture. She reached into a side pocket of a fully loaded small black leather purse searching for it when a business card from the radio station fell to the ground. Out of courteously, Mandy stepped forward and retrieved the card and was caught by the name on it. She looked up and put both face and name together.

She put her hand over her mouth and continued to look at the card, "Oh my . . . oh my gosh! It is you. I knew I recognized you. You're that . . . oh my gosh . . . you're that woman from the radio show." Her demeanor briefly changed. "Wait . . . you *hate* Christians. We've been praying for you for a long time now . . . um . . . years."

"Well, things have changed. God has touched me and now I am a different person . . . like you,"

"Grreeaat!" she yelled and raised her hands to Heaven, running back and forth across the street praising God. "What a wonderful day! To GOD be the glory. Whoa, we kickin' some devil booty now!" She looked down toward the ground and Hell, "Dawn McIntyre is on our side now. What cha gonna do now? You're a loser now and you will always be one . . . cause the Bible says so!" She marched back and forth in unbridled celebration.

"She is really a great person. She just . . . gets excited some times. We are out here every weekend and we're getting hammered by Satan and seeing very few victories. I guess this news was good enough to compensate for all the abuse we have taken over the last several years and she feels the need to celebrate. As far as she is concerned it doesn't matter at all what people think about her. But, she isn't nuts. She calls it 'being in the spirit'. Before today I had never seen angels, but I have also never experienced anything like that. To tell you the truth, sometimes I am jealous of her freedom to express herself. It really is a gift she has," Josh said.

"She's great. I could hang out with her. Can I ask you a question? Have you seen this person? This picture is kind of old," she said handing the picture to Josh.

He examined the photo and concentrated. "No, I can't say that I have. Mandy, can you look at this?"

Mandy calmly walked over and handed the business card back to Dawn before taking the picture and pushing the loose hair behind her ears. She paced across the street and back again cutting through the crowd and examined the picture for a second, "Yes! I wasn't sure at first . . . I mean that I recognize the face and she looks so young, but the earrings gave her away."

Dawn moved over to Mandy. "Are you sure?"

"Yeah, I'm sure. The earrings gave her away. Put in a nose ring and lip piercing and that is your girl."

Dawn retrieved the picture and looked more intently. Mandy reached over and pointed and gestured for Josh to look. He returned with a look of uncertainty.

"You don't remember her? How can you not remember her? You are such a goober-brain," she said. Mandy turned to Dawn. "You see, when we witness, we use the Ten Commandments . . . what we do is take a look at a person's life through God's Ten Commandments. If God were to judge us according to His Commandments, how would we fare?

"OK. Well, we see this woman walking through here all of the time. There is always this mad at the world look on her face . . .

she is not very approachable. Anyway, we were determined to talk to her one day. Then we saw her and we tried. She was down by the old nasty club where the plastic legs are swinging in and out of the wall. I call it Tacky Wacky's," she said while simulating the motion with her hand.

"Oh! Ok. Yeah . . . I think you are right," Josh said.

"I remember this woman and looking at the earrings. It is a flat oval with an Old English 'M' in the center of it. They were white gold . . . I guess. They match the earrings this girl in the picture is wearing. I am ninety-nine percent certain. Plus, this looks like her, with a few more miles, some piercings . . . it's her. He just didn't see it at first because he's mental." She said pointing at Josh.

What were the odds, Dawn thought? Why would she wear those earrings on the day that these same people tried to witness to her? Certainly she had other earrings she could have worn. But, Dawn reconsidered the thought as Amy was a drug addict. It is a miracle that she hadn't hocked them out of desperation. The odds were clearly against Amy wearing them.

"Josh here," she said while looking at him, "actually got 'the queen of mean', that was our nickname for her . . . sorry . . . to stop and talk. She looked like she had been crying and actually seemed like she wanted someone to talk to. She was alright at first. She took the liar, thief and blasphemer part alright, but BOY . . . when he told her she was an adulterer at heart, she kicked him right in the . . . you know . . . male area."

Dawn turned to Josh, "Are you alright?"

"He cried like a baby. I don't think he peed for two days," Mandy said with a serious but childlike expression.

Dawn fought the desire to laugh and would have openly done so had it not been for the trauma endured by Joshua's privates.

"Do you happen to know where I can find her?"

"No, I'm not sure. We don't usually see her till it's late, or morning." Mandy said.

"There is this couple who used to be missionaries and now they kind of rescue prostitutes and drug addicts. They don't come around much these days. The pimps threatened to kill them if they kept taking their women away. I haven't seen them tonight, but I can try to help you track them down. Before the threats, they really worked the streets and if anyone would know, it would be them. They should have some idea about who she is. Wait . . . or, do you know who she is already?" Josh asked.

"She is my sister," Dawn said unashamedly.

Mandy and Joshua stood silent and motionless digesting the revelation. "How can that be? You're like a celebrity and you sister is wondering the streets and you don't know where she is? Have you just not seen her for a while? What . . . did you two have a fight and just haven't talked for a while?" Mandy asked, pressing for information.

Dawn looked down and said, "Well, something like that . . . I've . . ." she said, swallowing a lump in her throat. "I'm here to find her now."

Chapter 18

"Thank you Lord . . ." Marcus was giving praise as he walked up to Dawn. "Man, I thought that guy was going to die. I was really worried about him. He is still breathing hard. He was really scared. Did you see what happened? It was like he had no protection at all and God let him have the full experience. He slapped him with a hard dose of Hell. Demons were all in his face and . . . that was more intense than I had expected. I didn't want to make the guy have a heart attack."

"Well, I think God gave him what he needed. This guy was apparently possessed by something and really had it coming," Dawn said.

"Maybe, but we need to be really guarded about this. I think we need to be more reserved about who we show this to. This is a little scary and we have a lot to learn about this . . . anointing or gift or calling. I need to learn more about this whole work that God is doing. It's powerful. I just don't want to misuse it. A lot of people back there are asking questions.

"OK. I think we are ready to go," Marcus said as they resumed the trek toward Bourbon St. "This whole area has been . . . kind of . . . well, changed for the better. Even the ones who didn't experience anything are intrigued. Despite the normally high drug and alcohol saturation levels and typically strange people, this is pretty radical . . . even for New Orleans. There must be twenty people down right now. The more sober people seem interested and want to know more about what is going on."

The crowd became increasingly dense, as did the demonic presence. New numbers of drunken revelers joined the party and began whooping it up and mixing with their new brothers and sisters of indulgence.

The Demonic presence was now everything Dawn had feared. The frantic and continuous movements of the fallen spirits limited Dawn's ability to tell one apart from another. The streets looked like a black and grayscale-colored fog or torrents of thick, billowing smoke, as if the entire Quarter was on fire and smoldering.

Marcus looked at the spiritual mess before them and wondered how they would be able to continue. The battlefield was a continuous flurry of activity and would be an impasse for both of them unless God cleared a way. Visibility was less than two or three feet.

Dawn turned from the scene, looked back toward the Moonwalk and considered leaving, as it now seemed impossible to proceed.

"Lord, I am just not strong enough to do this. I cannot possibly go into that crowd. It is too soon. There are too many. We need help," she confessed.

God stirred her heart to patience and faith. She released the fear and lunged forward into the mess of brawling and warring spirits. Five angels, near twelve feet tall, whom she had never seen before, walked up from the scene at Hurricane's and joined with Tios and Goad. The angels wore matching armor of golden plates that covered their pectoral and abdominal areas. Aramaic writing coated each plate, ascribing to the superiority of the Lord God Almighty. The lower rib and sides were protected by chromed steel that wrapped around and protected the lower back beneath the second pair of wings and were etched in a feathery pattern. Their forearms were covered by plates of chromed steel, which was fastened together, as Dawn observed, by silver cables the size of shoestrings. Eight foot long swords were housed in sheaths of bronze and copper. Graven images of a roaring lion and creatures unidentifiable by Dawn coated the housing and seemed to move as if the metals were alive.

Larger demons became aware of the heavenly offensive that had gathered and fell back to get organized in preparation to take on the intruders lest they get sent to the abyss. Several demons equal to Tios and Goad settled on the front of the battle line and stood to face the approaching angels, who were making easy sport out of the spirits before them.

The crowd of flesh slowly materialized when liberated from the oppressive spirit fog. Revelers laughed, drank, smoked and carried on completely oblivious to the demonic shroud that had previously covered them. One man looked at his drink as if suddenly losing the desire to continue consuming it, and tossed a white styrofoam container into a metal trashcan on the curb.

The source of the radiant dome as it had appeared from the Moonwalk was unveiled. A countless number of angels stood on balconies, parked cars, rooftops and hovered in the air. In front of each were large open scrolls positioned at a distance and angle that optimized their ability to scribe. Each angel wrote feverishly as they looked upon the crowd. Dawn watched the quills move quickly from right to left. The scrolls rolled, moved by an unseen assistant allowing the angels to maintain their full attention on their subjects. Angles moved with the person who was their charge.

"So, they are making records of every thought . . . action . . . everything," Marcus said.

Dawn thought back to her personal sins and asked, "What do they do with these scrolls after we have been forgiven?"

"I'm not sure, but they will never be used against you again. I have always had it explained like . . . our sins are bottled up and sealed, then cast into the deepest sea never to be retrieved or used against us again."

Marcus looked left toward Canal Street at the demons now standing observantly in a defensive posture, intending to block their way. Tios and Goad looked to their brothers telepathically discussing strategy and quickly agreeing on a course of action. An angel with short white hair pulled up his sword and moved aggressively toward a demon on the south sidewalk that had taunted him and blasphemed God. After several steps the demon retreated and disappeared below the asphalt. Others followed and moved back, acknowledging the authority of the angelic hosts.

"I guess we need to follow him," Marcus said as Tios motioned for the other angels to push forward and clear the rest of the block. Demons scattered in all directions and swarmed like enormous bugs on a fog light in a swamp. Marcus turned in time to witness Argo and Asher overpowering an attack from the rear. The two fought with perfect fluidity and skill.

"Do you think he is taking us to Amy?" she asked.

"I hope so," he replied.

Marcus and Dawn moved in behind the angel and made their way through the river of people, which moved into both directions in multiple currents and controlling their pace. The demonic activity moved in waves in accordance to the density of the people.

Red and blue plastic cups, napkins, beer cans and bottles littered the street and moved beneath their feet. Marcus worked to watch what he was walking on, keep up with Tios, dodge the patrons who danced and acted up in the street and look upon the scores of angels as they wrote on the scrolls.

They entered another intersection and Marcus realized that they had only covered a block and were on Toulouse Street. Tios turned to them and motioned toward a souvenir shop with two single pane wooden windows protected with rod iron bars. The gray paint revealed strong evidence of sloppy application, as it had randomly splattered on the glass and concrete.

The storefronts were full to capacity with items native to the New Orleans region: Mardi Gras beads, a local brand of coffee and chicory, beignet mix, coffee mugs, DVD's and t-shirts with dry humor. Marcus was thankful that it lacked the sexual innuendo that seemed to be the main theme of the other stores.

As they approached, an African American man of average height and broad shoulders met them. He was casually dressed in dark green slacks, a white polo, loafers and a black hat embroidered in the center with a fleur-de-lis.

"Hello, I'm Chancellor Reed. Everyone just calls me Reed." He reached out his hand and smiled.

Marcus and Dawn looked at each other and considered the scene just a block away. They nodded and declined to shake hands with the man and risk another event. They would share their secret when they knew who he was and that God had intended for them to do so. They looked upon the golden radiance and wondered if this was the man the kids had told them about. Marcus felt like the man had been expecting them.

Two angels stood behind him and were similar to Tios and Goad. The angels exchanged pleasantries and brotherly embraces, before turning their attention toward the building interest of the demonic hosts who had gathered. Their numbers grew at the realization that something out of the ordinary was going on. This was the sacred ground where they ruled and this provoked increased angst about the movement of God that was taking place.

"Mama, they're here!" he yelled to the back of the store.

A thin woman in her mid-forties emerged and moved past a shelf of spoons and tea cups and to the front of the store to greet them. "Wow, that was quick," she replied.

"This is my wife, Paris," he said.

Dawn stood uncomfortably with her arms folded into her chest and made no attempt to accept Paris' hand. She pulled back, confused but not offended.

The couple looked at each other, wondering why the two strangers had refused the customary handshake of good will between new acquaintances. Marcus decided that it was better not to explain and wanted to simply move on and get to the matter at hand as time was of the essence. He noticed the knots and bruise on Reed's arms and the badly damaged elbow. He wasn't sure what to think about it.

"Is there a place where we can talk?" Marcus asked.

"Follow me. God told us you would be here," Paris said as she led them into the shop and out of a side door into courtyard at the base of a narrow alley.

"God told you we were coming?" Marcus asked, glancing down the alley to make sure that it was safe.

"Of course, God has been stirring my heart for the last two hours to come over here . . . to Brother Marco's shop. Paris does his paperwork for him . . . you know taxes and billing. All that stuff.

"He is a new brother in Christ and we have been ministering to him and helping spiritually where he needs it. It has worked out really good for us. He is a good guy and we trust him and Paris makes some extra money," Reed said.

"Why do you need to trust him?" Marcus asked confused by the comment, "wait . . . are you the couple the kids down the street were telling us about? You are the ones who have been helping the prostitutes," Marcus asked.

Reed paused and said, "Well, we have been working with some women who are now former prostitutes as well as former cult members."

Dawn stopped and considered what he had said, "What is your mission work? What exactly do you do?" She asked.

"Prostitutes and drug addicts primarily. We also try to reach people involved in the occult."

"I bet you have angered somebody. Prostitution is a big business around here." Dawn said.

"We have gotten the right people angry. I can assure you of that. They threatened to kill us if we are ever seen talking to their women again. And yesterday, they tried," Paris said.

"OK. So . . . how can we help you?" Reed asked.

Dawn pulled out the picture of Amy and passed it to Reed. "We are looking for this person."

He took the picture and moved closer to a light and put the picture several inches from his nose. Paris moved in and looked over his shoulder. He looked up and politely asked, "What do you want with this girl?"

Paris looked at the two with a disturbed countenance, "We tried to talk to her yesterday. Gave her some food and a soft drink. She looks like she hasn't eaten in a while. Anyway, that was when he was attacked."

"It wasn't that bad," he said. "Who is she to you, may I ask?"

"My sister . . . she is my sister," Dawn replied.

He looked at Dawn and for the first time realized who she was and chuckled lightly after putting it all together. Reed looked up and pointed to God, "You got me on this one. You really are doing something big right now. Well, praise to you . . . praise to you." He looked down and said, "So, you are Dawn McIntyre and you are in search of your sister Amy."

"I didn't realize that so many people recognized my face," she said.

"Well, I knew that I recognized your face. But, I was unable to put it together until now. I have to admit . . . your show . . . I find it . . . uh . . . quite entertaining," Reed said.

"Why do you hate God?" Paris asked, setting up an opportunity to witness to Dawn.

"You mean, used to?" Dawn replied.

"You have accepted Jesus?" Paris asked.

"Yes," Dawn answered.

Reed sat in stunned silence while Paris raised her hands and gave praise to God for a mighty work.

"It is kind of ironic that we were reaching out to your Amy . . . your sister and now you are here." Paris said. "Anyway, we received some information about her from a woman we recently helped. So, we prayerfully decided to reach out to her. What do you know about her circumstance?"

"I know that I haven't seen her for almost thirteen years. I know that she is a drug addict and possibly a prostitute." She struggled with the reality of the admonition.

"Sorry to seem harsh, but she is definitely both of those. But, she is in a far more difficult position right now. Helping her will be tough." Reed stood slowly and paced several feet in front of Marcus and Dawn and continued, "Look I need to tell you something. Your sister is in deep and helping her will be a risk, but a risk that I am afraid must be taken.

"Our mission field isn't just simply the lost, lonely and hurting people of this city. As I told you earlier, God has called us to reach out to the occult," Reed said.

"Devil worshipers?" Marcus asked.

"Satanic groups or however you wish to label them. For about a year I have been following members of a movement called the Black Altar. The New Orleans chapter calls themselves 'Fils de Gaia.' That is supposed to be French for the Sons of Gaia the mythological earth goddess. Very hard belief system to understand, but they worship the devil as the father and their version of the Savior is Gaia. Totally off the wall and different, but they are a group of psychotic tree huggers that hate the human race. In a *nut*-shell," Reed said, making reference to Dawn's on-air insult. He chuckled, "Hey, I thought it was funny. It didn't offend me."

"There are two men who have been primarily responsible. George Butler is the Supreme High Priest and seems to call all of the shots. He has the ultimate decision-making authority. The second is Jeff King . . ."

The name struck Dawn like a dagger in the back, drumming up old wounds. She tried to hide her discomfort as her initial reaction nearly gave her away. She fought the anger and silently called out to Jesus for help.

"Do you know him?" Marcus asked.

"I'm not sure," she replied. "Please continue."

"Mr. King is in the position of 'Most High Bishop.' Last month I got a tip from a close friend and partner in ministry, Asa Brooks, do ya'll know him?" Reed asked.

"No," they answered in unison.

"Anyway, something big was going down on the island of Jamaica. That is a hotbed for satanic activity and violent crime these days. Those poor people are under a strong spiritual attack. They need our prayers. Anyway, I followed both men to Jamaica.
"Women and babies are being kidnapped at an alarming rate. It is believed that this has to do with cult rituals . . . human sacrifice. To make a long story short, the trail led us to an old shack in the woods west of Ocho Rios around Dunn's River.

"Asa and I rigged up this device. I have this little black lapel pen with a camera in it and it can send information up to several miles away to a remote computer and record the continuous data feed so that we can have proof of what ever happened.

"The ceremony started off like most that I have seen, but very quickly took a horrific turn for the worse. About thirty minutes in, they brought out a child and placed it on the altar. Asa and I were mortified.

"A child? I thought that was just Hollywood," Dawn said.

"Correct me if I am wrong," Marcus said, ". . . but only sometimes is the child actually killed in a sacrificial offering. Most of the time, the child is marked for future service by molestation, prayers and other really crazy stuff. The people basically put curses on these children."

"Right, that is fairly accurate. It isn't that common so see a child in a ceremony, that's why it caught me off guard. I almost panicked and prayed for an opportunity or a window to do something. The high priest put a bowl by the altar and pulled out a knife and began chanting. When he raised the knife as if he was going to stab the child, I hit him in the back of the head with all the strength I had and grabbed the child and ran into the woods."

"I'm guessing they didn't just let you walk out of there with the child," Dawn said.

"No, they came after me, and let me tell you, God was working. I don't know how I was able to gain as much ground as I did. They ended up tracking me with dogs and I didn't realize where we were at geographically, but I saw a stream or river and got in and followed the current till it dumped out onto the beach. There was a catamaran tied off on the beach and a couple helped me and the baby escape. At first they thought that I was the kidnapper, but they decided to trust me when they saw the cult members in their uniforms coming into our direction.

"Now, I tell this story for a reason as it pertains to this situation. Asa was able to get the car and the video on the computer. We had a lot of information to process. We were able to clearly make out and trace several of the attendees here to New Orleans."

"Amy?" Dawn asked.

"Yes. She was naked and on this altar that was right behind where the sacrifice or whatever was supposed to take place. A second person—"

"She is in a satanic cult? She was going to watch them do vile things, or even murder a child? What kind of monster is she?" Dawn's sympathy for her sister instantly turned to intense rage and disgust.

"Now, hold on, before you get too judgmental remember, she was so drugged up that she didn't know what was going on or what planet she was on. She was out of it. Having said that . . . your sister is in deep. Who knows what things she has seen? If she is a potential witness against them, they will have to kill her. She will never be allowed to just walk away. You know that . . . right?" Reed asked.

Dawn thought of the demonic influence and calmed down, "You're right. I just want my sister out of there and clean."

Dawn hated the deceiver for what he had done to her and Amy, but more for what he had done to the children and the war that had been waged on the innocent. In the womb or out, the beast sought to devour them. She was greatly disturbed and burned with righteous anger.

"There's this heavily infused element of sexuality, hence the nude . . . altar . . . thing, that people are really attracted to. People can't control their lust for sex and it seems to be everywhere and in everything these days. Anyway, group fornication and all kinds of weird ritual stuff takes place after their ceremonies. Often they will use the prostitutes to initiate the . . . well, use your imagination."

"I can only imagine," Dawn said.

"In their so-called 'doctrine', they blame man for all evil . . . get that! They look at everything else as evil in the world and they are the ones worshiping the devil. The one that the very word was created to describe! The irony! I don't get it!" he said excitedly. "Anyway, all of the evil in the world, things like global warming, air pollution, deforestation and all this other stuff. They follow the environmentalist belief that there are about five billion people too many in the world. They don't seem to know or care which of the five billion should be gotten rid of." He sarcastically added, "as long as it is not them. This is where their doctrine gets in line with Darwin, Hitler, *Mein Kampf* and the whole 'natural selection' or 'survival of the fittest' garbage. Obviously this is how they justify hate and murder. To them, they are doing the world a favor and speeding up a natural process and the world will be better for it. Like I said, it is crazy stuff. I can't make it up. All of these freaked out cults and radical environmentalists seem to walk that line.

"It is only recently that they have gotten into human sacrifice. It's dedicated to Satan as a payback for the sin of man. Because of their 'oneness' with the environment, they have most of their ceremonies deep out in the woods somewhere and that makes it a little hard for us to find out exactly where they are. We haven't been able to follow them yet and learn more."

"They seem pretty bad?" Dawn asked.

"I need to share something else with you," Reed said.

"Sure. I want to hear more."

"Not only is Amy a part of this cult, but she prostitutes herself out to support it and her habit. Her reward is drugs and a small paycheck. She seems to have a pretty serious drug addiction. There's about a dozen or so women in the same situation. They perform their services to support their drug habits and a little money for themselves. Most of the money goes to the Supreme High Priest who dispenses the money according to his will."

"So, how do we get her out?" Dawn asked.

"Well, it's going to be difficult. We are dealing with drug addiction and a demon possessed group of people who aren't going to let her go without a fight. They have already threatened to kill us," Reed said.

"He was beat up over her yesterday. Look at his arms. That was because we tried to give her some food and drink so that we could talk."

He looked sternly at them and said, "I will tell you where I think you can find her if she is working tonight. Earlier she was shaking from withdrawals. I'm sure she is doing all she can to get a fix. Possibly headed over to the Hell House."

"Where?" Dawn asked.

"Hell House . . . that is what we call that building where all this stuff happens. It's just down the Quarter a bit. The girls go and get high in one room, then move into another room that is kind of circular shaped. The girls sit at the bar or dance on the floor. The 'customers' are given rooms with doors that open to this central spot for easy access, they can watch, pick out who they want and . . . use your imagination." Reed said.

"Where is that?" Marcus asked.

"That will do you no good. Unless you're Rambo, you're not getting in there. If she's going, she would be there now.

"This is a private club and is very difficult to get into. They have taken extra measures to avoid the authorities. If you want to go, I will tell you how to get in, but you better get prayed up first. Satan lives in that place. I can feel it just talking about it," Reed said.

"OK," Dawn said.

"Sorry. You cannot go. Mr. Dillon here will have to do it. He will have to get her. I do not think you should go, sister or not," Reed forcefully stated before turning to Marcus. "Hell House is a tan building with green shutters directly on the corner of St. Louis Street. Walk up St. Louis Street to the metal gate that has a keypad on it. Enter . . . 32166654. I'll write it down. Anyway, follow the sidewalk behind the building. There will be a man standing at the door. He will try to make small talk with you. DO NOT talk with him, it is a test! Just say 'Rastafarian.' That is the code. Don't look phony and don't try to make small talk with anyone. They are very sensitive to small talk. It is a dead giveaway that you don't belong there.

Reed walked into the store and returned with a cigar box that held several golden coins. "Take this doubloon," he said while retrieving it from the box. He held it up for Marcus to view. "Show it to anyone who stops you. There are only several members who have these coins and they can let any one of their friends or business associates use it."

"Why do you have it?" Marcus inquired.

"Like I said, Brother Marco is a new Christian. God got him and one of the prostitutes at the same time. They know about Lexi, but not Brother Marco."

Marcus looked back at the store, "He has that kind of money?"

"Brother, you don't know the stuff he was involved with. Maybe one day he will give you his testimony. This guy was bad news. I'm not exaggerating," Reed said as Paris nodded in agreement.

"Someone will come to your room; just request Freedom Girl and she will be notified when she is free. Just be patient and when she does, see if you can get her to leave with you. Proposition her. Get her to leave. Don't talk to her there. You will certainly get yourself in a lot of . . . well, trouble.

"There is a restaurant across the street on the second floor called Drake's in the Quarter. Get her there and you guys can try to talk to her. But, she will be loaded and may be hard to reason with. She can be violent, as you can imagine with the life she has led. So, be careful. If she calls out to one of the goons, you may get somewhat roughed up. Call me," he demanded.

"Call you after I get her?" Marcus asked in confusion.

"No, call me now. That way your phone is preset on my number and all you have to do is hit send. Your phone will automatically call the last number dialed and we will get help," Reed said before calling out the number. "Hopefully no one else will call you between now and the time you are out of there. But, if you run into trouble, just hit the send button and I will get the authorities there as quick as humanly possible."

"These people are that dangerous?" Marcus asked.

"They can be. We just want to be smart about things. We will stay with Dawn and keep her company. When we see you and Amy crossing the street, we will move to a different section of the restaurant or leave. Let's pray before we go."

CHAPTER 19

Dawn stopped and reached out for Marcus's hand as he was several feet behind her. The practice was trending toward habitual. At first it was simply out of necessity as she found it comforting. Dawn realized that holding his hand was more than sharing their gift or an experience together. She could genuinely acknowledge an increase in her comfort level while in his presence. She reached out and held his hand as they took to the street.

The first obstacle was the two block trek through the spiritual battlefield while attempting to act as if there was nothing unusual going on in the company of Reed and Paris. The battle was noticeably more intense than it was just before they had entered the shop. Acting normal, despite what they were seeing, was akin to sitting in a boat in the middle of Pearl Harbor during the invasion and acting like nothing was going on. They were surrounded by chaos and at times it was hard to discern with any certainty which side had the upper edge.

Marcus looked up as something moved quickly toward them, demanding his attention. From down the alley to their right, a demon moved swiftly from right to left then turned in a tight arch and made a line toward them. Marcus knew that the evil spirit could not physically harm him and he trusted the angelic guardians, but his flesh temporarily got the best of him and he reached up with his left arm to block the unclean spirit's impact as it hit and bounced off of him and into the grasp of Argos.

Reed and Paris witnessed the blocking maneuver. It seemed a little exaggerated if he were blocking a huge insect. They looked at each other, searching for an answer, "Bugs?" Reed asked.

"Yeah . . . a big one," Marcus answered.

"That is it," Reed announced as they stood in front of Drake's, looking across the street at the two-story tan building.

Marcus looked upon the structure and wondered if the building had in fact been painted tan. Spirits hung off of the walls like bats in a cave and smothered the building. Only half of one of the green shutters was temporarily exposed to him. There was constant movement as the demons were anxious. Marcus looked on feeling his stomach begin to turn in knots. The building looked like the first stop or rest area at the end of a portal connected directly to Hell itself.

"You can't go in there. There has to be another way," Dawn said horrified by the vision she and Marcus shared as demons of many forms clung to and flew through the walls. Thousands sat on the roof or hovered above.

Under normal circumstances, nothing on the outside would have given any indication to Marcus as to the debauchery taking place behind its walls. It looked like a normal uneventful place, with the exception of the busy spirits. His nerves began to creep up and he quickly rebuked it and cleared his mind.

A short chubby man in a football jersey and baseball cap turned from the crowd toward the gate. Several demonic spirits accompanied him as he entered the property.

"Let's get this over with," Marcus said as he looked at Dawn. "I will see you in a few minutes." And with that, he walked away.

"This is Drake's," Reed said as he opened the wooden door and gestured for the ladies to enter.

Dawn paused and turned to watch Marcus as he punched numbers on a key pad hoping that he would turn to give her a final nod of assurance that he was OK with going in without her. She felt guilty about asking him to do something she was unable to do. She considered abandoning the restaurant, running across Bourbon St. and going in regardless of what Reed said.

A group of demons looked at Marcus with great interest as he stood at the gate. They looked at each other then back to Marcus and back at each other again, trying to figure out what to do with him.

Without looking, Marcus pushed the creaking iron-gate open, passed through and released it to the spring that forced it back to the locking position. The finality of the clicking sound of the lock as the gate returned to its closed position killed the idea of making such an attempt. She bowed her head and began to pray for his safety.

"Is the lady with you?" a man from the restaurant asked as Reed and Paris entered the staircase leading to the second floor dining area.

Dawn turned to face a man in his early seventies in black slacks and a navy blue sports coat. He had a full head of gray hair that seemed to glow as it bordered his sun-burnt face. His warm smile invited her in. However, she looked upon him and noticed that the glow or mark of every saved person she had encountered was not on him. A large demon stood at his right . . . whispering. Dawn looked upon the poor man and wanted to reveal to him the menace, but was afraid of touching anyone and bringing any unnecessary attention to herself.

"This way ma'am," the elderly gentlemen said, making a second attempt to get Dawn's attention. He motioned for her to go up the stairs.

She looked around the restaurant for the first time and noticed red carped with gold trim and exotic patterns on the storefront drapery. Large potted queen palms rose to the ceiling from within a large indoor fountain where lush tropical flowers and exotic plants arched to the tile floor.

The man led Dawn up a huge wooden winding staircase with dark walnut stain on the railing and heavily worn carpet. Paris and Reed were placing napkins on their laps when she made it to the table. The gentleman pulled out a chair that presented a perfect view of the tan building across Bourbon Street.

Dawn turned to thank him and unexpectedly found herself nose to nose with a demon nearly four feet tall. Wild nappy black hair flew into different directions as it animatedly yelled and screamed at Dawn inches from her face, causing her to recoil. Empty black eyes temporally stirred up fear despite the conflicts with the other much larger and more menacing creatures.

"What? What is wrong?" Reed asked as he leapt up from his seat and scanned the room.

"I thought I saw something," Dawn replied quickly shaking off the disturbance as Tios grabbed the little demon and effortlessly tossed it out of the building.

Dawn looked across the street and wondered what demonic trickery plagued Marcus's attempts to find Amy. The deceiver was cunning and certainly would have some obstacles for him to overcome. The thought of Argos accompanying him gave comfort. She placed her hands in her lap and began to pray for Marcus and Amy.

The activity in the restaurant was rapidly increasing since entering. She looked down into her lap to get her attention away from the demons that were floating around the room and looking at her. Dawn thanked the Lord as they moved on. She considered telling Reed and Paris about their "gift" or new calling, but was unsettled without Marcus.

She turned back to the window and looked across the street. The numbers around the building were growing as it became increasingly difficult to view. The spirits' covering had now grown dense enough to block the entire building, including all light, from her view. Demons climbed up the exterior brick walls and were sitting on the roof. Others attached to the walls and stuck their heads into the building as they watched the sinful activities of the lust filled mortals. Many fought in the air and knocked other spirits out of the way, vying for positions that offered better opportunity for the manipulation of the lust-filled heart of man. Small clusters of the unholy hosts gyrated in exuberant celebrations at the distasteful actions of their subjects.

"Look, I don't want to pry, but I can't help but believe that you know Jeff King." Reed said. "You seemed really . . . intimidated when I mentioned his name. Do you have some sort of relationship with him?"

Dawn looked at Reed and said, "I am not sure. Do you have a picture of him?"

Paris pulled out her cell phone and punched the keys until she found the digital file with the image on it. She handed the phone to Dawn who reluctantly took it. The pain of the memory of him was much to bear. To know that this same man could be connected, or even worse, an obstacle to her ability to help her sister was beyond belief. She didn't want Marcus to know about the incident and the reality of his involvement could certainly frustrate her efforts of secrecy.

Dawn accepted the phone and looked at the image and instantly became weak and nauseous. Despite the high forehead from a receding hairline, it was unmistakably Jeff King. She stared for a few seconds until the phone's energy saving mode turned the backlight off. She set the device down on the table.

Without thinking, she blurted out, "He raped me." Sympathy covered Paris' face and she reached for Dawn to offer comfort, but Dawn pulled back. "I'm alright."

"Did you go to the police?" Paris asked.

"No. I didn't want anyone to know. I just kept my mouth shut and did my best to move on," she said.

"I'm sorry," Reed said. "Does Marcus know?"

"Please don't tell him anything. He doesn't have any idea. I don't want to lie to him, but we aren't exactly in a situation where he needs to know about this . . . yet."

Marcus punched in the code and instinctively looked back to see Argos with his sword drawn. Three angels walked with them and Marcus was grateful for the extra protection. He took a deep breath and went forward in faith fully trusting God. He never imagined that he would have the need to enter such a foul place. It was a foreign concept, as he didn't understand the sexual perversion that drove men to such lengths. This was a mere call to duty and he prayed that God's strength was upon him.

Hedges lined a dimly lit path made of poorly maintained brick pavers that were coated in mildew and had grass and weeds growing out of the mortar joints. The walkway turned at the corner toward the back of the building. A husky young man in a polo that looked like it was several sizes too small looked at him.

"Heck of a game last night, wasn't it?" He said.

Marcus looked at him recalling what Reed said about small talk and said, "Rastafarian."

"Ja must be readin' yastarday's news, mon. Dat be da wrong flaver," the man said in mock Jamaican patois.

Marcus paused briefly realizing that Reed's information was out dated. He had no opportunity to think or consider options as it would be a certain sign that he didn't belong there. He felt the Holy Spirit talk into his mind and say, "Pasco," which he repeated in single-minded faith.

"Pasco gets a pass-o," he said in a silly tone. He paused briefly and studied Marcus's face searching his mental database for an identity. The man briefly fumbled through a set of keys before settling on one and sliding it into a worn brass door knob. He pushed open the sun burnt mahogany door and waved for Marcus to follow. He stepped in and grabbed a key that had a black round piece of plastic with the number twenty-four attached to it. "You will have number twenty-four, Mr . . . ."

"Rogers," Marcus blurted out.

The young man looked humorously at him and smiled while nodding his head, "Rogers. Right . . . . Rogers. Well, you're the forth one this week. I will tell you like I told that last fruit loop, we don't supply any shoes. You dig? But hey . . . if it works for you and the girls go along with it, who am I to judge? Right?" He placed the key into Marcus's hand, "Well, have a good time there . . . Mr. Rogers." The eccentric young man then slipped out of the door to wait for the next arrival.

Marcus stood in a small room for several seconds thinking about the man's comments and the supernatural revelation of Pasco, which he had never heard until that moment. He had forgotten about the coin and could have used it. But he was in.

The room opened into both directions where dark halls disappeared to the left and right. The lower third of the walls were covered by square four foot wooden panels that formed a continuous border. A dark, blood-red flat paint with a coarse texture covered the walls above the panels and ran to the ceiling, adding to the gothic décor.

An urgency to move came upon him and he tuned to his left where he saw a large man walking down the hall towards him. He wore a suit and hat and chewed on a cigarette. The man passed the foyer and looked at Marcus while continuing down a hall to the right. Behind him was a demon in the form of a dragon. It stomped and snorted while swinging its head back and forth. It looked at Marcus and snorted at him and continued to follow the man.

The door knob on the main door clicked and the door began to swing open. Marcus moved quickly forward into the darkness of the hall to avoid being spotted by the door man or the new client. The damage to his reputation and testimony could have been irreversibly damaged if he just happened to be seen by the wrong person. Demons flew in and out of rooms and darted back and forth busily.

He passed a black wooden door and searched it but was unsuccessful in finding any identifier on it. The head of a demon popped out through the door and snapped at him. Argos punched it sending the beast flying back into the room. From behind the door he heard the voices of a man and woman and moved on.

He thought of what it would have been like for Dawn if she would have been with him. He could only imagine the demons and activity taking place within the walls. What a vile and evil place it was.

A second door appeared in the darkness and he pressed in for a look. The number twenty four was in the center as if it were a hotel room. He was relieved when the key worked and the door swung open.

Four spirits moved around the room and one stood in the corner making obscene noises. The active demons moved closer to Marcus intrigued by the new human. When Argos entered the room behind him, the spirits became restless and gathered together. The angel of God stepped forward and challenged the demons who decided to seek other opportunities and disappeared through the walls.

Despite the darkness of the room, he could see a table. He fumbled for a light switch and threw it. A very dim lamp in the middle of the table came to life. Marcus looked around. The walls extended out to nearly twenty feet and angled inward toward ten-foot accordion door. He walked over and cracked it open to see where it led. Beyond its covering was a dance floor with several scantily clad women performing their routines and using a large chrome pole for a prop. Several rooms had the accordion doors pushed open as unidentifiable men entertained some of the women. Those who chose not to indulge in the entertainment and remain completely anonymous kept their doors closed.

A man noticed Marcus as he peeked from behind the door scanning the area for Amy. He yelled several obscenities and called him a pervert. The irony of being labeled a pervert by someone in this lowly place that was seeking prostitutes was almost laughable and ignited a little ember of anger. He walked back to the table and nearly jumped out of his skin when the voice of a woman called out to him. He didn't hear her enter and had no idea that he wasn't alone in the room.

"So, sweetie, what floats your boat?" she asked.

"Excuse me?" Marcus asked.

"Are you hear for some action, or are you just a watcher?" she asked. "My name is Candy."

"Well Candy, I really was hoping for a specific person. I hope that she is available," he said.

She looked at him and lit a cigarette. The flame revealed enough for Marcus to be certain that she was not Amy. She dropped the lighter on the table and simply looked at Marcus anticipating a name while releasing a large cloud of smoke into the air. Her face revealed a long and hard fought life. She had been beautiful once, but was now old beyond her years. He was sure that it was the same old story of drug abuse and stress. Sorrow filled his heart.

"I'm here for Amy," he said, forgetting her alias.

"A request? High school sweetheart? Had a crush on her in school, found out she was working here and came to see what you were missing? Is that it? Whatever . . . around here her name is Freedom Girl," she stood and walked toward the door. I'll see if she is with a client, if not . . . she will be here," Candy said before closing the door.

Marcus felt dirty, foul and low. He was becoming anxious and hoped that she would find Amy quickly.

CHAPTER 20

"But he raped you?" Paris persisted. "How can you just let it go?"

"In college . . . he . . . look, I am over it. I don't want to talk about that. It was a long time ago and I am over all of that," Dawn said, regretting that she had blurted anything out.

From the tone of Dawn's voice, Paris realized that she was not fully honest about her current emotion in regard to the incident, but wanted to portray herself as a strong and independent woman as seemed to be her nature. "Why didn't you get help? You went through that alone? Didn't you have anyone to talk to?"

"No, I didn't need to talk to anyone. I just wanted to put it behind me. That's it."

"Is that the way you are now?" Paris said as she reached out to offer Dawn comfort. Too her surprise, Dawn pulled back in a reactionary manner just before any contact was established. Paris sat in confusion with her hands remaining in the middle of the table for a second before pulling them back into her lap and sneaking a puzzled look at Reed, searching for an answer.

"I am sorry, Paris. But you don't want to touch me. Just trust me. You don't want to touch me." Dawn said. "It's hard to explain."

The oddity of Dawn McIntyre caused Paris' intrigue to peak.

Dawn watched as one of the demons moved behind Paris. It stood for a second and listened to her thoughts as she had undoubtedly opened a door with something negative. Certainly her actions had to seem strange to these new acquaintances, but the alternative was to let them see the unseen and she was not prepared to share the 'gift' with just anyone who crossed her path. Discernment was important. Who did God intend for her to expose to the spiritual world? Only He could make that determination.

The beast bent at the waist and was now close enough to the back of Paris' neck that had it been mortal she would have been able to feel its putrid breath. It whispered into her left ear and Dawn wondered what manipulating thoughts must have been going through Paris's mind. The beast worked both sides of her, speaking into both ears in soothing and unsuspicious tones, working its deception. Paris' posture changed as she sat upright and with a bent brow, suggesting to Reed with a look that she was ready to leave Dawn to her own problems.

Reed ignored the unspoken request and continued, "Can I ask you a question? Can you, as a Christian, forgive Mr. King?"

Dawn looked at him as she had yet to entertain the idea of forgiving him. The notion seriously challenged her as thoughts began racing through her mind. She knew what the answer had to be, but was initially unwilling to accept it. "Yes, if God gives me a peace about it. I can," she said.

Paris and Reed both became increasingly concerned for the sanity of Dawn McIntyre. Her unsettled eyes were perplexing.

"What's wrong?" Reed said as he reached out and touched Dawn's hand in order to get her attention.

Dawn wasn't fast enough to avoid him this time. The demon standing behind Paris was the first thing to get his attention as it continued to work on her thoughts. Reed leapt back in his seat and stood to rebuke the spirit away from his wife and let go of

Dawn's hand. The image disappeared. "I rebuke you in the name of Jesus Christ! In Jesus' name, be gone, demon!" He demanded yelling into the air above Paris' head.

Her mind stopped racing and she looked at her husband as if he had lost his mind. "What in the world has gotten into you?" she asked.

Dawn turned to see the demon being removed by an unidentified angel.

"How did that happen? I touched you . . . and . . ." Reed said

"I tried to tell you. I . . . ," Realizing that she would now have to come clean she reached out and offered a hand to each. Now Paris was the one pulling back. Reed panned the restaurant and was astonished. Watching the expressions of her husband intrigued Paris and she reached out and took hold. She nearly fell from her chair at the instant onset of the reality of what it was that congregated around them and the other patrons.

Images of evil pierced Reed's heart and he quickly tried to understand what he was witnessing. Remembering Marcus, he quickly turned toward the building and saw the unprecedented concentration of spirits wreaking havoc on the flesh of the fallen men in the brothel. He wanted to rebuke and war with the demonic hosts himself.

He prayed openly for Marcus and his safety. Patrons looked on and snubbed their noses at him. Dawn looked around as the deceptive spirits were outraged by the intervention. They viciously cursed Reed and Paris and moved in to make an attempt on them. A white cylindrical wall of light shot from the ceiling and engulfed the spirits nearest to the table, dragging them through the floor.

Marcus sat patiently and prayed for God to give him the proper dialogue by which to pull off the stunt. He was unsettled on his approach to their conversation and knew that it would need to come quickly. To Amy, the notion that he was not there to fornicate with her would undoubtedly seem suspicious. He prayed that he could somehow pull it off without lying or getting himself beat to a pulp by the thugs that patrolled the building. He struggled to find the spiritually correct way to address the situation.

The door opened and he nervously sat up in attention as a soldier ready for an inspection. A woman in a short black skirt and low cut white blouse entered the room. The limited light did not allow him to discern her hair color, only that it was long and straight like Dawn's.

"You were looking for me?" she asked.

"Hello . . . Amy! How are you?" he asked

"Why, are you writing a book or somethin'?" She said. "High School Sweetheart? I never liked anybody in school. Who are you?" She moved in for a closer look, "No, I don't remember you. Did we go to school together? How do you know my name?"

He was unsure about how to answer the question without being untruthful. "I didn't suggest that I was a high school sweetheart. That was Candy. I thought she was just joking. I was told specifically to ask for you."

"A referral?" Amy asked.

"Something like that," he replied.

She walked over to the table and sat down. Amy was beautiful but tired and thin. Her blouse was open exposing parts of her anatomy. Marcus focused on her eyes as he did not want to look down. Amy found his discomfort and willingness to not lust over her as strange.

"You haven't been with a woman before, have you?" she asked, amused by the obvious nervousness he displayed. She leaned in, enjoying his reaction.

Marcus was taken aback by the question and her actions. He pondered the pros and cons of his answer. "What would be wrong with someone who was a virgin at my age? What is so bad about that?"

"It just doesn't happen, especially with men."

"Well, there is no rule that makes it unacceptable," he argued.

"I agree, but it is still weird. So, now you came to me to take care of this situation for you?"

"Something like that, only not here," he said. ". . . dinner first."

"You want to take me out to dinner first? Look, are you looking for some action or what? This talk is wearing me down."

"No, just dinner," he said.

"Dinner? All you want is an escort?" Her tone changed as she was confused.

"Something like that," he replied.

"You really don't want to do anything with me but eat dinner?"

"No, I don't. Just the pleasure of your company for a little while," he replied.

"It's your dime." Amy said.

CHAPTER 21

Paris looked around the restaurant somewhat spooked and paranoid. She tried to envision the locations and activity of the unclean spirits in the restaurant, wondering how many currently surrounded their table. She remembered Marcus swatting at something on the walk down Bourbon Street from the shop. She really didn't want to know what that was all about or what that walk had been like for the two. Judging by the concentration of spirits in the restaurant, she realized that it must have been a continuous battle.

Paris second-guessed grabbing Dawn's hand and knew that she would never be the same again. The images were haunting. She reflected back to the times in her life when she had made bad decisions or acted irrationally, or when something simply unexplainable had taken place. Were they really acts of her free will, or were they pieces of some demonic plan? How often had there been angelic intervention? How in control had she really been over the years? A flurry of thoughts briefly overwhelmed her.

The scene in the restaurant was more horrifying than any Hollywood flick Reed had seen, and it was real. He would have to dive into his Bible and spend a lot of time on his knees to learn all that he needed about the invisible world that was more prevalent than he could have possibly conceived.

Despite decades as a Christian, his understanding of spiritual warfare had been surprisingly weak. He knew the scriptures, but did he fully understand them or have a watered-down belief? Reed knew that demonic spirits had been at work within the cult and its members, but the scene in the restaurant was a little more than he had considered. *The irony*, he thought, about being commissioned to infiltrate cults and his view of powers and principalities was lacking and misguided. How could he not have studied and read the scripture and sought a full understanding of the unseen world around them? He could certainly understand things from a fresh perspective. The experience, if applied properly, would help him. He would better understand some of the unusual things he had been told during conversations over spiritual matters.

Reed was torn between his excitement of the truth and the horror of reality. His strategy would have to be revised and built around what he had just seen. Perhaps he would have achieved greater success in the past had he been more receptive to the harsh reality of the truth.

Dawn stirred in her seat and looked through the window at a cloud of activity around the building. If Argos had not towered over the crowd of agitated spirits, she would have had no clue as to whom or what was moving into their direction. Argos fought with the demons as they crowed Marcus.

"Here she comes." Reed said.

"Well, we need to move before she sees us. Seeing us here wouldn't make things any easier for you. We will be in constant prayer for you. God bless," Paris said encouraging Reed to follow her away from the table. They moved to the opposite side of the stairs so that they could exit without being seen when Amy passed. They held hands and agreed in prayer.

Despite the activity surrounding him, Marcus walked in silence, thanking God to be out of the bordello. The place emitted a presence of evil that he didn't need to see in order to experience. His feet couldn't carry him away fast enough.

"Look, slow it down? I'm in heels here, not tennis shoes," she said.

"Sorry. I am just ready to get to the restaurant."

"So, what kind of person are you? You just need someone to eat with? That just seems strange," Amy said.

"No, I think you are exceptionally beautiful."

The comment nearly knocked Amy off of her feet. Since her father's death, no one had said anything remotely close to that to her. She didn't know how to respond and toned down her attitude a bit and asked, "Well, what is your deal? You seem like a nice enough guy. Why did you want me? You never told me how you knew my name."

"Let's just say that I know someone who thinks that you are extremely special and has told me all about you," Marcus said while opening the restaurant door for her. He wasn't sure where Dawn had been seated, only that they would request a table on the second floor. The older gentleman escorted them upstairs and turned left toward the back of the restaurant, seating them in a private corner.

Dawn watched Marcus and Amy as they moved from the stairs and to her right with the company of demons following her. The spirit entourage consisted of nine who were very distinct in makeup and, she assumed, responsibilities. Two were very short and wore black robes. One gripped a leather scroll in its right hand. They were positioned directly on both sides of Amy and continuously spoke into her mind.

Three larger demons of seven feet tall formed a wall behind her. Their swords were drawn in anticipation of God's desire to free Amy from her bondage. They would fight anyone who tried to steal her from the grip of their master. She was doing their work and furthering their master's kingdom. She was a prized human and worth fighting for. Satan had already lost one mighty warrior and he was not about to let her sister switch sides without a fight. One of the beasts looked toward Tios and Goad and arrogantly chuckled in an effort to taunt them. It looked down at Dawn, daring her to try something.

Four demons between five and six feet long moved on all fours to the corners of the room, then stood erect and watched the dining hall. They were the first line of defense should any angelic hosts try to secure Amy.

Marcus looked for Dawn and was unable to locate her and was unsure of what to do. Certainly she hadn't left yet. He pulled out the chair that would face away from the dining area and invited Amy to take a seat and pushed her chair in for her.

With all of the demons assigned to Amy, Dawn was grateful and surprised that Marcus was able to convince her to accompany him. Dawn watched Amy and wept. She looked tired. Bruises were on the inside of her left leg above the knee and right arm at the bicep. Her hair hung down the sides of her face, possibly to hide some other marks or injuries. The damage done by years of drug abuse was painfully obvious

Two four-winged angels entered through the ceiling above them and stood on the sides of the table in front of Argos. This agitated the three demons who were not willing to be intimidated and were hungry for confrontation.

"Amy," the voice called out.

Marcus looked up to see Dawn as she approached.

The three demons turned to see the new intruder only to find her accompanied by two more huge angels. The reality of being outmatched from the perspective of ability defused their lust for confrontation and they fell back into their original positions and regrouped. Tios leaned into the face of the demon who had laughed at him seconds earlier as the entered the dining hall. His face was an inch from the teeth filled snout. With his large index finger, he forcefully jammed the beast in its forehead and waited for a response. The beast flinched and Tios grabbed it and flew through the rear wall of the restaurant behind Marcus and returned a few seconds later, alone and satisfied.

From the four corners of the restaurant, demons moved in to give support for the fight that was about to take place. The smaller bald demon with the scroll jumped on top of a seat and screamed for them to back off. Dawn assumed that the spiritual stronghold would remain in firm possession of the evil spirits if God did not soften her heart. Satan's grip on her was strong and all the demons had to do was allow the deceivers to conduct their business. "She wants us here and there is nothing they can do about that!" the deceiver yelled.

"Amy!" Dawn called out.

Amy recognized the voice of her sister and looked at Marcus. "So, I knew you were up to something," she said without turning and acknowledging Dawn. "I really thought that you had a problem with women. Now that I see you know my sister, I'm positive you have a problem."

Dawn took a seat across from Amy and ignored the insult, "So, how are you?" She tried to look away from the smaller demons as they worked on her mind from both sides. Dawn wanted to jump up and rebuke them.

Amy's face turned cold as she looked at her sister. "Oh, I'm great. I'm living the dream!" she said in sarcasm. "How do you think I am doing? You know WHAT I do for a living since you sent your boyfriend over to fetch me like a dog instead of coming yourself. It's just like you to do that. Send someone else to do your dirty work for you. The high and mighty queen! You were always like that!"

"Amy, I am sorry. I would have come myself, but . . ." Dawn attempted to explain.

"But . . . what?" She interrupted. "What do you want Ms. High and Mighty. Took time off of your ego trip to stoop down and reach out to lowly me?"

"Amy, I want to help you," Dawn said sincerely.

"You want to help me . . . really? Well, you're about thirteen years too late for that. Besides, what happened with that private detective you hired to track me down? Wasn't that all about helping me? Or, was it that you wanted to help me until you found out what I was. Then helping me wasn't worth your time. I'm just an embarrassment. The story wouldn't look as good on national news since I am a prostitute."

Dawn's expression gave her away. She didn't know how to handle this line of dialogue and had no idea that Amy had known about the detective. Her motives were pure. It was genuinely about helping her. But in the end, Dawn chose to walk away. For that, she was wrong.

"Yeah, that's right. Your private de-tec-tive came around asking questions. He liked the package," she said, motioning to her body, ". . . and we made a deal. We had a good time for a couple of weeks there. I am willing to bet that every dollar you gave him went straight to me. We partied down," she proudly confessed.

Amy paused and her countenance changed, "I waited for you. I was excited because I thought that maybe you cared. Every day I thought, 'This is the day. Today she will show' and you never did. I waited for you and you never came. You never showed up," she began to weep and quickly turned back to anger. "You were ashamed of me. The big-shot radio woman was too ashamed of the whore she had for a sister and tried to keep it all quiet. Quiet! When you never showed up, I thought of going to the press myself just to embarrass you!"

Dawn felt dirty and worthless as she listened. Amy was right. She had chosen her career over family. The embarrassment would have been too much to deal with and she chose to take the easy route and do nothing. "Amy, I am sorry. I did want to help you."

"Now, you send this guy over to fetch me like I am some dog," she said angrily.

"No, that's not it at all. You don't understand," Dawn said.

"Oh, I understand. You are too big . . . too important to get your hands dirty. And now I am supposed to believe that you want to help me?" Amy asked.

"Let's understand one thing here, I didn't force you to run away or torment mom and act the way you did. I am not the reason you are a prostitute. It is not my fault. Those are decisions you made. But, I understand now why it happened and we can help," Dawn said. "Besides, I did come to your house."

Amy perked up and asked, "When?"

"Remember Donnie Dye? His car was in your driveway. I walked up to the door. I knew he was your pimp and I wanted to beat the crap out of him. When I got to the door . . . I could hear you begging. He was giving you your fix and you begged like you were going die without it. He was playing with you like you were an animal. He laughed as you begged. It was disgusting and I felt sick to my stomach. So, I left." Dawn said.

Marcus was surprised to see Dawn reach across the table and attempt to take Amy's hand. It was too soon for that, he thought. She wouldn't understand and who knew what the result would be.

"I am here to help you now," Dawn said.

"Oh, really? You can help. What if I don't want your help? Who needs you?" Amy asked.

Dawn was tired of watching the deceivers manipulate Amy's thoughts and called out to God again for support. Suddenly Tios and Goad were thrust into the air by two demons that had shot up through the floor beneath their feet. They were of equal size and tremendous strength as they sent the two angels flying across the room.

Goad landed on his feet and road out his backward momentum before making a charge toward his assailant who was already engaged by Argos. He was surprisingly cut off and separated by a rising wall of Satan's warring spirits. Meanwhile, Tios tucked and rolled before springing to his feet and unsheathing his sword. He was simultaneously smothered by demonic soldiers who slashed at him as he worked to fight them off.

Idio appeared through the ceiling and swung his sword at the demon that had tossed Tios across the room and fought along the side of Argos. They managed to push the huge spirits back against the wall and outside of the building. Platoons of demons entered the building from the floor and walls and intensified the attack on Tios and Goad. Tios had been taken by surprise by the number of demons who poured in all around them and was struck in the middle of his back, leg and chest before falling to the floor writhing in pain. Goad charged and quickly took a position over Tios and retrieved his sword. He fought with swords in both hands and the demons found it difficult to cut him down and further injure Tios.

Legions of angels darted in from the ceiling in all directions and began a rout of Satan's military. Demons began to scatter and flee from the restaurant at a pace quicker than their entry. Within minutes, the room was clear of every noticeable fallen spirit.

The illumination from the angelic hosts was nearly blinding to Dawn. She fought the urge to squint her eyes as she faced Amy. Dawn felt that her sincerity wasn't getting through to Amy. She appeared as a fraud. A part of her was fighting a righteous anger and the desire to leave Amy to herself. It wasn't her fault that Amy was a prostitute. No one wanted that for her. They tried to look for her for years after she ran away and was able to find nothing.

How can she blame her? The reality of Hell returned and cured Dawn's anger. She suppressed the thought and continued to search for a way to help her embattled sister.

Goad bent down to help Tios up. The mighty angel was severely injured. Goad wrapped his mighty arms around his fallen brother. His huge wings separated and they both darted up through the ceiling. Idio moved in position behind Dawn. The room was filled by angelic warriors standing with drawn swords in preparation of a second offensive.

"Amy, you need help. There is a lot you don't understand. Let me help you," Dawn pleaded.

"You can help me by getting out of my life!"

"I am a Christian," Dawn blurted out. "Christ has changed me. I know He can help you," Dawn said.

"Jesus? The cross and all of that nonsense, is that what you believe? That's a riot! Maybe you should go back and listen to your show. Christians aren't exactly your friends. You're such a hypocrite," she said rolling her eyes. "So, now you're one of those . . . people. Oh, well . . . that makes all things different! So, let me guess . . . your God is great and is big enough to help you with . . . the prostitute and embarrassment?"

"I never said you were an embarrassment." Dawn said in defense of herself. "Hell is a real place. I have seen it. I have been there. I don't want you to spend an eternity there."

"Hell is right here. We are living in Hell, honey. Sitting here listening to this crap is Hell. As a matter of fact," she said motioning with her index finger, "why don't both of you go there? OK!" She quickly rose from the seat and threw something at Dawn. Several pieces of paper glided through the air and spread out as they drew near the ground on both sides of Dawn. She turned and stomped toward the exit.

Clear green eyes were now staring at Dawn, reading her like a book. They seemed to glow despite the artificial light of the restaurant. A demon remained in a sitting posture in Amy's seat after she stood and stomped out. It was hairless and looked much like a man, but with the pigment of a dead person. Its green eyes cut into Dawn's confidence and she felt intimidated by the evil spirit. It was the one who had ultimate possession of Amy and had remained behind to taunt Dawn in a show of strength. The beast whispered to Dawn that it intended to take Amy to Hell. It took great satisfaction in the horrified expression. Slowly it descended through the chair and floor and disappeared.

Hours of searching yielded no results or leads to Amy's whereabouts. Dawn grew tired and the constant battling of the angels and demons became draining. A mutual agreement was reached to call it a night and try again after church which was about seven hours away.

They walked back up the stairs toward the parking lot and noticed the vagrant who was sleeping when they had first arrived was now awake was eating food that looked to have been dug out of garbage cans. Empty cups and bottles covered the ground. The man looked suspiciously upon them as they drew closer. The demon that once stood over him was not visible and Dawn assumed that it had taken its residence in the homeless man.

"Dead . . . is she!" A voice from a second man who sat on the ground behind a large planter declared.

The voice startled them as they initially had not seen anyone else. Marcus followed the direction of the sound and turned to the man asking, "What did you say?"

"Kill her, they must. So . . . dead . . . is . . . she! Dad, daughter . . . then mom make three." He coughed and continued, ". . . life will end . . . catastrophe," he said tossing his hands into the air then letting them fall into his lap.

Marcus knelt by the planter and looked into the face of the man who spoke the words of warning to them. "Who are you talking about?"

Dawn looked at the man and was surprised that she was unable to see any spirit on him at all. Many were certainly present, but had dwelt so far within that they were invisible to her.

"Amy her name is, but this you know. The road of life for her . . . not far to go."

Dawn looked at the man continuing to search for the demons that were inspiring the dialog. Her first response was to rebuke them and cast them out of the man, but quickly decided to wait and see where he was going and if the creature would slip up and give them vital information.

"Die she will . . . up on the hill."

"Where?" she demanded.

"Matters not . . . by the water is rot!"

"What are you talking about?" Marcus demanded.

"Burning sulfur makes a bed . . . screams day and night when she's dead."

Having heard enough, Marcus seized the huge planter and pulled it away from the bench and wall exposing the man. His cloths were ripped at the seam on his left shoulder and a cut was above his right eye. He reeked of alcohol and perspiration. Blood was caked around his lip.

"Man, you've been beaten up," Marcus said. He looked upon him in amazement and asked, "You're Hal Sutton? Quarterback of the two time Professional Football League world champion Minnesota Storm! I saw a news report about you just the other day. You just walked away from football, your family and home. No one knew what happened to you. Now you are here? On the streets of New Orleans? Why?"

"Voices . . . voices, night and day . . . keep talking, won't go away," Hal said in a sick monotone voice.

"Look, we will help you, but what do you know about Amy?" Dawn asked.

"Have her, they do. Tomorrow night, all will be through. Tell me they say . . . feel pain all the way!"

"How do we find her?" Dawn asked excitedly.

"No finding her . . . lost souls have she."

"Dawn, these spirits are just taunting us," Marcus said.

"Laugh, they do . . . not worried about you" Hal's body said.

Marcus kneeled by the man and raised his hands to God giving praise for all the mighty things He had done that night. His faith had become bulletproof and feared not those who possessed Hal and trusted God to do a mighty work. Moving from his knees and into standing position over Hal's legs, Marcus called out to the demons and bound them in Jesus' name.

Suddenly, like bees in a disturbed hive, the spirits stirred. Movements covered his body. The tip of an ear, claw, several feet and wings moved in and out restlessly. Marcus was amazed at the incalculable number that resided in the poor twisted soul.

"Legions are we . . . lesions on he!" the demons taunted.

Hal rolled over and grabbed an empty bottle of wine and slammed it against the ground. With the broken bottle neck, the demons steered his hand toward the exposed left wrist. Marcus stopped praying and lunged at the bottle and fought with Hal's body to get it away. With all of his physical strength, he worked to reverse the direction of the jagged glass before they sliced the wrist. Marcus felt powerless, like a boy who had challenged a grown man to a fight.

"I rebuke you! In the name of Jesus . . . . BE GONE!" he yelled while fighting with both hands to pull the broken bottle from Hal's wrist as it hovered less than an inch away from causing a serious injury.

"Death, death is his fall . . . death, death to you all!" he screamed. Marcus found himself supernaturally thrown off of Hal and into the planter with enough force to knock the planter over, sending it rolling down the concrete steps toward Decatur Street. The rounded planter chipped and broke with each step as it descended.

Marcus recovered and lunged toward Hal again, but it was too late. He jammed the bottle into his forearm and sliced down toward his wrist. Marcus grabbed the hand once again and pulled against the resistance. Hal pushed at him again, but Marcus was prepared and leaned against the pressure. His foot slipped and he crashed to the concrete while holding Hal's hand. Suddenly, a movement by Marcus's head caught his attention. Beneath the planter the concrete was damaged and a small piece had been left behind. Marcus reached out and grabbed the loose concrete that was three times the size of his hand and forcefully drove it into Hal's hand at the broken bottle. Shards of glass flew into the air and littered the ground. The hand opened and released a small remnant.

Hal fell backwards and grabbed his chest like a man experiencing cardiac arrest, fighting for air. Marcus and Dawn laid hands on him and called out to God once again. They watched the spirits as they fled into the night like excited bats in a cave. Hal's breathing became normal and he sat looking around in amazement. Marcus ripped a section of his shirt off and wrapped the free flowing laceration at tightly as possible. Dawn dialed for emergency support.

Marcus and Dawn fell back on to their butts on the concrete next to Hal and looked back and forth at each other attempting to take in the number of spirits that had possessed him. What a strange night it had been.

Hal moaned in pain and looked at the two strangers sitting next to him. The forearm was throbbing and extremely painful. He was now fully coherent and puzzled about his situation.

CHAPTER 22

A peace accompanied Dawn as she rose from her knees. Since Marcus dropped her off, she spent most of her Sunday afternoon in prayer and devotion seeking a deep intimacy with God. She stood spiritually naked in *confession* withholding no emotion or thought. The Spirit of God moved powerfully through her.

She raised her hands and sang the chorus of a song she had heard in the worship service with no concern for who might hear. Tears rolled down her cheeks and she felt the presence of God. She repeated the verse several times in continuous praise.

Dawn walked into the kitchen and was surprised by the time. She looked in the refrigerator and pulled out a clear glass plate with tortilla wraps, sliced celery and carrot sticks. She removed the clear plastic covering and tossed it into the garbage and noticed six disposable takeout containers that had been discarded. It was a reminder that she needed to go grocery shopping.

She turned and slid the plate on an open section of counter that separated the kitchen and living room. On the right side of the counter next to the golden leather purse that she had used for church that morning were the pieces that Amy had carelessly tossed at her.

Dawn walked around to the open bar area and sat on one of the raised chairs. She re-assembled the torn pieces of the 5x7 picture. Dawn walked back around and into the kitchen and pulled a roll of clear tape from the utility drawer. With four three-quarter inch-wide strips, she secured the pieces in their proper place and then sandwiched them between two sheets of lamination.

The original McIntyres, she thought. The photo was a group picture of the McIntyre family just before death had torn them apart. Destroying the picture was Amy's way of childishly declaring that they were no longer a family.

Dawn reached into the purse and pulled out a ball point pen and small spiral bound notebook she kept convenient for last second notes or ideas. She flipped it open to a blank page and recorded the words the demon had said through Hal: "Kill her they must. So, dead is she! Dad, daughter . . . then mom make three. Life will end . . . catastrophe." Was this an indication that dad was indeed in Hell? Or, was this just more deceptive rhetoric that was a part of the plan to taunt, and drive her to madness? Amy was next, then mom. A mild anxiety began to well up once again. She felt apprehensive.

A knock at the door followed by Marcus's voice calling out rescued her from depressing and unfruitful thoughts.

"In here," she called out from the study.

Marcus said anxiously while moving quickly through the front door and foyer. "I just got a call from Reed. He and Paris were out . . . somewhere I don't remember . . . anyway, they spotted that Jeff King guy and followed him. He got into some SUV, so they tailed him and he picked up Amy and some other people at some old abandoned warehouse by the Julia Street wharf. They are on the Twin-Span right now. Reed will stay with them and keep in contact with us, but we need to get going. This may be," he paused, "well . . . it may be an opportunity."

Reed and Paris slowly drove into the parking lot praying that they would not draw any attention to themselves. Reed didn't want to appear nosy or get caught staring and looked forward acting disinterested and on a mission disassociated with the gathering.

Paris, who was less visible from the passenger side, in the manner of a good play by play announcer, gave an account to Reed on all that was visible to her. "Amy is out of the car and is being escorted . . . well, I *say* escorted; the guy is jerking on her arm and yelling at her. He pushed her into some boat that is nosed up on the right side of the ramp. King is jawing with a man who is launching another boat. He is really mad at him. There looks to be several boats in the water toward the lock kind of in the grass. I can see the waves from a boat and a little light that has left and is heading out."

A small flickering light caught Paris' attention, coming from the cab of a dark colored Buick with a dented front bumper and a severely cracked windshield. On the driver's side a dancing flame faded from blue to yellow and wrapped around the tip of a cigarette and was followed by the bright orange glow of igniting tobacco. Light refracted off of the cracks in the windshield resembling streaks of lightening. The flame disappeared and the heat of the burning tobacco increased as the unidentified man took a long hard drag.

Paris wondered if the man had wanted them to see him, or if he simply had not perceived them as a threat to whatever it was that was taking place. If connected with the group, he was either announcing his presence as a form of intimidation or was foolishly careless.

"There is a man in a car in the middle of the outside lane . . . not too far from the car Amy was riding in."

"I wonder who that can be. Some sort of lookout or watchman?" Reed considered.

"He doesn't seem too bashful. He could have waited for us to get further away before lighting a cigarette and giving himself away. Thank you God for revealing him to us if he is a threat," Paris said.

"There may be more than one. So, we will need to really consider our options here," Reed said.

Reed was thankful that his love for fishing had occasionally brought him here and he had acquired a fairly reliable understanding of the geography of the area around the lock. He turned right and continued to the river side of the lock and nudged into a parking spot that was nestled behind several pine trees. The concentration of trees was sufficient enough to provide a decent covering from the group at the launch site and the watcher.

Reed searched his pockets and handed Paris his wallet and car keys. "What is this for?" she asked.

"I am going to check things out. If I get caught looking around, I don't want them to be able to trace me to you. I don't want them to ID me." He noticed the increasing look of concern on her face. "It is just a precaution. I will be alright."

"What are you going to do? What am I going to do?" Paris inquired.

"I am going to make my way over to the party and see what I can find out. There is a trail in this patch of woods that will shelter me and lead me alongside the lock. I will take a look from there and circle back with a game plan. There is a levy on the other side of the lock, which means that I will need to cross over. A couple of miles up the canal there is what is called a spill way. I hope that they are somewhere between here and there. Anyway, I am going to do my best to find out where they are. The canal is only about seventy feet wide, so I can cross over at any time if I need to. I will come back before I do anything."

With his left hand, Reed reached up to a dial on the dashboard and turned it to the left, killing the dome lights. He moved maps and papers from the center console, tossing them into the back seat, and pulled out three electronic devices.

With each device, he held down a button at the top near a small antenna and held firm until two three inch LCD screens came to life.

"What is this?" she asked.

"Our means of communication," he said, handing one over to her for instruction. "This is somewhat of a short range surveillance tool. On the top left there are three buttons. The top puts it into text mode. We can communicate with text message, there is a full keyboard. The messages will stay on a single screen and you can scroll down them like a forwarding e-mail. I will have my back lights off, so I will do my best to send you accurate messages, so you may have to make sense out of some things since I will be kind of blind.

"The second button is for the video function. We can send each other live video feeds. If you send me a video signal, my Compact will automatically record it. I can either keep it as one long video or mark segments to folders and review it at any time. You can also control the zoom so you can enhance your recording. Each Compact holds up to eight hours. The third is a GPS. You can track my device from yours. I have already set it up. Just push this button, and you will know where I am and how to get to me."

"How short or long range are these things?" Dawn asked.

"Accurate for about seven miles and goes downhill fast from there. What I need you to do is wait for Marcus and Dawn to get here. Call them on the cell phone and tell them where we are parked or whatever useful information you can think of. I want to scout out the area and will send you back information. If . . . if something happens . . . just leave. Don't get out of the car and don't stop for anyone. Someone gets in your way, run over them. Don't stop!"

Paris looked at him as if he were a madman. "I am not leaving without you. Don't worry about me."

Reed leaned over and kissed Paris, then prayed. He retrieved a foot-long strap and clipped one end to his Compact and the other to his belt loop. "Give one to Marcus with a strap. Oh . . . don't worry about getting them wet. They're good up to one-hundred and fifty feet.

"I am going to make a pass and then swing back here and make a decision on what to do next. It shouldn't take twenty minutes."

Slowly the door of the Montero swung open and Reed calmly stepped toward the tree line. It was dark and the moon had yet to light up the area. The woods provided the perfect covering and he slipped quickly through the pines. Reed sought refuge behind a large water oak and surveyed his surroundings. There was no other watchman or lookout close to his position in or near the woods. Reed moved behind the tree and took a trail to his right that led directly through the heart of the overgrown wooded area toward the lock.

The echoes of screaming outboard boat motors laid a temporary siege to the chorus of croaking frogs and humming insects. As is in every aspect of creation, the sounds of man easily drowned out that of nature.

Reed realized by the continuous launching of boats and diminishing crowed noise that the group was quickly leaving the dock area. He found the trail and moved quickly nearly falling over a downed pine tree that was hidden by the shadows. Visibility was near zero and he continued to press forward walking into large spider webs and endless thorn bushes.

A halogen light from the lock lit up the end of the trail and Reed stepped out of the clearing from behind the undergrowth. Reed got down on his stomach and worked his way to the clearance, looking from right to left in search of anything that could provide an advantage. Several more boats had yet to leave as a few last minute arrivals were quickly jumping out of a Ford truck and snatched duffle bags from out of the bed.

Two of five street lights worked properly and were alive with swarming insects. Reed spotted the old Buick Regal with a motionless figure behind the steering wheel. The location and angle of the Buick in relation to the streetlights presented the man as a multi-layer silhouette from which Reed learned nothing.

"Let's do it!" a man declared as he jumped into one of the boats and started the engine. A second man followed and pushed the boat from shore before accidentally stepping into the water and hurriedly climbing in. He rolled over and kicked his foot, trying to shake water from it while yelling obscenities.

The last boat took off and was quickly enveloped by the darkness. Humming engines faded after the first bend in the waterway and the boats became silent. The sounds of nature once again took over. A repetitive, "tap, tap, tap," of bugs drew Reed's attention toward a light on the edge of the lock. He looked around and noticed a hole in the fence that was reachable from the wood line. He felt God stir his spirit and noticed the four panels used to control the lock doors, which were primarily responsible for controlling the water levels between the Pearl River and the man-made waterway that was commonly referred to as "The Canal." Reed instantly realized that if properly utilized, the opening of the lock would cause a seriously strong and effective current by the huge volume of water that would rush through it. The swift current may provide them with an advantage. He was compelled to inspect the control panels and explore such possibilities. He moved toward the fence.

A movement by the car caught his peripheral vision and Reed turned back in time to hit record on the Compact and see the man as he kicked the door of his car open. A loud thud rang out when a dark gray Mercedes that was parked too close to the Buick was impacted by the momentum of the door. The man rose and looked around snickering as the dent in the passenger side door extended upward by the release of his three hundred-plus frame on the Buick's suspension system.

The man stood less than six feet with a head of thick black hair that was combed straight back. He wore blue jeans and a baggy short-sleeved button up shirt. The stranger was round, but solid. He reached back into the car and retrieved a phone from off the dash and flipped it open. With his right hand, the man grabbed the Buick door and jerked it free from the Mercedes, causing more damage.

His voice was inaudible as the man circled to the back of the car, lost in his conversation. A swoosh sound came from the compression of the rear shocks as the car slumped downward from the weight of the man as he plopped down on the trunk. He faced away from Reed's position, making it impossible to make a positive identification.

Reed saved the video to a file for further review. He moved down the tree line to the hole in the fence, recording his movement and keeping watch on the big man. He slid through the gate and wasted no time hiding in the shadows and making his way to the control station. He inspected the panel and realized there was an ignition for which there was a key required to start the motor in order to activate the giant wall that suppressed the water. Reed searched the control base and ran his hands looking for a key or a loose panel where the key could have been hidden or stored and found nothing. He ran his hands against the concrete and into a built up pile of dried grass from a cutting earlier in the day. A faint noise that sounded like that of metal sliding across concrete moved to his right after his hand passed through. Reed brushed the grass aside and a small reflection of light made the object visible. *Why in the world would they just leave the key out here?* he thought. He wondered if God had smiled down upon him and made a way for the key to be where it could be found. He was thankful for this good fortune despite not knowing how to benefit from it.

He retrieved the key, which seemed to have been lost for a long time, and cleaned off the caked on dirt and dry grass from within the grooves. Reed looked back at the big man who was still on the trunk of the car talking on the phone and turned to look at the key as he held it up in the increasingly present moonlight. "God, do you really want me to open the lock?" he asked in a voice no louder than a whisper. Reed felt God press it upon his heart to insert the key into the control and leave it. Reed questioned the voice of instruction. Acting against his desire, Reed pushed the key in till resistance and moved away from the control with faith that God had a plan.

After sending Paris a quick video of the operational procedures of the control panel, Reed walked over to the end of the lock and climbed down a ladder made of steel pipe that had been imbedded in the concrete structure of the lock. He hurried down and leapt onto a concrete landing at the base and swung under the railing toward the shoreline on the river side. Large chunks of concrete that had once been construction debris now protected the lock from erosion and had been spread across a twenty foot high area of bank.

Reed was circling back around to Paris and paused long enough to send her a warning from the Compact so that she would expect him and would not be frightened. He turned and continued to follow the shoreline and noticed an elongated black object that was stuck in a cluster of cypress trees. The sixteen-foot aluminum boat sat like a gift trapped in the cypress trees and ankle-deep water. A single oar lay flat on the bow. The rear seat was smashed, but the plug was in and there were no signs of damage to the outer shell that he could see. Reed noticed a dark substance that had been splattered over the bow. He reached down and swiped it with his index finger and brought it to the light.

"Blood!" he said aloud, uncertain if it was human or a large animal.

Paris was reviewing and watching the videos and messages sent by Reed when, despite the warning, she was startled by a figure exiting the woods and moving toward the Montero. He opened the door, climbed in and wasted no time, "Have you heard from Marcus and Dawn?"

"They are almost here and I told them to drive and park on the other side of the ramp from us," she answered.

"You are not going to believe this, but God led me to the key that opens the lock."

"I saw the video you sent. But, you're not really going to open the lock doors . . . or whatever they are called?" she asked, uncertain.

"Well . . . I'm not sure. It's just and option. Just think of us being chased by angry armed men in boats and those lock doors are open. It may just even the odds a little bit. Anyway, I found the key in some dry grass and put it in the ignition and left it there. If we need it, the key should be there."

He replayed the video. "Just in case you have to do it . . . basically each door is controlled by the same type of device. This key starts the motor . . . the ignition is here," he said pointing to the monitor, "spin this wheel counter clockwise to release the lock and push this button to open. If we get into some situation and God puts it upon your heart to open the lock . . ." Reed talked while sketching a diagram of the lock on a tablet. The canal side was to his left and the river side to his right. He marked an X on the box closest to their location. "The key is here. I would start at the first gate here and get this one going. Now, don't wait until it is completely open. Pull the key, leave it running and head across to the other side. You will have to cross over the doors themselves, so move fast or you will get stuck. Do them in this pattern," Reed said, drawing a horseshoe. "There is a cut out in this section of the fence by the control. You can enter here and cross over. Then move to the canal side and work your way back. If you can completely drain the lock before opening the canal side, it should increase the strength of the current and become nearly inescapable."

"What about the man in the car?" Paris asked.

"I am not really sure what to do about him, yet. But, at least you have an idea of what to do about the lock. We need to get moving. Where are they? We need to get going."

CHAPTER 23

An up-tempo contemporary Christian song was playing on an MP3 player through the radio's auxiliary port while Marcus tapped on the steering wheel. His adrenalin was flowing in anticipation of the task at hand and the dangers associated with it. The song did little to soothe his nerves, but the beat and lyrics mildly sedated his conscious mind. Loose gravel flew from beneath spinning tires as the Rover lunged forward in front of the landmark of wooden six by six posts that supported a hanging sign marking the geographic location of the lock.

Lock No.1 was one of three locks completed in 1956 as a part of the Rivers and Harbors Act of 1935. Each lock measured sixty-five feet wide and three hundred and ten feet long. Twenty miles of canals dug eighty feet wide and seven feet deep separated the locks. It had become a prime area for water recreation and fishing.

"Well, at least we know that we are close." Marcus said.

He sped down the winding road looking intently for moving objects hoping against hope that by some miracle Amy would have escaped and was walking down the road. Perhaps she had come to her senses and realized the danger she was in and managed to escape. Maybe God would make this one easy.

Large branches of mature live oaks loomed above, giving support to ominous masses of drooping Spanish moss that brushed the top of the Rover as they passed beneath. The sight spoke a warning into their hearts. Dawn looked intently searching, fearing that there would be an assault launched from above as they passed beneath the haunted canopy.

"I feel like I'm in one of those Scooby-Doo cartoons! This is really something," Marcus said.

Dawn remained quiet and only acknowledged his remark. She prayed that no matter what God's will was for Amy, if they rescued her, or if they did not make it in time that Dawn would not witness her sister's death or see the lifeless body.

During the greater portion of the ride, Dawn beat herself up for not pressing more diligently and looking through the night. If Amy were to pass on, how much of the blame could she place on herself? A mental picture of standing in front of the mobile home came to mind. What if she had knocked on that door and confronted Dyenomite or turned him over to authorities for the crimes he was committing? What if she had gotten her sister some help with the drug addiction? Why did she take the easy road and walk away? Any contact, even with a negative result, would have made things easier at this point. Amy resented her because she knew about her walking away. That must have been like pouring acid on her heart, the ultimate rejection. It didn't take much to realize the potential embarrassment of having a prostitute for a sister as a leading motivator. What was blood worth? Did it have any value to her? The most pressing question was why didn't she tell her mother where Amy was and let her deal with it. Certainly she would have reached out and done something. Dawn questioned her quality as a person and began to despise herself again. She silently cried out to God for mercy and forgiveness as she felt lowly.

Dawn pulled down the visor to use the mirror and saw the deceptive spirit that was attempting to manipulate her thoughts against her. She loudly rebuked it and it fled without hesitation.

The Spirit of God ministered to her soul. Despite the attempt by the Holy Spirit to place peace upon her heart, Dawn felt undeserving and refused to take any comfort until Amy was safe.

Marcus decided against the slow and cautious approach and felt a spirit of anxiety push the gas pedal. He was often obedient of traffic laws and unaccustomed to high speed navigation. Each curve carried a potential for unseen dangers as it was impossible to forecast obstacles on the back side. His heart pounded forcefully at the thought of staring into a pair of lost and frightened eyes that met with an unavoidable and potentially deadly impact. He prayed without ceasing for God to clear the way.

Several minutes later the headlights revealed a large yellow steel column that supported a gate that was open and pointed in toward the lock. A triangular sign riddled with slug holes and shot gun spray retained only random touches of yellow paint.

"That's inviting," Marcus said, pointing at the sign. "I guess we have arrived."

For the brief second he had taken his eyes off of the road, the Rover slammed into a metal grid that crossed the passage way that was used for keeping out free roaming cattle. It was too late to slow down and the front end of the Rover lunged upward briefly with enough force to pull the front tires from the security offered by the ground. The rear tires met the grid multiplying the downward gravitational pull on the front end slamming the Rover into loose gravel. Rocks and dust clouds were thrust into the immediate surroundings.

"Sorry," he said looking briefly at Dawn as she braced herself and held on.

"This is more like a movie every second," she replied and readjusted the seat belt.

They both noticed the man sitting on the back of the Buick just as Paris had warned them about. He was startled by the commotion and held a cell phone up by his ear while watching the stuntman's entrance.

Marcus tapped the breaks and pulled in front of four large wood panels that posted information about the Pearl River Navigation System and the success of the reserve. The Rover firmly rolled to a stop. A cloud of dust ten times the size of the Rover moved freely into the air.

The headlights revealed Plexiglas panels covering panoramic images of lush foliage, soaring bald eagles, swallow-tailed kites, osprey, blue herons and the infamous American alligator were posted on the large informational billboards championing the success of environmental conservation.

Dawn looked at the line of cars on the left side of the parking lot. "There isn't an open spot over there. Are there normally this many people on the water at night?" Dawn asked before being distracted by a bat that passed only inches from the windshield.

"I'm sure some of these are campers out roughing it."

Dawn turned to her right and panned the area hoping to make a mental connection with the description given to them by Paris, "I thought we were supposed to go somewhere to the right and follow it to another boat ramp or something over there."

"That's what Paris said. After my wild and crazy entrance, that guy will certainly have his eyes on us. We need to do something to lead him to believe that we are not a threat or interested in whatever he has going on. We can't take anyone for granted."

"Before anything happens, I just want to let you know how grateful I am for all that you have done and are trying to do," Dawn said.

"You have already said that, but I am just glad to be in a position to help. Watching God work through you is a blessing in itself. Thanks for letting me help." Marcus replied.

Of all the abilities and character traits of Marcus, Dawn continually marveled at his selfless, servant's heart and the fact that he was there with her. "I also want you to know, that I've never been an outdoors type of person," she said in pre-apology for what may result from her lack of experience in the wild, if that was where the trail led.

"It seems like a lot of cars," he observed and agreed with Dawn as he scanned the parking lot for a sign of life outside of the man who was standing behind the car and was watching them. "Nice beauty mark on that fifty thousand dollar Mercedes."

Marcus continued to follow the directions Paris had given them and followed the gravel drive to the right. He could see the Murano and the top of the second boat launch and pulled to the parking area by the water.

"Hey!" Reed called out softly, hurrying them over to the car where Paris was standing with the Compact in hand, "They took off. Amy was on one of the first boats that left at least a half an hour ago. The last boat left maybe fifteen minutes ago," Reed said as he pulled the two behind the security of the tree line and began filling them in in on all that he had learned.

"Well, then let's get to the levy and see where it leads. God willing, we will find her," Marcus said.

"What about guns. What if they have guns? How do we get to her?" Paris asked.

"You both need go somewhere safe." Reed said looking at Paris and Dawn.

"No! I am not leaving. I am going with you. I have to go," Dawn declared.

"Look, I'm not going to leave either, but I am not crazy about going in those woods in the dark. Besides, if you need me to open the lock, I need to be here," Paris said.

Marcus looked back at Paris with a confused look trying to understand the comment about opening the lock. "You can't stay here alone with that guy hanging around," Marcus said.

"I will back the car up over there," she said pointing to an open area that made it impossible for anyone to sneak up on her. "I will keep the engine running and I will be able to see him. If he moves, I will leave."

Reed reached into the trunk, pulled out a junior sized aluminum bat and offered it to Marcus. He declined. Reed kept it and pushed the trunk shut.

"Well . . . we've walked pretty briskly, despite having to climb over all these pine trees," Reed said while jumping over a fallen trunk that was lying across the crown of the levee.

To their right was as six-foot high fence of welded wire and signs indicating that all trespassers would be shot on sight. "Warming and so inviting. I bet this guy is a great host," Marcus said sarcastically.

"At our pace, we should be at least a mile out by now. I can see something right up there. Looks like several boats up in the trees," Reed said.

The soft radiance of the moon blanketed the canal and provided the perfect balance of illumination and concealing darkness. Marcus turned to Dawn, attempting to get a read on her condition as he was concerned by her silence. During the brisk fifteen minute trek she had not complained once and kept pace despite the obstacles of fallen tree trunks, broken limbs and numerous overgrown areas of stickers. She exhibited no extraordinary signs of stress and looked focused and ready.

Dawn was thankful that she had dressed for the occasion properly and had provided herself with the best possible defense from scratching plants and parasitic bugs. Blue jeans were now a wonderful gift from God.

Her long hair was pulled back in the traditional pony tail and was tucked into the back of her shirt. Vanity was not a part of the equation. In the event they had to make a quick move, she didn't want her hair to get caught on anything. She needed to move as freely as possible especially if she was to be a productive member of the rescue team.

Since leaving the lock and journeying down the levee, Dawn had not seen any demonic spirits since there were no souls to manipulate. She feared the spirits less than the snakes that hung in the trees over the water, as they often did at night. Each dangling serpent sent chills down her spine and gave extra motivation to keep pace.

Marcus thought of calling the police. But he considered it to be a fruitless option. How would they provide enough evidence to warrant any intervention? He imagined the conversation:

"Yes, I believe that a lady by the name of Amy McIntyre is in danger."

"By whom? Who has threatened her?" The police would ask.

"A satanic cult. She is out in the woods with them right now."

"Have they made any direct threats to you about Ms. McIntyre?"

"No."

"Then how do you know they intend to do her harm?"

"Well . . . my friend, I am sure you have heard of her . . . Dawn McIntyre, the one from the radio. Anyway, she and I have this gift and we can see demons and one told us that it was going to kill her. So, we think she is in grave . . . bad word . . . serious danger."

"Demons . . . huh! Sounds like you're the one who needs help! Look, if these nut jobs want to go out into the woods, dress in sheep skins and howl at the moon, I can't stop them. If there has been no credible threat to this Amy McIntyre's life, then I can't move on supposition. Did they force her to go by kidnapping her . . . at gunpoint or something?"

"No . . . she got in the boat on her own."

"What I can do is pick you up and bring you down to headquarters for a blood alcohol test and psychoanalysis. Call me again and I will do just that!"

It wouldn't be a pretty or productive conversation. Their options were limited without credible evidence.

"We are close," Dawn said. "They are everywhere . . . glowing eyes. Several began circling us about two minutes ago. Tios and Goad took care of them. But, I see more activity up ahead. We have to be close."

Marcus looked up to their right several blue and orange eyes shifted and moved upward into several tree limbs. Above Reed, a demon sat perched on a branch, looking down upon him like a predatory bird watching its meal.

Marcus's sixth sense stirred. He turned to a cold stare by a crouching silhouette at the water's edge. He had seen thousands of demons since they were empowered, but for some unknown reason chills ran down his back and he became keenly aware of the one before him. There was something about this demon that shook his soul and conjured a powerful fear. Marcus studied the beast. It was tall, lanky and rested on its right knee like a camouflaged killer minimizing its body mass to avoid detection by its unsuspecting victim. The beast's facial features were human in a basic form but covered in layer of satin textured scales that reflected a dull portion of moonlight. Emerald green eyes stared back at him, refusing to break contact and receiving gratification from the hint of fear they detected. Spiked thick hair like that of porcupine quills covered its scalp and was lying down in layers toward its back.

"Hello, love!" a voice said in his mind.

Marcus stood frozen in thought, wondering why this thing had such a stronghold on his attention. "What do you want?" He was surprised by the stupidity of his own question, an even greater indicator of the effects to his psychological condition.

"Just to do the same favor for you," it replied in a grainy and calm voice.

"What do you mean 'same favor'? I don't need anything from you! I just need for you to go to Hell."

Reed could hear Marcus and became concerned that someone had caught them. He watched Marcus staring at something by the water's edge and realized what was taking place. He considered intervening for the sake of alerting the cult of their presence, but decided against it. This whole demon thing, despite believing in the spiritual world, was new to him and would take some adjusting. He almost wished that he had never seen into the realm at all.

"Yes love . . ."

"Stop calling me that! You don't know the first thing about love. If you had, you would have never turned on God. All you know is hate and deception. You're a fool and no matter what you do here, you will suffer eternal torment. Day and night you will suffer!" Marcus wondered why he didn't rebuke or bind the demon, but conversed with it.

"Love . . . or was she your love? Did you love her, dear Marcus? It was I who spared her the horrors of this world. Peaceful in the grave now . . . she is!" the beast said, looking to strike an emotional wound and take down Marcus by using his most painful experience. The blow hit the mark.

"Rot in Hell demon!" Marcus said, losing all sense of fear and stepping toward the satanic spirit.

"Oh what a night," it tauntingly said while rising from the ground to face Marcus eye to eye. "I took that lonely, drunk and worthless soul and convinced him he needed something stronger . . . ." It laughed briefly. "Got some bad stuff for him. I had it all set up. He was so high he didn't know what side of eternity he was on. It was beautiful. I escorted him to your house that night. He did just as I had prepared him to do."

Marcus felt a tremendous weight come upon him and he began to drift back and reliving the minutes when he held Allison's dying body as she bled profusely. He wanted to fight the demon. He wished for the beast to take on a physical form so he could beat it to Hell and back.

"I came for you, but got her. It was an even trade . . . I guess. The big guy was happy either way."

Marcus stepped forward to rebuke him, but Argos lunged forward and got to the beast first. But the scaly spirit quickly stretched out its membranous wings and shot upward like a missile. Argos was after it, and in a matter of seconds returned to the surface next to Marcus with the squirming beast in his grip. The hulking angel unsheathed his sword and sliced the demonic soul in half. The beast let out a blood-curdling scream as it fell to the ground and was absorbed by earth.

"Thank you," Marcus said.

"Are you OK?" Dawn asked.

"What?" Marcus asked trying to sort out the experience. "Yes, I'm fine.

Reed returned from inspecting the area and gave the all clear to proceed with caution. Marcus shook off his thoughts and joined Dawn as they moved forward and came upon the boats. Reed was standing looking at the Compact taking a picture and looking at the GPS while standing before an open gate. As the warning on the fence had declared, a large sign indicated that trespassers would be shot.

Reed stepped through and waited for Dawn and Marcus. Before him was a trail that led straight into the woods. An inspection of the ground revealed that all-terrain vehicles had been used to transport supplies and/or the satanic congregation from the canal to the location of worship.

"We have no time to waste," Reed said as he moved quickly.

The trail was cleaner than the one on the levee. There were no fallen trees or debris. Grass and foliage was pushed over and several low areas retained rain water and was chopped up by the tires of an ATV. They pushed forward with more caution than before.

Within a matter of minutes the humming sound of a generator became audible. Reed turned and nodded with approval and seemed to have a gleam in his eye. Marcus wondered if the retired soldier was back in his element and enjoying the opportunity. He was a man true to the wild heart given to him by God. Marcus was quickly growing very fond of Reed and saw him as a warrior.

They stealthily continued their push forward and moved closer to the outdoor temple. Lights became visible. There was a large area several hundred feet in front of them that was well lit. A bridge was constructed by placing eight rail road ties side by side, filling in a low area that served as run-off from rain. The generator sat on far right side of the bridge and continued to hum loudly and steadily.

Four sheets of plywood were used as a temporary casing around it to deflect the sound waves away from the ceremony and toward the canal. Reed thought of pushing the off button or throwing the breaker just to mess with the deranged cult, sending them into a physical darkness to match their spiritual condition.

Several yellow twelve gauge chords stretched out weaving back and forth set in the straightest line possible in accordance to the foliage and density of trees. The rescue party moved quickly following the power source. With each step, strange ceremonious chants grew louder and more discernible. "Oh high god, mighty intercessor Gaia—goddess of the earth, creator of all things given by our father Satan . . ."

Marcus looked at Dawn with a confused look on his face. She simply shook her head, at a loss for it all. He nodded back in agreement and a spirit flew right in front of his face without stopping. Dawn instinctively drew back. He wished he could help her, but only God could take the supernatural ability away.

Reed stopped, turned and pulled them off the trail behind a cluster of holly bushes and a flowering Mayhaw tree. Without speaking, Reed held out his hands with eyes closed. Marcus and Dawn quickly conceded to the need for prayer and joined him. The prayer was not verbal, but united nevertheless.

Before their departure on this mission of mercy, the collective minds had no clue in regard to layout of the wooded satanic cathedral. Formulation of a game plan was not possible, as neither had any knowledge of exactly what was taking place. They set out with the faith that God wanted them to move and in return He would move.

Reed whispered, "Look, we are going to get dirty and muddy. There is some kind of structure over there. Let's see if we can't use it to hide us while we try to understand what it is that God wants us to do."

They both nodded in agreement and followed his lead. Reed slowly moved down to his stomach, prostrating himself on the ground. In the manner of a trained soldier sneaking up for a surprise assault, he began to crawl on his belly and slither beneath the brush and tree limbs away from the path. The ground was damp by the moisture trapped by the canopy of the woods and covering of fallen leaves.

Dawn was apprehensive about getting intimate with the ground. Even as a little girl she had avoided getting dirty and messy and had been successful till now. The tom-boy mentality was difficult to understand. She had no desire for grit and grime and now willingly lying face down in mud.

She soon found herself caught by briers that were ripping at her forearms and legs through the denim. Marcus was behind her and reached up to pull the drooping branches free from her legs. The thorns grabbed like razor-sharp, Velcro refusing to let go without leaving scratches. Marcus's hands were cut while pulling her free. With his teeth, Marcus pulled out the splinters of broken thorns from his hands before continuing his passage.

An open pavilion was now in view. Round steel posts supported twelve inch beams on which sat a shallow-pitched hip roof covered with corrugated tin. A raised floor or stage matched the outer dimensions of the structural beams and provided protection from minor flooding. A two-foot overhang extended outward and added some extra protection from damaging rain water. Circular open trays of smoldering incense were mounted to each of the posts. The smoke from the ash cubes danced upward in tight lines like a cobra seduced by a charmer.

A short stubby man in a hooded robe moved in the center of the stage and spoke in to a microphone. A large black book sat open on a wooden podium as he referenced it. The man shook a crooked index finger at the worshipers while proclaiming the word of their master. Men and women clothed in dark green, red, blue, white and black hooded satin robes joined in simultaneous cheers and chants in support of hate-filled dialog of the man at the podium.

"How many times have you driven by a church and seen the whole parking lot full of SUVs the size of buses? They laugh at you if you care about Mother Earth-our dear Mother goddess." The raspy voiced man ranted and screamed, damning profane insults about the followers of God and the scourge they had always been on society. They had been the real workers of iniquity and purposefully sought to mislead the world and usher in the future destruction of the earth so that the new Heaven would descend. Global warming was one of the accelerators. He stood in place and stomped both feet in the manner of a spoiled child in a temper tantrum, calling for justified genocide of anyone who lived a life "unworthy of our father" before irreversible damage had been done.

The congregation whaled and hollered and gave up shout and praise in the height of their spirituality. They seemed oblivious to the observers in the woods, completely absorbed in the charismatic lecture of the man in the red robe.

To his left on the ground was an altar constructed of cinder blocks and concrete. It was built four blocks high and was painted black. Around the outer edge was a continuously concaved area appearing like a concrete river that meet at a collection point and spout.

Twelve torches circled a rather strange-looking tree at the center of the gathering. Marcus was unable to tell what was distinctive about the tree, but there was certainly something unique. He was able to conclude that this tree was part of the attraction of the group to this site in the middle of woods.

Marcus was astounded by the number of people and compared to the number of boats and cars at the lock. He counted sixty standing on the outer rim of the flaming canisters and estimated that over a hundred men and woman had been in attendance. Where had they all come from, he wondered?

To their left, near the outer range of the temporary lighting, stood a wooden building with a shingled roof and vinyl siding. The building was sixteen feet wide and would offer them ample protection with the support of the trees. Lighting was sufficient enough to offer them some visibility.

Reed raised his left hand to signal for them to make a move to the wall when someone awkwardly walked from around the side of the building. The two figures moved from the left, which was the least-lit side of the small building.

"What are you doing? Stop pushing. Why are you bringing me over here?" the female voice demanded.

"What is the problem? What's your problem?" A man with a deep voice demanded as he rounded the corner shoving the woman to the ground.

"I'm tired. I just don't want this no more. I've had enough. You can beat me, or threaten to kill me . . . it doesn't matter anymore. I want out," the woman said through tears and a broken spirit while regaining her footing.

"Look, tramp. I have had enough of you. You're hanging on by a thread. You get back, get right or I will take you out myself!" he threatened.

Reed cautiously raised the Compact and hooked the strap around a leafless branch. He triggered the Compact and sent a live feed to Paris' device to record for future use. He was determined to get as much information as God would allow, for the sake of exposing the unlawful activities of the group.

The man viciously struck the woman with his right hand, sending her back toward the small building. She bent over to the right side, temporarily disoriented by the blow. She cupped the impact point on the left side of her head in an attempt to protect it from another punch.

On many occasions she had suffered abuse at the hands of the men in the Fils de Gaia in various forms. She learned that fighting back only meant more intense abuse and that there would be no victory. She no longer cared. The woman had her fill of the abuse and longed for death if it was the only way out.

Brown knotted hair hung down around her face as she was bent over trying to recover. She blinked repeatedly trying to resolve the blurred vision. The man stood over her ready to swing again.

While securing the Compact, Reed had placed the bat on the ground. Dawn began to push herself up when she saw the movement of the right hand. She hoped that the man would not see her. An old, discarded soda bottle rested half submersed in the mud from years of settling in the saturated soil. She anxiously pulled the bottle free and wiped the excess mud off to lighten the projectile. Throwing from a lying position was odd as her motion was limited and she was glad that accuracy was not warranted. With an arching motion, she heaved the bottle into the woods by the cult member's right side, away from the injured woman.

Leaning against the structure were several three foot long pieces of rebar. The woman reached down and grabbed one. She was done with the abuse and would die fighting.

The man took great joy in his domination of a physically weaker person who he knew had no ability to best him. All of the times he had been called in to control her, she had never cried. Now she was truly broken, and the convulsive crying was better than a trophy. Maybe he had broken her for good, he thought. She would be all the wiser to listen to him.

Instinctively the abusive man turned briefly to investigate the sound made by the bottle. Enraged, the woman swiftly and relentlessly retaliated with the rebar, swinging it upward, driving it against the side of the man's head directly over the ear lobe. He fell to his side in agony. She drove the rod between his legs and into his privates. Unsatisfied with his pain, she swung the rebar hard across his upper left arm, then the ribs and back to the head and arm. She then focused on the ribs with several more full swings, then back to the private area for a final strike. He fought to breath as the pain consumed him and rendered him completely defenseless. Out of breath and exhausted, the woman stood over her injured abuser thinking of the numerous times he had hit her. The woman wanted to kill him, but was out of breath and energy. If given enough time to recover, she would finish off the thug.

She turned and looked into the direction of the canal as if looking for a path to escape. The moonlight finally revealed her identity: it was Amy. Dawn could not resist the need to get up and rush to her aid. She no longer cared about the cult, its members or anything outside of helping her sister.

Amy turned back and stood over the man looking as if she wanted to inflict more pain and damage on the woman beater if he wasn't already dead. She lifted the rod and put it back down.

Dawn stood in a small clearing in the thicket. It was the only clearance where she could stand fully erect without being jammed in the head by limbs or mauled by stickers. "Amy!" she called out.

Amy turned to see the source of the voice coming from the woods. She was unable to spot Dawn, who called out a second time. "Who are you . . . where are you?" she asked.

A hand reached out from the darkness of the shed and grabbed Amy from behind. A white rag covered her mouth and nose. Amy fought and squirmed while attempting to scream. Dawn yelled, not concerned with who knew she was there at that point. She searched for a way through the thick brush and briers and began to force her way to Amy.

Reed stealthily made his way over to the man, who was more concerned with the struggling woman then the strangers in the woods. Leaping out of the weeds, Reed drove his bat into the base of the man's neck, temporarily paralyzing him. The cloaked man let go of Amy, but Reed was too late to help her. She fell limply to the ground and was unconscious.

CHAPTER 24

After moving the Montero from the refuge of the natural barrier of topless pine trees and water oaks, Paris watched and prayed for the makeshift rescue team. The fore view was now of distant lights and lifeless parked cars. To her right, the rising moon glistened across the still waters of the manmade waterway. The tree tops slowly swayed in the gentle breeze.

Paris found no added security had been offered to her by the move and thought it was highly probable that the man would eventually find her. She remained in the driver's seat with the engine running, where escaping was simply a matter of engaging the transmission and stomping on the accelerator. The spirit of fear began to plant seeds in her mind. *What if it isn't fast enough? Can you outrun a bullet? What if you panic and can't get the car into gear . . .*

Frustrated with her thoughts, Paris reached into her purse, blindly searched through its contents and secured the cayenne pepper spray. Any manner of defense was better than none.

She quickly realized she was losing the battle with her mind and desired a distraction before a full blown panic-attack set in. She prayed a second time.

The thoughts subsided and she picked up the Compact and selected the file containing the video of the man by the Buick. She looked up and panned the area and saw no evidence of any activity outside of the swarming bugs. The trees blocked her view of the Buick's exact position, but she would have enough warning if the stranger approached from the lot entrance.

"What if he was in the woods next to you? He can just reach over and do you in right now, or just shoot from the woods. Either way, you are dead," she rebuked the relentless spirit a third time and focused on her faith in answered prayer and divine protection.

She touched play on the screen and watched the playback of the stranger's assault on the Mercedes attempting to identify him or pick up other useful information. Paris and Reed had watched the group for nearly a year, but she had never seen this man before. He was new. Nevertheless, she began to question his affiliation.

"Why would he . . . as the person assigned to watch or guard the parking lot, tear up one of the cult member's cars and be so cavalier about it? He seems proud of what he did," Paris pondered aloud.

It didn't make sense, but she wasn't sure what to think. "Well, they are a satanic cult after all . . . they can't be the most logical or possess the most stable minds," she continued.

The only thing certain was that the man undoubtedly had issues and could prove to be a threat to her and the objective. She found herself becoming equally intrigued and fearful.

As she did every few seconds, Paris panned the parking areas and saw nothing outside of swarming bugs and moon lit water. She returned to the screen and the replay of the man as he ripped the Buick door free from the Mercedes.

The video automatically stopped and returned to its file as a new live transmission was being received. The automatic record button illuminated briefly and faded away. Reed's voice, in a peculiar manner that seemed to possess a distressful tone called out to Paris's and directed dialog specifically to her.

"Paris . . . look, I need you . . ." Reed's voice trailed off.

As if jammed or from a weak signal, the audible blips and brief frozen images allowed Paris to catch only fragments of the transmission. She looked at her watch and added up the time since the boat had cast off and disappeared from the shore. Although it had seemed like hours, only forty-five minutes had passed, leading her to the conclusion that there was no way they had exceeded the Compact's range. Paris grew concerned and was unable to discern the nature of Reed's communication since it was not a text, but video broadcast. Reed said that he would not communicate that way unless absolutely necessary. He had instructed her not to reply to him since the back lights would be off until the objective had been accomplished.

As Paris considered her options she became even more uncomfortable with her situation. Rolling the window down and sticking the Compact out proved useless. She had to get a better signal and became anxious. What if Reed was in trouble and needed for her to call the police? What if someone was hurt? What if they found Amy near death and she need to call an ambulance? Endless waves of "what if's" came upon her.

Paris looked around fearing the loss of valuable time and turned the car's engine off. She opened the door and moved around the front toward the path taken by Reed toward the water. She continuously moved the Compact from side to side, up and down in search of the ideal vein of the frequency. She moved cautiously, panning the area and watching the screen, praying for a better signal so that she could return to the safety of the car. *I always make fun of those Hollywood movies when people in danger do stupid things that get them caught or killed. Now I am doing the same thing*, she thought.

"I should just call the police," she said in a low voice.

The signal cleared and she froze to listen, but was too late. The screen displayed mostly dark images. Panting, heavy breathing and the wrestling of leaves filled the ear buds. She had missed the message, but they seemed to be moving. She watched for a moment and there was no obvious evidence of excess stress or relay of important information.

Wasting no time, Paris turned swiftly toward the car. She froze in horror, realizing her greatest fear. The man from the Buick was standing by the passenger side of the car, facing her. He was a huge and ominous-looking man. His arms were hanging down by his side and he was staring coldly at her. It seemed as if all the blood in her body had somehow drained out through her feet. Fear left her paralyzed, cold and nervous. She immediately called on God for help and fidgeted with the Compact to start a recording of her encounter with the watcher.

The audible prayer struck the man and he asked with a deep angry voice, "Are you with them? Who do you call God? What God do you pray to?"

Paris looked and was too afraid to answer incorrectly. Had he seen Reed, Marcus and Dawn? Was this the "them" he was referencing? If so, they would certainly have fallen into a trap and would be in danger.

"So tell me . . . ," he demanded in an increasingly impatient manner, "are you with them?"

"Who?" she asked nervously.

He walked toward her. "Who were you praying to just now? The devil? You one of those sick, perverted devil worshipers?"

"No. I am a Christian!" she exclaimed.

"Oh, really? Then where is that man who was in your car? Where's the guy who thought his Range Rover was a monster truck and drove in here like a mad man? Maybe he was late for the séance or whatever it is that you screwed up people are doing in those woods. The man and that woman . . . where are they? Now, tell me if you are not one of them," he said accusingly.

Paris was surprised at the line of questioning and answered, "Sir, aren't you a watchman for that that cult? Why are you asking me these questions?"

Rage welled up in the man. "First, I will ask all of the questions. But I will assure you that I ain't in no cult."

"OK. Just calm down . . ." Paris pleaded.

"Calm down. You people stole her mind, drugged her up, beat her, abused her and killed her. She couldn't get away from you sick . . ."

The man was getting increasingly angry and on the verge of violence. Paris knew that she would be defenseless if the man attacked, which seemed immanent if she didn't find a way to convince him that she was truthful.

"Sir, we are here . . . ," Paris carefully considered her answer, "yes, because of the cult. The guy in the Range Rover, the woman with him . . . her sister is a part of that group and they are going in to get her. They fear for her life and are trying to find them now so that they can save her. They think she is going to be sacrificed tonight. Look . . ." she said, holding up the Compact. Her hands shook violently and she fought for enough control to work the electronic device.

The video played in sequence and she handed the device over to the man. His initial response suggested caution. He inserted the right ear bud and watched all of the video. He listened to Reed's commentary and video of him and the lock doors until he was finally convinced. He popped the ear bud free from his lobe by yanking on the thin wire. He passed the device back to Paris.

"Look, I am sorry if I scared you. And I am sorry if your friends get caught. But, no matter what happens, I promise you, it will all end tonight. They won't hurt anyone anymore. If I were you, I would leave. You don't need to be around here. I know their deal. After a few hours they will do their chanting and who-do crap. Then spend the rest of the night drinking and doing . . . well, I'm not going to say. In the early hours of the morning . . . when they are all out of it, they will be taken care of. I assure you."

"I can't do that. I need to help my friends. Why, what are you going to do?" Paris asked.

"Kill them. Every last one. They will all rot in Hell tonight! Each and every one of them."

"Sir—"

"Stop calling me that. I'm not a school teacher. Just . . . call me Ralph."

"OK, Ralph. You can't do that, you will go to jail," Paris said bluntly.

Ralph looked at her. Hate was at full blaze in his eyes. "They killed my little baby. My little girl is dead because of them and the police don't have enough evidence to charge anyone with anything. Scott free! The law won't do a thing. What's a man to do, I need justice? My baby girl is dead and they will be too!"

"Ralph. Help us. Let's get them another way. Not murder," Paris said.

"You said that you're a Christian . . . right?"

"Yes," she answered.

"Then how about 'an eye for an eye'? The life of each one who let my little girl die!"

"That's not what that scripture truly means. It has been taken out of context," Paris knew she had to minister to the man or delay him until Reed or Marcus made it back.

She guided him to the car and sat on the hood and offered him a seat. He declined and stood motionless in front of her lost in his hate and need for revenge. Paris pushed aside all fear and realized that she had an opportunity to minster to the man. Reed had too much of his own anger to deal with and would have been of no comfort to Ralph.

"I am here if you need someone to talk to. Can . . . will you share with me what happened?" Paris asked.

As if snapping out of a trance, he looked away, fighting not to show his emotions. After a few seconds he looked up at Paris. "It hurts. It hurts . . . but, it keeps me going. I wanted to die when they finally found her. If it wasn't for killing them, I would have killed myself." he said. "It hurts so bad . . . I hope you will never know what I go through every day." He took a deep breath looked up at the sky.

"Joann Bethany Crampton," he said in a continuous struggle against his emotion. "They called her, of course, Jo Beth. But I always like Joann. I hated it when they called her Jo Beth. Her Momma would get onto the kids if they called her Jo or JB or Jo B.

"I remember when she was eight and I was working on the car and . . . you know she just liked to hang out with me. Next to her mom, she is the only person in the world that ever wanted to hang out with me. The only person who ever really loved me. It didn't matter what I was doing, she was there watching and keeping me company.

"I asked her for a wrench and she handed me the right one and I jokingly called her JB. She turned and flashed her big blue eyes at me and said, 'Dad . . . you make me sound like a boy.'" He smiled through his tears at the memory. "She was so feminine and beautiful. All I got left is right here," Ralph said pointing to his head. "Memories," he reached into the open shirt pocket and pulled out a picture and gave it to Paris. She opened the car door to produce light so that she could see the photo.

"Wow! She is beautiful. I see what you mean about her eyes," Paris said.

He nodded his head in acknowledgement of her comment, "You know, we didn't always have a lot of money, but our family was close and we always spent a lot of time going to the park and beach and stuff like that. She never did anything wrong or bad. Never talked back and kept her room clean. Her grades were great. At least until she turned sixteen."

"That is a rough age for a girl," Paris commented.

"She started getting interested in boys and I just was not happy about that."

"That's understandable. You wanted to protect her."

"They don't see it that way. We really began to butt heads over her clothes . . . the way she was starting to dress. We began to drift apart. She said my wanting to protect her was pushing her away.

"March 12, two days after she turned seventeen . . . she disappeared. She and her girlfriends went out and someone pulled up in an old BMW and grabbed her. We looked for weeks and had little luck with anything. One day she called from Mexico. Mexico City or just outside of it. There was so many people looking for her, so they . . ." he said pointing toward the location of the cult. ". . . sold her to some sleazebag in Mexico so that no one could find her.

"They said they would kill me and her mom if she ever tried to leave or called the police or called us. She suffered through rapes and beatings to protect us. To protect us," he said angrily. "She told us everything that she could recall through the drugs. About the house where they took her and the things they done. At first they forced the drugs on her, then . . . ," he stopped.

"Anyway, one day some guy tried to help her. He got her and was gonna try to get her home. Like an idiot, I said that I would come and get her . . . wrong decision. Before I could get there, they found her dead in a pile of trash in some back alley with some guy. I guess it was the guy who tried to help her."

"I started talking to the cops . . . about what she had told us and nothing ever happened! The police believed that these cult people were directly responsible, but could never gather enough evidence to make an arrest! But, I know they were involved. I seen the house and some of the men. I've watched for months now . . . and now is the time."

"Ralph . . . ," Paris called out.

"Look, you can't stop me. This has to be done before another man's daughter is taken and abused and killed. These are sick parasites . . . and they must be exterminated."

"What if the police show up? What if you only kill some of them and maybe you are killed . . . then what? Will you enjoy that revenge in death or prison?"

"These animals are sick . . . and sick animals are executed."

"God doesn't want you to kill them. He wants you to forgive and let Him take care of them," Paris declared.

He looked at Paris as if she was his enemy and had played him like a pawn. "You're one of them. Aren't you?"

"No, I am a Christian . . . like I said before." Paris said.

"Where was God when Joann was taken from home, scared and suffering and in torment? All I need is for your God to remain consistent as He has through all of this," he said stepping forward, ". . . stay on the sidelines and do nothing. Sit back and enjoy the easy life in Heaven, if it exists."

Lights flashed from the Compact as a new live feed was being received. Paris picked it up from the hood and unplugged the ear buds to trigger the external speaker. A woman yelled and was hit viciously. Paris moved the Compact to where Ralph could see the screen as curiosity got the better of him. The video was a brutal assault on a woman.

"That is Amy. This is the woman we came for," Paris said.

They watched Amy as she defended herself with the rebar. Ralph almost cheered for Amy as she inflicted heavy bodily injury on the cult member. He became antsy and anxious by a deep inner need to help.

"Oh," Paris said watching Reed's assault on the man with the rag. He fell to the ground.

"I wouldn't move if I were you," an armed man in a black robe commanded.

A Q-beam moved back and forth between Reed and Dawn. Three men pointed weapons at them barking orders and making threats of what would happen had they not followed directions.

Marcus was thankful that they had enough presence of mind to not look back into his direction and tip off the cult members and give him away. He slowly began moving back when Dawn began to call out to Amy. Their capture was imminent at that point as they were heavily outnumbered and had given up their location and security.

Marcus made it back beyond the oppressive stickers and into the midst of thicket impenetrable by the portable lights. His position was safe. From an opening in the foliage, he watched as two men moved in front of Reed and Dawn.

A person in a black robe stepped forward and pulled down his hood, revealing his identity. "I think I will take you out nice and proper this time."

CHAPTER 25

Marcus was out of view and couldn't believe the turn of events. How could he help them? How could he as one man go against this entire group with weapons and no apparent qualms about killing someone?

He heavily considered what to do and worked to stay focused. He remembered the Compact, but didn't know how to use it properly and was uncertain if the back lights would come on and give him away, but it was a chance he had to take. He would need to get further away out of sight. Marcus looked up again and the lynch mob was forcing Dawn and Reed at gunpoint into the worship area.

Marcus decided to make his way back to the boats and search for a weapon or some kind of equalizer. He assumed that no one knew he was there or they would have given pursuit. When he returned he would kill the generator and cast the whole camp into darkness, but, for now Marcus had to take advantage of his invisibility.

The trip back to the boats only took a few minutes. It was much quicker than he remembered. Marcus looked cautiously around to make sure that the boats were still unguarded before rummaging through them. He waded in the water and began searching the boats. In the first boat he found nothing but life preservers and crushed drink cans.

The humming of an approaching boat became audible. Marcus wondered if it was an answered prayer. The boat approached quickly and the loud dialogue of the feuding men led Marcus to realize that it was not the police. He ducked behind a tree and watched as two robed men killed the motor and coasted forcefully into the bank, docking the aluminum boat and tossing a bow line over a tree branch.

"We are really late. Your moron, why couldn't be ready on time?" one of the unidentified men asked.

The men jumped ashore, pulled out their flashlights and began to move toward the camp. They fought and cursed at each other as they went.

As soon as it was safe to move again, Marcus realized that he had no option but to contact Paris and ask her to get the authorities. He depressed the button and typed, "Need police. Need some help now!"

Marcus resumed his search of the boats. As he did so, he pulled the drain plugs and pushed the boats out to the center of the water way so that they would sink and be of no use to anyone who tried to go after them. He inspected the twenty foot aluminum boat of the late arrivals and decided to keep it for their escape, however it was to happen. The electric ignition sold him since the key was still in it. It would save time and hassle from trying to pull-start the other outboards.

He pushed the boat into the water and maneuvered it slightly down from the docking point and hid it behind an overhanging tree limb. He pulled it back up to the shore and lightly tied it up.

He returned and continued to search and sink the boats. He found a flare gun, machete, several boat oars and then, a shotgun and a handful of six shot. With some hesitancy he grabbed the shot gun and shells then tossed the machete into the boat that he had put aside for their use. With all of the boats in the middle of the canal and sinking, Marcus started back up the trail to the generator. He was ready to do whatever was necessary to get them out of the camp.

On the trip back, he second-guessed his plan about shutting off the lights. The dark covering may have given more of an advantage to those who knew the layout of the camp and woods better than he did. It would also give away his presence and they would begin hunting for him. He made it to the worship area and moved back near the brier bush.

The two men who were running late were now standing in front of the group, getting an update from a member. Dawn and Reed were sitting at gunpoint on the ground. On the altar, Amy was lying motionless. She looked like she had been tossed onto the concrete without concern of injury. Long brown hair covered most of her face. One arm extended out from the alter, locked at the elbow. The left arm was twisted behind her body.

The demons moved in a frenzy of excitement. For Marcus, it was a lot like the experience in the French Quarter. In the limited light, he could hardly track them as they moved in and out of the illuminated area. The demons were excited at the new opportunity to take out two of God's people. They yelled and petitioned for the humans to kill the two and be done with it.

Something began to appear from the ground behind a bald man. It rose and looked like the earth was transforming and taking on life. Within seconds Marcus recognized it as the demon from the restaurant, only it was now much larger. The large beast stood behind the bald man in Reed's face. Its entire body looked like it was covered in mud or was made up exclusively of the earth. It was muscular and nearly fifteen feet tall. Its nostrils flared and it began to scream, working on the bald man. Its penetrating green eyes were fixed on Reed. It yelled without ceasing for the bald man to execute Reed. It wanted violence and death.

"Should have done you right there. All those people . . . it was your fault. You stupid Americans, like you always do, had to stick your nose where it doesn't belong. Maybe that will be the first thing I cut off—" the man said.

The killer that Reed had nick-named The Ax now stood before him. It was almost too good to be true. How he had longed for this opportunity and would not let it pass from him, even if it meant death. Asa had told him that The Ax was rumored to be in the area and what good fortune as it was finally time to close the chapter.

"The last time you ran like a coward after you hurt that woman. Come on. Let's see how tough you really are," Reed said.

The Ax walked away and came back with a hatchet. "How does this fancy you?" He turned to Dawn. "You look just lovely. You see, our friend here doesn't do a good job of taking care of the people around him. Is he going to let you die too? What do you think?"

Reed jumped from his knees and drove his right fist into the throat of the Ax and rode him to the ground. A man stepped forward to take a shot at Reed, but from the shadow of the trees Marcus fired a round into the man's back. The six-shot coated his body sending him running hysterically. He pulled off his robe desperate to get the hundreds of pellets out of his back, head and arms. Marcus fired off a second shot and the spread hit several cultists, knocking them down.

The shots sent the rest of the group into a panic as they realized for the first time that Reed and Dawn were not alone. They became fearful, not knowing how many guns were pointed at them and began to scatter.

Reed was on top of the Ax, focused and hitting him with all the strength he could muster and never stopping to investigate the shot or even caring who the victim was. The hatchet fell to ground just out of his reach. As it fell, Reed flashed back to Haiti and the woman. He looked at the bald man who was bleeding from his eyes, nose and mouth. He looked unconscious, and Reed was tired. His arms and fists ached from the continuous pounding he had just delivered, but he was not satisfied. He pushed off of the man and walked over and picked up the small ax.

Marcus prayed for God's help and continued to hold the gun up. A man with a rifle was scanning the woods and looking for him. Marcus took a third shot and hit the man across the thigh and lower abdomen. Marcus knew it was only a matter of time before they found him. Somehow he had to get Dawn and Amy despite the chaos and get them to safety.

Hearing a noise in the bushes to his left, Marcus turned to look and froze. Large bronze eyes were fixed on him as a massive coyote stood several feet away in observance. It didn't bark or growl, or appear aggressive. It sat and starred at Marcus as if trying to figure him out.

The canine's eye's radiated in the darkness. Its coat was full and the top of the coyote's back was nearly three feet off of the ground. He looked broad, proud and powerful.

The large coyote pointed its snout to the sky and began to howl. The woods instantly came alive with the shuffling of leaves, brush and moving tree limbs. Lunging out of the camouflage of the dark woods were dozens of large wild dogs, some coyote and others were mixed breeds that had once been domesticated before running wild. The unholy temple was under assault as the satanic members were attacked. Screams now filled the air as the dogs pinned them to the ground, biting random areas of the arms and legs while shredding the robes of the satanic worshipers.

Dawn watched as two angels attacked the mighty earth-born demon who had accompanied The Ax. The demon had the edge and was pushing them across the camp. It was strong and fought with amazing power and speed that was hard for the angels to overcome. The demon's speed allowed him to take advantage of an opening after an over-committed swing missed its mark. The blow struck the angel down. The angel in charge of Reeds care continued to fight. It grabbed the sword of his fallen brother and began to push the demon back. He swung madly and hammered away at the beast with all he had. The demon swung through a block by the angel striking him in the chest. The angel flew backwards losing one of the swords. Sensing victory, the demon moved to finish the angel.

A brilliant light descended in front of the wounded warrior of God's army. Asher now stood between the angel and the demon. The beast became angry and yelled blasphemies, not wanting to be denied. The demon raked its long claws over the ground and drew a line in the dirt issuing a challenge to Asher.

Asher was prepared and was dressed in golden armor. He looked equal to the green eyed demon in height, but not width. He unsheathed his sword and went on the offensive. The demon's nostrils flared as it snorted. It wings opened up. Claws were open and at attention.

Asher attacked and put the demon in a defensive posture. The beast soon became severely agitated and screamed. It swung its sword and flexed its muscles. In wild desperation and unbridled rage the beast flew at Asher and knocked him back. It raised the sword to take him down. The hand and sword fell free at the wrist and disappeared beneath the earth. He then fell quietly to the ground, paused for a second and was absorbed into the earth. Asher had cut the demon's hand off and then took the opening at the mid-section, cutting it in two.

Reed had the hatchet and was looking at The Ax. He moved forward and had second thoughts about killing a man who was unconscious. But Reed quickly realized that he had to do something to make sure that the killer would never be able to hurt anyone again. A light grey coyote moved between him and the injured bald man and pushed Reed warning him to back off. Reed was irritated by the interference by the animal and considered hitting the canine with a stick. But as he looked around, he realized for the first time that the dogs were on their side.

"God, you mean to tell me that I am this close and you aren't going to let me finish this? He doesn't deserve to live," he said out loud.

"That is not for you to decide," God said to his heart. Reed felt convicted. He wanted to take on the role of God because of the emotions he couldn't control. His heart was filled with hate and that was not of God. Defending himself and Dawn and beating The Ax to the ground was justified, but he crossed the line when he went for the hatchet to kill someone who was defenseless. It became murder and not self-defense at that moment.

Reed glanced at The Ax and threw the hatchet deep into the woods. He looked at the canine with respect and turned to survey the scene. He felt like he had been in a trance and had no idea what had been going on around him.

He looked up and saw Marcus and Dawn dragging Amy off of the altar and ran to meet them. He and Marcus grabbed her arms and put them over their shoulders, dragging her feet behind them. They moved quickly out of the camp and down the trail toward the boat.

The three stared at each other, amazed that they had been spared in the attack. The screams of the Satanists were sickening, but their focus had to be on getting back to safety as quick as possible. They turned and almost felt like they had celebrated too soon. Three large black and grey coyotes sat on the trail waiting for them.

"If they wanted us, they would have attacked," Reed said, readjusting his grip on Amy.

The dogs stood and positioned themselves as on queue. One moved to Reed's right and one on the left of Marcus who continued to carry the shotgun. The canines escorted the three to the path.

"I have a boat," Marcus said and passed the shotgun to Dawn.

"Go and get it ready, I will take care of Amy," Reed said.

Reed grabbed Amy and scooped her up with both arms. Marcus killed the generator, pulled the plugs and slid it into the runoff. He ran down to the levy and toward the boat. Dawn followed between the two, making sure of where Marcus was going and helping Reed.

Dawn was instantly horrified when she reached the water's edge and said, "All of the boats are gone."

"I pulled their drain plugs and pushed them out. They aren't completely sunk, but out of commission for the most part." Marcus said.

Dawn looked out and could barely see the bow tips of several sinking boats. She was impressed and thankful for his actions.

Reed fell to his knees in exhaustion when he and Amy had finally made it to the shore. Amy was lifelessly lying cradled in his arms. A noise from down the trail indicated that several of the men had gotten free and were in pursuit. Reed astutely jumped up and placed Amy in the boat. For proper weight distribution, he positioned her near the center of the vessel where Dawn could sit next to her. Marcus would take the seat at the console and he would take the bow.

Dawn cautiously climbed into the aluminum boat. She had a vision of it rolling over and sending them into the water. She feared that she would mess everything up. The shotgun was bulky and heavy and she slipped. In a panic, she dropped the weapon into the water. She paused and looked up at the two men who were now staring at her with blank expressions and were considering what to do about the new circumstance.

"We don't have time to fish for it," Marcus said.

Reed nodded in agreement and began pushing the boat out while Marcus lowered the engine in the water. Dawn sat down, giving a panicked looked at Reed. The rocking of the boat assured Dawn that she would not enjoy a second of the ride and she vowed to never subject herself to boating as a mode of transportation ever again if they were to make it back to the shore. She desperately hoped that guns would not come into play.

Marcus pulled the leaver back, engaging the reverse, and quickly backed the boat out to the deep water in the center of the canal. He pressed the throttle as far forward as it would go and the engine began to scream. Marcus turned to his right and toward the lock.

The sound of sporadic gunfire began to break out. To his horror he saw two boats that had been docked some thirty feet from the other boats and he missed them. A helpless felling came over him. They were anything but out of the woods with the cult members and still had the watchman to deal with. He began to consider their options and prayed for guidance and deliverance from the situation.

He pointed to the shore and Reed turned in time to see the moon reflecting off of the outboard motors of the docked boats. Marcus could sense the disappointment and shared concern. It was too late to sink them or make any move back toward the shore. They had to make an escape—or at least an attempt.

Reed realized the obstacles and decided to focus on the watchman. If he was at the dock, the only option would be to bull-rush the man and pray that the watchman didn't get a weapon out before he could get to him. Reed was tired and sore, but he knew that the watchman had to be taken out quickly.

Reed looked around and found an industrial sized flat-head screwdriver that was rolling back and forth with the motion of the boat. He picked it up by the shaft and tested it in his grip by banging the handle soundly against the side of the boat. The weight was pleasing and it was better than nothing.

"Did they travel by boat or on the levee?" Ralph asked.

"They walked up the levee," Paris answered. "I don't think that they will make it on foot. I assume that somehow God was going to get them back faster. I guess by boat."

"You know that by the time you can beach a boat . . . or whatever the plan is, a boat that is close behind can easily get several shots off. How exactly do you guys plan to escape?" Ralph asked.

"I'm not really sure. We didn't have time for any real planning. We just acted in faith," Paris answered.

"Even without guns, it takes a few seconds to dock or beach a boat and get out . . . right?" Ralph persisted.

"Yes, but there is nothing I can . . ." Paris remembered the lock in mid-sentence. "I guess God really did want us to . . . yes," she thought out loud, giving no heed to Ralph despite the fact that he was hardly more than a stranger. Perhaps God had put this man here at this particular time and place specifically to help her. "Boat,' she blurted out, "I think they will be coming back by boat. That is why He gave us the key. We need to open the lock. Certainly we can stir things up and give them a chance."

"Open what? What key? Who gave it to you?" he asked, almost amused by the adventure.

"Open the lock. We have the key to the lock. It's in the first control on the river side," she said confidently. The tone of her voice sold Ralph on the plan. He stood and briskly walked toward the controller. Paris fought to match his stride.

"Tell me, how exactly did you get this key?" Ralph asked.

"Reed found it lying in some mud or something while he was looking around."

Ralph stopped as he was insulted by the response. "Look, I'm not a moron—"

"No . . . it is true." She pulled up the file on the Compact.

He reviewed the clip a second time as they continued to walk to the slice in the fence line. Ralph paused briefly in amazement. "Talk about a needle in a haystack . . . well, in this case, old grass. I'll be . . . ," he paused and reconsidered the use of profanity. "This is incredible. That was worse than a one in a million shot. He walked right up to the thing. Isn't that something?" He said shaking his head in disbelief.

With the stealth and grace of a foraging armadillo, Ralph kicked the fencing inward to the left and out of the way. Ducking his head beneath the cross bar, Ralph moved in and observed the controller. He turned and looked at the water level in the river and realized that the lock would drain completely once opened. This would initially maximize the volume of water that moved from the canal.

"Well, it is obvious that the riverside is a lot lower than the canal. But each door has to be opened separately," he said pointing to four podium shaped controllers at each corner. "I am not sure how much time we have, but if we open these doors and let the lock drain as much as possible, when we open the doors on the canal side, the current should be swift and will pull everyone and everything through . . . depending on the timing."

Ralph turned the key and cranked the steel wheel, releasing the gears to motion. Metal teeth and groves connected and the giant door came to life. Water began to shoot out of the growing gaps. A current of brown water and foam poured into the river and began to create minor erosion. Sand and rocks shifted and moved under the direction of the overbearing pressure of the once restrained water. The noise was growing with the increased volume of rushing water and communication became more of a challenge.

The door moved slowly but continuously and Ralph wondered how much time it would take for it to open completely. Time was probably minimal and may not offer them sufficient opportunity. Like an impatient child, Ralph pinched the key with his index finger and thumb and was surprised to find that the key was not locked in the ignition and released without killing the motor. Sensing good fortune and great opportunity, he ran across the moving door and leapt to the north side door, grabbing onto the fence to maintain his balance and avoid falling backward into the water rushing out of the lock. He quickly repeated the process and the second door began to move inward and once again, the key released.

Ralph ran the length of the lock to the canal side and crossed the closed doors to where Paris was watching him. "The only problem is that if we don't close the lock back after we open the canal side, the river may flood." Paris pondered.

Paris stood and watched the emptying lock and wondered when they needed to open the two canal side doors. She had no idea what had happened to the rescue party.

CHAPTER 26

Dawn became increasingly anxious to reach the dock, which seemed to be an eternity away, and she pleaded with God for the boat to increase its pace. Dawn watched Reed as he smacked the bow of the boat with the large screw drivers and wondered what in the world he was planning. She looked past him and the lock was nowhere to be seen. Her anxiety peeked. She turned toward Marcus and noticed a pair of running lights had moved from the shore and was out in the middle of the waterway behind them giving chase.

"They are coming!" she yelled to Marcus, who turned and nodded.

Dawn looked down at Amy. She was lying on the floorboard of the boat with her head resting on Dawn's lap. She caressed Amy's hair trying to keep her mind focused. She brushed it aside exposing her face. The large knot on and above the left eye gave great concern to the possibility of a concussion resulting from the vicious punch from the abusive stranger. Dawn marveled at Amy's ability and strength when she struck back at the man and took him down.

A piece of the synthetic leather pad that made up the seat to the left of Amy suddenly ripped and was forced upward. Marcus and Dawn shared a concerned look as they were now being shot at and had no way of taking cover or protecting themselves. Dawn realized that firearms were going to be an issue and felt even worse about what amounted to her tossing the shotgun overboard when she had lost her balance.

Dawn looked back past Marcus and noticed that Argos was flying behind the boat while Goad flew on the port side and Idio was starboard. She looked at Reed and could physically see that he was once again a soldier ready for action. His posture suggested that he was focused, undaunted and ready to take down anything that was dumb enough to get in his way.

Reed grabbed the Compact from out of his pocket and sent a message to Paris, "under fire. we r going 2 have 2 make a quick escape. have Amy. will need to have motor running waiting for us. get SUV."

Unexplainably a sense of urgency came upon Ralph and he moved hastily to the northern lock and pressed in the key. As the previous times before, the gears obeyed and moved the giant steel door. Ralph looked up and ran back across the lock. He pushed in the key and activated the door on the south side. All four doors were now in operation.

He looked up the canal and in the distance saw two lights round the final bend before reaching the lock. He was certain that he was hearing some small arms fire. He was unsure who was in the boat and what to expect. What if it was some of the cult members and they sought an escape. He couldn't let that happen. He remembered the shotgun in the back of the car.

Paris looked at the light as the Compact came on. She read the text out loud to Ralph. "They are under fire! Someone is shooting at them!"

"Yeah, I kind of figured that one out already."

"Go and get your vehicle and I will stay here and try to help. You better move quick, they will be here in a few minutes."

Paris ran around the trees and to the SUV while Ralph turned and wondered if their little plan would either trap the very people they wanted to help or somehow truly ensnare the ruthless thugs. He pondered the things Paris had shared and thought most of it to be either a coincidence or skewed to suit her religious desire and the need to fabricate the results of her faith in God.

He was surprised at the thoughts that began flowing through his mind. What if He was real, what if there was even the slightest percentage of a chance that Heaven was real? Want if Jesus was standing right behind him? The thought conjured up a chill that paraded up and down his spine. There was something physical he was experiencing. The hairs on Ralph's forearms stood at attention and he turned.

Standing before him was an angel equal in height. He had two wings and was robed in white linen. Ralph felt the angel's gaze upon him. The celestial being penetrated his spirit, which for the first time he could distinct as definite part of his being. The angel opened his mouth wide and fire shot out and covered Ralph. He fruitlessly tried to shield himself by raising his arms, but quickly realized that the fire was not hot or scorching. Ralph felt an awesome flow of positive energy and a great peace surging through every inch of his body.

"Ralph . . . I love you! You are a child of God and He loves you," an audible voice said loud enough to be heard over the raging water.

Ralph fell to his knees and looked up. The angelic being was gone and the headlights of the SUV were now fixed on him. Paris ran around the driver side door and over to Ralph.

"Are you alright?" she asked.

"That was incredible. I saw something. I saw an angel or something," he said. "He covered me in fire and it felt good . . . and he talked right into my mind."

Paris didn't want to discourage Ralph in regard to the supernatural experience he'd just had, but the sounds of approaching motors and tapping of gunfire demanded that she stay focused on the mission at hand. A bullet struck the railing on the walkway over the lock door and embedded in the side of the control panel. Dawn tugged at Ralph's arm in an attempt to move him to safety, but the large man was unresponsive. She fruitlessly tugged again.

Marcus watched the lights of the dock as they grew closer. He grew increasingly concerned for the safety of Dawn and Amy and he was still fighting to formulate an escape. His mind raced and deliberated the same question of how he would get everyone to the vehicles while being fired at.

Dealing with an unconscious woman created an especially difficult scenario. Amy would need someone to carry her out and that would take time. They had come too far and would not leave her behind under any circumstances. He considered slowing down and letting Dawn and Reed jump out of the boat near the bank and then taking a turn hard to port and ram the oncoming boats. But what would become of the defenseless Amy? There would be no time to formally disembark. The window was less than thirty seconds.

Three darting objects moved like missiles and quickly descended upon them. Three angelic beings robed in armor and flaming swords flew in a tight disciplined formation and trailed behind Argos. Their faces were expressionless, like a Navy SEAL on a mission, focused and ready to fulfill their God-ordained duties.

Dawn reached back and touched Marcus with her foot. He looked up at Goad and Idio. While holding her wind-blown hair with her left hand, she pointed into the direction of the three new angels, which he looked at briefly before returning to his navigational duties.

Goad moved suddenly and forced the boat to slide toward the south shore of the canal. Marcus and Reed looked at each other as they both felt the impact of the mighty angel and the force he used to direct the path of the water vessel. Marcus understood what he was doing and steered the boat starboard.

Argos moved down and grabbed the boat by the transom on both sides of the motor mounts. The bow rose and the aluminum boat picked up its pace and moved forward beyond the capacity of the ninety-horsepower motor moving toward the now visible dock.

Reed pointed up to the lock as the gates were undoubtedly open. Rushing water was clearly visible. Distinct movements and patterns in the water indicated that an extreme current had developed and was sucking everything into the lock.

The three new angels slowed down and waited for the boats with the armed cult members and swiftly moved in. Two of the angels drew their swords and sliced through the outboard motors, rendering them inoperable. The two motors were silent and unresponsive. The boats were no longer able to control themselves. The Satanists were dead in the water.

Goad steered the boat while Argos continued to push it toward the shore. Marcus, Dawn and Reed braced themselves when they saw the dock approaching with little evidence of stopping or even slowing down. Reed shoved the screwdriver into his back pocket and turned forward and held on to the rim of the boat as it met with the mud embankment and then the grass on the shore line.

Argos killed the motor and raised it out of the water to prevent a violent reaction from the crash with the shoreline.

The boat lunged onto the solid ground and slid across the grass, cutting a deep trail. It continued upward nearly reaching the gravel parking area before stopping suddenly. The momentum and quick stop ejected Reed, sending him flying three feet off of the ground. His feet met with the loose gravel of the parking area. He spread his feet apart while using his hands to maintain balance. Reed was a boardless surfer sliding across the parking lot gravel. The soles of his shoes pushed into the loose gravel, digging shallow ruts. After stopping, Reed paused for a second in disbelief of what he had just accomplished and was amazed that he hadn't gone down face first.

He quickly scanned the parking lot and the watchman was nowhere to be seen. Reed turned, retrieved the screwdriver from his back pocket and ran back to the shoreline checking on the status of the other boats. He nearly laughed when he saw them floating and helplessly spinning around in the currents. The living water now drowned out all other sounds of the night.

The energized water seized control of the pursuing boats and moved them mercilessly toward the open lock. One boat was entering the lock backward and the other sideways. Several men worked feverishly to get the motors to start back up in order to regain control of the vessels. A man yanked on the pull-cord and the motor weakly turned over and made no attempts to start. He tried again and again with the same result.

A man sitting on the bow held up a gun and was attempting to get off another shot before riding out the rapids. He pulled the trigger and there was no report. The gun jammed and the man angrily examined the gun trying to remedy the cause of the misfire.

Reed looked again at the open lock and remembered the key. He didn't recall asking Paris to open them, but nevertheless, they were open. Where was she? Did the watchman have her? He looked for her and saw the running SUV with its lights on and the passenger door opened.

Where was Paris? What happened to her? Did the watchman do something?

To his left at the top of the lock, Paris looked to be in a struggle. The watchman was on his knees and looked to have Paris by the hand. The scene looked peculiar, but Reed had no time for discernment. He ran over the arching road of the boat launch and across a small grassy field to a gate that protected the lock from vandals and other unwanted intruders. Reed maintained focus on the struggle at the top of the hill while he ran to help her. The large screw driver was out and ready and the handle could deal out a lot of damage.

As he approached, Paris turned to see Reed making the charge, stood in front of Ralph and raised her hand. "Stop! He's OK."

Puzzled, Reed asked, "What was going on then. He wouldn't let you go."

"He opened the locks for us . . . ," with little time for an explanation said, "I will explain it all latter. I just want to get him up before we get shot."

The two boats moved briskly into the rapids. The first boat entered backward striking a small concrete wall where the water cascaded into the larger lock chamber. It went end over end dumping the men into the water. They struggled to keep their heads over the surface as the rushing water and undercurrents drug them down. Within seconds, they popped up and were launched from the lock and toward the river.

A shot rang out as the second boat entered. The lost, blank and confused expression on Ralph's face from the angelic visitation morphed into painful helplessness. He looked down to the small hole that was oozing blood in his left pectoral.

"Oh no . . . he's been shot!" Paris screamed. She fell in front of the big man who now took on the personality of a hurt and frightened child. "You are going to be alright! You will be alright!" She began to panic. "Get an ambulance!" She yelled in desperation. "Ralph . . . they will not do to you what they did to your little girl," she said through growing tears. "You're going to be OK!"

Reed called 911 and emergency personnel were dispatched. He requested a chopper for an air lift.

Marcus watched the second boat speed and tumble over sideways when it entered the lock. The gunfire had seemed less ominous than a firecracker as the sounds of the living water owned the night. He turned to Dawn and Amy and noticed her stare into the direction of the lock. For the first time he saw Paris and the watchman together. Their body language suggested a rather desperate situation had befallen them. Uncertain of the circumstance, Marcus thought it best to continue with the mission of getting Amy to safety. She was their priority.

He moved quickly to the side of the beached craft and fought to retrieve her limp body by himself without causing further injury. He couldn't have imagined the difficulty in lifting the small but limp body out of the water craft. Years of maintaining his body would pay off as he reached down and cradled her like a child and brought her to his chest. He stood and made his way to the waiting Range Rover, where he placed her on the rear seat.

Dawn looked hypnotically toward the three and climbed over the side of the boat using her hands to feel the way. Dark spirits were gathering from the air, woods and canal.

In the sky was a sight she could only compare to the Northern Lights as seen in Alaska. Living streaks of multi-hued light moved in waves traveling in all directions.

She looked up the lock where Reed now knelt beside Paris in front of the stranger. Dawn watched as the three angels that had kill the motors of the cult member's boats and directed them into the current, now stood with swords drawn in a semi-circle fifty yards at the back of the stranger. They focused on the area in front of them as the dark line of the woods seemed to be moving. Within seconds, four huge angels descended and joined the formation between the man and demonic spirits, who sought the soul of the dying lost man. The light of Christ was not upon him. They had every right to claim him.

Dawn turned to make sure that Marcus was alright while taking care of Amy before charging up the mound to the upper control of the lock. Time was short as the demons began to crowd the area.

The line of twisted and deformed bodies of the cursed angels parted near the center. A large dark hooded creature moved to the front of the line to confront the angelic hosts.

"You have no claim on him. You can't stop us from taking him. This man is not safe from us and you have no right to get in the way!" The echoing voice of hooded spirit demanded.

Desperation came upon Reed as he knew that time for the watchman was short. He knelt in front of the bleeding man and found the entry point just beneath the shoulder blade and placed his hand over it. He cupped the exit wound in an attempt to cause no further discomfort but stop the blood from pouring out. He called out in a loud voice toward the heavens in an appeal to the Father, "Oh Father, let not this one be cast from you. We pray your mercies and grace to abound. Father in the name of the Most High, I call on you Lord for you are the Mighty Physician and can heal. Please, Lord have mercy on this man and we claim a healing in Your holy name and glory!"

He pulled back and examined the injury. A puncture wound one-quarter of an inch in diameter remained at the entry point beneath the shoulder blade and exit point above his left nipple. The exit point was larger resulting from the effects of the impact on the bullet that caused the lead to flatten out and damage a larger area to insure death as it was designed to do.

Ralph looked over to Paris and asked her, "Do you think that God can forgive me?"

Dawn watched as the angelic hosts moved aside. They had no legal right to refuse the demons to their claim on the man. They had bought Ralph all the time they could. Several of the unclean spirits moved past and made their way toward Ralph. They too had a sense of urgency and wanted to get to Ralph before the Spirit of God could fall upon him. The large demon who had confronted the angels drew his sword and held it high as he moved closer in order to save time as he moved in for the kill.

"Yes, He WILL forgive you!"

"Help me. If I'm going to die, please help me," Ralph pleaded.

Dawn looked at the commanding demon, who had fire in its eyes and smiled with delight at the opportunity to lock up one more lost soul to an eternal separation from God.

"You're not going to die! Don't talk like that," Paris said then grabbed his hand and raised her right hand and began to pray and led Ralph in a sinner's prayer which he repeated from the heart. The sight of the angel and fear of death snubbed his pride and anger.

The beast had not made it but decided to continue the assault. Goad moved from Dawn's side and confronted the wicked spirit and drove it back. He swung mightily at the demon that lacked the strength to match.

Dawn watched as a flash of light fell from the heavens and entered the newly saved man. A peace came upon his face and he no longer seemed afraid. "I think I just saw the Holy Spirit enter him," Dawn said to Reed.

Dawn reached over touching Reed and Ralph and told them to look to the sky. The waves of light descended and revealed the source of the illumination. Hundreds of angels of many shapes and attire now filled the sky above the lock dancing and celebrating the new brother in Christ. They seemed to beckon him. The light from the spiritual presence was blinding to Reed and Ralph. The Glory of God now filled the area over the lock.

"They celebrate for you," Reed said to Ralph. "For in the scripture is it is written that, 'there is joy in the presence of the angels of God over one sinner who repents.'"

Ralph looked up through the physical pain and tried to smile and became weak. He fell to the ground and landed on his stomach. Paris rolled him over.

With one motion the angelic warriors began chopping down the adversary in a wave of overwhelming force. The demons that had arrogantly stood before them now scattered and sought the refuge of the thick woods and the depths of the earth. Seven angels maintained pursuit while two remained behind for security.

"We can't wait any longer for an ambulance. Can we get the car? We will need to take him now," Paris said.

"Paris, you can't move him . . . he's dead. He's gone home," Reed said, checking the man's pulse. He pressed against the wound, trying to minimize the bleeding and began to administer CPR. "You guys get out of here. I will stay and tell the police what happened. Get her to safety before some of these stupid cult members show up and shoot all of us."

Paris wept and slowly turned toward the parking lot and moved no further. She froze in stride, giving no consideration about moving toward the car. Hurt and pain from the loss of Ralph had already affected her, but she stared blankly to her left.

Marcus's mind flashed back to the gunman and considered the amount of time they had lost while taking care of the wounded man. Subconsciously his mind began calculating the time and distance the raging waters should have carried them before they would have been able to get to the shore and make their way back. He turned, expecting to find that they had run out of time.

Sitting on its back haunches was the large coyote. Its back was turned to them and it focused attentively into the darkness toward the river side dock. The canine's ears stood at attention, occasionally turning back to check on the humans that were standing behind him. The mighty animal stood continent to trust what was behind him and remedy the unseen danger approaching from the dark.

Marcus looked at Paris and nodded his head in assurance. "I think he is on our side. Don't ask me why, but I think . . . ," he turned back to examine the dog once again, "that this dog just helped us get away . . . I think. I'm not really sure how he got here so fast, but it looks just like the one. We really need to get a move-on. Is there an ambulance coming?"

The coyote's head began to waggle and it stood at attention locked in on something they couldn't see. The canine began to growl. Its withers stood at attention as an indication of distress and the beast ran into the thicket where Reed had previously spied on the watchman.

To her horror, Paris watched as the man ran around the corner with his pistol aimed at Marcus, who was making his way over to the Rover. Laser sights moved up his leg toward his chest. Seeing the light, he leapt to the side and rolled a microsecond before the shot was fired. The red laser moved across the ground, dancing with each move Marcus made to avoid providing an easy target. He moved ceaselessly, rolling back and forth in search of refuge while pulling the gunfire away from Amy.

The man violently screamed in agonizing horror as the coyote rushed him from behind. The canine had circled around and charged from the wooded area. The coyote viciously lashed onto his arm and shook its head side to side ripping the muscles of the killer's arms. The gun separated from his flailing right hand and slid across the grass in into a thick patch of brush. The canine maintained the intensity of its assault. Marcus heard the tearing of clothes and witnessed the breaking of the man's arm as the huge beast relentlessly mauled the demon worshiper.

Abruptly, as if by command, the coyote stopped and took several steps back from the reeling man, who was now in no position to provide a threat to anyone. It sat and panted and watched into the darkness in the same general direction from which the previous threat had come. The coyote stood once again and darted into the safety of the wood-line. Seconds later, more screams filled the night as the coyote took down another cult member.

Chapter 27

Marcus fought the surging pain in his lower back, forearms and biceps and did his best to maintain control of Amy while getting her to bed. The trip up the stairs to the second floor apartment above the LeJune Studios had pushed his muscles to their limits and seemed on the verge of going into spasms.

It wasn't solely the steep forty degree rise that made the task excessively taxing, but the two and a half feet of width between the sheetrock and banister. Marcus climbed up sideways to the point of nearly walking backwards and dragging the back of Amy's legs up the railing. Never had he envisioned carrying anyone up the stairs, but then, he found himself doing a lot of unique things since stopping to knock on Dawn's door just a few days earlier.

Dawn followed him and spread a large blanket over the bed in order to keep it clean from the blood, dry dirt, crumpled leaves and dry grass that had covered Amy's body.

Marcus placed Amy cautiously on the bed then gently attempted to brush off the grass and debris while inspecting her for injuries. Cuts and bruises covered both sides of her head. He was no forensic expert, but the injuries looked both old and new, the result of long-term continuous abuse. His heart mourned for her and all she had suffered. How trapped she must have felt;

subjected to a relentless struggle to satisfy her body's need for drugs. Marcus wondered what she was on and how difficult it would be for her to go through withdrawals and eventually kick the addiction. He brushed her face clear, moving the knotted hair to the side while inspecting for other facial trauma. She was beautiful, and the resemblance to Dawn was undeniable.

His heart began to ache for Amy despite having limited knowledge of all she had endured. He envisioned within her a desperate child that mourned the loss of her father, a lost teenager who made bad decisions. He saw a beautiful woman who still had a lot of life ahead of her if she could make the turn. From his heart, Marcus called out to God for Amy. He prayed for wisdom and guidance as the task ahead was not without its challenges. Amy needed a lot of love, help and support. However, the first step was spiritual. Marcus knew the scripture and that God had empowered all that followed His Son with the ability to cast out demons, but each situation was unique. With Dawn, she was affected by the experience of Hell and the seeing of spirits. She was willing to pray and accept mostly because of what she had physically seen. What would be the challenges for Amy? He called out to God for legions of angels to be sent down as a battle of epic proportion was about to take place. Satan was surely not going to let go of her.

For the first time Dawn stood over Amy in the light in search of the spirits that possessed her. She looked around and saw no evidence of any evil presence. On the side of Amy's bicep, her skin changed in texture and color. A three inch charcoal gray area coated by small reptilian like scales pushed to the surface then faded. Then her cheek and right forearm. The demon was moving within her body, unable to remain still. Red grainy textures briefly surfaced on the left arm and lower leg.

"I'm not sure how many are tormenting her," Dawn said.

Marcus retrieved a small white packet of smelling salts and activated it. He placed it beneath Amy's nose and moved it back and forth from nostril to nostril. Amy immediately reacted and waved her head in an attempt to escape the pungent odor as if it was painfully eating away at her sinus cavity. The muscles of her face jumped and contorted and she pushed away with both of her hands.

"She woke up on the way over, but she is just exhausted," Dawn said.

"Stop, just kill me . . . I can't take it anymore. I'm tired of you treating me like an animal. I don't want to live like this anymore. Kill me . . . just kill me," Amy covered her face with her hands in anticipation of being hit or possibly shot.

"Amy, we don't want to hurt you. We are here to help," Marcus said leaning closer to Amy as he tried to give her comfort.

Dawn gasped when a large head matching the first reptilian texture leaned out and stared at Marcus. Horns curled outward from its face. The beast snorted in disgust and rolled its brow down tight over its eyes. Marcus looked back undaunted and ready.

Amy looked up in confusion and thought momentarily that she might be in a dream. For so long mental and emotional abuse was the only human interaction she had known. She rubbed and tried to adjust her eyes to in order to identify the person that made such a foreign claim. She recognized Marcus and turned to see Dawn at his side. "You . . . you came for me?" Amy asked half coherently. Her words were slurred and ran together.

"*We* . . . came for you. Well, not everyone is here." Dawn said wanting to give acknowledgement of the selflessness of Marcus, Reed and Paris for putting themselves in harm's way. She walked around the bed. Dawn welled up at the thought of their sacrifice and the opportunity that she now had to help her sister. Without their help, Amy would most certainly have been killed by the angry cult. God had placed the three in her life at the right time that she may have a second chance to do the right thing. Once again, God had displayed His abundant mercy.

"We need to get to a hospital and get you checked out," Marcus said as he leaned back over and inspected the cut on her face from the brutal punch. The image of the demon was hard to push aside and he had to step away for a second. Marcus was angry and wanted to punch the smug expression off of its face.

"No! No hospital. They will just find me there and . . . will come and get me," Amy said less lethargically. Concern came across her face once again. "Where's my purse? I need to go to the bathroom."

"I'm sorry. We just got out of there as soon as we got you. There was no time to look for anything. Is there anything I can get you?"

"No. I just need my purse. Where are we? What is this place?" she asked while pushing herself up to stand. Amy looked around attempting to peer out of the widow in order to get a sense of her location.

Dawn feared letting her know that she was back in the city. Withdrawals would soon take control over Amy's actions and mind. This was evident in her twitching hands and increasing nervousness. As was typical behavior for drug dependent people, desperation would certainly lead to violent behavior. The only thing that would matter would be satisfying the need for a fix. Dawn feared the situation and she was uncertain how to help Amy. Doubts began to creep into her mind and were soon followed by a new fear—one of total failure. What if Amy, despite the situation, acted like her mother?

Even if they were to manage getting Amy off of the drugs, without God's continuous help she may always be tempted to go back to her old life style. There was a long tough road ahead.

What about those who wanted to do her harm? Certainly many eyes would be on the lookout for all of them and it was only a matter of time before one of them would be found and followed. Dawn's house was certain to be under surveillance. Marcus considered. They would need to contact the local authorities in the morning and focus on what to do. Thankfully Reed had managed to retrieve the Compact as evidence of everything that had happened.

Marcus pulled a cell phone from a leather pouch that had been clipped to his belt and walked into the hall in order to give Dawn and Amy some privacy. Dawn could discern by the conversation that he was talking to Reed about the stranger, apparently named Ralph. It seemed that he was unable to be revived and was pronounced dead on the scene. As he continued talking, she overheard the story of Ralph and how he had opened the lock doors. He hadn't been a watchman for the cult. It was possible that his efforts had saved their lives and afforded them time to get Amy out. *What about the strange activity of the canine assault pack?* Her mind wandered to the huge animal at the lock and the screams in the dark. *What become of those people?*

Amy returned from the bathroom and willingly got back into the bed. She had cleaned herself up to best of her ability with the limited toiletries in the bathroom. Dawn fought the desire to reach out and comfort her. She wanted desperately to embrace and hold her, but was afraid of her potential reaction. Amy was already in a highly vulnerable and weak state and she didn't want to risk adding to her trauma. She needed to cover Amy in prayer first and allow God to move.

An unseen and unexplainable presence suddenly filled the room. Dawn looked anxiously around and could see nothing with the exception of the unclean spirits in Amy. She moved to the hall and looked at Marcus, then quickly back into the room and peered out of the window. Floating before her was a wall of dark and demonic spirits that had surrounded the building.

Screeching and writhing began to come from Amy. Dawn turned to see her gyrating and starting to foam at the mouth. Marcus ran into the room and tried to hold Amy down by placing his hands on her shoulders. Amy stopped and looked at him. The once blue eyes were now black. The frail and tired woman gained strength and pushed him forward with ease. Veins in her forehead bulged grotesquely running in random lines. She was like a threatened animal backed into a corner and viciously attacked Marcus. Wildly she threw her fists and clawed at him. He maintained his ground and climbed back on top of her and caught her wrists. Marcus tried to leverage his weight and force her into submission, but the attempt was fruitless. Once again she tossed him back.

"Amy! Stop!" Dawn yelled.

"In the name of Jesus I command you to stop!" Marcus yelled.

Amy stopped and looked at Marcus, "Jesus . . . Jesus," a raspy voice said and laughed. The beast controlled Amy's body and turned to Dawn. "Hey sweetness, did you tell your boyfriend your little secret?" It laughed.

"I rebuke—"

"Yeah, yeah, yeah like I ain't never been rebuked before," it said, cutting her off. Amy's head rolled back to Marcus.

"Shut up! Come out of her," Marcus demanded.

"Can't do that. She wants us here. She would die without us. Kill her, I will. She belongs to the master. She is his special pet. Oh how he adores her. Now leave us alone or the master will kill the both of you!"

Amy's feet lifted up from the bed and shoved them into Marcus's chest. The blow forced him over the foot of the bed and onto the wood floor. He landed on his back and rolled over to his feet. He looked back at Amy. She stood, paying no attention to

Marcus or Dawn, and walked toward the bedroom door. Marcus was uncertain of what to do. He couldn't legally detain her.

Dawn moved to the door and once again called for Amy to stop. This time Amy obeyed. She stood emotionlessly staring at Dawn. "How could you let this happen to me?" She asked. This time it was Amy's voice. "Why didn't you help me? All I needed was your help . . . years ago. You hated me and left me to die. You left me to live a life of filth and abuse. Why was I not good enough for you?"

The words tore at Dawn's heart. What she said, in a sense, had been true. She had let Amy down. There was a movement to her left and she turned. The humanoid green-eyed demon form the restaurant moved through the exterior wall and into the room, stopping in front of her. Demons slowly seeped through the walls and into the room. They clung to the walls and ceiling in observation.

"You are not wanted here," Marcus said forcefully, hoping to impose his will on the evil spirit. "This is a house of God and you have no authority here."

"But I do. Here to protect my master's investment." The green eyed demon was hollow and unable to express emotion. "You cannot deny me this right I have to her. If you try, you will both be destroyed."

"Well, you will have to go through us!" Marcus declared.

"How are you so certain of your authority . . . your ability? Has God Himself told you so? Has the mighty Creator brought Himself down and sat before you . . . eaten at your table? My master rules all. My master has all power and authority. Your name is not in the Book of Life and your soul is still up for auction. It looks like I am the only bidder. My master has given me the authority to take both of your souls."

"Pithius! You are but a liar full of deceit. Cunning with your tongue and sharp with your deception," a voice forcefully declared from behind Dawn.

Marcus and Dawn turned toward the angelic voice and saw Asher standing with a staff pointed at the demon. A brilliant radiance blanked him. The demon lifted his hand and called out to the host of Hell that had covered the walls like fidgeting overgrown insects. He boldly called out for the spirits to attack and they did so. In unison the demons leapt from their crouched positions in a full aggression. Asher seemed unfazed by the assault. The offensive was brief as Asher spread his hands and called on the strength of God. The dark spirits fell from the air as if sucked down by an unseen vacuum.

"Your salvation is not in question," Asher said, looking at Marcus. "And your future is certain too . . . and I know that you don't question that," he said, turning to remaining demon.

"You know the law. She is ours. She has not denied my master. God has no claim on her. You cannot deny my master his right!" Pithius said.

"Then send your master to get her! Leave us you worm!" Asher said and put up his hand. The faceless demon launched viciously backward and through the wall.

"Her soul lies on the edge. He will come for her. The Father will not interfere. She has rejected His help time and time again. Some of the saints, even your new friends have been hurt trying to reach her for God. She has chosen unwisely. You must help this child and she must call on salvation herself. If she calls, the Lord will save her. But, she must call in humility and repentance. Make sure that is not just an emotion but from the heart. You don't have much time," Asher said, then ascended.

The imbedded demon's body jarred as if being physically struck. The unclean spirit levitated from Amy and moved into a standing position next to the bed. It looked mercilessly down at her unconscious body. It turned back to Marcus and snorted then opened its mouth and screamed. The demon's lower jaw hung open, deformed by abnormally large teeth. The creature opened its mouth wide and closed it several times and seemed to laugh. Suddenly the beast's head moved forcefully down and jammed its teeth into Amy's shoulder. The vile creature growled like a lion. Chills ran through Marcus and he began to fear the creature for what it was possibly going to do to Amy.

Amy screamed as four large puncture wounds with an arching line of smaller teeth marks above were now in her shoulder. Saliva and blood followed the natural pull of gravity and eased down her chest. Reacting instinctively, Dawn swung at the beast to get it off of Amy. It bit a second time and a third, leaving deep bleeding puncture wounds. Amy panicked and did all she could to protect herself as she looked frantically around the bed and room, unable to see her attacker.

It struck again, biting her neck and arms and then moved down to her legs. Dawn realized she had no option and reached out and touched Amy's foot so that she could see. Instantly Amy saw her assailant as it moved to bite her again. She became wide-eyed and screamed in fear. She frantically swatted at the demon's head it as it came in for another bite on her left thigh. This time it moved in slow motion adding to the excitement of the torment and with little fear of opposition. Amy moved her leg and the beast stood and growled grabbing her leg and pulled it back toward its mouth. Amy's body helplessly slid across the bed and into the mouth of the demon. The creature bit several more times in succession, leaving a trail of imprints, blood and saliva.

Despite his constant rebukes and attempts on the creature, Marcus was unable to levy an effective offensive against it. The unclean spirit turned and leapt at Dawn before sensing something and turning toward the exterior wall. Before the wicked spirit could brace itself, Idio slammed into the demon and began ripping it apart with his huge hands.

Amy was crying and looking horrified wondering if the monster was really gone. She curled up like a frightened child against the headboard. She inspected her body and the bite marks. Breathing became a chore and she was hyperventilating and fighting to remain in the conscious world.

Dawn climbed on the king sized bed that was now a mess of bunched up sheets and covers. Amy tried to move away from her. "Don't touch me. Please, don't touch me. Leave me alone," Amy pleaded.

"No. I don't want to hurt you. I am here to help." Dawn said.

Amy wasn't easily convinced. Marcus ran out of the room and returned with a cloth, tub of water, gauze and some first aid tape. He touched Amy and she jerked back.

"Amy, I know that this is a hard thing to understand right now, but you have to listen. That thing you just saw was a demon. That was a real honest to goodness demon who wants to hurt you. Listen to me, God is real and He is reaching out to you. There is a demon that is attacking you and wants to kill you before Jesus can help you. Jesus is real and is the only way you can stop them from physically attacking you. Please trust me."

Reed and Paris had just made their way to the studio and followed sounds of the disturbance upstairs and to the room. They knew exactly what had been taking place and they kneeled next to the dresser by the doorway in prayer. They pleaded and begged for His intervention and that He would prepare Amy's heart to understand and receive Christ as her savior.

"How do I do that? How do I . . . ," her eyes rolled back and a second demon began to manifest in her.

"Got to do better than that. Weak as she is she can't just let go. We have her and she is ours. She wants us here and we don't have to leave. How she loves to get high. It helps her to handle rejection, like the kind that comes from a sister," the spirit said.

The building began to shake and the lights flickered. They all looked at each other puzzled by what was happening. "We don't have earthquakes in Louisiana. What in the world is going on?" Reed asked.

A tall, oval-shaped lamp fell over and landed on the floor. The shade popped off and broken glass from the bulb scattered across the heart pine floor. Stress lines began to run through the sheet rock as several of the taped joints separated from the pressure of the shifting structure.

Marcus moved to get Amy and position her in a door frame when the building suddenly stopped. Each was looking around inspecting the damage and wondering what had just taken place. The density of Louisiana soils and the high water levels absorbed shock waves from underground tremors.

"Are we in California?" Reed asked.

"I'm not sure what just happened," Marcus replied.

Before Marcus could leave the room and inspect the building, a foot penetrated the wall passing through the sheetrock. Dawn took take a step backward. A man casually passed through the 150 year old bricks near the same area Idio had taken out the demon. He casually walked in as if stepping off of an elevator.

The heels of his shoes clanked on the floor as he moved several feet away from the wall nearly to the center of the large room. He stopped and looked at each person making direct eye contact with those who had been staring at him. He was exquisitely clothed in an extremely expensive white linen suit and silk tie. The man was neatly groomed and handsome beyond anyone the women had ever seen. His thick black hair was combed perfectly with each strand in place. The texture of his skin was perfect. Blue eyes sat atop a huge and warming smile.

Marcus recalled the drawing Sarah had shared with him of Satan. Despite the black hair and lack of a beard, the man looked like the drawing. The eyes of the man in the drawing had been disturbingly accurate.

Dawn, Paris and Amy were instantly drawn to the being. The attraction was powerful and they struggled for control their thoughts of this strange man. It was Paris who offered the first rebuke realizing who the man was. She stepped forward and demanded that he stop messing with her mind.

"The Good Book does say to control your mind now, doesn't it?" To which he just laughed and ratcheted up the attack. Paris was undaunted and stared coldly at him and launched another rebuke.

Amy fell down and crawled on her hands and knees toward the visitor. She mumbled and spoke with slurred English. She kissed his feet and worshiped him.

"Aren't you going to worship me?" the man asked Marcus.

"No, I'm not. Who are you?" Marcus asked, not fully certain.

"I am the Alpha and the Omega. I am the God of mankind. I am ruler of the heavens."

"You don't look like Jesus to me," Marcus said sarcastically.

"Jesus . . . Jesus. He is so overrated . . . *so* two thousand years ago." He said waving his hand. "He managed to get a few of the riff raff to lift him up as an idol and worship Him. But, in the end He ended up becoming one with a tree . . . now didn't He?" The visitor said. ". . . and so weak. Look at the world, it belongs to me."

"So, you are claiming to be Satan. If you are, you were defeated at the cross!" Marcus yelled.

"Yes, so I have heard. But, yet here I am. Are you so sure? How can you be sure? How are you one hundred percent on anything? Your knowledge comes from a book. Mere ink and paper all created by man."

"By God . . . not written by man," Marcus interrupted.

Undaunted, he continued, "How can you ever be sure where it came from? You claim that it was inspired by God. Come on you know you have doubts. I can read your mind. You wonder why He put that stupid tree in Eden in the first place. Why even leave a possibility for 'evil' to enter the perfect world? What kind of non-sense was that? Why He punished all of you simply because Eve ate some fruit . . . then they had to cover it up and blame it on me. Seems a little like a story the Greeks would have made up, doesn't it?

"I'll give you a few new ones to think about. Why did he design you with certain . . . needs and desires then put all kinds of restrictions and limitations on your desire to act on something that by design is natural? Got to be married if you're going to fornicate . . . whatever. I just help people to live their lives. The flesh is weak, but didn't He supposedly design you that way? Take a look at your attraction to that woman. You want her, I would even call it lust . . . but, that's me."

Dawn shook her head free of the interference from the deceiver and looked over at Marcus. He was embarrassed about the comment, but had never had any "lust" for Dawn, only love and respect. He didn't see her as a sex object as the creature portrayed.

"An all-loving God? Created the world, created man, put them in the Garden of Eden naked and unprotected. Talk about vulnerable. Then placed temptation before them and allowed me to test them. Then man is corrupt and sin drives God to kill everyone besides Noah and his family. NOW THAT IS LOVE!" he yelled animatedly.

"He destroyed His own creation! Where can I get some love like that? And somehow you humans squeezed out enough babies to repopulate the entire world. What a hoot! Let me put this in perspective for you, let's say you have ten daughters and sons and they all multiply. Then they choose not to worship and live the way you do and go about their own way. You see the way they live as sinful. Instead of going and confronting them face to face, you send out a couple of messengers to warn them. They don't listen to your messengers. So, you kill them . . . woman . . . children . . . all. Your family, your descendants . . . you kill them. Now, is that love? Where is the mercy in millions of drowning children? Babies died who were 'born into sin' but hadn't had even a chance to sin. Children have a special place in your heart . . . ever just throw one in a river and watch it drown? He did. And you say that I am evil?"

"I have heard enough from you! Now what do you want?" Marcus demanded.

"I'm not done! You mentioned the cross, how do you know any of it is true? Have you seen Jesus? He is supposed to be so full of love for all of His miserable converts, but he really never reveals Himself to you . . . now does He? For nearly two thousand years I have heard, 'For God so loved the world.' You guys are pawns and He has just been playing this game for the last six thousand years with you. Well, four thousand anyway. Everything at the beginning was wiped out. You're like a bunch of dolls and God is playing house with you. You're His toys. He is bored, so he creates you so that He can be entertained."

"Well, you have admitted something that we knew already. God is the creator. And I know that you are the deceiver!" Marcus said, fully discerning the intentions of Satan to plant seeds of doubt in their minds.

"Get out of my head Satan," Dawn demanded.

"See. Everyone knows who I am. I am the angel of light, bringing light into a dark God-oppressed world. I allow people to live, while God wants to punish them for doing so."

"Enough! We have heard enough," Reed said. "It wasn't God who slaughtered an entire village. It was you!"

"Look, everyone dies. Life is trivial. You're going to die . . . the only secret is how and when? Is it going to be horrible or slow or painful? You just don't know," he said mockingly.

"They were butchered with machetes," Reed said.

"So?" he replied.

"They were innocent!" Reed yelled.

"They deserved to die! Did your God stop me? No! I do what I want. This is my kingdom!" Satan screamed before turning to Dawn, "I must admit, I really miss having you on my side. You were my right hand. A lot of people will always be with me because of you. I just want to thank you personally. You were quite the influential warrior. You just don't know!" He laughed and took pleasure in Dawn's reaction. "You, babe were one of a kind. But, you weren't the only one.

"The nations serve me. You should to. I am the living God. I am the king of all you see. Come and feast your eyes upon me." He said raising his hands in the air. The white suit disappeared and Satan stood naked in his arrogance. He turned so that all could look upon him.

From out of Amy came three spirits that knelt at the feet of their master and worshiped him. Amy, now out of the trance, looked around and moved away from the naked man. Bewildered, she looked around the room, awake for the first time.

Marcus rebuked him again.

"Yes . . . yes . . . whatever." As he spoke he began to transform. His once blue eyes turned black and long gray fingernails grew out of his fingers. "You tried to take something that was mine and I want her!" he said, looking at Amy. He raised his hand and she fell to the ground and began sliding across the floor towards the transforming beast. "She is mine and God cannot have her. She serves *me*!"

Amy looked dead despite sliding across the floor. Dawn fell on top of her trying to weigh her down. The force was too strong and she rode Amy across the floor desperately trying to help her. She wept and called out to Amy trying to wake her up.

Satan continued to grow and morph. His skin texture became scaly and a multi hue of red, black and grey. Six membranous wings opened from their position on his back. Razor sharp teeth and the black tongue filled his mouth.

His voice changed and became deep and penetrating, "You see . . . you should have left what was mine alone. He pointed to Amy and a red spirit that had been worshiping him got up and returned to her. It reached into her chest and she curled up in pain.

Dawn fruitlessly swatted at the demon and rebuked it repeatedly. Despite the jabbing effects of the rebuke, it continued to dig its hands into Amy's chest. She cried out and gasped for air. Her face turned red, then blue.

Oddly, the room suddenly grew silent and the red demon began to frantically look around and removed its hands. It stood and ran through the wall disappearing from sight. Amy was unconscious and looked to be in the world of those who had passed on.

Asher descended into the room. Behind him a second much larger angel had entered. Marcus felt an overwhelming emotion. He looked up at the fourteen foot high ceiling. This new angel bent at the waist and stood a few inches below the ceiling.

"Michael!" the horrid beast growled and leapt at him. The mighty archangel grabbed Satan by the throat and tossed him in the direction of the exterior wall and charged after him. The building shook once again and new cracks formed in the sheetrock where they had passed through. Marcus moved to the window and watched as the archangel fought with Satan, who was now of equal size. They seemed to be of equal strength and the battle went back and forth for several minutes. Then Michael, as if he had been toying with the demon king and had decided to get serious, charged and delivered a series of destructive punches and wounds from his sword.

Other demons began to ascend from buildings and beneath the surface of the ground and join in support of their master. Each was matched by angelic warriors who gathered from random places. Swords smashed against one another and both sides took on injuries.

Ascending from beneath the floor, a familiar presence entered the room. The hooded demon with the illuminating green eyes who had promised to take Amy reemerged to take his turn.

Asher returned and moved over to Pithius and drew his sword. "God has specifically instructed me to protect this girl. And to deal with you!"

Pithius removed its hands from the pockets of the black robe and held them out. From the palms of both hands swords with blue flames appeared. Asher swung down on the demon but was met with skill and force. Pithius moved the mighty angel back across the room swinging both swords skillfully. Asher fought the assault and managed to swipe the lower torso of the demon. He yelled in anger and continued to charge. The demon's momentum carried it a bit too far allowing Asher to spin and deal a lethal strike above the shoulders. The black robe fell to the floor and the demon disappeared.

One by one the dark spirits began to fall. The numbers of angelic warriors increased and began a rout of the opposition. Satan looked around at his defeat and like a coward, darted into the earth away from Michael. The mighty archangel gave chase and entered the earth.

Asher knelt over Amy and reached in, pulled out a screaming demon and tossed it. "The demon had his hands cupped around her heart, but he was unable to stop it. It tried to cause her to go into cardiac arrest. There is strength in her. Nurture it and help her.

"God gave her a second chance because of your prayers . . . all of you," he said. "The sacrifice you made to save her has deeply touched God. For it is written, 'Greater love has no one than this, that he lay down his life for his friends.' You put yourself in harm's way to save this woman. He wants to see her well and alive again. This He wants for all man. But she needs to make the decision. She will need to fight the spirits as she has invited them in and must make sure that she closes that door. If she does so, then she will live and be well. But, if not, she will continue to be as she is now. You must cover her in prayer and continue to give unconditional support. Right now she is influenced by nothing but her own free will. The spirits will stay away for now unless she invites them back. She will wake up and you must tell her." Asher moved upward through the ceiling.

Chapter 28

Amy opened her eyes and looked at Dawn. She quickly sat up and scanned the room for the beast that had attacked her. She pulled her hands up to her chest and neck area and felt the bandages. The line of punctures on her leg were clean, but had yet to be covered.

"It is alright. We're cleaning you up," Dawn said.

"I'm cold," she said pulling a blanket up over her shoulders. "What was that? What just happened?" Amy asked.

Dawn thought that it would be better to just give an honest and simple answer, "They were demons."

"I thought you didn't believe in those things," Amy replied.

"Well, seeing them will change your mind . . . don't you think?" Dawn asked.

Marcus turned to Reed and Paris and asked them if they wished to join him in another room and give the sisters some privacy. They moved silently across the hall to a small spare bedroom.

"Look, as of last Friday I didn't believe in God, the devil or any spirits. That whole world just seemed made up to me. As a matter of fact I hated Marcus—"

Amy interrupted, "I heard your show. Is that guy the one who brought me to the restaurant?"

"Yes, that's him."

"I could tell that he didn't belong there. He was just too nervous. I thought of an altar boy the first time I saw him." Amy said about the time he was in the brothel.

"I went to Hell. I called God out and He showed me. He sent me to Hell. I guess I was there for about fifteen minutes, but it seemed like a lifetime. It was the most indescribably horrific place or experience in my life. It is everything you've ever been told and more. Just the darkness alone is constricting and oppressive.

"I looked into the face of a tortured soul. She was suffering and begging me to help her, but I couldn't help myself. Looking into her face and knowing that I was going to suffer the same way forever was . . . the most difficult part of the entire experience.

"That experience had an enormous effect on my way of thinking. I never want to ever go there again. Never! And you don't either," Dawn said.

"I had an experience too," Amy began, but paused in confusion. The drugs and long nights made her days run together, "What day is it?"

"Well . . . Monday morning. Really early on Monday morning."

"Some time Friday, I had this strange experience. This guy knocked me out . . . that's a part of what's wrong with my face right now he beat me pretty bad. I woke up and this beam of light was shining across the room. Someone . . . or something put a Bible by the sink and left it open. The light was shining right on some sentences. When I read it, it was like the words were for me and only me. I can't remember how to find them again. But that was really strange. I felt something that wasn't from the drugs."

"I've had some rather unusual things happen to me too. Life has been a little crazy. I mean, look at Marcus. I hated him. Now . . . we're friends. That in itself is absolutely something to behold. It certainly has been a strange sequence of events.

"Look, God brought me back from that Hell experience and I felt dirty. Like no bath could ever clean me. I was just nasty.

Marcus helped me understand what was happening to me. I realize that the whole spiritual world is real. God and Satan are real. You just saw evidence of that. The entire story of Jesus is true. Angels and Demons are real. You've seen that too. I have seen a bunch of them the last few days. You can't deny what you've seen. Heck, they attacked you. The bite marks are here to prove it."

"I saw one . . . and he was beautiful," Amy said.

Dawn was a little surprised by the comment and sought clarity. "What? What was beautiful?"

"An angel, he told me not to worry. He spoke into my mind, but I saw him," Amy said looking into the spot where he had previously stood. She turned to Dawn. "Do you realize what I have done. You know what I am. I'm a—"

"Child of God. You're a child of God! Forget all of that and give God a chance to make a difference in your life. He will love you and all of that stuff won't matter."

Amy started to cry and asked, "What if I can't do it. What if I can't?"

"Do you mean being perfect? That isn't gonna happen. There is no such thing as a perfect person. No one is perfect," Dawn passionately explained. "Do you want to know Jesus?"

"Yes!" she cried.

Dawn's heart leapt for joy.

The kitchen in the LeJune Studios was barren of anything that could be deemed healthy. Sugar-laden snacks meant for a quick boost of energy filled the shelves. Amy and everyone else would need a good meal in the morning and Marcus decided a trip to the grocery store was needed. It wasn't often that he would venture out in the early morning for groceries, but these were strange times.

On the way back to the studio he passed by Dawn house to make certain that everything was in order and that it hadn't been ransacked or vandalized. He deliberated about what they were going to do in regard to the rest of the cult members. He wanted to know if they were seeking vengeance and were out in search of them especially if they were staking out Dawn's house since she was the most recognizable member of the group.

He wouldn't make his passage obvious to anyone who may have the house under surveillance and just do a simple drive by. The chances were zero that anyone would recognize the maroon LeBaron he was driving. He simply needed to know if the place was being watched and what the impending dangers were.

He was alarmed to see Keri McIntyre's car parked in the driveway and became worried about her well-being. She had no idea of what had happed in the previous hours and no idea about the cult and was certainly vulnerable despite her nasty disposition. Her attitude was no match for a gun. If they knew where Dawn lived, and that was possible, men would be sent out to watch the home to get to Dawn and eventually everyone involved.

He noticed nothing that he considered to be out of the ordinary and considered passing peacefully by. But, nagging thoughts of the potential danger that Keri was in ruled his conscious mind and he just couldn't take the risk. He realized that he had no option in this situation, but to stop and do what his best to make certain that no harm would befall her. His thoughts would allow him no peace until he knew that she hadn't been abducted by any of the cult members seeking an equalizer. He could never forgive himself if he just drove away and something happened, especially considering his failure to protect Allison.

Marcus pulled the LeBaron up close to the arching brick structure that housed the mail box and moved quickly up the dimly lit pavement to the mahogany door and taped on the wood next to the leaded glass. There was no reply. A second knock yielded the same result.

He knocked harder the third time and the door slid open. A chill ran up his spine and he began to have a legitimate fear that something was amiss. The door, despite the time of night, had not been locked or completely shut. Marcus pushed the door back, fearing the worst and uncertain how to proceed. He leaned in for a look and was relieved to see everything as normal as he had remembered it since the demonic attack two days earlier. Marcus took a deep breath and entered the house. He moved quietly and cautiously past the foyer and peered in all directions for any clues of movements. Rope lights above the kitchen cabinets gave Marcus just enough illumination to see without tripping and falling over the furniture. The living room and kitchen both appeared to be empty.

He decided to check the bedroom and turned down the hall. The bathroom door opened. Marcus's heart stopped and he froze, unsure of what to do. Keri stepped out. She saw him and jumped backwards and let out a scream. He reached out and slapped the hall light switch and called out to her. The shock subsided at the recognition of the intruder's identity.

Obscenities began to fly, and this time Momma McIntyre held nothing back. Marcus felt stupid and stood helplessly uncertain of what to do like a confused deer about to be sent into the afterlife by a speeding eighteen-wheeler. His instinct took over and he was able to duck as a porcelain tooth brush holder was on line to strike him in the head. It crashed into to wall behind him adding yet another dent into the sheetrock adding to the collection of imprints from imbedded projectiles. A thud came from the toothpaste and a bar of soap that crashed in nearly the same location near his head.

"Hey! I am sorry, I didn't mean to scare you. I just wanted to make sure that you were alright."

"Where is my daughter? Did you take her? Look at this house . . . holes in the walls, food stains on the floor all of the dishes are broken. What have you done to her? I'm calling the police!" Keri ran to the counter for her purse and began digging for the cell phone.

Marcus met her at the counter and pleaded for her to listen. He promised Keri that Dawn was more than fine and offered to bring her to where she was. With severe apprehension, she agreed. Although she did not trust Marcus, she wanted to find out what was going on with Dawn and that she was OK. He decided against divulging any information about Amy and simply absorbed the verbal assault without a retort.

Had he not entered the house without invitation or permission, despite his intentions, and had assumed to be involved in some criminal mischief by the Diva of Odium herself, Marcus would have slammed on his breaks in retaliation to being followed from what seemed a very liberal three inches from his rear bumper. Keri had really graded on his nerves with her self-righteousness and coarse language. Marcus had never realized the number of profanities a person could squeeze into a single sentence. He wondered how it was humanly possible for Dawn to be so mellow in her previous state, and chuckled at the thought.

For the third time he punched send on the cell phone hoping to make contact with Dawn and warn her of Keri's approach. He wasn't sure that he had done the right thing. It just seemed to be the only option at the time and he hoped that Dawn would be receptive to her mother.

He began to fervently pray for Keri. Jesus spoke of people who could watch a man rise from the dead and still not believe. Marcus feared that Keri could stare into the face of a demon and would deny its existence.

Paris and Reed had taken over Maryellen's desk near the lobby. It was covered with two open Bibles, an exhaustive concordance, notebooks and loose papers. They were discussing and drafting a log of the evening's events and didn't notice Marcus and Keri enter the room. They spoke loudly as they cross-referenced events and questions with scripter preparing for the next time they had to confront demons or even the devil himself. The printer was actively working to complete its assignment and Paris feverishly flipped through a writing pad in search of a note she had made.

At the site of the active couple writing and talking excitedly, Keri stopped and listened for a moment then looked at Marcus, "You're just surrounded by morons . . . aren't you?"

Reed and Paris looked up at Keri and then back to Marcus. They weren't sure who she was, but considered the possibility. They stood to greet the new acquaintance, but Keri rudely brushed them off and continued to pace the foyer.

"Where is my daughter? I want to know right now!" she demanded, raising her voice at Marcus.

When he turned to go up the stairs, Dawn was looking down at him. She smiled at the sight of her mother, which gave Marcus some relief. She ran down the stairs greeting Keri with an excited embrace. "How did you get here?" she asked.

"You can thank Tweedle Dumb here for that. He nearly gave me a heart attack sneaking around your house," she said, pointing at Marcus.

Dawn thought about what her mother had said and with a wrinkled brow briefly turned to Marcus. She was quick to defer the explanation to a later time. "I was going to call you first thing this morning. I have something exciting to share with you."

"If you tell me that you and Mr. Nut Job over there are engaged, I'm going to jump off of the High Rise."

Dawn rolled her eyes refusing to let Keri's perpetual negativity get her down. She looked at Marcus and leaned over and kissed him, "Thank you," she whispered.

Dawn turned and began to go back up the stairs, but Keri pulled away, "Why are we going up there? I just came to get you. Get your stuff and let's go! I don't need a tour of Loser Central," she demanded.

Dawn looked at Marcus and realized that he had told her nothing of Amy. He had afforded her the opportunity to do so. She would look forward to hearing the story of how he managed to keep the secret and get Keri to follow him.

"Mom, you have to go up these stairs with me," Dawn persisted.

"NO! Now get your stuff and let's get out of this nuthouse!" Keri demanded.

"You don't understand. There is something you need to see."

"They are brainwashing you in this place. The only thing I need to see is you and me on the other side of that door in the car driving away," Keri said.

Dawn paused and looked at her mom with a startled expression. "No one is brainwashing anyone. You never talk to me like that. What I want to show you is more important than you can imagine."

"I'll tell you what I can imagine. I lost one daughter to who knows what. Now these religious bumpkins are playing with your head. These two over here are talking about demons and talking to Satan. This guy goes into your house in the middle of the night," she said, pointing at Marcus. "What the heck was he after?" She turned to him, "You are so lucky I didn't have a gun! I don't care if it had a hundred bullets, I would have emptied it out on you!"

Reed looked up and prayed openly, "Lord please forgive me for what I am about to do." He stood and calmly walked over to Keri leaned down and got face to face with her while a profanity was rolling off of her tongue.

"Will you *please* get your mean . . . cranky butt up those stairs before I throw you over my shoulder and carry you up there MY-SELF! Either way you are going up those stairs and I don't give a crap what your lawyer thinks about that! You may think you are a pitbull with a big bite, but to me you're just a loud annoying Chihuahua that needs to get over herself and get up those stairs . . . NOW!"

Keri didn't comment but stared back with a scowl. She was not intimidated by the threat made by the stranger, but decided in favor of attending to the matter that was at the end of the stairs. "This better be for a good reason."

"Why? Either way there's nothing you can do about it! Now get moving," Reed demanded.

Without saying a word, Dawn ran childlike up the stairs and watched Keri, waiting for her to follow. She paused briefly at the top before running excitedly over and pushing open the door to a room. She stood aside and gestured for her mother to look. Amy was sitting up in the bed, eating some crackers and drinking a Sprite to settle her stomach. Keri stopped at the threshold, dropped her purse and became weak in the knees. Dawn almost reached out and supported her, but remembered before making contact. Keri became overwhelmed by an instant tidal-wave of emotion. Nervous and shaking hands reached up to her mouth as she gasped and fought for the proper response.

"Amy? Amy, is that . . . really you?" she moved as fast as her shaking legs would carry her. She wrapped her arms around her daughter and wept and held no emotion back as she let out years of worry and pain.

A box of tissues slid from behind the door and across the floor. Dawn walked over and saw Marcus. Dawn moved to retrieve the box and caught the door. She looked at him through tears of immeasurable gratitude and thought about all he had done.

She reached out and touched his cheek. "Thank you . . . for everything."

He simply looked at her and said, "No. Thank *you*. It's OK. Go and be with your family. It's been a long time coming and you all deserve it." He closed the door.

Dawn moved to the bed where Keri had yet to let go of Amy and was crying uncontrollably. The reunited family apologized repeatedly and began re-establishing the once strong bond. They vowed to never let anything come between them ever again.

Keri turned to Dawn, wiping the tears from her face while trying to breath and asked, "How did this happen. Apparently you two girls have a story to share."

Dawn paused and was uncertain how to proceed with the truth. It had been an adventure . . . a spiritual one. This was something Keri would refuse to understand.

"Well, out with it!" she demanded.

Dawn and Amy looked at each other. They had discussed their mother, but had not been prepared for this moment.

"What is with you girls? Just tell me."

Dawn stood and walked across the room to a window and pushed the treatments back. She looked for second and spoke without turning. "Remember that day when you came over and Marcus was in the house. The foyer table was broken. The coffee table was broken and the house was a total mess."

"You mean like it still is?"

"Well, Marcus saved my life that evening."

"Saved your life? You don't mean what you tried to tell me before I left the house?" Keri asked.

"I didn't think you would understand. There was an intruder. But not the kind you're thinking of. It was a spiritual intruder . . . something normal people cannot see," she said, turning to her mom.

"Oh come on, not this! Not now!"

"Can you come to the window?" Dawn asked.

"Why?"

"Please, for once just trust me. You want to know what happened, you need to know everything."

Amy nudged her and said, "Go. You need to see this."

Confused, she walked up to the window and looked out, "OK. I'm here, now what?"

"Look across the street at that single story building, the one on the corner." Dawn instructed.

"Looks like an old liquor store. So what?"

Dawn pointed to the building again. "Keep looking at that building,"

She reached down and grabbed her mom's hand. A huge figure appeared at the corner of the building on the roof. It had two wings and exaggerated deformities that assured Keri that it was something quite unique. The creature hunched over as it searched the street. It was three times the size of a normal man and moved actively across the roof. As if sensing it was being watched, the beast looked up at them. Sharp glowing red eyes met with Keri's and she froze in fear.

Dawn let go of Keri. She blinked and looked outside again. The beast was gone. Dawn grabbed her hand a second time and the beast reappeared.

"That is a demon. And he is looking for either someone or an opportunity to use his particular skill or whatever."

The beast jumped into the air and flew straight at them and landed on the brick wall at the window. It opened its mouth and screamed into their faces. Keri jumped back and let go.

"I didn't think those things were real. That is stuff for the movies and not real life," Keri said. She was challenged beyond all comprehension. "I should have known that night when you started talking about God that something really big had to have taken place. But I had no idea. That thing out there is horrific. How can you make me see that? How did you do that?"

Satisfied, Dawn motioned for Keri to return to the bed and followed. She shared everything with Keri. When she heard all that Marcus and the others had done, a deep conviction penetrated her soul.

Keri was taken aback by all that she had learned. It was a lot to take in at once. She loved her daughters and was glad for the opportunity to have a second chance with Amy. This man who she had condemned and ridiculed had risked everything to help both of her daughters and was not so loony after all. He was a saint.

Of all the man-made places in the world, Marcus loved his studio the most. The sentimental value was priceless. It was where he could create or just be alone. It was his refuge at times. Music helped him serve and draw closer to a God he so loved. It was his therapy and worship.

A napkin with some words on it hung down from the top of a music stand. Marcus sat on a wooden bar stool holding a box guitar with his back to the door. He felt his way through the notes on the guitar and the studio was alive with the sound of music. When he was satisfied, he matched them with the lyrics.

"Cutting loose . . . from what I've known
This life of sin . . . empty all alone
I need you . . . to pull me through
Bottle up all my sins
Thrown away never again
Can be used . . . I'm cutting loose
Picked up the book . . . so good to read

Pages alive now inside of me
To be used . . . You've cut me loose

Once trapped inside the lie
Stuck in the world I cry
I need the redemption
Your words had mentioned
Come and save me
. . . For all eternity

Cutting loose . . . I look to the throne
Lost world is so alone
They need you . . . to pull them through
Open their eyes . . . let them see
Soften hearts so they can be
Used by you . . . cut them loose
Wash us now . . . of our sin
Second chance to start again
Lord we thank you . . . they're cutting loose."

He continued to strum the guitar, recycling the notes and pondering them.

"That was really good!" an excited voice said from behind him.

Marcus looked up in the picture window and saw Dawn's reflection as she entered the studio clapping her hands. "Thanks." He simulated a bow. "How's the family?"

"Well . . . a family and a little overwhelmed by everything. All of our lives have changed so drastically in such a short span of time. No one really knows what to do. The amazing thing right now is that Amy has no desire to smoke or any signs of withdrawals. She seems fine. She isn't fidgety. It's an absolute miracle."

"That's awesome," Marcus said.

"Yes it is, but so are you," Dawn said moving closer to him and taking his hand.

"That's nice, but you don't have to say that. We just wanted to help. All of us did what we knew was the right thing. It was just as much of a blessing for me and Reed and Paris that we were able to help. To be completely honest, after the last . . . I don't know . . . five years or so of praying for you and for God to not only let me know about your salvation, but to be a part of it was incredible. I kind of feel like a chapter of my life has now closed."

"Has a new chapter started yet?" Dawn asked.

"What?"

"Are you starting a new chapter?" Dawn asked.

"I hope so," Marcus replied.

"How would the first words in this new chapter read?"

"Well, if I were a writer . . . 'the most beautiful woman in the world punched me in the nose' . . . no, that's the old chapter." They shared a laugh. "Let me try again—"

"No, let *me* try . . . 'Marcus Dillon was a brave and honest man. There was this woman who didn't deserve him, but very much wanted him to be a part of her life. The only question was . . . would he?'"

"I have to admit . . . this book sounds like a winner. Marcus Dillon would say . . . yes. He would like that very much." Marcus replied. "No reservations?"

"No. Not anymore." She leaned in and for the first time, truly kissed him.

Marcus felt a sensation of guilt come upon him and pulled back. Dawn looked back at him. "I just want you to know that I didn't do anything or act in any way to win your affection. There was no preconceived plan. While I cherish your affection, what was done was done to please God and because it was the right thing. If I was doing all of this to win you over, then I would be a worthless phony. I am crazy about you, yes! But, I had no pre-set goals or false motivation."

"Just stop," Dawn said and continued to kiss him.

Marcus pushed the guitar aside and held her close. He wrapped his arms tightly around her and prayed. He would now have to move on with life and leave as much of Allison to rest as possible. He never wanted to forget her, but just as the tattooed man on the beach had told him, it was time to move forward.

CHAPTER 29

"Last night when that demon or Satan or whatever that was in the room, it thanked me and called me an 'influential warrior.' It said that many people are in Hell because of me. That hurts. I realize what I have done and I need to make things right, or as right as possible. I know they are deceiving spirits and God has given me a peace about everything. It's not as if I can go into Hell and get them out. Just knowing that I may have had a part of anyone ending up in that place is a lot of guilt to deal with.

"I want to go on-air and tell the gospel. No one at the station knows that I have changed. You know . . . saved. I am not sure what to do. I need a chance to go on air in front of that audience and tell them the truth. No matter what it costs, I need to do it. Do I tell them up front what I am going to do? Or, just keep up a front and then when I am on the air . . . just let it all out? Which case, they may pull the plug on me.

"I can't give a 30-second speech and expect that to be enough. To do this right, it will take time. I need at least fifteen minutes for a basic message. Longer for detail," Dawn said.

"What if you witnessed to someone first? Tell them your story and use your ability to convince them. I mean, so far you are one-hundred percent in the witnessing arena. Well . . . except for that tarot card reader," Marcus said.

"It's not just one person. Scott is the producer, Sonny is my co-host and Mike is the station manager. I don't really have time to formally witness to each one. I had originally planned to go back tomorrow. I've already arranged for a fill-in for today so that I can prepare for tomorrow."

"How do you want to do it?" he asked.

"Go into the studio and let it all out. But, I just don't know how . . . there is just no way that they are going to give me the air time I need."

"Really? What if you show them that it is all true? Is there a mirror in the studio?"

"Not a big one.

"So, we'll just bring a big one with us."

"You're going to help?" Dawn asked.

"Living for the adventure," Marcus replied.

The ding of the elevator caught the attention of the receptionist. She looked oddly at the delivery man as he approached her with a thin square package wrapped in red paper and sporting a big green bow.

"It's not exactly Christmas," she said.

"No ma'am it sure isn't. I just deliver them," he said handing over a folded sheet of typed paper. "These are the instructions."

"Instructions?" she asked, raising her eyebrows.

She opened the paper and read aloud, "'For Mike—I will meet in your office at 9:00.—Dawn McIntyre. p.s. Don't open until I get there.' Can you please take it to the first door on the left?"

Dawn smiled as she walked into the office. Mike stood to greet her and was surprised when she waived him back down suggesting that there was no need to get up on her account. Mike looked at the gift and wondered what Dawn was up to.

"So, what is this?" he asked.

"This is only part of the gift. It isn't even the real gift," she said. "Well, I want to share with you an experience of a lifetime, one that I have had over and over the last three or four days."

Mike leaned in, intrigued. "OK."

"I've been kind of lost and in need of direction," she replied.

"Direction? You're a national celebrity. You've made lots of money. As we speak people are waiting to eat out of your hands. What the heck else do you want? How much 'direction' do you need? There are millions of listeners who look to YOU for direction."

It was Mike's last statement that caught her off guard. It was true and exactly what Satan had told her. She felt the loss of lost souls as a burden and would not miss the opportunity to correct her mistake.

"Do you believe in Hell?" She blurted out.

"No! But, you don't believe in Hell either. Why ask such a question?" he inquired.

"True, I didn't," Dawn said.

"'*Didn't*! It kind of sounds like you do now?" Mike replied, confused.

"I want to show you something," She turned and pulled off the red wrapping paper to reveal a square four foot mirror.

"I thought it was a picture, I didn't realize it was a mirror. I don't get it."

"Let's make this simple," Dawn said setting the mirror on the arms and back of a wooden chair Mike used for visitors. She pulled the mirror closer to Mike positioning it where he could see. She walked around the desk and stood next to him. "Please look into the mirror and tell me what you see."

"Do I really have time for this?" Mike paused for a second and conceded. "I see a man who needs Dawn McIntyre to get back on air. That's what I see."

Dawn touched his hand and power surged through him. Mike's eyes opened wide as he looked in the mirror and around the room. His breathing became shallow and fast. In the mirror he saw the presence of evil fading in and out of his reflection. The demonic grin of a demon faded in and out in line with his face. One second Mike simply saw himself and the next, his image transformed to something he had never seen before. The demon toyed with him. "What is that? What is that? How are you doing that? Is this some kind of trick? What is going on?" he asked as the demon faded back and then stood next to the window. It moved casually down the wall and stood in the corner of the office and Mike turned to watch the spirit as it looked angrily back.

He turned to face Dawn and looked through her, noticing Idio standing at attention. Mike stared taking in as much detail as he could. In his heart he was convinced what he was seeing was the truth. Idio stood stoic and focused on the demon.

Mike's pulse raced. Dawn let go of his hand. She walked back around and stood next to the mirror. "Sorry to have to do that to you. But it seems to be the only way people believe."

"What about having faith without sight?" Mike asked looking crossly at her. Instinctively he reached over to the bottom right hand drawer and pulled it open. He pulled a flask and slapped the lid off. Mike quickly raised it to his mouth and turned it up.

"That's not going to help. As a matter of fact, that will just make it worse. How did you know about having faith without sight?" Dawn asked.

"I grew up in church. I went my whole life until college. I haven't been since."

"There is a presence of good and evil in this world and we need to realize it." Dawn said.

Mike leaned back and kept turning to the corner and looking. But the demon was no longer visible. "So, that was a demon?"

"Yes," Dawn replied bluntly.

"What about the angel?"

Dawn turned to the door, "That is Idio. He is one of the angels that takes care of me. And his hands have been full."

"Come on, Dawn. How did you do that? This is all a joke, right? I'm on a hidden camera. Come on you can't fool me. That did seem real. I'm not sure how you did it, but I would sure like to know. You trying to take David Copperfield's gig or what?"

"It was no joke. It was real."

"So you come in here like some new Christian when you happen to be the biggest atheist to ever walk the earth. You've made a living off of it. You have proved to a lot of people that religion is stupid. No, this has to be a joke. Come on. Tell me what's going on. No more games."

Dawn was stunned and looked at Idio, pondering what to do. She was unprepared for such a situation. A word of knowledge came over her, "Your father was a deacon in the church. He drank a lot and beat on you. No one believed that he was abusing you."

"How did you know that? That is impossible that you would know that. I've never told you. I haven't talked about it since I left that wretched place. How did you know?" he demanded.

"I can only say that God told me. He also says that He loves you and wants to show His love for you," Dawn said.

"Why are you doing this to me? All of this is crazy and just has to be explained logically. This isn't happening. I just need—" He paused as the papers on his desk were moved by an unseen force. The out files magically mixed with the in files. An empty fast food container fell over onto its side. A yellow piece of paper containing a list of items needing his attention slid off of the desk and into the garbage.

Dawn watched Idio. He smiled back at her and continued about the business of doing his work. She wondered why he didn't simply appear before Mike. He looked at Mike and spoke, but Dawn could not hear what Idio said.

Mike looked oddly at Dawn and said, "Blessed is the Lord God of Israel. His kingdom has come upon you . . . or, I guess me. A voice came into my mind was saying that."

He pulled the paper out of the trash can and inspected it. No strings or strange breeze had planted it in the garbage.

"Let me see again!" he demanded.

Dawn reached down and touched his hand and the angel appeared to Mike. He looked at Idio and asked, "Did you do that to my desk?"

Idio looked at him and nodded yes.

"Did you just talk into my mind?"

Again Idio nodded in affirmation.

Mike turned and looked for the demon and could not see it. He panned the room until looking back into the mirror. In the reflection the demon was standing next to him speaking doubt about God into his mind. Its head leaned down next to his ear. Mike jumped up and moved away from the desk.

Without help from Dawn, Mike called out to God for mercy and help. He stumbled through his words and worked hard to pray.

Dawn sat overlooking the river from a bench as she considered the future. Ships and barges moved about their business, transporting cargo up and down the river. She knew that many of the show's followers were going to rebel against her and attack her over her new-found faith. Many would try to label her as a hypocrite or even a phony. She would need to grow thick skin and learn how to deal with being on the other side of the assault on Christians. She was once blind to the truth and now had to stand for what she knew to be the truth . . . that Jesus Christ is the Lord and Savior of the world.

About the Author

William Songy has spent the last decade tirelessly studying and learning about the world of the supernatural. After an incident with his son at the age of two, he sought to find the truth about the spiritual realm. He and his wife, Darnell, have three children and a grandchild. They live near New Orleans, Louisiana.